LOST
in
ARCADIA

LOST
in
ARCADIA

SEAN GANDERT

Text copyright © 2017 by Sean Gandert
All rights reserved.

Published by 47North, Seattle

www.apub.com

Amazon, the Amazon logo, and 47North are trademarks of Amazon.com, Inc., or its affiliates.

ISBN-13: 9781477848531
ISBN-10: 1477848533

Cover design by Shasti O'Leary Soudant

Printed in the United States of America

For Jacob Corona

THANKSGIVING 2025

Gideon tells me that back then dad was almost never around. And after I hit elementary school, mom was so busy catching up with work that she was mostly gone too. But I guess when we were still living in the old house—where the door to mom and dad's room scratched against their king-size mattress every time someone entered and me and Gideon shared one bedroom so that Holly could have her own—we used to have this sort of mandated family time every week. Mom always thought the five of us didn't spend enough time together and was so afraid that we'd turn out like her family that she made staying home on holidays and Friday evenings compulsory. None of our friends could come over for dinner. Dad wasn't allowed to code at the table. No to everything but the family. I don't even remember when she came up with the idea, but even dad treated these nights seriously after he came home late to an evening of family time and it resulted in one of their big, annual fights. From then on, if he needed to stay late on family nights, first he'd come home, loosening his tie (Holly says he liked to call it his "corporate noose") and joining whatever activity we'd decided on that week without complaint. Only when family time had definitively ended would he head back to the office for another all-nighter.

We'd put on sweaters, go to the den, and pick out something to play from the game closet. The den was always freezing or sweltering, an addition to the house that had never been insulated. Holly used to say that if you stayed there long enough during the winter, like to watch all of the Saturday morning cartoons, you'd lose feeling in your face and wouldn't even know that a trail of mucus was running from your nose to your chin. She liked to complain that you shouldn't be able to see your breath indoors, but mom just said that if she had a problem with it, she could always watch less TV. Depending on their moods, this would either be ignored or lead to an ugly argument.

Inside the closet was an entire story of games, some of their boxes dating back to before we were born. *Trivial Pursuit* from 1978, a *RISK* set with wooden pieces, puzzles we had neither bought nor opened. My favorite part of the closet was an entire shelf of dad's old *DnD* books, filled with terrible black-and-white drawings of dwarves and dragons and buxom princesses. He didn't play anymore, but he didn't have the heart to sell them, so they sat there. I used to get them out to stare at them, even before I knew what they said. Below them were fantasy games, like the one I wanted to play that night, *HeroQuest* or something like that. But my brother was with me and he wanted to play *Sorry!*, which I always hated because it was all luck and no skill. The two of us were arguing, then he pulled out the *Sorry!* box and said that because he was older, he got to choose. According to Gideon, I grabbed at the box, and as I tried to pull it away from him, he let go and I fell backward. The top flew off, launching plastic pawns and cards into the air, primary colors cascading across the room.

Gideon says he noticed that I hadn't gotten up after falling to the carpet, and it became clear that I was struggling to breathe. He didn't know what to do, so he started pushing on my chest like they do in movies. Mom and Holly came in to see what all the noise was about, and then mom screamed for dad. Gideon says that he kept pumping on my chest and yelling at Holly to do something, but she was frozen in place, staring. Mom was on the ground comforting me and trying to clean up the mess, worried about dad slipping on the pieces.

"Do something!" she screamed when he entered the room. He pushed Gideon away, who'd given up on the chest-pushing business and was now brainstorming how he could duck the blame. Holly cried and called 911. Dad asked Gideon what he'd tried so far. Gideon said he'd pushed on my chest like Bruce Willis, and dad just got pissed off.

Gideon says that dad tried another round of Heimlich-ing me but decided it was futile, so he opened up my mouth and thrust his finger down into my throat, trying to manually yank out a green pawn lodged in my windpipe. Everyone waited and waited and finally an ambulance arrived, with mom crying and Holly watching, standing perfectly still while they removed the pawn, placed me on a gurney, and put an oxygen mask around my face.

When I woke up the next day I couldn't remember anything after dad came home. I was lying down in a white bed with a pleasant humming sound in the background, looking through a plastic sheet onto a silvery roof with tubes above me. I kept lying there, staring at the roof for so long I had time to wake up again. Maybe that's why it came to mind now, staring up at nothing again, waiting for some indication that everything has worked out.

Gideon says that he and Holly were sent over to our next-door neighbors, who after hearing about the accident fed them a big meal with turkey and stuffing and all the rest, and even gave them ice cream for dessert. Gideon tells me that was the first time he tried Neapolitan and that it turned out to be a really fun evening after all until he and Holly came home and the only sound in the house was mom alone in her room, crying and crying. I guess that was the first time dad left. He just disappeared, not answering his phone or anything and no one knew where he went off to or what he was doing. He returned before I got home, and everyone pretended it had never happened, but even I knew everything had changed. After that, he kept leaving for longer and longer until one day he just didn't come back.

1

TWELVE YEARS LATER

Devon planned on spending the entire weekend in his room.

The only real exception would be attendance at the practically mandatory dinners with his mom, the two of them at adjacent corners of a battered and stained kitchen table that could easily seat eight, trying to pretend they had something to say to each other. Missing dinner was on par with smoking pot in the house or getting a large tattoo of a snake on his biceps. Autumn pretended not to care, that she was fine with the only person living under the same roof ditching her for the evening, but Devon had tested those waters before, only to discover her crying when she thought he wouldn't notice, alone in her overly large bedroom with her face planted into a pile of pillows.

Other than dinner, he was free to do whatever he wanted. That meant sitting at his computer, logged on to Arcadia.

After another interminable day at high school, Devon walked through the front door and headed directly into his room, throwing his backpack on the floor by his bed. He pulled his sneakers off with his left hand while his right navigated through a simple but powerful UI he'd helped his dad beta test more than a decade ago, back when it seemed like Arcadia would never be completed. He'd be the first to admit that his room was a huge fucking mess, cleaned maybe three or four times a year under extremely specific circumstances. Autumn appreciated it if the house was tidied before Christmas, even if they weren't spending the holiday at home, and when someone (almost always a semi-unknown relative) would be staying over.

Not that any visitors ever saw his room, since even when it was clean, he kept it off-limits. Letting a stranger into your room was begging for judgment, and he was certain there would always be something to snark about, whether it was an old stuffed animal lying in easy view or his poster of Gravedigger, who remained controversial despite mainstream success.

Since Christmas there had been no visitors, though, and Autumn had been out even more than usual, working on a line of high-concept western paperbacks hitting before the end of the year—so lately she hadn't even had time to feign disbelief at the room's disarray. As a result, it was fully his, soda cans covering every flat surface, trash bags overflowing with used tissues, decks of *Magic* cards scattered across the floor alongside pewter fantasy figurines and dice.

Although they'd moved in more than eight years prior, after his dad finally acquiesced to Autumn's demand for more space, Devon's room wasn't heavily decorated. Teenagers on television always seemed to have elaborate setups, whole worlds of music and rebellion surrounding their beds in a swirl of safe anarchy, but the only kids who decorated like that grew up to be set designers. In a world with the infinity of games, the infinity of all media sitting right there next to your bed, who had time for that crap—who had time for anything else?

Three posters hung on his otherwise unadorned walls. The most prominent one depicted Gravedigger, wearing his trademark jester's cap and looming over a tiny white king in the foreground. It wasn't a great photo of the rapper, but it was signed, a birthday gift from

Gideon three years ago. The other two were pieces of promo art for Arcadia that his dad had given him before the platform was even released. Devon liked them both, even though they said little about either Arcadia or even the launch title they were designed to promote, *Kingdom Without a King*. The first showed a lord fleeing a mob of peasants at the front of his castle during a storm, and the other featured a beautiful woman crying over two children's bodies while a knight in the background looked on angrily.

The mess reached an apex at the desk opposite Devon's bed, where a monumental desktop computer, three feet high and a foot wide with a translucent cover, was dwarfed only by the twenty-seven-inch monitor that sat beside it. On top of and adjacent to the desktop were figurines of a few of Devon's favorite game avatars, versions of himself used in Arcadia's chat program and games, manufactured by an acrylic polymer–based 3D printer and purchased at minimal cost. The only other figurine on his desk was a small ceramic tortoise, given to him by his father probably ten years ago.

Devon checked in on his clan, the Baby Eaters—who was offline and who was online and what if anything the rest of his cohort were doing. He'd entered his room less than a minute before, but because his computer was never truly off (instead using sleep and hibernation low-power states that he'd customized to keep him logged in to Arcadia), no loading screens were required. Not that he needed to stay permanently in Arcadia—it probably added another fifty dollars to their monthly electric bills and cost half a mine's worth of annual coal production—but it was worth it not to wait for his computer to boot up.

Staying logged in all the time was also a show of commitment. All of the higher-ranked members of the Baby Eaters, the primarily Albuquerque-based clan he'd cofounded during the first weeks of Arcadia's release, were online all the time, even if they weren't always available. His account's characters could be called up by any of the other leaders if needed with a bot program, or in direst of circumstances played by someone else. The expectation was that you'd be there when the clan needed you, one way or another, "real life" be damned. Anyone worth playing had their priorities straight.

Devon left his avatar idling in his digital house while checking his emails and PMs. Most of Devon's effort in Arcadia, after earning enough "points" (easily converted to and from dollars, but with no monetary value so as to create tax loopholes and leave the platform's publisher, Electronic Arts, inculpable) to keep buying new games and playing for free, went into his online real estate, building a small mansion and then giving it a classic look and feel that was comfortable and inviting, a place to relax on his own or socialize with the clan.

The clan's channel, |3ə—a common space that functioned as chat room and general hangout for members when they were between games—had a few dozen members in it, as always, but no one Devon particularly felt like talking to at the moment, so he pulled open a menu to put on some music before joining in and outlining their plans for tonight's raid. Although he'd never bought an album, LP covers adorned Devon's living room walls and a genre-alphabetized collection filled a huge shelf, complete with wood-paneled turntable hooked into a virtual surround-sound set that changed the mix based upon where Devon's avatar was located. The recordings were high-fidelity vinyl transfers, all so well captured digitally that they had been proven by even the most anal of audiophiles to be indistinguishable from the real thing. Some people preferred more traditional high-bitrate digital feeds, 320 kb/s digital transfers that had been the standard since before he was born, but Devon had heard that these tended to flatten out an album's highs and lows. Gideon told him once that Gravedigger used a special digital-to-analogue technique that made listening to his tracks on digital recordings more authentic than the physical copies hipsters insisted on buying in stores, a sort of inside joke to the web junkies who made up so much of the rap superstar's audience.

Devon liked the little touches that made his house feel more authentic. It wasn't an ostentatious Victorian manor like Disney's or a Lovecraftian mess like Steve's, who considered the point of virtual real estate to be creating a home that couldn't exist in reality and filled his abode with impossible feats of engineering and rooms with variable gravity. Devon's place was like the classy Hollywood houses he'd seen in movies, well lit and spare, yet inviting, with elegant curves on the outside and a sensible floor plan within, containing even completely unnecessary bathrooms and a laundry room. Devon's favorite part of the house was the bar/lounge area, where he and his friends could get together for "drinks" (which, due to his father's insistence when designing the alcohol simulation part of the program, actually affected the behavior of their avatars based upon body mass index and "tolerance") or sit around and play poker at a felt-covered table. They could have just as easily met in a standard-issue chat room, but the lounge, with its pool cues and dartboard, its glass tumblers and abstract paintings, was a nice conversation piece and helped Devon get a reputation in the clan for being classy. He liked being the leader whose avatar wore a blazer and hosted cocktail hours, even though he'd never touched a sip of alcohol in his life and truth be told had been left a bit paranoid about the stuff due to stories that had trickled down to him about his dad, Juan Diego, ever since his disappearance.

Unlike at home, in Arcadia Devon felt he had complete control. His character didn't need to go to dinner, and didn't get a bit winded running up the stairs. In Arcadia, all the games were meant to be winnable, and that made all the difference between playing *NCAA Basketball 2k29* and shooting hoops during gym. School had been more of a grind than usual this week, but his space online was always an oasis (hell, he could control the weather and make it a literal one if he wanted). In a few minutes he would be back among the clan, with all the pressure and excitement that would entail, but for now he moved his head close to the screen so that it filled his entire field of vision while Gravedigger's "Festival of Fools" played through his headphones, watching as his avatar toured La Casa de Reyes from the hot tub to the master bedroom and enjoying the orderly perfection of everything he'd been able to accomplish here.

2

She couldn't really blame him for being so pissy. Holly knew full well that Robert was on this trip for her, not because it was something he wanted to do, as he'd kept repeating since they left their driveway that morning. They weren't even close yet and she'd already heard this complaint, with slight variation, at least a dozen times, whining that what he said wasn't a whine but just "an observation." Still, Holly believed it would be worth all the grumpiness in the world when they arrived. Robert had always been obstinate, but he wasn't oblivious, wasn't stupid enough to miss something extraordinary when it stared him right in the face.

Quemado was a tiny town, one of an endless number of them that made up New Mexico's febrile 120,000 square miles. The entire settlement was just a speck in the desert, taking up less than a square mile and situated seemingly at random. No rivers ran through Quemado, and there were no hills to mark the location as unique. No field or naturally forming arroyos made it any different from the endless expanse of nearly identical dirt and shrubs they'd passed by on the way over. Situated at the intersection of two deserted highways, few drove along either of its sun-cracked roads except truckers bringing supplies to Quemado or Red Hill or Omega or any of the other out-of-the-way particles of civilization that hadn't yet been beaten back into dust.

They parked in the only café or restaurant either of them saw in the town. The faded turquoise sign above its doorway said simply "Café," with no indication that it had ever aspired to distinguish itself with a proper noun. The same man who took their order grilled their hamburgers and brought them to their table. He was the only person they'd seen since arriving in Quemado. After fixing their meal, he disappeared to the back room again.

"It's not that I don't trust the food out here," said Robert, tentatively nibbling at his burger as grease dripped down his fingers and onto his knuckles. "It's just that what with a new E. coli or salmonella epidemic nearly every week, I don't think it's safe to put our lives in the hands of, let's face it, hicks who more than likely can't read and have never heard of, much less used, a meat thermometer."

"We're not in Paris sampling the local cuisine. It's a fucking hamburger, be an American and eat it."

They spent the rest of the meal in silence, eating slowly. After finishing their plates they walked past a single shop to the Diaz building, a large white structure double the size of the café, easily the tallest thing in sight. They were apparently the last ones to arrive and their group was waiting outside the building, next to a van that might have once been sparkling white but was now coated with what looked like twenty years of dirt and mud. A couple in their sixties stood nearby, endlessly asking questions to a bored-looking driver sitting in his vehicle. A pair of youngish men leaned awkwardly against the building, using its shade to keep off the sweltering midday New Mexico sun.

"Seriously, we have to live with them?" Robert asked softly as they approached the group.

"We don't live with them, we just share a common space. Now try to be nice." Holly stood up straighter and pretended she was at least a little less sweaty and irritable than she felt. She was disappointed when Robert didn't follow suit.

The driver introduced himself, as did the rest of the group, and they filed into the van. Holly and Robert sat at the very back, hoping to avoid conversation. As they drove away from the city, even the talkative older couple became silent. All the passengers stared out the windows as they headed away from the vestiges of society, out into the true desert. No birds flew across the sky. No lizards scampered into bushes, and as they drifted down a barely perceptible dirt road, it felt like the ubiquitous straw-colored weeds trailing alongside them were decreasing in number. Far in the distance, Holly could make out what might have been a tree, but otherwise they were driving into pure space, an expanse defined by its absences. The barely sloping hills looked almost like a palette-swapped Martian landscape, made up of hard rock with only the tiniest bits of gray-green plants poking through the crust to remind them they were still terrestrial.

The drive lasted less than an hour, but it seemed like a trip through time, or to a different dimension. As they drove, the land became somewhat more green, but it was all tiny shrubs and weeds. Finally, a cabin in the distance, constructed of unpainted wood. When the van approached, they could see that, though the building looked its age, it was still solid. The most striking thing about it was the impossibility of telling when it had been built. No concession seemed to have been made for modern convenience. The cabin appeared as if it had always been here, and the same was true of the wooden benches and rocking chairs that rested on its porch.

It took Holly a few moments to figure out why the cabin was so striking: there were no trees in sight, or at any point along the drive over, that could have supplied its lumber. The wood was an aesthetic design choice rather than a necessity of the land. The people who built the cabin here could've just as easily put up a more modern building, but chose not to. The cabin itself was part of the experience, as much a conscious decision as the size of the group and the drive leading out here, each step leading pilgrims further from civilization.

They piled out of the van and onto the porch. The driver told them how he could be reached in case of an emergency, then abruptly left. Everyone waited until he crossed over the distant horizon before moving, en masse, into the cabin.

Holly thanked God that the driver assigned them the one room with a double bed. If they'd been given a pair of singles, she knew that Robert would never let her hear the end of it. She closed the door behind them and lay back onto the bed to soak in the moment, surprised to find that its mattress was thick and plush. The walls were all unfinished wood, the only furniture a matching unfinished dresser, bookshelf, and the bed—no hint of tacky hotel art or "tasteful" pillow arrangements in sight. Holly knew the mattress had almost certainly been bought in a furniture store somewhere, shipped from some Chinese factory where it had been made by seven-year-old girls earning six cents an hour, but she turned that part of her brain off. She closed her eyes and breathed in deeply, luxuriating in the room's organic smells and imagining the tiny bits of wood dust entering her pores, becoming a part of her.

She sat up and looked at the room's window and saw no buildings or cars, just wood and glass framing an unpeopled world that stretched out to the horizon. No polymers made from petrochemicals. No bisphenol A or polyurethanes or epoxy resins with styrenic copolymers to worry about. The only polyvinyl chloride was what they'd brought with them. This was a holy space, sanctified by simplicity.

Robert entered and sat down on the bed beside her, immediately pulling out his phone. "I know it's not supposed to work out here, but I just want to make sure. Goddammit, does this place really not even have power outlets? I forgot to bring a real book, so when my phone dies, that's it."

Holly stood up and pushed him down onto the bed. "Relax. Just take a breath for a second." He sort of acquiesced, at least he quit talking, but with her head resting against his chest, Holly could hear his heart still beating quickly. She knew what would relax him, and began unzipping his pants.

After they finished, Robert seemed more content, or at least not so apt to criticize everything. They walked outside the cabin and joined with the other visitors, who still hadn't found much to say to each other. "Wanna go check it out?" asked Robert, and the group assented.

Not that they needed to go far. The field was directly in front of them, a collection of what looked like almost-but-not-quite-invisible toothpicks poking out of the ground. As they walked forward, these transformed into sticks and then finally poles, standing completely straight at intervals that looked to be regular. The cool air and lack of wind highlighted the alien nature of these jutting fixtures. Now that they stood in front of the field, it didn't feel like a Martian landscape as she'd thought before. No, it was like entering a post-human world. Wilderness, as desolate as it might be, had retaken the land, but these poles remained, standing as proudly perpendicular as the day they were first planted.

After a few more minutes of walking, they arrived at the first one. Made out of an almost silvery steel, the pole was easily four times her height, reflecting down at her the light emanating from the cloudless blue sky. She wrapped her hand around it and felt that the pole, despite its brilliance, was cool to the touch. She pulled on it, but there was no give.

Holly wondered how deep it went, what kept it there. It felt so firmly placed in the ground that she had no doubt it would still be standing in the same spot a hundred years from now, but how about five hundred? How about five thousand? Would there ever be a time when archaeologists found just one left, and what would they make of it?

There were four hundred in total, spread out evenly across the plain. Holly touched Robert on the shoulder and pointed out a direction to wander. He silently followed. Behind them, one of the men was taking photos with his digital camera. The older couple talked silently to each other, occasionally tittering. It seemed a sacrilege, and Holly wanted to get away from them as soon as possible.

They drifted to the west, passing by several poles as the landscape rose and fell slightly under their feet. All the poles rose to the same elevation, so that while some were taller or shorter relative to the ground, if you put a giant plate on top of them, it would rest perfectly flat.

"What do you think?" she asked, when they were finally on their own. She hoped that Robert felt the same power of the place that she did.

Being here was something you couldn't photograph or experience through a skilled Hollywood film crew working with top-of-the-line 3D technology. You had to walk past the poles yourself to understand it.

"The guy is a genius."

"Completely. But what about the field? I mean, you understand why it was worth the trip now, right?"

"Not exactly . . . but I don't regret it. I'm just really impressed by the way this De Maria guy was able to get people to experience his art through such an extreme route. It gives me an idea. I mean, if someone has to pay this much money and spend this much time to see his sculpture, visiting a crappy shack with annoying roommates, then they pretty much have to say it's good. They have to say that the experience lived up to the hype, otherwise it's not so much a judgment on the piece itself as on their own choices. It's an insurance policy against a bad review."

"It's not a question of good or bad, it's whether the piece moves you." Holly felt her voice rising with irritation, but she tempered it. "Try to act like you're not in competition with the creator for one second and just experience the piece."

Robert's voice slid into the patronizing register that always made her want to smother him with a pillow. "Honey, that's like saying to turn off my brain. I can't do that. I can't help but think about his motivation, his ambition. This is the twenty-first century—it's been more than a hundred years since anything you found in a dumpster could earn millions at an art gallery because you had the right critic in your corner. If you don't have the artist, you don't have the art. If I have to be honest, I'd much rather read a biography of De Maria than come up here. If nothing else, it would be less time-consuming."

"Try to see it without context for one second. See it like you're an explorer who's just arrived at these poles knowing nothing about them beforehand."

"Then all I see is a bunch of poles sticking out of the fucking ground." He paused and seemed to consider if what he was going to say was a good idea. "Honey, I've seen fence posts before. They're not that exciting. I've seen wood shacks before, and they're equally uninvigorating. I'm happy to be here and do something for you, but I can't change who I am, and who I am is a thoroughly bored person who's wondering how he's going to pass the next eighteen or so fucking hours without going crazy. I don't want to ruin this for you, but it's just one of those things you enjoy that I don't."

Goddammit, why did he wait until they arrived to be like this? If he'd acted like such a cock on the way over, they'd be through with this bullshit by now and could just enjoy the trip.

"Fine. I don't mean to force you to do anything. But you said you were interested in—"

"And I am. But being interested in a topic and wanting to stare at poles for an entire fucking day are two very different things. Look, maybe it's because I'm a sculptor that I can see through this for the self-promotion it is."

"Well if you're finished here, then why don't you just go back to the cabin and read or whatever for a while. I'll see you when I'm done."

"If that's what you want, I will. If you're really fine with it and not just saying that."

"Yes, go do what you want. I just want to be alone for a while."

"Okay, I'll see you in a bit."

Holly wished that he'd stormed off in a huff, but instead he kissed her cheek and leisurely ambled away. That he didn't care about being uncaring annoyed her most of all. She couldn't fault him for not getting it, but it felt like Robert refused to even see the point of trying.

Not that she felt like she totally understood what was going on at *The Lightning Field*, either, but she knew it went beyond the artist or the poles. There was something magical about this precise configuration, and she walked through the work knowing that there was a power here, even if she didn't understand it or know how to respond appropriately. She understood the other couple's giggling as a natural response to seeing the sacred and lacking the ability to appreciate it after a lifetime of television and malls and blue plastic rosaries with a government-mandated "Made in China" label stamped on the back of the crucifix. The photographer was simply trying to take it home with him, having not yet realized that it was impossible to capture an experience like this on digital film. Some things can't be re-created or mass-produced—even a second trip out here would never have the same enchantment.

Holly walked farther into the field and sat down, smiling as the sun embraced her skin, basking in its glow, trying to take in the enormity of what surrounded her. She thought for a moment about how she would paint this in her studio at home before deciding that would be even worse than the photographer, than her dad thrashing together and selling a *Lightning Field* video game for $1.99 online. She watched as the sun set, and the poles' shadows drifted hazily toward the horizon, growing with every second. In the noonday sun they had been pins, but now they loomed, the silhouettes of giants' spears resting across the sand.

The sun plummeted slowly from view, a spectacular reddish glow that lit up a pair of distant clouds, giving them a pink tint, and across the field, poles reflected this light and cast an infernal hue. Wild grass and weeds were the color of fire for just a few moments, while the angle was perfect. Then the sun dipped away entirely and the plain was left in the dim, brilliant aura of the magic hour, when it was still light enough to see clearly but the radiance's direct source was missing. Visibility was still strong at the absolute end of the day, but only through reflection and fragmentation. The poles, each exactly 220 feet apart, stood like sentinels, guarding the field from the vast, unending wilderness that threatened to overwhelm it.

Holly decided she was ready to return to the cabin, even though Robert would be there. She didn't know why she'd thought that he would understand the place. Maybe because he was also a sculptor obsessed with large, ungainly visions, and the majesty of the area would speak to him. Ha. Maybe she was just searching for something, anything for them to share; the list of things they had in common seemed smaller with every passing week. She walked back to the cabin thinking of how much better this would have been if she'd come alone. His presence was an infection, throbbing in the back of her head and reminding her of his arrogant dismissal.

Robert stood next to the door when she arrived, smiling broadly. "How was it? See any lightning?"

She had to smile back at his joke or risk ruining her remaining time here. "No, not yet, but I still got a spectacular show." In the cabin, everyone else was already in the midst of conversation. "I'm starving. We get food, right?"

"There's a brick of vegetarian lasagna in the refrigerator to heat up, but it's still undecided whether or not we should classify that as food."

He closed the door behind her, and Holly saw that someone was missing. One of the two men who'd come alone hadn't returned, though she also hadn't seen him in the field on her way back. "Where's . . . Taylor? Tyler? You know, the other guy?"

Holly had been trying to speak quietly, but the male half of the older couple butted in. "I think he's still out there, doing peyote. Not that I have anything against that or anything—I think it's really important to expand your mind, I really do. But maybe we should go out there and check on him?"

"Do you think he knows what he's doing?" his wife responded.

"I sure hope so. I just don't know why a person would come out here and take peyote. It ruins it for the rest of us, doesn't it?"

Robert smiled broadly again, and Holly saw that he wasn't in a smirky, jackass mood like she'd feared. He was in his people-pleasing mood. With his smile pasted on, Robert reminded Holly of her father when he was trying to get people to do things for him, subtly manipulating them into agreeing with him even when it was against their best interests. She tried her best to ignore this thought, reassuring herself that Robert wasn't like that, wasn't a guy who would disappear from his family without so much as a voice mail, but it was hard to shake when she heard him speaking with the same plying tone of voice. "I'm sure he's fine. A guy like him probably does it all the time. Let's just heat up this food and have dinner. We'll save him a piece."

Holly found herself disappointed that the cabin had a refrigerator and an electric stove, though fortunately they were set off in a small kitchen area, apart from the rest of the otherwise ascetic decor. While the lasagna was pretty tasteless, Robert apparently felt great. He and everyone else were in a good mood. The couple had brought up a bottle of champagne for the occasion, which they drank with dinner and shared with everyone. Robert asked the single guy what he did for a living, and they learned he was one of those people restoring the Florida coast following the hurricane. Holly had to admit that Robert made an effort to be pleasant.

They finished the champagne, and Robert pulled a bottle of Maker's Mark from his bag, reminding Holly why she loved being with him. On her own, Holly would've probably shut the door to her room and stayed there, or else just stuck it out in the field. But he'd always been the life of the party, the charismatic center that everyone else liked to swirl around. She no longer knew if she was in love with him, but she loved being in his presence, being the one he rested against while talking. He told them all that they'd driven in from Truth or Consequences, how he thought it was the real artistic center of the state, not Taos or Santa Fe, which were no more than the great tourist traps of the Southwest.

Sipping the sweet liquor made Holly feel warm inside and out, and she wanted to exit the cabin again, to sit and watch the field under the light of the heavens. Everyone else thought it was a good idea, too, and the couple pointed out that they might also be able to spot their missing companion.

The air was so clear now that the moonlight shining down on the poles lit them up like torches, though surrounding them was complete darkness. They were the only illuminated elements in a black, gaping expanse that stretched on past where the eye could see. De Maria's search for the right location for *The Lightning Field* was supposed to have taken years. Not only did he wish to find a place with a high incidence of thunderstorms (according to a pamphlet Robert had been reading in the cabin, they were still exceedingly rare, despite their increased frequency due to climate change), it also needed to be completely isolated—hopefully, for all time.

Holly pictured De Maria trudging across this land decades ago. In her mind, he carried with him some strange tool with two handles, and he'd chuck it into a hole and then kindle the stone at the bottom with it. He did this methodically, hole by hole, traveling across the land as a pilgrim himself. He marked the path alone, but behind him a team erected the poles, and if someone had seen him, it might have looked like he was marking the land with fence posts or planning the route of a railway, but his purpose couldn't have been more different. Each hole seemed to owe its existence to the one before, building something new upon a landscape cleared out by the blood and violence of progress, generation by generation.

A loud rumbling filled the air. Even Robert stopped talking, and everyone looked out at the field. The noise continued unevenly for a few seconds, then a single bolt of lightning crashed from above into one of the poles. The sound was deafening, like the sky ripping in two, and the pole lit up in flames. Holly thought the rumbling had disappeared, but her ears rang so loudly that she couldn't tell.

Robert screamed, "Did you see that? Now that's some motherfucking art." He ran out into the field, headed toward where the post still smoldered. The rest of the group followed after him, though more cautiously. There were no clouds in the sky, so the lightning seemed to have come from nowhere.

Robert was already at the pole when Holly arrived, and the fire had completely dissipated. "Don't touch it," he said. "It's still incredibly hot. Look at the way it melted the whole thing." The pole was now toppled over, its steel melted and blackened by the strike. The base still stood in the ground, but now slanted at a fifteen-degree angle. *The Lightning Field* had to have been made for this, but it felt to Holly like the strike had destroyed a temple, and she had to stop herself from crying.

"Let's go back. I don't want to be here, it feels wrong."

"Just a second, I've never seen anything like this before." Robert took off his scarf and wrapped it around his hand. He picked up a piece of blackened, glassy rock from the ground. "A souvenir from the trip."

As they walked back to the cabin, they heard loud footsteps behind them. It was the missing member of the party, shirtless and with some weedy foliage sticking out of his mussed hair. His strides looked too large and his movements too dramatic, and it was immediately clear that he was still high on peyote or whatever he'd brought with him. "It's an omen," he said. "A sign."

Robert laughed. He always thought it was funny to watch people who were drunk or high when he was sober. Holly found it cruel. "A sign of what, exactly? A storm?"

"It was struck by a blow from the sun." He said this with some solemnity.

"A cloud, but you were close," said Robert, though the sky was clear. "Hey, why don't you come inside with us, it's getting cold."

The man joined them, but he was in no mood to discuss what they'd all just seen. Once inside the cabin he walked straight into his bedroom and shut the door. Holly and Robert hung around the common area for a few minutes, waiting for the rest of the party to return. Then, after saying a quick goodnight, they went to their room.

Holly fell asleep to pleasant thoughts of seeing the field again in the morning, wondering how it would appear in a different light, but when she looked outside the next day, it wasn't like she'd dreamed. The missing pole ruined the entire sculpture, like a book with every other page gone, or one of those movies with all the good parts edited out. After a couple of minutes, she went back to bed and slept in until the driver showed up again.

On the way back to Quemado, Robert and the rest of the group were still in high spirits. They talked about having had a *true* experience, beyond what they'd hoped for. The driver told them that in the seven years he'd been taking groups out, only a couple dozen had even seen lightning, and it was only the second time a pole had been struck.

"So do you guys replace the pole or what?" asked Robert.

"Well, we did once, five years ago, but there's no money for it anymore."

"Oh. So it just stays broken then?"

"I guess so." The driver's voice dropped at the end of his sentence.

"Maybe that will increase the value of the work," offered Robert. "In a way, it's part of the sculpture."

"Maybe. I don't know. Visitors are less frequent these days anyhow, and the foundation's pretty much broke. This might be the sign that it's time to close up shop."

Holly was dismayed. "You can do that? Like, is that an option? I didn't think . . . I thought that, I don't know why, but I thought it would always be there."

"I suppose it might be. I mean, we won't break it or nothing like that. It'll still be out there, waiting in the sun like always. But I wouldn't be surprised if this was the last season we're taking groups up. I love *The Field* as much as anyone, but I'm not going to keep driving people up to it for free. I've got a family to support. Everything's gotta end at some point."

The van's jubilant mood dissipated, and what had been a quick ride on the way over now seemed to stretch into an eternity. To their sides, the desert stretched past the horizon in every direction, a hill-less expanse of rock-hard dirt without even the shadows of clouds to offer relief.

3

When the last tire of Gideon's car slid off the driveway, that really was it. That was a true good-bye. Whatever they'd said about remaining friends or keeping in touch, he certainly hadn't meant. He had no intention of ever calling Claire again, of pretending that he wanted to see her. What would be the fucking point?

A hastily packed trailer bounced behind the car, spilling all of his worldly possessions into a heap on its metal floor before he'd even made it two blocks away. Gideon had rented a small apartment in downtown Stamford, about a twenty-five-minute drive from their—correction— her house three towns away and as close to a train station as he could manage. He didn't plan on seeing anyone. For the first time in his life, Gideon felt that he understood his father's wish to disappear entirely, to pull a big Houdini on the world because it had become too much. Not that he forgave the bastard.

Two divorces by the age of twenty-five had to be some kind of a record, at least for his graduating class. Had Gideon not been in the middle of a project requiring constant oversight, he probably would've made good on those claims of vacating the tristate area, maybe gone back to New Mexico to visit his family. But since separating from Claire two months prior, he'd thrown himself into his work, tiring himself out so much that at the end of every day he had no energy left for crying or self-pity. He tried to keep his mind on unpacking the trailer, cutting open boxes, placing his meager belongings in an apartment that seemed at once far too small for him to fit in and far too big for what he owned, tried to keep their final conversation from echoing in his head yet again. He gave up before finishing the last load, falling asleep on a new bed he still hadn't purchased sheets for.

Gideon woke up with the sun. He added curtains to the mental list he was keeping of things to purchase for the apartment. He hurried to the train station and pulled up his presentation on his phone while he waited. Anonymous Propaganda had been even more demanding than usual lately, not to mention revolting. When he first took the account to AP, the head of Universal Music Group, Spencer Hutz, had told Gideon straightaway that he was only interested in making money and that not only was he deaf, he'd also never bought an album before joining the company. But as Gideon's boss, Eric McTeague, liked to say, if it wasn't an interesting problem, they wouldn't have come to us.

It was probably Hutz's disregard for music that had led them to Gideon's original proposal. When UMG first approached the firm a few years earlier, Gideon's name was still riding high off the success of the Great Wall of Freedom, and they insisted that he be put on the account. Of the five ideas that Anonymous Propaganda pitched Hutz, Gideon's was far and away the strangest, but unlike the others, it had both a base cynicism and historical precedent on its side.

At the time of his first big presentation to UMG, he'd still been a cocky kid. "All right. I'm sure you're all aware of what our basic idea is," he'd begun. "But I'm going to show you how we take that to the next level. Now, industry-made artists are nothing new, especially to the people in this room." Light chuckles from everyone, as planned. "What makes our plan different is simple: for the first time ever, the artist will be one hundred percent made by us, including background, history, family, friends, etc. We're not packaging a person. No, we're making a person from scratch to fit the packaging and then selling that product to kids. The artist we make will be as flawless as a Barbie doll, as streamlined and perfected as Coca-Cola.

"The Monkees have been done to death. What we need is an artist who can't become undone by fame, can't be caught with hookers and blow unless that boosts sales, won't be on a sex tape unless we produce and sell it, won't endorse sunglasses unless they're manufactured by us. No espousing trendy political causes unless that's how they draw in the youth demographic, no bad haircuts unless they need more tabloid coverage. No DWIs or bastard children. You ask how that's possible? It's possible because this person doesn't exist beyond what our publicists determine."

Here Gideon paused to make it clear he was finished. The woman sitting next to Eric responded, "I think I get it, essentially, but corporate adoption is still relatively unpopular with the public. Plus, the process takes way too long. We need to start thinking about how to spike next quarter's sales, not next decade's."

"I couldn't agree with you more, ma'am. Those are all problems brought in by living, breathing people—but we don't need one. Even if we raised someone, that person would always have an ego, whims. We'd lose our hold. There would be husbands or wives, rock-star excesses. No, we need something different, and we can finally make it happen. We have all the resources necessary to create an entirely computer-generated artist, but more importantly, we can create one that no one knows isn't as real as you or me."

That had been almost three years ago, and since then the "artist" Wyatt Collins Jr., aka Gravedigger, had been Gideon's bread and butter. Because it was his proposal, Gideon had talked his way into becoming the project lead, despite his age. Eric told his team that he had faith in Gideon, saw great things in his future, and left it at that. No one voiced resistance, as no one who had a problem with Eric's whims tended to stick around AP for long.

Today he was presenting the outline for a new album and its accompanying tour. Gideon felt anxious, couldn't help second-guessing every detail. He'd spent hours agonizing over which publications should be given interviews and what track styles to copy. Not that he suspected anyone would argue with him about the details, but right now he needed something to be good at, to prove that he still had some worth despite his crumbling personal life.

Gideon's train came to a stop and he rushed off with the rest of the commuters, heading up to the street and walking along Park Avenue before turning left on 57th. He passed the Universal Records Store and entered the building's lobby, then showed a security pass to the rent-a-cops and headed to the elevator. Waiting for it, he tried to psych himself up, silently repeating, "Don't fuck it up." He knew that some people responded better to love and support, others to abuse, but he hadn't the foggiest idea what worked best for him.

The elevator arrived, and he rode upstairs with a group of unmemorable men and women, their faces as blank as their streamlined outfits. The lift reached the office space of the UMG headquarters and he walked by rows of felt gray cubicles, the din of conversation from a few phones barely audible in the otherwise muted room. Men, almost all men, stared at computer screens in their white shirt/slacks/tie combinations, nearly identical in their dress and grooming, but even so he could pick out their pecking order from a distance just by the way they held themselves. A few cubicles had album art posted on their sides, and a series of gold records hung on the far wall, but this did little to enliven what was at its heart a place of business.

He made his way to the conference room without engaging anyone, even in eye contact. Three men and one woman were already seated, one fiddling with his phone while the others waited in bored silence. Gideon attached his own phone to the room's projector and opened up the first slide of his presentation, then joined the others in waiting. A minute later Hutz and his sign-language interpreter came in with Eric and they shook hands, Hutz saying in his too-loud, slightly slurred pronunciation, "Happy to see what you've got in store for us."

"It looks like everyone's here," said Eric. "Go ahead and get started."

Forty-five minutes later Gideon could barely recall what had happened, but he glowed with success, troubles with Claire completely forgotten for the moment. That was what he loved about work, the tangible results, the fact that good and bad were easy to understand, success and failure easily quantifiable. Success, in this case, hadn't just been about whether they agreed with Gideon's decisions. They didn't, as usual, with every member of the committee butting in with their own "suggestions" for changes, their own utterly strange ideas about what should be done that Gideon would spend more time minimizing in the future than he would on delivering a quality product. No, the important thing here had been whether he was able to arrange it so that he could do his job managing Gravedigger's career from home, far away from Claire, whose office at AP's headquarters, Gideon could tell you, was precisely one hundred fifty-seven steps from his.

As he walked back to the elevator, Gideon began unbuttoning his navy Oxford shirt. Once he reached the lobby he almost ran back to Grand Central, already impatient for the train that would whisk him away from the looming skyscrapers and honking cars. Away from nine million people and into a solitary box he could call his own.

4

USgamer
Published online at 12:00 AM on April 23, 2037
USgamer Celebrates Arcadia's Tenth Anniversary
By USgamer Staff

A decade is an eternity in the world of video games. Ten years is more than just the gap between console generations, it's the jump from one era of games to the next. In a medium that moves at the exponential speed of Moore's Law, anything that remains consistent is an oddity, but because of that Arcadia has been the exception in video gamers' lives that proves the rule.

Arcadia's ubiquity—its overwhelming enveloping of the gaming landscape, its reshaping what we think of as the value of online social interaction—has overshadowed just how revolutionary the program initially was. Arcadia's success at "game-izing" the entirety of the Internet was controversial at the time of its launch, as was its procedural generation of new video games. Ten years and billions of dollars later, it's easy to forget that many critics believed Arcadia was destined to be a big enough flop to sink Electronic Arts entirely. Likewise, its creator Juan Diego Reyes, now regularly listed among video game greats like Shigeru

Miyamoto, Will Wright, and Chris Avellone, was at one point a controversial figure.

In celebration of its tenth anniversary tomorrow, over the next week the entire staff here at *USgamer* will be focusing coverage on Arcadia. Check back every day so you don't miss any of our features.

Monday

An Oral History of Arcadia's Beginning: We piece together Arcadia's origins, with new information and interviews from deep-behind-the-scenes sources like Randy Pritchard, EA's ex-CEO; Eric McTeague, the head of Arcadia's initial marketing team; and recently rediscovered archival interviews with the notoriously reclusive Juan Diego Reyes.

Tuesday

Top 10 Procedurally Generated Games: The cream of the crop in games that Arcadia came up with itself. Believe us, it was difficult to limit ourselves to just ten—post your own favorites in the comments section.

The Controversies that Shaped Arcadia: Despite its enormous userbase, it's been a bumpy ten years for Arcadia. From concerns about privacy to creators' rights and royalties to the mysterious disappearance of Juan Diego, we take a look at how controversies have changed Arcadia's landscape, for better and worse.

Wednesday

Where in the World Is Juan Diego Reyes?: Speaking of controversies, we take a look back at the media circus surrounding the sudden and still-unsolved disappearance of Arcadia's creator Juan Diego Reyes five years ago, the effects it had on Arcadia's development, and the latest theories and rumors as to his current whereabouts and activities.

The Strange Realm of Juan Diego Reyes's Gameography—From Apopudobalia to Zero Sum: We played through and ranked all of Juan Diego Reyes's pre-Arcadia releases so you don't have to. See which games held up to the test of time and are still worth spending your points on.

Thursday
The Ten Easiest Ways to Rack Up Arcadia Points: Not earning enough while playing *Duty Calls*? Here are ten ways to rack up points in no time and keep the free-to-play system free.

Friday
The Future of Arcadia: We interviewed acting head of Arcadia Jake Simmons about what's next for the program. He answers our questions about new releases, upcoming changes to the UI, the effects of EA's merger with Monsanto-Halliburton, and whether rumors about Arcadia 2.0 have any truth to them.

5

At its most basic, concrete level, the concert was being performed in a small office space in lower Tribeca. While the operative voice replicator and mo-cap-to-CGI programs had been designed years ago and tested countless times, it was still a live event, and as such someone needed to be monitoring and manipulating the various tiny parts of the show that made it, in every sense except perhaps the most important one, authentic.

Little things had to go wrong. Maybe a song started a little bit off, or a person tried to rush the stage and briefly got on before getting pulled away. These details had all been preapproved and tested, but their timing would be up to live operators working to craft a perfect simulacrum. Or, as they liked to put it, giving the fans a real show. The crew put many possible scenarios into the performance AI, too, reactivity drawn from top-of-the-line video game middleware that was so sophisticated not even its designers could fully anticipate its responses. At some level, though, you wanted a human involved in order to make sure things went smoothly. This was the responsibility of five "creative" personnel, who were wired up with their supervisor, working out of Connecticut, and two technicians (focused not on the performance itself but on Arcadia's infrastructure) based in the EA office in Albuquerque.

Eight people may seem like a lot to make just one program run smoothly, but the concert's expected attendance was six hundred thousand, so AP liked to have some insurance. If an error were to occur, it usually hit in the first ten or fifteen minutes, and so far the show had been going smoothly. The live stream hadn't hiccupped once, and Gravedigger excited the crowd exactly as he was designed to.

Searle Díaz—Disney to his friends, for reasons largely forgotten—watched the concert in his bedroom. He'd blacked out its windows years ago with three layers of curtains secured to the walls by electrical tape, allowing only the tiniest glimmer of light from the outside. He'd never figured out how to adequately block out the light coming from the crack beneath his bedroom door, but since his grandmother was away on her night shift, every light in the house was off, the only radiance in the room coming from his computer screen and the neon diodes on its casing. This was, he typed into the Arcadia channel |3ə, the ideal way to view a concert. With no one else at home, Disney cranked up the music; bass beats pumped out beneath his desk while avatars on the screen in front of him jumped up and down to the rhythm of "St. Florian" and Gravedigger's shout-singing of the chorus: "Took all them police to bound me/fought fire til they drowned me/Don't fucking surround me/I do this on my own."

Dizknee: Hey, who's in the crowd?
Dizknee: Cause it looks like a serious shitstorm down there to me.

A swooping crane view of the arena filled Disney's monitor (there was no actual crane, of course), then cut to other carefully chosen shots of Gravedigger's performance. One corner of the screen was taken up by a virtual camera Disney had positioned himself, a permanent view at the center of the stage. The main camera dived from the back of the room through the ocean of people, which looked to him like maybe a couple hundred thousand strong, not quite as overwhelming an audience as some had predicted. That could mean attendance was disappointing or, equally likely, that a lot of people had opted for semi-omniscient views of the performance like Searle had.

DevolChilde: Hell yes, and it's fucking crazy.
DevolChilde: I don't see anyone I know, but whatever. Being down here is a beautiful thing. This is a real goddamn experience.

Devon nodded his head to the music, swiveling his whole body in his desk chair. He wore a Gravedigger T-shirt and sang along silently with almost every word in the song. A few minutes earlier he'd been doing so at his normal talking volume, but when he heard Autumn in the hallway he'd stopped out of embarrassment. Of anyone to have heard him stumbling his way through rap lyrics, his mom was the worst. She would never understand why he needed to proclaim his love for "Tapping hos' behinds/so fast they have to form a line." They were close, but not that type of close.

DevolChilde: Best part about this: I don't have to smell everyone.
ʃeter: I'm stuck at my grandparents' house. Couldn't get out of it.
ʃeter: I'm still watching it over here, but I may be in and out.

Pedro Esqueda wasn't lying about his situation, the most irritating part being that while his grandparents would've understood him skipping the visit to attend a concert, his parents wouldn't. They asked why he wanted to be there tonight when he could just buy a recording. Pete wanted to explain that just because his dad could watch recorded sporting events didn't mean he'd lost his interest in watching or attending them live, but he knew it was an impossible argument. As a result, Pete was accessing the show from his phone in a bathroom he'd been in and out of all evening, having told his parents he didn't feel well after forgetting a Lactaid pill.

M1: Whoa, dude, I hope this set is fucking long.

TeslaTank69: The digger you know he doesn't cut any fucking slack. Tells it like it is y'know.

TeslaTank69: It's like he says when he says how it's like being the court jester to the American fucking people right and slamming down on that truth.

ʕeter: Looks like a good 150 or so members in the house, Diz. Not bad for a school night.

Dizknee: So are those women on stage supposed to be real people, like their avatars, or are they just programs?

SpicnSpanish: Does it make a difference?

ManicPixelDreamGrrl: Don't be such a perv. Spank on your own time.

DevolChildə: Goddamn Saintly Sinning is a great song. If I could only listen to one song this would be it.

DevolChildə: Or No Afterlife. I hope he does that one too.

StackAttack: Hey what are you guys doing later?

NealOrDie: Smoking a spliff. Then maybe smoking a blunt.

IcarusSr: What about Paint it Black? I thought you were really into that one. Or am I thinking of Billiam?

StackAttack: Dude, those are the same thing. Also, Neal, you're not in the 505, and I'm pretty sure you're like 13.

Steve's Slave Until He Has Proven Himself Worthy of His Own Screen Name(Which At This Rate Seems Unlikely To Ever Occur Before The World Ends): Goddamn some of these people are fucking pushy. Why couldn't they have made it so physics didn't knock around my view?

NealOrDie: Fuck you they're like totally different. One's like for a quick hit and one's big and deep.

NealOrDie: And fuck you if I just want to get nicely toasted. I'm 28 I'm way older than you.

BigRalph: Dude that's kid's stuff anyhow. Go get yourself some e or k or shut the fuck up.

Dizknee: If you're in the crowd there's ragdoll and collision physics for your avatar. That's why it makes sense to go omniscient-style and just observe.

Disney thought he heard a sound in the house but ignored it. More than likely it was his grandmother returning home with somebody or another, the latest in a long line of men come to replace her deceased husband, in which case she'd be more than happy with music as loud as Disney could make it. And on the off chance it was a burglar or something, he figured it'd be safer to just let them take what they wanted from the rest of the house without interruption.

DevolChildə: I like it, I suppose, but black also isn't so bad to me. I mean, it's just nothingness, I don't have the whole sadness connotation that he does.

Steve: Neal shut your head hole. I just checked your fucking age and Jeff was spot-on, you little prepubescent dipshit.

Steve: You wouldn't know good weed if it was growing between your nostrils.

Estéban Vásquez had Gravedigger's performance playing on his screen in a windowed format while he compiled a program in the background and ran his usual display of porn and clan stats on the side. His PC struggled to perform all of these operations at once, but he didn't really mind watching things a bit choppy. He lay back on his mattress, resting directly on the room's shag carpet, sheets covered in crumbs, and took a deep swig from a box of wine he poured directly into his mouth. Nothing better than relaxing to good music while harshin' n00bs online.

CompanionBot112: Shit is anyone else's feed breaking up?

LeanMeanGrillingAutomoton: Nah man. Comcast?
CompanionBot112: Comcast :-(
Bill.I.Am: I'm here to the back left side. Contrary to popular belief, I'm even enjoying the show, although I still don't see what all the hype's about.
Bill.I.Am: Have to admit he's better than I thought he'd be. Even if he's a sellout.

William Voluminous Jr. had the concert playing on the left side of his screen, while on the right was the clan's statpage. His legs rested on his plywood desk and he wasn't lying, it was a pretty damn good show, though the lyrics were still typically terrible Gravedigger drivel. He tried to tune them out and just hear the beats, the inexorable thumping that carried the music forward and made Billiam's heart rattle in his chest. His door was closed so that he could keep his legs up and relax without being bothered by either of his parents, who each liked to stop by his room at least a few times a night because it offered an excuse to look down the hallway and make sure the other wasn't enjoying himself.

Billiam's house had the oddity of being in nearly every way symmetrical, with the exception that the kitchen on one side was mirrored by a parlor on the other. Billiam had the master bedroom because it happened to be in the perfect center of the house. Years ago his father had won what he later referred to as "the motherfucking lottery." Not the full jackpot, but still a substantial sum of more than eight hundred thousand dollars. Up until then William Sr. had been a preacher, and gambling was his one little vice, so minor (he only bought a ticket or two every few months) that his wife Irma didn't complain about it, even though their religion said it was a sin. In fact, since the money earned off the lottery went almost directly into the school system, she helped him overcome his guilt about it by rationalizing that the tickets were a form of investment in their son's future—and if President Haight's government not only approved of but encouraged gambling, then how bad could it be? It wasn't like they were Mormons; it was his right as an American to have a chance at the jackpot, and she would gladly defend it to their neighbors or congregation if the secret got out.

For a while they even made a little event out of it, the whole family sitting in a circle around the television set while the local news reported the Powerball numbers. Not that they ever expected to win, but with every ticket, Billiam and his parents loved how "close" they got to a jackpot.

No one was prepared for a win, least of all William. They had been watching television in the living room and because it was a Saturday night, an old movie was on, a musical with so much singing and dancing, so many odd slapstick jokes and stylish flourishes, that he couldn't put together what the hell the plot was. William had his laptop open, hitting refresh every few seconds so he'd know the moment the winner was announced. Suddenly he jumped out of his seat and started screaming that he'd won. He ran up to Billiam and Irma, hugging and kissing them again and again. Irma cried tears of joy, and Billiam started laughing, images of the life of the world to come flickering through his mind.

After a few minutes of jumping and yelling, they opened up the only bottle of alcohol in the house, a cheap white wine stored in one of those ugly green bottles that skunks beer, downing its contents like they'd found a river of salvation at the end of a desert. Even Billiam, just fourteen at the time, got a glass. Then William yelled for champagne, saying that a real celebration called for the good stuff and that he was headed to the bars downtown to get some. Irma should meet him there, call him when she finished preparing for a night out. Billiam asked if he could stay up all night now, after all it was Saturday and who needs church when your family's loaded? In his good mood, William said sure, why the hell not—given their income bracket, his son should start getting used to having his way.

William headed out immediately, while Irma danced and sang around the house, cranking the TV's sound way up and pretending she knew the songs in the movie. She struggled into a dress she hadn't worn in more than a decade and Band-Aided her feet so that the heels that made her legs look amazing wouldn't give her blood blisters.

Billiam went to his room and pulled up Arcadia, telling the Baby Eaters clan that some crazy shit was going down over at his house and that, as a result, he'd soon be treating everyone to some new levels and loot. Then he dropped out and pulled up some porn, thinking about the way girls would start treating him now that he could afford to take them out to the nicest restaurants in the city, the Artichoke Café and El Pinto, while the usual chumps were still headed to the Frontier. After he came, Billiam lurked invisibly in the clan channel and enjoyed hearing speculation about what it all could mean. Steve thought it was an amazing prank and was jealous he hadn't come up with it, while Devon seemed concerned that Billiam was going to give them all his shit and then kill himself, which Billiam thought was just fucking hilarious.

Once he hit the bars, William loudly announced his good fortune and forgot the champagne in favor of beer. The whole room became a party. One person had him yell out his numbers and then everybody cheered. A couple of girls latched on to him, and when his phone rang with a call from Irma asking where he was, William immediately silenced it. Someone from across the room asked to see the ticket and he passed it across, loving the way everyone marveled in the meaning of its numbers, its metamorphic aura. Each time someone saw it they bought him a round, and then someone else asked to see it, and the good times stretched on into the evening, a stream of laughter and hugs and dancing that William could barely believe was happening even as it all occurred.

One of the women who'd been hanging on to William said she lived nearby, and he wandered with her and her friend out of the bar. Trying to show off to them along the way, he pulled out his phone and called up the church office, disregarding dozens of texts and voice mail messages from his wife. William had always hated the bastards who attended his church, a bunch of fundamentalist dickwads who wouldn't know Jesus if he were hanging from a crucifix on their lawn. He spoke his drunken, unfiltered mind at them and left a scathing six-minute message on the church's voice mail before texting everyone in his congregation that they could blow his rich motherfucking cock. Then he fucked those two girls, the first women other than Irma that he'd been with since his sophomore year of college.

It wasn't until the next morning that he noticed the Powerball ticket in his wallet wasn't the same one that he'd bought.

God said that Billiam's parents had to stay together, at least that's how Billiam heard it explained, but that didn't mean they had to be happy about it, and a few days later Billiam's house was divided down the middle by a large painted line. Billiam didn't think it was as weird as it sounded, and it rarely had much of an effect on his life. How often did he really need to talk to his parents anyhow?

6

It would be categorically false to say that Gideon hadn't left his apartment in three weeks. It would, on the other hand, be no exaggeration to say that he hadn't gone farther than a thousand feet from his bed. Stamford turned out to have an exceedingly good food-delivery service, with prices barely more expensive than a grocery store's, so every few days Gideon opened up a green plastic bin filled with milk, eggs, butter, fruit, and other essentials packed with dry ice. Admittedly, a lot of what he had delivered went to waste because he preferred ordering pizza to cooking, but having perishables lent his life a sort of domestic normalcy that he appreciated.

He'd even set up a small fitness room in the back of the apartment so that he wouldn't need to head to a gym or worry about how constantly staying inside—almost always either sitting or lying down—might ravage his body. Not that it mattered here, since no one would see him, but Gideon knew that one day he might wish to return to the rest of the world. He had a bench set up, plus free weights and an elliptical. He hadn't used them with anything approximating regularity, but they were always there waiting for him, and because of their presence he felt fully self-sufficient.

Never having to leave the apartment meant more time for himself, more time to do what he, rather than his ex-wife, wanted. More time watching movies and listening to music, no tedious shopping or worries about what the apartment looked like if someone wanted to pop over. More time for relaxing in bed, more opportunities to roll over and see that it was eleven o'clock and then, since there was no particular reason to get up, falling back asleep. (As an experiment, he spent an entire day in bed, apart from using the bathroom, to see if he liked it. At first he did, but at the end of the twenty-four hours, he felt awful, wracked with unhappiness for reasons he hadn't been able to decipher, and hadn't tried it again.) The cogs he'd set into motion for his job required a fair amount of effort to keep turning, but not as much as he'd guessed, and being out of the office meant that he got back all of the time most people wasted on nonsense, the coffee breaks and meetings and progress reports that until now made up what he knew as adult life. Most of all, staying in the apartment meant endless time online, endless content on Arcadia. And that meant looking at women.

None of the streaming girls were around all the time, in fact most of them were pretty damn unpredictable, but that didn't matter too much to Gideon. Sometimes he had two on in different windows, but usually he just watched whichever of his favorites happened to be streaming at the time, the result of hours spent searching through camfeeds until he found someone he couldn't get enough of. One he followed because when he first happened upon her channel, she was masturbating with her mouse and he'd never seen anyone do that before. Another reminded him of a girl he'd known in college, something in her eyes or maybe smile. She was pretty tame by web standards, only stripping or lightly playing with herself, but he still liked sitting in on her sessions and watching her giggle.

He'd spotted his newest favorite at the end of a long day, more than ten hours of staring at his computer screen. He had begun to doze off, and at first he thought he was hallucinating. She had long dark hair, skin nearly the same shade, and eyes that seemed too big for a real human, more like an idealized version of a face than one that could occur by nature. With most girls he didn't even look at their faces—what was important was the way their body parts fit together, like pieces of a puzzle—but with hers, he couldn't look away. Gideon had since become what was known as a "devotee" or "regular." Not a stalker, but more than just a guy who visited frequently. A lot of the more popular girls had some, and even he had to admit it was a strange relationship, as regulars tended to be more defensive of the girls' privacy than the women themselves were—jealous of anyone asking too many questions, like a spouse or significant other.

He'd found her soon after separating from Claire, first visiting her occasionally and then subscribing so that he'd be notified whenever she turned on her camera. He knew what music she liked, that she didn't like her hair so long, considered cutting it regularly but never did. He knew that her nose had a slight crinkle to its left side and that sometimes she became so absorbed in what she was reading or playing online that she completely forgot she had a camera running. Despite their lack of titillating content, these were some of Gideon's favorite times with her. He knew from watching her bedroom for hours that she read a lot but only physical books, never on a reader, which was either quaint and old-fashioned or a hipster affectation, depending on who you asked. He knew that she used K-Y lube and preferred wearing dark colors regardless of the season because she thought they went better with her skin tone. He knew that she was so embarrassed about her face that she refused to look in mirrors. He knew that she had a brown mole right next to her anus and that she was the tiniest bit bowlegged. He had seen all the contours of her body, was more familiar with them than he was with either his own or his ex-wives'. While he'd felt theirs, he had never just stared at them, examining every inch of skin for hours like a masterpiece in a museum.

What Gideon didn't know was her name. That is to say her real name, not the screenname NightXAngel that she unfailingly used online. Or where she lived, or who she was friends with. He was fully aware that they were not in anything remotely approximating a traditional relationship. But none of that made his feelings for her any less real.

"So today I was thinking we'd play a game of Truth or Dare," she said, speaking directly into the camera mounted above her laptop monitor so it looked like she was addressing each member of her audience individually. "But you know that there are some things I won't talk about."

She smirked and touched a finger to her lips. "Let's keep things completely sexual here."

Which was probably fine for almost everybody else in her channel, but he wanted more. Her name, of course, but really he'd be happy with any glimpse into her life outside the hour or so a day she spent on camera. What was she like when the computer was off?

GetItOn: Truth
SpanksfortheMammaries: Dare
Guest113: Dare

"I heard a truth first, so what should I tell you guys?"

Guest244: Dare
JonsonsJohnson: How many guys have you slept with?
SurlyDizknee: Dare
Guest113: Do you like it up the butt?
Guest12: What really turns you on?
GetItOn: Do you live alone?

"I think I'll answer . . . Guest Twelve, who asked what turns me on."

SpanksfortheMammaries: Fuck that, let's do a dare.

"I like a man who's really . . . faithful. I like it when I don't have to worry whether he's a big horndog sleeping around the town. If I know he has eyes only for me then I want to fuck his brains out."

Guest88: Cmon bitch do a fucking dare and show us your cunt.

"Guest eighty-eight, I think you should leave."

Guest88 has been banned from the channel

"That being said, I gave a truth, so now let's do a dare."

Gideon minimized the window. He knew how things would go from here. She'd stick something into an orifice and pretend to be getting off on it, which the guys would love and in return send her "tips" in the form of Arcadia points and positive reviews. And he couldn't complain, because most of the time he spent watching camgirls that was what he hoped for, too. But he kept her window open and the sound on so he'd know if she went back to talking about herself.

He pulled up the analytics on last night's show and started preparing for a presentation he'd be giving (via videochat) next week on the plan for Gravedigger's next few months. Five minutes into it, though, he became distracted by noise from the channel and maximized her chat window again.

When she logged off for the day, he cleaned up his desk with tissues before diving back into work with a whole new idea for what Gravedigger should do next week on *The Tonight Show*, which in deference to the lead guest would be shot in Arcadia using avatars for the host, band, and audience. He knew his boss would love it, not that Gideon gave much of a fuck about what he or anyone else thought at the moment. He felt too unhappy to register anything but the task at hand, and concentrated on losing himself in writing the fucking inane banter that would make this appearance go viral when it aired several weeks later. Her video streams were the closest thing Gideon had to human contact these days, and when they went off he felt not just alone, which was why he'd cordoned himself off in the first place, but lonely—not that he could admit that fact, even to himself.

7

Teresa stabbed a piece of chicken with her fork, but noticing her grandmother's glare from the far side of their dinner table, she left it on the plate. "Slow down a second," said Granny T. "We need to say grace." They always started meals this way, but she still always hoped they would forget, that they could just eat like a normal family without this arcane speed bump.

The three of them bowed their heads. "*Gracias te damos Señor por el alimento que nos has dado y que las almas del santo purgatorio descansen en paz. Amen,*" said her grandfather. It seemed like the hungrier she was, the slower he spoke, but there was still something soothing in these words she'd heard repeated thousands of times.

They sat around a small, square wooden table on chairs with homemade cloth covers, sewn by her grandmother when their seats ripped apart. Teresa ate quickly, out of both hunger and a desire to leave the table as fast as she could. Her grandparents always made dinners last an entire evening, stretching them out until her energy and patience had been sapped away by inane questions, but sometimes when she finished, they'd let her leave.

They ate in silence for several minutes, devouring reheated chicken enchiladas from yesterday that tasted just as good as they had the night before. Granny T didn't like cooking, even though she was the only member of the family who'd ever made a meal more complex than a sandwich, so she tried to do as much of it as possible at once and to stretch her dishes out for an entire week sometimes.

"And as I was saying about tanning," said Granny T.

That was the other problem with dinners. Teresa was stuck, forced to listen to how her loving but undeniably out-of-touch grandparents viewed the world, and worse, how they wanted her to live in it. She'd ducked out of this conversation earlier today, knowing it could lead nowhere good, but that didn't mean her grandmother was ready to drop the subject.

"I don't understand, it's not like I even . . . Granny, who even needs to get tanned in a bed—we live in a desert. If I want to get tan, all I have to do is walk around outside for five minutes. It's so bright out there you can actually watch as the cancer grows on your skin."

"Bullshit," said Granny T. Her ancient back was straight, and this posture made her look younger than she was, despite her gray hair and lined face. While she was stout and had the worst resting bitch face Teresa knew, Granny T was also quick to smile or laugh. The only truly talkative member of the family, she was also never willing just to be quiet and agree in order to make life easier, which Teresa thought was both admirable and stupid. "Folks said that when I was growing up, too, but kids used them back then, and I'm sure they do now. White girls always want to look like they've got some brown in them, eh? If you do it, though, you'll just look like burnt toast, and who wants that?"

"Mm hmm," said Grandpa Luis. He was too busy trying to make a straight cut with his knife to really care what else was going on in the room. He was the same way with everything, approaching tasks slowly but with absolute devotion. Even with his hands shaking he could carve a turkey cleaner than the food in catalogue pictures, or cut wood in perfect curves while working in the garage. He was regularly consulted by neighbors for advice on problems too tricky for them to work out on their own. Teresa had heard them refer to him as wise, saying that his unflappable, dawdling pace was a sign of his intelligence, but usually it just drove Teresa crazy. The math lessons he'd given her years earlier had been some of the longest hours of her life, so excruciatingly time-collapsing that she'd briefly fantasized about running away from home just to avoid them. The one time he'd needed to write an email, Teresa let him use her computer and returned two hours later to find him still editing its three sentences.

"Granny, everyone's known those things are dangerous since before you were born. UV rays aren't exactly a new discovery."

"That doesn't mean people don't do it. Don't pretend you haven't smoked a cigarette, and everyone knows what cancer sticks do to you. I'm just saying you should be careful about what you try on yourself. I'm sure those makeups you buy online are chock-full of hazardous materials, toxic waste and, and parabens and whatnot. Unless you grow it yourself, you can't be sure it's safe."

Luis and Theresa (Teresa had been named after her grandmother, but apparently her mother hadn't known the correct spelling of Theresa's first name, so her daughter ended up with a name inspired by, but one letter different from, her grandmother's) watched the local news three times a day and were some of the few remaining subscribers to the *Albuquerque Journal's* print edition, a luxury that they justified by living with practically no other luxuries whatsoever. They tried to keep informed about the world but distrusted almost everything they read or watched, saying the media exaggerated constantly to keep viewer and reader numbers high. Teresa had almost no memories of what they'd been like before retiring, but now that they had, the pair rarely left the house except for church or groceries. She assumed that everything they told her about the world and the people in it came from either dubious reporting or events that occurred before she was born, in which case their recollections were at best outdated and most likely riddled with specks of dirt and dust.

"I don't use 'cancer sticks' and I never did. But if I did, it'd be with the full knowledge of what I'm up to, same as with tanning beds. I'd never use one, but if I did I would do it as an adult, fully aware of its possible consequences."

"Okay, dear," said Granny T. "It's just you've been wearing a lot of makeup lately. And I know you may be hearing things about what it takes to look pretty, what boys like and all of that nonsense."

"Is it a crime to care how I look?"

"No. I know that. We both know that, don't we?" She looked back to Luis for approval.

"Mm hmm," he said, dipping a tortilla into the remaining sauce on his plate. He liked to eat his food one item at a time, which drove Teresa crazy whenever she noticed it. Afterward he would drink in the same manner, but never while he was eating because he was so engrossed in the food. Back in high school, when she'd first moved in, Teresa used to wonder whether he enjoyed eating more than she did, whether for him it was a wonderful experience while to her it was just like filling a car with gas.

"And I was just seeing that on the news the other day," said Granny T. "I don't know when it was but I made sure to remember it because it was something you missed and I knew, I just knew that it would be something you should hear about."

Teresa simply stared back at her, having decided that the best possible way to leave the table was to let her grandmother ramble. That was always the way. They talked, she listened, and while she loved her grandparents dearly, this was also why she so desperately wanted to move out. Having nearly finished with their lives, all they had left to do in this world was to advise hers.

"There was this young girl, about your age I think, maybe a little older," said Granny T. "And if I remember correctly she was trying to impress some boy or something. Wasn't that it?"

Grandpa Luis looked up, swallowed his food, and answered. "No. No, they didn't actually say why she did it."

Teresa was shocked by this reaction, and so, it seemed, was Granny T, who took a few moments to recover. The pair rarely disagreed and for the most part functioned as a unit. It was sometimes hard even to think of them as separate people. Sure, Luis would be out in the garage making table legs while Theresa spoke on the phone with faraway friends that she rarely ever saw. But for the most part they seemed like two organisms that had somehow combined into one, with memories, thoughts, and feelings that only ever complemented each other. They'd been together for more than sixty years, at least that's what Teresa guessed, though she was far too embarrassed to ask. She could probably figure it out if she knew one of their ages, but she'd never asked about that, either. While they'd always been old to her, their aging seemed to have slowed down so that they were perpetually old yet never decrepit or enfeebled. Age attached itself to them, adding more wrinkles and liver spots but leaving their routines and personalities untouched.

"They . . . are you sure?" asked Granny T.

"Yes," said Luis.

Teresa interjected. "Not important. What's the rest of the story?"

Granny T looked back at her husband, but he was already back to his second helping of enchiladas. "Well I thought it was about . . . well anyhow, it might've been a lot of things, but this girl . . . for whatever reason she goes into a tanning salon to get herself prettied up. You know there are legal limits on how much time you can spend in one of those things. Just because they're legal doesn't mean the government isn't aware that they're bad for you."

"I know they're bad. I don't need to resurrect the FDA to tell me what I can and can't do to my body," said Teresa.

"What with Haight in the White House deregulating everything he can find and erasing immigrant rights, saying that the federal government shouldn't be—"

"The story, abuela? El cuento?"

"Sorry, I just get so frustrated sometimes with those politicians. What I was saying, dear, is that after they make her leave one tanning salon, she goes and visits another one. She visits . . . I think it was four salons a day?" Granny T looked up, then continued when Luis made no move to respond. "It must've been four a day for maybe like a whole week. Or it might have been longer, I can't remember. But then she started smelling funny."

"Eww. Really?"

"Everyone around her starts noticing it and some of them even mention it to her. Can you imagine? She visits her doctor and the doctor tells her, 'Honey, I'm afraid to say this to you, but you've cooked most of your internal organs and unless we can find you a number of transplants, I don't think you have long to live.' The news program, I think it was *Action 7*, not that grubby *News Four* team I can't stand, they had these pictures of the girl and she looked like an absolutely gorgeous Chicana, though I guess she was white. Maybe she was trying to pass, ha. Her parents came on, sobbing, talking about how they hadn't known what was happening. They noticed she was getting a little tan, but thought maybe she'd just been out getting some exercise."

"Wow. So did she die?"

"They never did a follow-up. Maybe? I think it's like those people on TV who can't stop getting plastic surgery, even when it makes them look worse. She got addicted or something to the rays, or maybe the tanning beds cooked her brain a little bit so she didn't realize what was going on. And she was still a pretty girl. Even with all her insides cooked, it was a nice shell of a person they showed on TV."

"I hope she survived."

"Me too. It would've been a pretty sorry way to lose a life. So be careful with what you're doing to impress boys."

"I'm not going to cook my insides. And as you said, I'm already 'tan.' Grandma, Grandpa, may I be excused?"

"Certainly, nieta. Just put your dishes in the washer first."

Finally. Teresa cleared her place, walked down the short hallway to the back door, and exited the house. Her room was a converted garage, which she'd insisted on after turning sixteen, not because it was a great space (it wasn't), but because it wasn't connected to the rest of the house. Her grandparents had never been invasive, but at the time it made her feel like she was an adult, living on her own. Her grandfather worked with a plumber to create a bathroom for the garage, and even added windows cut into the back walls, thinking that she'd want some light in her room. She'd covered them with thick green curtains as soon as she'd moved in, but she had appreciated the gesture. Despite her laziness, she tried to keep the place clean to show her appreciation and because when it was cluttered, it still felt like a garage; adults, at least the ones on television—which were the only ones outside her family she'd ever seen—kept their homes streamlined and organized.

She flopped onto her bed and lay there for a moment without moving. But as soon as her eyes shut, she started wondering if something worthwhile was happening online. Maybe one of her favorite celebrities had posted a photo or she'd been emailed a limited-time coupon. When she was online, half the time she was bored with everything, reading the same blogs and watching the same shows and playing the same games on Arcadia. But as soon as she was offline she got an itch to check, to be connected, to hear something that drowned out her self-critical thoughts. It wasn't like she had any particular reason to rush away from dinner, but she couldn't shut off the part of herself that would rather have a mouse in her hand, refreshing her feeds until something, anything, happened to take her away from her life.

Teresa turned on her computer and checked to see if anyone she followed had updated their Arcadia profiles, but nothing seemed interesting or relevant. It was supposed to be easy to meet people through Arcadia. That was why they insisted that it was as much a social-networking OS as it was a game platform, but most people had friends through work or school or even organizations. Teresa always thought it was funny that her grandmother was warning her off boys and sex when either one would require a willingness to leave the house that she fundamentally lacked.

After a few minutes of screwing around, looking at news and hoping something would catch her eye, she sighed and pulled up freechatgirlz. com. In fifteen seconds she already had a couple of users in her channel, two named and two guests.

Guest317: What do you have planned for today?

"Umm," she said speaking at the screen, her voice picked up by a microphone resting below her laptop's keyboard. "I think I may wait a couple of minutes and then you'll get to see." This bought her time to decide. She hadn't logged on with a purpose; she'd gone to the site because she had no reason not to. It was something to do online, and it kept her thoughts off herself for a few more minutes.

GetItOn: What's that you're wearing? I don't think I recognize it.

"Probably because for once I am in fact wearing something. These are just my normal clothes. I wasn't really planning on having a session now, so I didn't put on anything lacy or kinky or whatever. But I figured, if I was going to be online anyhow, I might as well let you guys have a peek."

SpanksfortheMammaries: Can we get a preview . . . ?

"Oh, all right." Teresa stood up, turned around, and pulled up her skirt so that the camera got a view of her panties.

SpanksfortheMammaries has left a tip

"Thanks, Spanks."

Guest4123 has entered the chat
Guest93 has entered the chat
Jeremiahsbullfrog has entered the chat
LezBProud has entered the chat
Guest103439 has entered the chat
CaptainMCHammer has entered the chat

"Looks like a few more of you are here now, so I guess I should get started with, umm, something. Don't forget to tip if you like what you see."

8

According to most students and even some members of the faculty, Albuquerque High School was designed by a prison architect. The story goes that back in the 1970s, when the district school board decided that AHS should move locations, the city was still coping with student protests, which began the previous year when Jane Fonda spoke at UNM in protest of ROTC programs on the same day as the Kent State shooting. Students held the UNM Student Union Building until the National Guard was brought in and stabbed at least a dozen with bayonets, a move that backfired when it turned out that half of the victims were journalists or photographers there to cover the protests. The school board worried that AHS would be next, since the city's most central high school always had a strong connection with UNM and its new campus would be even closer to the university.

While this may sound like one of those things seniors tell incoming freshmen, the school's design made a pretty convincing argument. No room in the building had windows looking outward, which was said to be a safety measure, and as a result every classroom was lit by fluorescent ceiling lights. What windows did exist opened onto the school's courtyard, so that the building looked only at itself. Another design oddity was the school's single-story construction, said to be a defensive measure. The only exception was a watchtower overlooking the central hallways and courtyard. AHS's cloistered design was better equipped than almost anywhere else in the city to withstand a riot, though not particularly well suited to function as a place of learning.

The school had slowly grown during the years since its founding, including an addition for science classrooms that was as devoid of windows as the rest of the building but featured skylights. Fearing student vandalism, the powers that be installed metal crossbars in the roof, and the trickle of sunlight that did filter through multiple panes of industrial-strength safety glass was crisscrossed by classic prison silhouettes. It wasn't until the school's most recent addition that it broke free of the windowless motif, adorning the building's front with a wall of ever-so-slightly-green-tinted glass that transformed AHS's face from prison to corporate headquarters.

Some teachers in this new part of the building found the green light that passed through the windows sickening, covering their windows with blackout curtains and relying solely on the fluorescents. Mr. Hogan's class was notorious for its flickering bulbs, and while he tried to fix this periodically, the maintenance staff was unable to solve this problem for longer than two or three days at a time. Steve had dubbed Hogan's class the strobe room, and the name had stuck. Hogan had even put problems about his lights' rate of flicker on the winter exam, a move that while not quite clever was still appreciated for at least trying to relieve the monotony of AP test prep.

Mr. Hogan had a terrible sense of humor, but at least he tried. And lucky for him, he only taught the school's AP and honors math courses, which left him both his sanity and his self-esteem—had he taught pre-algebra, he wouldn't have lasted a semester. Mr. Hogan never seemed particularly concerned about whether his students noticed his Monty Python references, let alone his lessons, making him a particular favorite among second-semester seniors. Hogan liked to say that he was preparing the class for their AP exam, and anyone who wanted to pass it and earn college credit should pay attention. But he wasn't a babysitter, a point he'd once made to Ms. Phillips and Coach Nick, only to be laughed out of the teachers' lounge. Like a lot of his students, he spent most of his time alone on his computer, and felt little more at ease with his colleagues than with his classes.

Because of Hogan's leniency, his students regularly ignored his lessons. While most classes banned phones, in AP Calc II they were required for coursework (dedicated calculators having long ago been rendered obsolete), and this, combined with Hogan's turning non-confrontational teaching into something approaching an art form, meant that some of his students thought he'd almost be disappointed if they didn't take advantage of his leniency and spend the period online. At one point during the previous semester, eighteen of the class's twenty-six students had taken part in a three-day *Dead or Alive* tournament that, so far as anyone had been able to tell, Hogan never detected.

AP Calc II was Devon's favorite course at AHS—aside from the occasional test, it was just more games and chatting with his friends online, almost an extension of Arcadia. Hogan guessed correctly that his students wouldn't ignore his lessons entirely, but it's not difficult to pay enough attention to crib notes while chatting online at the same time, especially if you'd spent the past fifteen years of your life typing to friends regardless of whatever primary activity you happened to be simultaneously engaged in.

Devon's mind was split between whatever Hogan was talking about at the chalkboard, something about the difference between convergence and absolute convergence in a number series, and Disney's story about the dimensions, density, and spring coefficient of a girl's ass he'd seen while riding the bus up to the game store over the weekend.

Dizknee: It was so taut that if you threw a tennis ball against it, the ball would bounce back at you even faster than you'd thrown it.
Bill.I.Am: You're exaggerating.

It was five minutes until fourth period ended, and Devon had by now completely lost track of the day's lesson. Since it wouldn't be necessary until Wednesday's exam, it wasn't important. He picked up most of the course's material from the textbook or notes taken reflexively during class, and anything else he could copy from either Steve in front of him or Billiam to his right, neither of whom minded. Steve encouraged cheating as part of some weird vendetta against grades and rankings of any sort. In the three years of math classes they'd had together, Devon had never seen him take anything approximating a note, and he frequently went whole weeks without turning in homework, but that didn't prevent him from regularly acing tests.

Some students really gave a damn about their grades and deserved their stunning report cards. But Devon secretly thought they were a bit dimmer than his friends, who took the same classes as the future valedictorian yet barely tried, with resulting GPAs that only differed by two-tenths of a point or so. Try too hard and you ended up a scientist working sixty-plus-hour weeks at some corporate lab and earning shit for a living. But don't give a fuck, and do it with style, and you're already middle-management material. It was like President Haight said in one of his more famous election speeches: "You achieve what God wants you to, and no amount of hard work can change that in this world or the next one."

Devon had never told anyone, not even Steve, that he loved AHS, that the school so many others saw as a prison sentence, as some sort of personal insult against their autonomy and personal enjoyment of life—he dreaded the idea of it all ending. He liked the regimentation, knowing what he'd be doing the next hour, the next day, the next year. The way he saw the same people and had essentially the same conversations, only about newer games or maybe a different girl Disney was fixated on. School was something Devon was good at, a reassuring, real-world game engine where, after years of experience, he had mastered the rules. What came after graduation was a dark unknown that he did his absolute best not to think about.

School was a known quantity, an easy segue between games, and that was all Devon really wanted. He knew this made him weird. Everyone else had that one thing they couldn't take, be it a never-ending stream of date rejections or the conjugation of Spanish verbs, and you either figured out how not to let it bother you or dropped out. AHS had a high dropout rate, but there were also the flame-outs. Boys who showed up one day and started smashing security cameras with bricks and peeing down a row of lockers. Girls who couldn't take it anymore and decided that it really was worth the prison time if it meant they got to stab the bitch who'd made their lives hell for the past decade. While not everyone saw Karl Hong's body swaying slowly from the basketball hoop, everyone knew he'd taken his own life after being replaced as a starting forward by some freshman.

The bell rang for lunch, and they rushed out of class. Devon and Pete walked as quickly as possible to the halls outside AHS's courtyard where they ate most days. Devon waited on the bench where his friends ate every meal and pulled his phone from his backpack. Pete did the same. As they played, they talked about the previous night's raid, as they did every day. There was always a new game, or raid, or pvp map.

Up-tempo salsa music began playing from the courtyard while their friends joined them, pulling out their own phones and intermittently snacking as they made their way through *16 to Doom*, a puzzle-shooter Steve had gotten everyone hooked on. Every time someone opened the courtyard door, it blasted the area in sound, but Devon didn't even notice, already engrossed in the game and figuring that if they did well, they could get through the current level before fifth period.

9

Autumn looked in the mirror and didn't like what she saw. The red dress she wore was far too sexual, too low-cut. It had been her favorite for years after she first bought it, but that was . . . twenty years ago now? She could still remember finding it on the rack, marked down enough times at the outlet center between Santa Fe and Albuquerque that she could justify its purchase. It was still expensive, at least by the Target-or-Thrift Town standards they were living on at the time, but she'd decided to treat herself, just this once. Even Juan Diego, who seemed pathologically incapable of offering a compliment no matter how much she dressed up, had said that it looked "pretty nice" on her, which meant it looked stunning—plenty of men claimed they were interested in a woman for her mind, but he was perhaps the only one who seemed to be speaking the truth when he said this cliché, had told her on multiple occasions that he loved her because she was the only woman he'd ever met who was smarter than he was. The dress seemed tailor-fit for her body then, long and thin in a way that seemed luxurious, like a movie starlet walking down the red carpet.

Now, though, it looked way too young. It made her think of a child playing dress-up, or a seventeen-year-old trying to seduce an older man. She was still skinny, but not all straight lines anymore, and even slight lumps in the fabric made it look cheap. She took it off and decided on a simple black dress, no laces or frills or attempt at giving her the cleavage that even after three children she still didn't have. It was elegant, looked proper for someone her age. She matched it with black heels and a pearl necklace, both purchased, like the dress, since he left. Everything needed to look right, to emphasize the fact that she was doing well, that his disappearance hadn't touched her in the slightest.

She looked in the mirror again and liked what she saw, though she noticed the wedding band still on her finger. She didn't know why she still wore it. Five years earlier, when Juan Diego disappeared for the last time, unlike all the blogs and news outlets and social media of the gaming world, she'd seen it coming. It was a natural progression, like a puddle slowly evaporating into the clear desert sky. He'd always been mercurial, passionate about one project for months before dropping it entirely and moving on to something else, and that was as true with his family as it was with his video games. Eventually he'd stopped coming home for a night or two a week in favor of working on parts of Arcadia, its networking structure, its growth algorithms, its UI. Sixty-hour weeks became seventy became eighty until he didn't return at all.

They'd been married for nearly twenty-one years, but she understood him less as time went on.

She kept wearing the ring after he left, because as far as she was concerned, she was still married, even if they were separated. She had a family to take care of and only redoubled her efforts to create as stable and safe and normal a life for her children as she could. The ring gave everything a sense of normalcy, as if at some point Juan Diego would walk right through that door and everything would continue as before.

After six months, though, following a terrible day at work—with the Advanced MRI–based DayCart computer program still having trouble producing a readable manuscript for Glosster and her first deadline approaching at an alarming pace—Autumn needed someone to vent at. She needed someone to blame, personally and at great length, to unleash her fury on the one human who truly deserved to be screamed at—Juan Diego. Autumn had never raised her voice at anyone, had once overheard a colleague at the University of New Mexico refer to her as "fundamentally incapable of showing that much emotion," but at that moment she was ready to inflict real violence. She longed for it, to hit him with some large, blunt instrument until she collapsed in exhaustion. She had headed out to where she assumed he was still working, but once she had exited the freeway, the adrenaline rush subsided. She pulled to the side of the road and threw her ring, which bounced off the window and landed on the passenger seat. She cried one more time over his departure, over the years they spent together, drifting apart, over being the kind of person who assumed things would get better if only she pretended they were okay for long enough. And then it was over. She fixed her makeup, drove home, put her ring back on, and exited the car before cooking a well-rounded meal with a minimum of starches or butter for herself and Devon, as if nothing had happened, because as far as the rest of the world was concerned, nothing had.

Now, with a final glace at herself in the mirror, she left the ring beside her jewelry box and headed to her car, surprised that she didn't feel naked without it. She didn't feel any difference whatsoever.

Autumn placed the contract on the seat beside her, making sure everything was there. She'd had her attorney file the divorce papers on the assumption that there would be no response. Instead, Electronic Arts's lawyers contacted her and said that Juan Diego would be willing to sign the divorce papers only if she brought them to him in person. If that was all it took, she was willing to see him one more time.

Autumn drove her Prius up the winding hills leading into Mesa del Sol, the planned suburb of Albuquerque where EA and its parent (Monsanto) and related (e.g. Anonymous Propaganda, General Mills, and portions of the United States Defense Department ever since it became privatized) companies had headquarters or satellite offices. The compound's light brown walls topped with barbed wire came into her view and she pulled into the security gate.

The guard, a white man in his twenties wearing mirrored shades, asked what her business was.

"I'm here to see my hu—to speak with Juan Diego Reyes," said Autumn.

Perhaps taking her for a fan, the guard smirked. "I'm sorry, ma'am, but he doesn't work here. At least not recently."

"I understand that. But could you look on your list and see if there's an allowance for Autumn Reyes?"

He sighed. "Just give me a second . . ." He typed her name onto a tablet. "I'm sorry for the inconvenience, ma'am. I didn't, umm, does that mean he's here?"

"No problem. Could you just tell me where exactly it says I should go?"

"I guess so. Can I see an ID? It says here that you're allowed in Building C, that's the little one off to the left, Office 12."

"And parking is . . . ?"

"Right beside the building."

"Thanks," said Autumn, rolling up her window. The main parking lot was located on the other side of the compound near most of the offices, and there was no traffic, in vehicle or on foot, on her way to the small, unmarked building the guard had pointed to. Parking spaces alongside the building had numbers indicating who was assigned to each spot, but Autumn ignored these and parked in the first empty space she found.

Inside the unmarked building, windowless hallways and white floors glared from the harsh fluorescent lighting above. The doors to each side of her were stainless steel and heavy, so that the hallway looked as much like a clinically sterile corporate headquarters as it did a fortified bunker. She followed the row of identical doors down to the end, stopping finally in front of one that looked identical to the five before it and the six across from it, except for the cheap plastic "12" to the right of its handle. She slammed the handle down and opened the door.

He was lying on top of a disheveled bed with a laptop to his side. His head was propped up on his arm and the computer screen lit up his face, but otherwise the only illumination came from the blinking lights of a thousand diodes and what leaked in from the hallway. Autumn held the door open while she reached for a light switch. She flicked it on, and the man who was still legally her husband shielded his eyes.

"Did you have to do that? It's so bright, my God. It's like looking into a supernova."

"Yes," said Autumn. "You can deal with it."

"Well, what is it you want?"

Autumn took a moment to glance around the room. Electronic equipment seemed to coat every surface, with uncoiled wires spewing out of not just the walls and floors but even the mattress he lay on. Mixed with this were equal parts dirty clothing and takeout boxes, giving the room a fetid smell like a wet trash bin. Juan Diego himself looked haggard, with dark circles beneath his eyes and several months of graying facial hair obscuring his face. He'd grown a belly but lost muscle mass, his skin starting to pull tightly around his bones.

She had heard rumors about his absence, of course. Even with everyone around her doing their best to stay tactful, she'd heard the speculation: that he'd been using his money to fund a full-time orgy, that he'd given it all away to ride the rails, that he'd never existed in the first place and was just a media construct of EA's. Autumn had always assumed, though, that he had gone on his midlife crisis vacation for a year or two, whatever that might have entailed, then headed right back to living and working the way he had when they met—just another grad-school slob too immature to pretend he cared about the opinions and lives of other human beings. She found herself both gratified to be correct and more than a little disgusted by her present surroundings.

"I have the divorce papers for you to sign."

"Fine. Leave them here and I'll have them sent to your lawyer once mine have gone through them. I'm glad you came, though, there's something I wanted to talk to you about."

"Just sign the papers now. Your lawyers said there would be no problem if I came in person. I'd like to get this done and then leave as quickly as possible."

"You're not interested in what I've been up to, what my—"

"No. Just sign."

The divorce had been a long time in coming, but it hadn't felt right, hadn't felt necessary until now. With Devon's graduation just a few weeks away, she needed to move forward too. In the fall she would be the only one in that huge house they'd purchased together, and she wanted something besides its sepulchral silence to greet her at the end of each day. She needed to see other people, or at least find out whether that was what she wanted. Autumn was tired of his presence haunting her life, and as he looked at her with his darkening hazel eyes, she was happy to find that she felt no more regret, no more anger. Just relief that this was finally happening.

"Fine. I will happily sign the papers. But that's not why I wanted you here. There's something I need you to consi—"

"I have nothing to consider. Neither do you. If you were interested in me, or the family, you would've done something ages ago. Don't draw this out."

"It's not about us. It's about your work with Glosster."

Of course it was. He hadn't mentioned a thing about her dress, probably hadn't even noticed it, or the perfume she wore or that her hair still didn't have a touch of gray in it. He hadn't even asked about their children. Now and always, he just wanted her mind and what he could take from it. "Since when were you interested in publishing?"

"I'm not, exactly. But the technology you've been using over there, the research you've gleaned from the AdMRI, the patented work you've done mapping neural pathways and the human connectome."

"Just sign the papers. I don't have time for this."

"Here, hand them to me."

Autumn stepped over the cables and pulled the divorce settlement and a pen from her purse. He snatched the pen away and flipped to the back, scribbling his name and dating the paper with a crude signature. He practically threw it back into her arms.

"Aren't you interested in reading the terms?" Autumn didn't know why she asked, but perhaps it was because all of this had been too easy. She'd expected a fight, or at least an argument. Words that acknowledged, even passive-aggressively, some sort of regret. The reality of things, that he clearly didn't care, perhaps had never cared in the first place, was harder to take. Autumn decided she was done here and turned to head back outside into the fresh air.

"I'm sure they're perfectly fair. I just want you to listen to me for a second."

"I want to know why you left." She wasn't planning on asking him, hadn't wanted to hear it, but it slipped out anyway.

He smiled. "I thought you didn't care."

"Did you ever love any of us? Did you ever consider that it wasn't just about you?"

"I don't know. That's a difficult thing to quantify."

"Maybe for you."

"I evaluated my priorities and realized there were more important things in life. I won't say I don't have any regrets, but what's done is done."

"There are no more important things—what you left *was* life. Me and the children, that was your life." The only thing on hand to hit him with was her purse, which was too soft. Should she grab one of his computers?

"Not in a literal sense, no. Listen, things have been . . . a little out of control lately, and I don't have time to waste arguing about the children. I can't say I haven't thought about them, if that answers your questions, but I'm sure they're doing fine. There are more important things happening, Autumn, bigger than us, more important than family. I need to be able to access the work you've been doing on the AdMRIs. We need to understand how to take that raw data, the uncompressed brain imaging, and represent that on Arcadia. Flawlessly."

"So this is just about the patents?"

"Yes, it's about the fucking patents. I'm not crazy, I don't expect you to be happy with this, or to work with me. I signed your paper, I just want you to consider my proposal."

" . . . "

" . . . "

"How much?"

"I don't even know," said Juan Diego. "A lot. More than you'll ever know what to do with. Money is the one thing we do have plenty of. You know we could just purchase Glosster."

Autumn had no memory of a life without work. Even in preschool she'd been told by her parents to work hard so as to get into the right elementary school, the right middle and high schools, the right college. She never even asked for vacation days. But she'd grown tired. She couldn't help but wonder, finally, what she'd done all of this for, whether life had some purpose beyond her job and what it could give her children. Maybe it was time to be done with all of that, maybe this was the beginning of the end, the goal she'd always been searching for.

"If I say yes, you'll stay away. We're done."

"Of course. I'm pretty good at staying away. Let me call my colleague Victor in, he can tell you more about the details. That is, unless you want to talk to me about it."

"I'll wait for Victor in the hall."

10

A lot of problems, it turns out, don't really have solutions. You can ignore them or rearrange them a bit, you can rename them or redefine them or sometimes even redistribute them, but you can't actually get rid of them. Not really. Once a glass falls and shatters, even though all the physical pieces are still there, each crystalline shard easily accessible, you still can't reassemble the original glass. Eventually you have to confront the fact that many things only work in one direction.

That's at least one explanation for where the Great Wall of Freedom initially came from, another being that a young Gideon Reyes came up with the idea because he really needed an "A" on a freshman marketing assignment and, only six hours before his deadline, realized that his previous idea wasn't going to cut it. Not having enough time to work out a complex, nuanced idea, he opted instead to show off something big and impressive, praying that the class wouldn't ask too many questions about it.

Methamphetamine was developed in Japan in 1919 and subsequently used by doctors to treat asthma and narcolepsy, not to mention its well-publicized use by bomber pilots in WWII. By the 1950s, it was commonplace, one of the drugs of choice for everyone from college students to corporate lawyers to gutterpunks. Use of the drug decreased following passage of the Controlled Substances Act in 1970 before increasing again in the 1980s and rising to epidemic proportions in the 1990s and beyond.

Meth was the most American of drugs, not just because of its universal clientele but because of the way it's produced. Cocaine, marijuana, and heroin were all derived from plants, and plants require cropland, harvesting, rainfall, etc. They're dependent on factors that can't be completely controlled. The weed in your house right now is different from what your neighbor has because of varying levels of CO_2, water, light spectrum, and soil pH, not to mention inherited genetic traits. Even the most highly processed heroin is dependent on these factors, and prices can fluctuate with a bumper crop or a fallow harvest. Anything organic is variable, which is why so many prefer that crops are treated with Monsanto's finest, a process that effectively turns organic produce into manufactured goods while they're still in the ground.

Meth was produced indoors, and with the right resources could be made with the same factory precision as a silicon chip. It had an insane profit margin, even outstripping cocaine, so that even the most modest of operations could expect impressive growth. It not only made users more awake, it also gave them increased concentration, self-esteem, sociability, and aggression, helping a population of increasingly sullen introverts to socialize. And best of all, whether smoked, snorted, injected, or taken as a suppository, it's startlingly, almost absurdly, addictive.

It should come as little surprise that meth had long been illegal, considering that its side effects were extensive and truly ghastly and its production highly toxic and combustible. But the United States didn't really begin cracking down on it until the 1990s, after the number of meth heads suddenly exploded. Especially in the Southwest and Midwest, where isolation was common—epidemic, really—the overnight proliferation of meth labs was universally seen as a law enforcement problem. Nothing could keep meth labs from cropping up, but pressure put a damper on the local manufacture of the drug and made it possible for other suppliers to break into the market. Surprising absolutely no one at all, those suppliers turned out to be Mexican.

The reigning drug cartel at the turn of the century, and throughout the next few decades or so, was Sinaloa. Large, organized, and with so much of the Mexican government in its pockets that it could practically operate in public, Sinaloa spent years building the meth market into a trade that, while illegal, could operate on street corners with impunity. For years there wasn't much difference between the cartel and any other corporation, and certainly it was little worse than any other organized crime ring. That is, until the Zetas decided they wanted a cut of the business.

Los Zetas existed in some form or another since 1999, when the original core group deserted the Mexican military to join a drug cartel. Eventually they left the cartel, too, deciding that they'd had enough of being told what to do and at the same time shedding any restraint that had previously kept them back from pure sociopathy. They turned violence into a language, and the dead bodies they left, stripped of various limbs, sent messages to any who saw them. A missing tongue meant the victim talked, missing legs meant they had changed groups. A missing head didn't mean anything different than it did in other circumstances, but that didn't make it any less clear, and Los Zetas had a well-known predilection for beheadings. The main message, though, wasn't in the particularities of each victim but in the sheer quantity of bodies.

Sinaloa had always been about the business, as profit-minded as any publicly shared company on the Nasdaq. The Zetas were equally concerned with dollar signs, but unlike the older cartel, they were short-sighted and, what's worse, lacked the familial scruples that allowed Sinaloa to rise to the top. Rather than restricting themselves to drugs, Los Zetas kidnapped, killed, extorted, raped, robbed, and more in order to turn a quick buck, including selling from Sinaloa's territory rather than the shrinking number of areas the cartel didn't claim. Initially outgunned, Sinaloa found itself literally blown away by the new competition.

The war between the Zetas and Sinaloa escalated. More than ten thousand were killed annually, many of whom were merely bystanders or only peripherally involved with the drug trade. Entire cities became uninhabitable. If you looked down from one of the taller buildings in El Paso, the border between countries was unmistakable: on one side, a modern American metropolis with Walmarts and office buildings and McMansions to the horizon; on the other, a mangled ruin of broken glass and chipped concrete, bullet holes in every surface and roving street gangs that seemed straight out of *Mad Max*.

For a while, the American government's solution to the problem was to ignore it. Mexico had become the country's noisy neighbors; they made a lot of ruckus and dealt drugs at all hours, but so long as they stayed in their own yard, you wouldn't call the cops on them for fear of possible retaliation. But after a string of disastrous Mexican presidencies, the problem grew worse. Most of northern Mexico gradually became a war zone like Juárez, and violence began seeping over the border with alarming frequency.

The United States found itself at an impasse. It had attempted to combat the spread of the war through funding for Mexican law enforcement, but results had been minimal at best. It couldn't move to a more gentrified continent, and if lawmakers still waffled on legalizing marijuana, there was no way they'd budge on methamphetamine. So what was the country to do?

President Haight, quick to change subjects from his end-of-the-world prediction that hadn't worked out as he'd hoped, did what he'd done many times in the past: he asked the publicity firm Anonymous Propaganda, whose recent success working behind the scenes of his presidential campaign only confirmed the importance of consulting them for all major governmental decisions, if they had any bright ideas. To Haight's surprise and delight, they did.

Gideon's initial project hadn't been called the Great Wall of Freedom—that was a title that came out of extensive market research—but rather the "Mending Wall." When presenting it to his class, he explained that coming from a border state, he was well aware of the problems in the Southwest and thought that a drastic solution was necessary, something much bigger than the antidrug and immigration campaigns already in place. When he was little, he remembered his mother explaining to his father that they needed a bigger house or their children would hate each other. Juan Diego, having grown up with three siblings in a tiny three-bedroom apartment, disagreed, saying that he liked the feeling of a packed house. Gideon's mother had responded that good fences make good neighbors, which not only shut him up, it also soon resulted in their move away from central Albuquerque and into the foothills of the Sandia Mountains.

The idea of subsidizing the Wall with advertising, which was really the heart of the whole project, only came to Gideon a few minutes before the presentation, when he realized that the country—many trillions of dollars in debt—would need some serious help if it wanted the Wall to span the entire 1,969-mile border.

Gideon's teacher—a friend of Eric McTeague's who'd always rewarded the best final project's creator with an internship at AP—showed the idea to his friend as an example of young Reyes's creativity, and McTeague instantly saw its promise. When Haight first hired the company to deal with the "drug crisis," McTeague had his creative team begin brainstorming ways to make it appear publicly that Haight was doing something effective about it. They'd already briefly considered a wall, as well as a moat, a mine field, and even an irradiation field, but had discarded all these ideas as far too expensive. When Gideon's idea found its way onto McTeague's desk, the firm had been getting desperate. This desperation spurred some creativity, but ideas like offering the Mexican government one hundred twenty million shock collars seemed less and less likely to succeed. By solving the funding problem, Gideon found himself with an internship. AP also purchased the idea for a not-small sum and offered him a job with the firm once he graduated.

Of course there had almost always been walls along the Mexican-American border, but these were mostly small affairs, wooden posts or chain-link fences topped with barbed wire. They helped, certainly, but did little to deter anyone who really wanted to enter, and drug runners easily found ways around them. The Great Wall of Freedom was to be made of concrete, a minimum of sixteen feet thick and twenty feet tall at all points, with a walkway on top for patrolling guards. Advertising space would be available on both sides and at any location along the Wall, though after initial construction few cared enough to purchase any on the Mexican side—despite exceedingly cheap rates—and most corporations smartly focused on the border crossing points, where travelers could be stuck for hours staring at the same famous basketball player drinking Coke.

The number of crossing points was reduced from dozens to one per state, and even on the American side, lines of cars stretched for miles at these points, which were like fortresses, blocks of concrete so thick they were said to be able to withstand five megatons of explosive power without giving way, garishly outfitted with advertisements that would've seemed more fitting in Times Square. At night, the lights of these crossing points shone out through the desert like embassies from Las Vegas, neon rays and multiple-story flat-screen commercials keeping those stuck at the border (often for days) from falling asleep, their closed eyelids filled with images of Google, Coke, Disney, Apple, Nike, IBM, Ford.

President Haight, who'd been up against a wall himself about revealing his promised "secret solution" to the "Mexican problem," a claim he'd come up with during a debate and had been regretting ever since, was ecstatic about McTeague's news and began funding the project out of his own pocket before it had even passed muster in Congress. By the time the House blocked the bill's passage, the Wall had already made it a hundred miles inland from the Pacific Ocean and, more importantly, had secured huge sponsorship deals with numerous corporations who wanted to be seen as part of the effort to clean up the country and keep it pure for Americans.

When Congress put a stop to the Wall, at least from a federal standpoint, Haight appealed directly to the American public. What was now known as the Great Wall of Freedom (other finalists had been "The Wall of America," "The Liberty Wall," "Mexi-Can't Wall," "The People's Wall," and "The Greater Wall of America") was a way of protecting good, hard-working American citizens from drug lords and terrorists, while spurring economic development and reducing the national deficit. Haight's carefully calculated talking points hit a nerve with many of the country's citizens. By the end of 2029, when the Wall was nearly a third finished, support for it had grown to such an extent that the House of Representatives, which only a year earlier had called Haight's American Autonomy Bill (or "Beaner Bill") quixotic and destined to fail, voted in its support. The Wall was here to stay.

It wasn't long before Haight declared the Wall an emblematic cornerstone of his foreign policy strategy that he'd been planning since before he was elected. He had long been famous for his worries about foreigners, made worse when, in early 2029, Islamic terrorists hijacked planes headed for Italy and China, protesting religious discrimination policies recently passed in the two countries. The Italian flight crashed harmlessly (for all those not on the plane) into the countryside, due to the heroism of several passengers, while the Chinese flight crashed into a small office building in Beijing, killing hundreds. In response to these actions, Haight greatly expanded the scope of the Homeland Security Department and rebranded it with the now-infamous dark hoods and white insignias. The black-and-white regalia, adapted from the old logo of Haight's Heritage Baptist Church in Dallas, became synonymous with his presidency.

Haight's other secret to slowing down the deficit was to cut the United States, whenever he could, out of all forms of international relations. Embassies were closed around the world, as were military bases. The president called this his "live and let live" policy and said that if the rest of the world wanted to deal with the United States, it knew where to look. His noninterference was praised worldwide, and he was even given the Nobel Peace Prize in 2035, though he was unable to accept the award in person. The last time he left the country was in 2031, and by 2035, he'd long since quit leaving the White House, though rumors proliferated that he traveled the country in disguise.

The irony of the GWoF (aside from the fact that it was officially "opened" on Thanksgiving Day) was that it did little to nothing to stop either Mexican immigration or drug traffic, let alone drug-related violence, though few realized this after those statistics were deemed national secrets and kept from the public. However, it had been as effective as hoped in raising revenue, and in 2037, Haight began talks with his cabinet about raising a wall along the United States' border with Canada. Haight understood that it would be a harder sell for the public, and despite the success of the first wall, his cabinet was split on the proposition. But, as his secretary of commerce explained, "The president and I are really hoping to bring in a profit this quarter, and we think that this may be the way to do it."

Haight hadn't mentioned to any of the cabinet that building crews were already headed to Washington State, figuring that whenever they and Congress came around to the idea, everyone would just be pleasantly surprised at how many miles had already been laid.

11

Autumn smiled at Holly from across the table. "So how did the exhibition go? You sell a lot of paintings?"

Holly tried her damnedest to take this question at face value—as a mother innocently inquiring after her daughter in a supportive manner. Ignoring the subtext, that her choice of profession and lifestyle were both mistakes, was the only real way to keep the meal civil. She smiled broadly in return. "It went well."

Autumn nodded and seemed satisfied with this response. Next to her Devon absentmindedly fiddled with the peas on his plate, knocking them about with his fork.

Holly remained awkwardly silent. She didn't want to talk to her mother through this bullshit. She'd briefly considered staying in a hotel during her visit but knew that doing so would've caused more drama than it was worth. Plus, she loved Devon and all his uncompromising geekiness, and probably loved her mother, somewhere deep down—at least that was what Robert always said. Whatever other problems she had with Autumn, at least the woman had stuck around. And that was what you were supposed to do when twenty-one years old and visiting your hometown: you meet with your parents and pretend you're totally content with the choices you've made.

"It was wonderful," said her uncle Nick, jumping to the rescue. "I don't know if anyone bought anything, but that's not what these things are about really. It's about getting her some exposure, you know? And like having her name out there. People don't really buy art in this city, so the thing is you just try to get good write-ups and all of that."

This was almost verbatim what she'd told Nick at the show, but that didn't mean it was incorrect. Still, hearing her pep talk repeated back to her made Holly feel like throwing up.

Her aunt Charlotte and uncle Nick were seated next to each other opposite Devon and Autumn, and as far as Holly could tell they were genuinely happy to see her. She had no idea why, since they'd never been close and had nothing in common, not really, but they were good to have around because they kept things civil. In the Reyes family, the more people you had around, the less likely it was that someone would bring up a contentious subject. A small family reunion she'd attended when she was eight years old featured more people talking with the utmost seriousness about the weather than any meteorology conference ever did.

"The food was great, too," said Charlotte. "It's too bad you couldn't make it, I really just adored some of those cheeses. What did you say that one was called?"

"Garlic Brie. I'm glad you enjoyed it," said Holly. She wasn't about to mention specifically requesting that her mother not attend the opening. She'd even asked Autumn not to talk about it when she did inevitably visit the gallery. Holly couldn't in good conscience forbid her mother from seeing her paintings altogether (or rather, didn't want to cause her mother to lie about it), but fuck if she ever wanted to hear about it. Her mother's idea of good art was, and had always been, whatever sold for the highest price.

"That's great, I can't wait to see them. I'm sure they're all fantastic," said Autumn. "Has Devon told you yet that he's planning on going to UNM?"

"No, he hasn't." Finally a topic that wasn't her. "That's cool, Devon. Do you know what you're going to study yet?"

Devon didn't look up from his plate, instead mumbling something at them that sounded like, "Haven't decided. Maybe comp sci? Or possibly, I dunno, something easier. Not really sure yet."

Four additional place settings had been prepared, as well as enough enchiladas, tamales, and salad for four more people. Autumn had also invited Juan Diego's sister Yolanda, along with her husband and children, as she did for every family gathering, even a small and holiday-free one like this, but as usual they'd opted out, saying that someone was sick or whatever lie they found most convenient this time. No one ever seriously thought they'd show up, but Autumn always prepared nonetheless, and when anyone made jokes about their "illnesses," she shushed away their criticism.

"Devon, I know you'll be great at whatever subject you choose to apply yourself to," said Autumn. "I think that if you want to do computer science, you should really go for it. Or, if you want to go into English, I still know a lot of professors working there."

"Thanks, I'll . . . I'll think about it."

This passive-aggressiveness always drove Holly crazy. It wasn't that Autumn was a deadbeat parent. If anything she was too on the ball, too coldly supportive. When Holly was caught with a Minor in Possession charge, her mother had picked her up from the police department and, without raising her voice, explained that the only thing that mattered was whether Holly was safe. In the future, if she wanted to drink, Holly should do it at home with her parents (less than a month after that, she would have to change the word to the singular) so they could keep everything under control. Holly could even invite her friends if she wanted to drink with them. They could have a little get-together, or better yet, a sleepover, that way everyone's parents could be certain their children were safe and cared for rather than wandering the streets, paying homeless men to buy them 40s.

What Autumn didn't understand was that drinking at home was completely pointless because she approved of it, that most of why Holly began drinking was to find escape, from her friends, from a world she hated, and most of all from herself. After a night out she could touch her toes and not recognize they were hers. One of Holly's favorite teenage moments came when she woke up without knowing whose house she was in or how she had arrived there. For a few hours she wasn't Hallelujah Reyes, thinking and rethinking every little decision, micromanaging every choice. Instead she lived completely by instinct. She saw pictures at school that convinced her that those lost hours had perhaps been the most fun she'd ever had, completely worth the aches and nausea. Her only regret was that she experienced the ride through stories and videos on her friends' phones, never through her own memories.

But you can't have real fun when your mom checks in on you. You can't lose yourself, become just a body ricocheting off the beats of a dance floor, if you're safely at home. The MiP night was the first time Holly ever threw up from drinking, and as Autumn held her hair while she puked her guts into the cold porcelain toilet, Holly cried, not because of the retching, but because she wasn't allowed to do it alone. The next weekend she woke up on someone's couch spewing green vomit that tasted like bile mixed with corn syrup, wondering what she'd discover about herself when pictures of the evening were uploaded to Arcadia.

"You might want to visit me in T or C before the school year kicks in," Holly said to Devon. "The summer between high school and college is supposed to be the best one of your life—you'll probably never be that free again."

"Yeah, I might do that. I don't really have any plans right now." Devon pulled a phone from his pocket to signal that this small bit of conversation was over. Orange and neon-green lights from some unknown game lit up his eyes.

Autumn's smile wavered a tiny bit before returning to its usual fixed place. No one else seemed to notice; Nick and Charlotte were oblivious as usual to the family's friction. Holly knew what her mom's look meant, though: the child who'd dropped out of high school made a recommendation, therefore it had to be a bad idea.

It was no secret that Holly thought her mother was the epitome of a corporate shill and so probably not a good influence on Devon, the one child that Autumn still had a hold over. At least Gideon was completely honest about his choices. He worked for a corporation he couldn't give two shits about and would happily leave if he could keep his paycheck. They'd argued about this in the past, but Gideon was so aware of his own hypocrisy that it wasn't even worth talking about.

Holly could never tell if her mother thought of her work as "just a job," or if she believed it had some sort of real value. Holly couldn't imagine putting in the hours her mother did for something completely meaningless, but bankers, financiers, CEOs, stockbrokers, ambulance chasers, and politicians never seemed to think it was weird to work more than sixty hours a week purely for the cash. In some weird, fundamental part of her, Autumn always believed in the best intentions of everyone, even when it was obvious that a person or corporation was acting purely out of selfishness. A lot of the books she churned out as an "editor" seemed to center around telling people that what they were doing was fundamentally good: letting the racist military agent be the hero because he saved lives by stomping on the necks of terrorists, or making the woman fall hopelessly in love with the man who managed a petroleum byproducts factory and paid for her dream wedding with a holiday bonus earned by laying off a dozen workers at the Christmas Eve party. Their narratives cleverly reaffirmed the status quo. Life in America was always full of hard choices, and the books Autumn published offered the tacit answer that what was best for the easy-to-identify-with protagonist was best for everyone, unnamed supporting characters be damned.

"You could also get a summer job to have some money for the school year," said Autumn. "Or I'm sure we could find an internship for you. Your dad's name still has pull in this city. I'm not saying you shouldn't visit your sister, just that it's probably time to start planning for the future."

"Your mother's right," said Nick. "I always had a summer job, and the discipline I learned there has helped me out in life ever since. It may not be prestigious, but trust me, it's worth it."

Autumn and Juan Diego both worked constantly for as long as Holly could remember. Her mother had gone straight from undergraduate to grad school to assistant professor to tenured faculty in a spectacular, almost unique rise in UNM's history, one that almost certainly wouldn't have occurred had Autumn not been adamant about staying in the area so as to give her children some stability. She had worked in the English department as a leading researcher in the so-called third wave of cognitive literary theory, through a partnership with the neuroscience department. Her early breakthrough was realizing that if you really wanted to understand the way a person watched a movie or read a book, the best method was to go directly inside the brain.

Even a few years earlier this would've been impossible, but with the advent of Advanced Magnetic Resonance Imaging—AdMRI, which scanned and detected the resonant frequency of a range of molecules not limited to hydrogen atoms, and thus was able to offer an exponentially greater level of detail—researchers could get a sense of what it actually meant to be a person reading a text or listening to a song. One of her earliest articles focused on a qualitative study of two pieces of music, Bach's second cello suite and The Beatles' "A Day in the Life," and compared them to other works in their genres. Her results showed that there were brain scan patterns that could be picked out when a person heard one of the two great works that differed from those of more pedestrian compositions. She controversially argued that it wasn't just a matter of preference. Great art tapped into something else, she said, communicating with the human brain in a completely different way.

Her focus remained on literature, though, because while she'd proven (according to some) that the same basic tenets applied across all of the arts, she remained a faculty member of the English department. Autumn began putting together algorithms to figure out the average reader preferences for the range of a book's vocabulary, the shape of its plot, its emphasis on character. Subjects would read in the AdMRI's slick metal tube, and she would study how much digression led a reader to become uninterested, what age a protagonist should be in a mystery novel, how many partners a character should have in a romance, how many pages a book should have, how many words, how long sentences should be, and what was the right mixture of description and dialogue.

Preferences were just a variable, she decided, and when the right equation was determined, it could be plugged into a scientifically rigorous process like any other hypothesis. Autumn's access to a digitized corpus of both the entirety of Western literature and knowledge of readers' innermost thoughts indicated a new understanding of what it meant when someone said a book was "good."

Soon after Juan Diego disappeared, his direct deposits into their bank account stopped, and she was left with a choice of whether to go through a lifestyle change, selling the enormous house they'd moved into in the scenic Sandia Mountains and cutting back her lunches at the St. James Tearoom and the Artichoke Cafe, or leave the city. Her children had assumed, as did much of the faculty, that when Juan Diego's desertion became publicly known, she would look for a higher-paying appointment elsewhere. No one suspected that she would leave academia behind entirely in favor of seeing if her research really held the practical applications she claimed. Autumn resigned just days later and immediately entered publishing.

Six months after Autumn began working for the startup publisher Glosster came the release of the first of the bestselling Duncan Hardy novels. The book's author, "Tabitha Silverstone," was a pen name for Autumn, two editors at Glosster, and a computer program that generated a first draft based on research she'd done into designing a "perfect" British spy novel. Since it was based on an early version of DayCart, the custom software that went on to make Glosster into one of the most prominent publishers in the world almost overnight, the draft required a fair amount of tinkering. But the basic story it generated was tight, its characters surprisingly well-rounded, and its set pieces exciting. The *New York Times Book Review* called it the most original debut novel of the year and the herald of a major talent. They said nearly the same thing the following year about *Tinkered Again*, a book based upon the literary fiction algorithm. And although critics bashed the romance novel by one "Janet Hawthorne," it still went on to record-breaking sales figures.

The positive aspect of Autumn's superhuman commitment to her post-UNM position, as far as Holly was concerned, was that it meant less time hovering over Devon. Even though Holly felt certain that he was mostly just playing video games, she liked to think that at least he was choosing his own path, that he did his own thing and had found his own freedom online, whatever that might be worth.

"How long are you around for?" asked Devon, looking up.

"I'm headed back tomorrow, actually. I just came in for the opening, but I want to get back to my studio ASAP."

"I'm just so glad you could be with us at all," said Autumn. "With you and Gideon gone, it can feel so lonely here. I know you're busy with your painting and such, but if Devon can't visit, surely you can make a longer trip later in the year."

"Oh I'm . . . I'm sure we can figure something out." Not fucking likely. Holly had planned on staying for a few days and packed accordingly. The trip was supposed to be a reprieve from work and Robert, to inspire and invigorate her, to convince her that the last few years of her life weren't a huge fucking mistake. She'd planned out locations and friends to visit while in town, maybe taking Devon somewhere to get him out of the house. But the visit left her tired and wanting to curl up in bed, where she'd see neither Robert nor her family and wouldn't have to crawl back to her studio to create another indifferently received painting. Every moment she spent with her mom she could feel a fight looming, and worst of all, she thought that maybe Autumn was right about everything. Even before Juan Diego disappeared, Holly had felt a hole in her life, in all of their lives. He used to joke that he was glad things weren't perfect at home because every happy family was happy in the same way, but that they were different, they were interesting. But she'd seen Robert's family and visited her friends' houses, and as she became older, she understood that the truth, the real joke of the statement, was that the only thing happy families had in common was that they didn't exist.

12

"The end is nigh, man."

"Eh?" asked Devon. He was logged on to Arcadia, and while his voice piped through the headset resting on his desk, Devon's attention was elsewhere. He slung off a white button-down shirt and slacks, which Autumn requested he wear when family or other guests were in the house, and tried to get comfortable. Dressing "like an adult," as his mom liked to put it, always made him feel like a kid again. It had a sense of make-believe to it, as if he were a five-year-old pretending to be the type of older guy who wore neatly ironed clothing and could discuss when it's preferable to use a seven iron.

Now that Devon sat in front of his computer screen wearing only his boxers, he felt a great deal more relaxed. He could've stripped totally naked, but even across waves and wires that made him feel uncomfortable. Outside of showers Devon always wore underwear, the poly-cotton blends somehow making him more complete.

"I mean," said Steve, "that the year's nearly over for us of the second-semester senior persuasion. I mean that there needs to be some big commemoration of this fantastic event and our newfound freedom from the clutches of tyranny that surround us. I mean that we should throw a crazy fucking party to finally show your sorry ass a good time."

This wasn't a new refrain for Steve. Probably because his parental supervision had always approached but never quite reached zero, the guy had begun drinking regularly at fifteen and was the one person Devon knew at AHS who had definitely had sex and tried hard drugs. When Devon had finally gotten up the balls to ask him about these experiences, Steve had pronounced both recreational activities great fun but generally more trouble to obtain than they were worth—not that this stopped him from trying.

"Hey, are we public now or are you whispering to me?"

"For some reason I'm whispering, though I can't say why this material would be so fragile that we'd want to keep it private," said Steve. "It's not like we're planning a bank heist or talking about info we ripped from another clan."

"I know, I'd just prefer it if this didn't become other people's business. Hey, let's do some grinding if we're going to be chatting for a while. I'll set the waypoint."

Devon clicked on his avatar and opened up a world map for their current game of choice, *Apartments & Accountants*. Members of |3ə were free to play whatever they wanted, but for the most part the clan moved from game to game as a unit because everyone hated being left behind, playing the same old thing alone.

Still, they had their favorites, some of them single-player titles. A lot of Devon's favorites were his dad's old games from around the time Arcadia was launched, or even before—*Agent Orange* and *Dangerous Dave in Copyright Infringement* and more than a few of the "avant-garde" (or, as Steve liked to call them, "artsy fartsy") games like *Eschaton* and *You Only Get One Life (Unless You Find the 1up)*. They were a nice change from shooting another alien or zombie for the five hundred millionth time in his life.

The clan loved *Apartments & Accountants* because although it took place in dreary offices and bland, Swedish-decorated apartments, its fundamental game system was the venerable ninth-edition D20 engine.

This meant that when an account executive dropped an attaché brief-case +2, they knew that to fight off the third-floor district manager, it would be better to use an unenchanted yet armor-piercing staple gun, because otherwise their blows would barely get past his Armani suit's damage reduction vs. blunt weapons (d8+2 damage - 6 vs. d4+1). And while the game also featured good graphics and a decent plot, more importantly it was supposed to have some pretty great achievements and loot to unlock.

"So is there any way I could actually convince you?" asked Steve, warping to join Devon at the bottom of a large office building in a city said to resemble St. Louis. His avatar, dressed in a smart gray suit with a skinny tie and enchanted Louis Vuitton shoes, followed Devon's into a five-story building. Both avatars were recognizable representations of the boys, but with adjustments. Steve's was tall, almost a giant, with very light skin (you wouldn't guess the player controlling him was Chicano) and walking with a purposeful gait, almost a strut, that Steve said he'd modeled after the president's. Devon's looked athletic and imposing, the body of a young Brad Pitt but with his own face and dressed immacu-lately in a tailored suit that made him look like James Bond.

The two applied for work at the building and, after a loading time representing four to six weeks of procedural waiting and interviews, were given entry-level jobs.

"I mean, I just don't like that sort of thing. I'd like to do something for the end of the year, but throwing a party sounds awful."

They began a melee with the first secretary in the building, and it took only a couple of attacks before she agreed to answer their phones and schedule all their meetings. It was the quickest Devon had ever gotten out of the mailroom, but their characters were pretty high-level.

"Well shit, I just hate thinking that you'll have graduated without living a day in your fucking life. But I guess having fun isn't for every-one, so what if we throw a crazy bash you are comfortable with? Let's host a game. I'm talking in person."

"Dude, let's start harshin' the fuckwits in the secretary pool and then move around back." The two of them dashed on to the next secretary and a few attacks later she was off to get them a Danish and coffee. They were overleveled for the area, but it was still a good idea to explore every part of a building to avoid ambush, so they wandered around the first floor searching for other hazards. This city was supposed to have a high chance of spawning confidential memos, too, one-use consumables that could offer powerful buffs against a vice president or lobbyist lurking in its upper stories.

"Okay sure, I'm down with that if you can get anyone else interested. Do you want this armor I found in the filing cabinet? Three-piece suits cut down on my dexterity bonus." They finished up the last of the secretaries and found a locker at the back end of their cubicles full of loot, some of which was sponsored by Texaco and redeemable outside Arcadia, though a full tank of gas required thousands more of these drops.

"Nah, man, it's much shittier than what I'm wearing. Thing is, it may be Jeff's last game. He's headed back east with his dad over the summer and then it's college. I would much prefer we threw a box social, but I'm also a realist and know that you'd just skip out like you always do." Steve's avatar was thrusting behind one of the secretaries, waiting for Devon to finish looting. Her lifeless eyes failed to register this, and she continued collating papers as if no one were in the room. "Hey, maybe we could even throw this at your place?"

"I was thinking we skip the IT guys in the basement, 'cause they never have worthwhile drops and they have cheap-ass auto-kill attacks if you haven't put enough skill points into tech-speak. And no, are you fucking kidding me?"

"No harm in asking. Remember back in middle school when we used to come over and stay up all night, playing *DnD* or *Warhammer* until we collapsed? Well this would be like that, only with booze and Disney puking on your bed because he's a fucking lightweight but won't admit it." They moved to the other side of the first floor and wiped out all the other mailroom boys, plus the rest of the low-level janitor and intern drones.

"Fine, but that's not an option. Move on to plan B. What about your place? Ready to go upstairs?"

"Yeah, man. Hey, I'm getting a message from Billiam saying he wants to join. I'm going to tell him to wait just a minute. You do know what my place is like, right? I don't mean to brag or anything, but no one on our block has been vandalized in almost three weeks."

"Fair point." Steve lived down in the South Valley, deep in one of the city's few truly Mexican ghettos. Even street signs were written in Spanish there, and while cop cars circled the area during the day, searching for illegal immigrants and "anti-American" activity, hoping to nail offenders of the so-called "no brown in town" laws, when the sun set they only showed up when called, at which point they brought in a full retinue of squad cars and riot gear, armed to the teeth.

When Devon first visited Steve's place a few years back, Steve requested that he stay away from the west side of the street, which still had one of Haight's billboards proclaiming the end of the universe, otherwise he'd be putting himself at risk. Two opposing meth dealers lived opposite each other, and they used light from the billboard to see when someone was coming. Devon was a halfie, a mestizo, to use his dad's term, but he looked far too light to make it down the street at night without drawing notice.

"Why don't we do it at Billiam's or Pete's like usual? I'm not exactly known as a party animal. I'm not gonna be trashing their shit."

"Don't you think I know that? You didn't go to prom, which isn't even a party, it's a fucking tradition. If it weren't for prom, Pete would probably be a virgin until he was twenty-eight. Instead he . . . well, he's still a virgin, but at least he's seen a girl naked without the aid of a computer. I just want this to be the big one, an unforgettable experience before we all head out and drift our separate ways. It's time we made a move on these low-level accountants."

"Hey, I'm going AFK for a sec." Devon switched his avatar from manual to bot mode while he went to grab a glass of water. From downstairs he heard Holly arguing with Autumn about the semantics of something stupid—it sounded like they disagreed on whether an event could qualify as a miracle to an atheist—and before he left the bathroom they'd begun shouting. They'd always argued, but these days it was like they didn't know to quit before drawing blood, and their fights usually ended with Autumn crying and Holly storming out of the house. While it sounded like Autumn remained the ice queen at work, Juan Diego's departure had left her perpetually vulnerable to the rest of the family, even when it made little sense. Devon snuck back into his room as quietly as he could in the hope of avoiding all possible involvement.

"Okay, what'd I miss? You ask Billiam about using his place?"

"Since you're so much of a wanker, I briefly considered it, but instead I used your absence to come up with a much better idea. Wanna hit some sales drones or just head up?"

"Nah, let's go for it. So what then?"

"Right, so you know about Hell and all, I assume."

"How stupid do you think I am? Just because I don't go to parties doesn't—"

"Yeah of course, dumbshit. Don't be such a baby. I'm talking about the tunnels." Steve and Devon's avatars walked through the building's third story, lined with endless cubicles and desks. It was lunch hour, though, so only a few unlucky employees were stuck at their computers, which made the otherwise difficult room manageable.

"Yeah, I know about the tunnels, but I always thought Hell was just some bs. Like when you're talking about that kid who was supposed to have died down there."

"Strictly speaking that wasn't in Hell, that was over by the university, but fuck you, dude, you know I wasn't lying. I never make shit up, and that really happened. Ask Billiam, ask anyone."

"Whatever you say."

"Fine, don't believe me. But, yeah, he didn't die in Hell. The tunnels go pretty much everywhere. You know the Whitehurst brothers? One time they strapped on a pair of spelunking helmets and biked for more than four miles down those tunnels before popping out in fear of getting lost. Four goddamn miles."

"Yeah, I get it. I've heard about the tunnels, but what's the big deal about Hell?"

"Well, the great thing about Hell is that for some reason its floor is warm. Most of the tunnels are pretty chilly, even during the summer. Actually, there's this awesome place down in the valley that's great for cooling off in the summer—when I was young, one of my uncles brought these buckets of water down there and we skidded around on the ice. But Hell's got this heat, so it's nice to sit on the ground. I guess it's on top of a hot spring or maybe some ancient machinery down there or something like that. Okay, when I open the door, we're rushing the department head."

"So that's why they call it Hell?" Both avatars rushed into the large corner office, trapping the head of local marketing behind his desk. Steve shut the door to prevent reinforcements.

"Partially, I guess. The other thing is that most tunnels have some light coming in. Something to remind you of the outside world, a concrete connection with your normal life. Hell is completely lightless, completely self-contained."

"Motherfucker! Dude, would you heal me here? I forgot how hard these guys can hit."

"Yeah, department heads have special authorization abilities that give them a damage buff. Just raise your AC so they don't hit you so much next time. Damn, dude, try not to die for one second here. The other great thing about Hell is that it opens up really close to school, so it's within walking distance for pretty much everyone we know. Except, of course, us."

"Cocksucking cuntfucker shithead, can you resurrect me? That sounds pretty cool. Ripe for a themed game."

"I'll pick up your corpse and take you to a doctor. Someone should be able to help you out, you're only at -3 hp."

Devon lay down on his bed with his headset still on. He heard a door slam outside his room, so he turned off its only light in the hope that his family would think he was already asleep. Or, short of that, that they'd take the cue that he didn't want to leave the room and deal with them.

"So we're a go on this, right? One last hurrah before college," said Steve.

"Fine."

"And don't worry, I'll think of something to make it special. Hey, I just got your body back to the doctor and it's no worse for wear. Let's join up with Billiam."

"Nah, man, I'm too tired. My sister's visiting and it's all sorta exhausting. I'll see you tomorrow."

"Okay, but I'm going to spread the word. Later."

13

For several weeks after Gideon moved in, he would stand at the apartment's threshold. The door stood open and he felt the wind from outside, carrying with it the scent of grass and tires. Clouds passed overhead, and he watched their shadows cover the ground. He watched ants crawl on the sidewalk in front of him and listened to dogs bark from the yards of neighbors he'd never met. He learned forward, tilted his head around and waited, unsure whether to move forward or not, but eventually someone would walk or drive past his small residential street. The moment he saw their eyes, even if they didn't glance back at him, he would slam the door shut. As the adrenaline subsided, he would return to his desk, wondering what had come over him.

Those periods of doubt were brief, though, and he spent most of his time sitting in a plush recliner and staring at his computer, sometimes with focus and drive and sometimes with absentminded fascination, jumping from site to site like he was flipping through channels on a television. He still worked long hours, sometimes insane hours, but to anyone observing him from in front, it would be impossible to tell whether he was reading pop culture lists or doing his taxes or shooting aliens. When he lay back, his body bent at a twenty-degree angle, the three screens in front of him filled his vision like a wide-angle lens, an LCD panorama that enclosed the entire world.

Late one night Gideon was trawling through an image board where someone was making fun of Japan. He skipped past the normal racism, sexism, and homophobia, until this troll mentioned more than eighty thousand hikikomori living on the island. On Wikipedia Gideon read that in reaction to the country's ultrapopulated public spaces, hikikomori locked themselves inside, willfully stranded in their bedrooms, apartments, and houses. The troll called hikikomori a disgrace to humanity and proposed that each of their caves should be permanently closed off, cemented shut, or buried like tombs. Gideon found them inspirational.

He'd had trouble rationalizing this existence, worried about what would be said if anyone found out but not ready to give up his lifestyle just because of that. He kept getting close to exiting his apartment but never quite managed. He didn't want to be a recluse or shut-in, words that implied damage, derangement—he just didn't want to go outside. Everyone looked at public reticence as a symptom. They said that Howard Hughes and J.D. Salinger didn't choose to be recluses, it overtook them like a cancer, invading and transforming an organ into a disfigured and dysfunctional illness. Before her own husband pulled a similar act, Gideon's mom wrote an article on how Thomas Pynchon's disappearance from the public imbued his novels with power and meaning, but Gideon thought maybe it was less a calculated marketing strategy than a guy just wanting to be alone. How was it anyone's business? Maybe it was a matter of preference, or maybe Pynchon was like Gideon, fed up with his ex-wives and the stress of trying to connect with other people. Even the thought of his first wife, Sandra, with her picturesque husband and son smiling at the camera on her Arcadia profile as if to say, "this is what you could have had," or his second, Claire, still working cheerfully at AP without missing a day or showing up with a hair out of place as she filed divorce papers, made him glad of his chair's warm embrace and the deadbolt on the front door.

People, as he saw it, were just too goddamn much—too forceful, too different, too happy, too sad—and at a certain point you couldn't take it anymore. You lived in a free society, and eventually you realized that even the decision to leave your house was a choice. That was the freedom that President Haight strove to protect, the sanctity of saying no more and turning inward. And with Arcadia always available, this choice of ignoring the outside didn't preclude leading an intellectually and emotionally fulfilling life.

Hikikomori weren't damaged or psychotic, they were living out a philosophy. Gideon loved their spirit of defiance. Thoreau expounded on the joys of living in the wilderness, the pleasure of living alone in a cabin without contact from other humans, simplification and isolation as transcendence. But for a hikikomori, that wasn't an option. For every one of them to live in an area the size of Walden Woods, Japan would have to be the size of Canada. Plus, hermits were quaint, old-fashioned. They were content to live in a world without high-quality stereo systems and the pleasures of The Suffragettes or The Beatles. They could sit and watch a sparrow fly across a glistening blue pond, but they couldn't know the beauty of a twelve-hour *Simpsons* marathon.

There were entire online communities devoted to hikikomori. Over the next week, he dived into these, learning that many hikiko-mori weren't just secluded, they were also otakus, the ultimate nerds of a particular subject searching for enlightenment through the things they loved. On one hikikomori forum, he'd read about a person who hadn't left his apartment in thirteen years, finding contentment in creating a model train set that mirrored the Tokyo transit system so well that he'd been consulted by the mayor about planned renovations. One in Ireland could recount entire sections of *Ulysses* by heart and tell you every change between its first three editions, while another had a com-plete set of the original NES library and was spending his years indoors beating every game, finding solace in their end credits.

Knowing about the thousands, perhaps millions of others gave Gideon confidence in his own choice, allowed him to admit finally that he wasn't going to be leaving anytime soon. His trips to the door became less frequent. It wasn't about living a misanthropic life in a cave, wishing the heavens would rain down death and destruction. It's just that for some people, including him, opening the door became too difficult, too frightening; sometimes it stayed that way for years, or forever. Many (perhaps most) hikikomori died in their rooms. News stories reported bodies that took a year or longer to be noticed and removed. If it weren't for the stink of a decaying corpse sneaking out from cracks of even the most secure apartment, it's possible no one would ever remember there'd once been a person living in that space.

Gideon began to work even harder on Gravedigger. A lot of hikikomori lived as burdens on their families, but he took pride in earning his own way, and with this, more successfully cutting himself off. He hit project deadlines with ease and enjoyed his work, returning to a more micromanaged approach to Gravedigger's coming album. He still needed to videochat with superiors regularly, but it had become easier to present to them. Everyone he worked with seemed to have adjusted to his new method, and he had a confidence that he hadn't been able to muster in person since he was straight out of college. Within the four walls of his house, he didn't need to fake a swagger—he felt it.

While at first he'd lived in fear of being called back into the office, of having to choose between his job and this lifestyle he didn't know if he could end, it never happened. Others on the Gravedigger project worked from home, too; he had no idea, and it didn't really seem important. Recently he'd been asked about moving off the Gravedigger project to manage some new Monsanto campaign—the details of which he was unclear about, but it sounded as if it was just another superefficient bioagent—but he'd opted out immediately. With any other project, he couldn't guarantee this level of autonomy.

Aside from a few Gravedigger posters and a small collection of physical books, most of Gideon's apartment was Spartan. He gave up on "normal" and stopped having the grocery delivery service bring him all the fruits and vegetables and meats he never ended up eating—even with all the free time in the world, he couldn't be bothered to cook anything with instructions more complex than a microwave time or, on special occasions, an oven temperature. He rarely left the "office," the massive desk at the center of the living room. He couldn't say for sure that he was happy, or even content, but inside his house Gideon knew he wasn't unhappy, and that was what mattered. From here he could luxuriate on his chair's plush cushions and watch life from a safe distance. As the chair seemed to swallow him whole, he closed his eyes and concentrated on its satiny fabric against his skin.

Gideon saw himself running across an endless hallway with every door on both sides wide open. On his left he saw the drones working in the AP building, talking about the awful products they had to advertise, not just poorly made but harmful, nefarious, possibly evil. A bell rang and they snapped back to work, lines of them in identical cubicles, room after room of them making the same motions at the same time. The longer he looked, the more constrictive his collar felt.

On the right side of the hallway were classes, from elementary school to college, and in all of them rows of desks stood facing the same blackboard. He recognized the students, though he couldn't quite remember their names. At the front of all the classes, someone gave a presentation, so he stopped to see what one of them was about. It was a high school physics course, but the student was younger, maybe eight, maybe his brother, and he was trying to explain to the rest of them about some incredibly complex experiment he was working on at CERN, drawing diagrams that looked like a game of *Hangman,* but no one paid attention to what he was saying. The other students were seventeen or eighteen, and the teacher was asleep, so a couple of them were dry-humping at the back of the classroom while others were play-fighting with meter sticks for swords, attacking at will in the name of defending the students' rights. One girl kept talking about how her project was so much better than the presenter's, it wasn't even funny. A guy in the back began rapping in Elizabethan English about his face on Gatorade bottles, and the room grew louder and louder. The little boy at the front tried to speak up and be heard, something about how his little project could be important for the future of humanity, but no one paid attention. A couple started drawing a caricature on the chalkboard, the kid as a baby in a diaper. Gideon couldn't look away, but he also couldn't get into the classroom to do anything about it. Then the kid began peeing his pants, at which point the teacher woke up and screamed at him for the mess, which only made the rest of the class shout louder. The teacher broke down in tears, repeating "¡*Mis hijos*!" but no one paid any attention to her, and her tears began filling the room and—

Gideon heard pounding at the door. He opened his eyes and did his best to stand up. His left leg was asleep, so his steps toward the door were slow and painful, as if his body were trying to punish him for not having moved the thirty feet to his bed. He hadn't ordered food, had he? No, they knew to knock once and leave it on the ground. Delivery Hero was good at getting that part right, even when the food itself bore little resemblance to the order he'd placed online. The steady beat of knocking continued, and he finally reached the door and put his eye to its peephole.

The sun hadn't risen yet, so the image he saw was both dim and strangely distorted by the convex lens. Even so, it looked sort of like his father, but too old and haggard. He wore a suit and held a briefcase. Juan Diego wouldn't be caught dead wearing a suit, and there was no way he could've known about this place. Not even Holly knew he'd moved out. Was he still dreaming?

No, it had to be another Jehovah's Witness, come to tell him the good news at an hour of the day when people were guaranteed to be home. It was just a trick of the light and the whispering of his half-asleep brain that made him see what wasn't there. But the man really did look just like his dad. Shouldn't he open the door, just in case? No, he needed to stay resolved, to keep himself inside regardless of whatever strange temptations the world out there sent at him to lure him back.

The hammering on the door was almost painful, so Gideon sat back down and waited, half-asleep but unable to do anything until it stopped. Finally the man quit. Gideon closed his eyes for a moment, but curiosity overtook him and he went back to the peephole. The man pulled out his phone and frowned at whatever it was he saw. He sat and waited on the stoop for a minute. When he finally left, Gideon felt relieved—take a hint and try peddling your Lord elsewhere in the future.

Gideon lay back in the chair but couldn't fall asleep. Eventually he opened his eyes and touched the mouse in front of him to bring his screens back to life. It was 6:37 p.m., and he'd completely lost track of how long he'd been lying there, whether the man outside with his face like Juan Diego's had been part of another strange dream or just a weird coincidence.

Gideon pulled up his list of Arcadia friends. BigRalph, his pal Ralphie, wanted him to check out a shooter mod one of his clanmates had made, in which the avatars' outfits were sheer lingerie and the guns were just Silly String canisters, so he played for a few minutes but soon found himself tired and bored. He sent his avatar back to his house/lobby in Arcadia and switched his attention to one of his other monitors.

He'd probably been sitting in his chair for six or seven hours, but it was still comfortable, well worth the five thousand dollars he'd spent on it, more than any bed he'd bought, even the nice one that Sandra really wanted. Or maybe that was Claire? Half-asleep, he could barely remember. Was it Sandra who'd gotten pregnant weeks after they broke up, or was it Claire? Whose parents lived by Silver City, and which of them had told him they'd be together forever, or was it both? His mind blurry, he pulled up an image board because he didn't feel up to anything else.

His eyes scanned more pictures than his head could process, and soon Gideon couldn't tell which ones he'd seen before and which he hadn't, which were fucking fantastic and hilarious and which were ungodly, disgusting things he should be ashamed to look at. He found himself wandering into Rule 34, an image board based upon the ontological argument that if you can think of it, there's porn of it online. Horses raping women dressed as porcupines, men being impaled with street lamps and getting off on it, Care Bears opening themselves up to Bill Gates, images assaulting his mind until he couldn't quit. Super Mario Brothers in an orgy with the Battletoads, a man taking a shit into a girl's mouth with a hole in the back of her head and another man slurping it up as it came out. He kept scrolling through them until the images onscreen lost all meaning. He looked at a man fucking a hole in a girl's amputated arm and felt nothing.

Still half-asleep and desperate to stop himself, Gideon pulled up freechatgirlz.com and watched as a girl giggled and talked to the camera. She was surprised this many people were interested in what she had to say and yes, she'd take off her bra for a few more tips and no, she wasn't a fan of the newest Batman movie but she liked some of the old ones from when she was little and no, nothing especially terrible happened today but sometimes you're just not super happy and she thinks everyone understands that not every day is great but you've got to go into work either way because of the money, so she's here, but she's not angry at any of them, no, she's just here, and her sonorous voice lulled him to sleep again, but this time he didn't remember his dreams.

14

So like shit, dude, it was maybe five or six years ago, possibly more. Nobody seems too sure actually, which is just the way with these sorts of things. Anyhow, so it was a bit back that this girl, I think her name's Tessa or Teresa or somethin' like that but I dunno for certain, arrives right here in the heart of the 505 with her mom, this woman who's headed down Southwest to take part in the tech boom that was just kicking off at that time, Arcadia and EA and all that shit. And it wasn't like she had anywhere else to go after a very messy divorce, with all the cheating and lying and things being said that can't be unsaid sort of thing that always entails. And so like this girl T was just entering high school at the time, she was fourteen or maybe fifteen but everyone notices her right away because that's how it is with newbs, you know, and like even during boom times a shit school like AHS only gets like maybe five or six new kids a year. But more than that it's because this girl is just fucking beautiful, and I mean drop-dead gorgeous. Fucking beyond gorgeous, this bitch is pulchritudinous.

Lo and behold a buncha guys are smitten. What am I saying, I mean like the whole straight male population is wanting to find out what's her deal, like is she down with shit yet or what. And there's not too much word going around about T 'cause she kept quiet about herself. She was a freshman new to the city and just wanted to feel her toes around in the waters, not jump right into the deep end into the arms of some asswipe. So T doesn't talk about herself, but she does ask a bit about what people do for fun here, like are there any arcades or especially like amusement parks or water parks or that sort of thing in the area. She'd moved from LA, where she was a regular at Magic Mountain and was just absolutely devastated when she learned there were no coasters or even anything close to that around. With her parents always fighting and all, some of her few really good memories had been from theme parks and she was into the whole experience, the carnival games, the big goofy mascots and the funnel cake, and best of all the rides. But after her family imploded it wasn't like she got a choice where she ended up—maybe she was living with her grandparents now or something, I don't know—and that's just how shit goes.

Well, the guys didn't care about what she was going through, what they cared about was that even at fourteen or fifteen, this girl had an amazing rack and the face of a Greek goddess and all they can think about is how to get with that. Every group in the school had their alpha guy claiming dibs on T, talking about how fast they're gonna pop her cherry and how she'll be licking up their cream like a good little pet before the week's done. 'Course it's all talk, just bullshit talk because most dudes especially in like high school are too shy to do anything about an intimidatingly beautiful girl, so while you'd think she'd be fucking popular as hell instead she's sitting alone at lunch for her whole first week.

One guy, though, he gets up the nerve to come and talk to her. He's saying that he's heard she's bored with the Southwest, but hey at least the state fair's in town now and maybe she'd be interested in heading over there, because while he wasn't claiming it was the best or anything at least it had cotton candy and churros and a few rides, weak as they may be. T says okay 'cause why not, anything's better than going home to her mother crying, and they meet up after school. He's goddamn giddy with excitement about the date, thinking that her luminous presence will change his life forever and that he'd be happy just to be near her for a few hours. And fuck it, maybe she's a secret slut and he'll get lucky.

So here they are after school and he's walking her to his car, which is probably something like a '16 Centrino sans air conditioning, but she seems perfectly content with things and happy that at least someone's reached out to her. They circle around the fair's big, fenced-in square and can smell the horseshit before they even get in and the attendant is this huge fat guy exuding even more grease and stink and the whole area is dank and nasty and all that. But at the same time they start getting whiffs of fried food, and after parking in a dirt lot and paying a couple bucks to get past the gate they're in the fair proper, surrounded by booths and toys and candy. This guy's trying to make a whole evening out of things, taking it slow and exploring the grounds, but T gets bored quick and wants them to head straight to the midway, so they skip out on the rodeos and the ethnically themed villages and the rest of the filler crap.

Let's cut to the chase. They play a few of the standard games, whacking moles and shooting birds with BBs and maybe he wins her a stuffed bear or some shit. They look around the area and of course she wants to go on the biggest roller coaster they've got, and while this dude's kinda afraid—he figures that if he mentioned his fear of rides she'd think he's the biggest pussy ever—he says okay because he wants to be with her. So they wait in line and step in the little cart together and the coaster starts heading uphill, and the guy's so freaked out that if she weren't with him he'd be in tears. But she is there, so instead he squeezes her hand and she squeezes back which makes it all okay. They drop down the first big hill and it's amazing. He's so happy he makes a move and this girl, vulnerable under the circumstances of having such a fucked-up family and being so goddamn alone in the city, reciprocates and they kiss a little while going up the next hill, and it's actually a first for the both of them. And while maybe she's doing it out of pity or whatever, that doesn't matter to him.

Now the problem with rides at fairs and carnivals and places like that is that they aren't always up to code. Three days before, when the carnies were settings things up, one of the screws on the left side of the track wasn't tightened as much as it should've been. I mean, it was tightened and all, but as the ride had been continuously used that little margin of error gradually grew until it slipped out entirely. With that one out, the one next to it started to loosen, so did one on the other side of the track, and soon so did the ones next to it. And it wasn't a particularly well-made ride to begin with, so the metal on the tracks had been slowly bending for years. Worse yet was that the cart this pair was riding in, which I guess I hadn't mentioned was the one at the very back, had a connection to the rest of them that had been slowly rusting away. So as the pair careened down the second big hill, when they should've turned to the side with the rest of the carts, sparks flew up as theirs broke the bent track and immediately snapped clean off from the rest of the ride.

T grabs onto the guy in a panic as they're careening through the air and he's got his tongue in her mouth, sucking on her face so hard she can't catch her breath. Time slipped for a moment and he was in the air forever, raising a family with her and watching as they're coming home tired from work and watching TV. Then they're arguing about their children's colleges and visiting an old friend in the hospital together, worrying about finding burial plots side by side. For those few moments of eternity they were raised up like angels floating on a cloud, and he held on to her as tightly as he could and she was holding him back and it didn't matter that it was so short because those seconds before they hit the ground together were the happiest in his life.

How I heard it was when they crashed into the dirt below they were still kissing. The dude who told me was like, Steve, her head went *all the way through his*, and that somehow cushioned the impact, and that's the only reason she survived.

15

For Holly, the worst part of any trip into Albuquerque—regardless of how much other bullshit might crop up while visiting her mother or seeing old friends who clearly would have preferred it if she'd disappeared entirely when she moved away—was visiting her grandmother. Growing up, Grandma Inez and Holly had been just shy of inseparable. While Gram had certainly been more thrilled by Gideon's birth than anything else in the twenty years preceding it, it wasn't until Holly's arrival that it became obvious to the family that what she'd really been waiting for was a granddaughter. Gram remained scrupulous in treating the Reyes children as equally as she could manage, giving them equivalent birthday and Christmas presents and keeping the same hardline approach to manners at the dinner table, but all it took was one gaze at Holly to see that this connection was stronger, this love was something special.

Grandma Inez's husband died when Holly was two, and following a quick funeral she left Vegas to be closer to her grandchildren. As early as Holly could remember, Gram had been the Reyes's default babysitter, helping Holly finish chores as fast as she could so they could draw with crayons or bake cookies or play with her stuffed animals. Holly's fondest memories as a child were with Gram, making dinner for their exhausted parents, *Wheel of Fortune* in the background, trying to guess words and phrases before the idiotic contestants. Gram always said she wondered how they found contestants so dense that her eight-year-old granddaughter could give them a whoopin'.

By the time Holly was ten, Gram had taken her granddaughter to get her ears pierced, much to Autumn's annoyance. She'd taught Holly how to count cards and spot a bottom dealer and how much baking powder to put into a cake without measuring. Autumn had long since returned to working fourteen-hour days in anticipation of tenure review while Juan Diego's schedule was as busy as ever, the intricacies of Arcadia's branching network structure leaving him in perpetual crunch time. So Gram practically lived at their house, and the "guest room" became "Gram's room," even though she still had her own small townhouse on the West Side. It was around that age that Holly began periodically feigning sick just to stay home with her grandmother, and while Autumn was almost certainly aware of this deception, she never said anything about it, knowing both of them enjoyed their days together so much.

Gram became not just a part of her daughter's family, but her son-in-law's as well. She began attending the same church as the extended Reyes family and meeting regularly with Nick and Charlotte, who reached out to her after her husband's death. Gram began telling Holly that she thought Nick was a wonderful man (perhaps better than the one her daughter had chosen, but who was she to judge . . .) and he helped her set up a workout routine in an attempt to get her interested in life outside her daughter's household again. She met up with them in the morning to go running, and while they were at work, she'd stop by to lift weights. When it was too cold out, she'd use their bike and Nick recommended some light rock climbing, maybe, if she thought she was up to it. Holly thought her grandmother was a bit nuts, but she seemed happier and no less doting and attentive. Eventually Holly couldn't even remember how her grandmother had spent her time before she's known her fitness-obsessed in-laws, mixing protein shakes and taking weeklong backpacking trips in the Sandias.

Holly was twelve when it happened. Nick and Charlotte were vacationing in Vegas on Gram's recommendation. They'd never thought of themselves as Vegas people, always saying that the city was too seedy for them. Its women were all strippers at best, whores at worst and the only entertainment was getting drunk and gawking at them. But Gram said there was a lot more to it than that, there were the shows, there were the rides, there was the adrenaline shot of almost winning big.

Holly arrived home from school and was surprised Gram wasn't already there waiting for her. She was worried, but Autumn soothed her and said that Gram was a grown woman and could look after herself. If she needed help, she would call, said Autumn. "I'm sure she just forgot." After school the next day, Gram still wasn't there, so Holly tried looking for her. She called Gram's house three times and still no one picked up. Because Gram lived far away, Holly decided to bike to Nick's first on the off chance that she was over there. The front door was unlocked and lights were on, so Holly walked inside relieved. She yelled for her grandmother, and after hearing no response she headed into their small gym, where Gram was collapsed on the elliptical.

Paramedics arrived shortly afterward, though Holly couldn't say how long it took. The only thing she could be sure of, the only thing that kept her sane during the eternity she spent crying alone, surrounded by fitness equipment, was that Gram was still breathing.

When Holly was finally allowed to visit her, Gram still breathed easily from her hospital bed but everything else about her had changed. She mostly kept silent except for a few instances when garbled words came out of her mouth. According to what doctors told Holly's parents, Gram seemed to react to physical stimuli such as being pinched or pricked by a needle. She seemed to feel pain, but was otherwise unconscious and completely immobile—a body completely disconnected from its mind. The first time Holly saw her now-incapacitated grandmother, she ran out of the room, screaming that it wasn't Gram there in the bed and why weren't the doctors doing something about this isn't that what they were paid for why did they tell her it was just a coma just a coma this was everything thiswastheworstthing oh my fucking God.

Gideon was sad about Gram, but largely unaffected. He seemed resigned to Gram's coma, as if that was just what happened to old people. Juan Diego seemed to react similarly, but after a few months he went off on an anti–exercise equipment crusade that laid waste not only to the family's elliptical but also to their treadmill and even the yoga ball. His rants about the dangers of solo exercise further traumatized Holly, though they mostly confused Devon—after seeing how Holly reacted to Gram, their parents decided that it was something Devon shouldn't know much about. Holly had no idea whether Devon visited her later, on his own, or if he just pretended that she was no longer alive, but Holly always felt an obligation to see her grandmother, even though the experience sometimes gave her nightmares for weeks afterward. Her mother felt no such obligation, apparently, a fact that further damned her in Holly's estimation and caused no end of fights until Holly finally resigned herself to her mother's seeming callousness and decided to never mention Gram in Autumn's presence again.

A month after Gram's stroke, Holly's parents told her the doctors were uncertain whether she'd ever come out of it. Something about her frontal and parietal lobes sustaining massive oxygenation loss and, in a way, death, plus a smattering of damage to her temporal and occipital lobes. Still, it wasn't enough to kill her, not quite. They always said to remember how unpredictable comas were, that people could suddenly snap out of them for no reason. But it was nearly a decade later, and Gram still lay in her bed as far from waking up as the first time Holly saw her there.

Holly didn't even know if what she saw when visiting was technically Gram at all. Sure, it looked like her, but so did photographs and digital images of her on a screen. If she'd wanted to, she could have moved Gram down to Robert's studio and, after taking a 360-degree image, printed out a life-size sculpture of her made from plaster and resins that would look, even to her family, as close to Gram as to make no difference. The difficulty Holly really struggled with was whether this newly created version, rendered and edited on a computer, would be any more real than Gram's current existence. In either case there would be a fully three-dimensional body that could be touched or held but contained no personality, no thoughts or feelings or dreams that could be communicated. Only one version of her was made out of slowly decaying flesh that smelled of urine and looked unnervingly straight ahead, while the other would be no more than painted dust. And Holly knew, in that part of her so deep down and essential to her being that she could never share it with anyone, that she would rather visit the sculpture that had always been lifeless than the ex-woman and her vacant eyes.

But here she was again, pulling up to the nursing home, which frightened her far more than any funeral home, more than any horror movie or the threat of crashing her car on the way over. Heaven's Gate kept Gram in an eerie ward at the back of the building, inhabited only by coma patients and their caretakers. Holly couldn't tell if it was just her mind playing tricks on her, but the moment she opened the home's door she smelled dead skin and urine covered by ammonia, a noxious fume that stank worse than two-year-old rotting vegetables. After signing in to see Gram, Holly walked past Alzheimer's victims wandering down the hallways in confusion and an open door to a room with two women plugged into respirators. She passed a room of people staring out a window that only showed the wall of the building next door and another filled with overweight amputees. No one stood without assistance and almost everyone had a plastic bag or two attached to them, tubes going in and out linking them to the chemicals that sustained them and flushing out the waste of their own bodies in convenient pouches.

She'd always hated visiting Gram at the hospital, but there it seemed like everyone was getting better, improving. The doctors weren't perfect but they still granted new years of life to people; here everyone was just in storage, larger boxes to prepare them for smaller ones. At Heaven's Gate there was no research or development. No useful thoughts. No brilliant economic theories wrestled with Haight's shaky theocratic ubercapitalism, no physicists pondered the meaning of existence, no artists created work that would ever be seen outside these halls. No one entered Heaven's Gate and walked out again an improved person. But then, no one entered Heaven's Gate and walked out at all.

Even the staff was gloomy. Giving a formerly respected city council member a wash because he tore off his diaper in a fit of confusion and took a shit all over his legs and the hallway. Trying to help a teacher remember the days of the week, the months of the year. Composing letters for those whose mouths couldn't speak a word and hands couldn't hold a pen.

Reaching the end of Heaven's Gate's single hallway, Holly finally arrived at the coma ward, where two bored-looking orderlies watched over twenty-four beds. One miniscule window offered the room a faint gleam from the outside but it was lost in the flood of stale yellow streaming down from rows of old fluorescent bulbs in the ceiling. They were remnants of when the building had been an office during the 1970s and had never been changed.

Holly sat next to her grandmother, as usual uncertain whether she should say something or not. Occasionally there'd been other visitors when she came and they usually talked with the patients. Sometimes they spoke about times they used to have together, which resulted in tears, and sometimes about what was happening right now in the outside world, whether they'd gotten the promotion or not and what their kids were up to and how those idiot politicians were screwing up this, that, and the other, a stream-of-consciousness dialogue with a person who medical science said was definitely not listening. When Gram first arrived, Holly had been in the first category, crying about their past, plans they used to make for the future, Gram's promise to go with her on a trip to Europe if she got into a good college, Gram's botched attempt at making sopapillas like Grandma Reyes. But by the time she'd left town, Holly'd become a rambler, just talking so as to fill the void. She told her grandmother about plans for leaving high school and a boy she'd met and how she was pretty goddamn certain that AHS's econ teacher was a full-blown fascist and probably a racist. But eventually she noticed the way orderlies listened to these stories and she started imagining that when she left they made fun of her, that they looked forward to her visits so they could hear more stupidity from the girl who dropped out of high school for what Autumn liked to call "no good reason I can see whatsoever."

Sometimes, when Holly spoke, Gram opened her eyes.

Holly never detected any pattern about when or why it happened. Midway through a sentence she'd notice Gram staring at her intently, as if some of what Holly said made it through to her. But she never moved, and her occasional burbling didn't come in response to words. While Gram's eyes seemed knowing, possessing the same wisdom that they'd had since Holly met her, they didn't follow motion or change positions. They kept staring at Holly or the ward's wall in front of her. At some point after Holly left, one of the orderlies must've closed Gram's eyes because they were never open when she arrived, and they were so unnerving that Holly never waited around to see how or if they closed on their own.

So now, when Holly visited, she just sat there, almost as still as her grandmother. The orderlies made the occasional noise behind her, turning one of the patients and scrubbing her body free of dead skin. Holly sat and watched Gram breathe in and out shallowly, her body, once incredibly fit for a sixty-five-year-old, now completely bereft of muscle tone. Holly saw veins through Gram's sagging, translucent skin, her straw-like hair thin and matted, fingernails a ghastly yellow. Holly didn't know whether or not she believed in souls, but if they did exist, she didn't believe that this body contained Gram's any longer. A layer of dust coated Gram's forehead and Holly decided not to wipe it off, because what difference would it make?

It had only been twenty minutes since she had parked her car, but it felt like hours had passed. She hurried out of the nursing home, past the orderlies and patients, keeping her gaze fixed on the door at the opposite end of the hallway. As she exited the building, she had to shield her eyes from the sun as they adjusted to the light. Holly dived into her car and once inside wasted no time heading straight to I-25 South, back toward Robert and as far from Gram and Autumn and the rest of her past as she could go. She hit ninety on the interstate and didn't slow down when she passed the city limits.

The road was practically deserted, as it had been for years since the Wall's construction drastically decreased shipping from Mexico, and the only people who took it were locals, mostly headed to or from Las Cruces. Holly always felt like the horizon was lower and she could see more of the world when driving across the Southwest, with just a pair of perfectly white clouds in the sky and the whole desert laid out in front of her. She picked up her phone to tell Robert she was already headed back, but the call went straight to voice mail. "Si, es verdad que Roberto Francisco Hernández-Romero is unable to take your call. If you leave your nombre y su número de teléfono, then he'll get back to you inmediatamente."

When she was in a good mood Holly could laugh at what she called his "stage name" and shrug it off. It's not like Andy Warhol's birth name was Andy Warhol, after all, so what the hell did it matter that her boyfriend had changed his in order to court success? Shouldn't you be able to choose your own identity after you become an adult, decide for yourself that you're really more of a Carl than a Tsing-pao, the same way you change your hair or your sex, without being judged? Isn't defining your own identity, choosing a path different from the one you were born into, pretty much the entirety of the American Dream, the realization of the self-made individual?

But his given name was Robert Johnson (middle name: Frank). One of his great-grandmothers was a Hernández, and his stepmother—who divorced his father just three months after getting her green card—was a Romero, so he claimed to have a legitimate reason for adopting his "nom de pinceau." The one time that a journalist brought up the question of whether changing his name so dramatically might, in perhaps some small way, besmirch the authenticity of his work, he'd deftly laughed off the comment. "Por favor, my friend, not every spic has to have dark brown skin, an oversize moustache, and be named Juan de Taco. Some of us leave our sombreros at home, gringo, and live on this side of the Wall without fear that Haight's dogs will toss us south. Ese, the name I sign doesn't mean my mama didn't write Robert on my birth certificate, it just means that I'm pretty sure if I didn't call myself that all the güeros out there would be too ignorant to take the time to figure out I'm not like them."

Holly left him a message. "Nothing sold and I fought with my mom the whole time and my friends were terrible and I just wanted to tell you I'm headed home." She instantly regretted saying anything, leaving a digital recording that could be thrown in her face the next time she talked about spending some time back in 'Burque. He always thought it amusing that she wanted to spend time back home given how happy she'd been to leave it, and she hated that all the more because he was right about how miserable it made her.

She threw her phone onto the passenger seat and slowed the car down to the seventy-five-mile-per-hour speed limit. Holly saw a sign on the side of the road noting how far it was to Truth or Consequences, wondering why she was in such a rush to return home anyhow, and hating that the highway only *seemed* to go on forever.

16

WIRED
Featured Interview
Published online at 2:00 PM on October 23, 2027
15 Minutes With Juan Diego Reyes
The Mad Genius of Indie Games Returns with a Budget . . . and a Vengeance
By Austin L. Murray

Arcadia is Juan Diego Reyes's first studio-published game, but this relatively scant CV doesn't include the series of brilliant indie games that put him on Electronic Arts's radar in the first place. Titles such as *Genocidal Freedom Force*, *Rated M for Partial Nudity*, *Gaping Ágape*, and *Gaijin Gaiden* were critical favorites, garnering enough awards at festivals and trade shows to make him a well-known figure on the independent scene. But five years ago, his constant stream of oddball releases came to an end when he was hired by EA. Following the creation of a new studio in Albuquerque, New Mexico, Reyes has rarely been heard from, although rumors about him and his work have remained constant.

Then, at E3 EA unveiled Arcadia, promising the title as a "next generation" universal gaming platform, social network, and operating system set to revolutionize the medium. Reyes was revealed as the project's director, and EA told stockholders it hoped to recoup all the losses incurred by the Albuquerque studio within a year of the program's launch. Much speculation has circulated about what exactly Arcadia is, and with the platform set to launch next week, Reyes finally agreed to speak with us about what he's been up to for the past five years, why he left the independent gaming scene, and what project he wants to work on next.

WIRED: While you used to be known for creating ten or more games a year, it's been almost five years since your last release, *Meaningless Repetition to Reach Predetermined Goal.* **Did you spend all that time working on Arcadia?**

Reyes: Whatever you've heard from conspiracy theorists, I wasn't abducted by aliens or anything stupid like that. New Mexico has always been pretty weird, but it's not *that* weird. No, I've just been busily working as usual. The only thing that's changed is the size of the project. When EA approached me a few years ago, they made it clear that they were interested in having me work on something bigger, not just one of my little doodles. Plus, when I started, I was used to working alone, or maybe just with an artist. Honestly, I spent a lot of my working hours just trying to figure out how to manage a team with more than 200 people, which is a skill I've never really possessed. I have to give credit to EA for not firing me on a number of occasions when I made some really poor managerial decisions.

WIRED: I know a lot of fans were dismayed when EA didn't just hire you to keep making the same small games you always did.

Reyes: That's certainly nice to hear, but it's not like there were a ton of people waiting with bated breath for those things. A few months back we finally hit 35,000 sales for *Docudramedy* and that's . . . well . . . for quite a few reasons that's always been my most popular game, and it took seven years to hit that minis-cule benchmark. Total sales for my whole catalogue are probably around 250,000 or so. I don't know. And I realize it sounds pretty big when I put it like that, but we're talking years of downloads on dozens of titles, and it's hard to raise a family on money like that. I'm happy that my fans are pretty loyal, but let's not kid ourselves, most people have never played anything I've made.

Also, I know fans liked seeing those things get cranked out, but after 20 years of that sort of thing, you get tired, especially when they only sell a couple hundred copies each. I wouldn't say I got burned out exactly, but it was definitely time for a change.

WIRED: So was money the primary factor in moving to EA?
Reyes: I don't know about primary . . . but money is a pretty damn important thing to have. Not a lot of people know this, but at the time EA hired me, I'd been looking for work at one of the majors for a long time. Everyone else always wanted me to move, and with my wife working at the university and the kids all in schools with their friends here and . . . for a lot of reasons, it just wasn't worth it. My family's been living in the area for a few hundred years, actually, and we've always had a hard time leaving it. Guess it's just in my blood. So in the meantime I kept scribbling away, hoping that someone would be in-terested in hiring me without requiring relocation, and finally EA came along and offered to build a new studio out here. So I thought, "Hey, what do I have to lose? If it doesn't pan out, I could always go back to making indie crap no one buys."

WIRED: Once they hired you, did you immediately begin working on Arcadia, or was there ever an inclination that you would do smaller games like before, just with more resources?
Reyes: I can't necessarily speak for the executives who hired me, but from my point of view it was always about doing something bigger.

My first job at the studio wasn't anything related to games, it was just hiring people who I thought were smart, either from around the area or just as often trying to entice developers to move out here. After that, I was working on a smaller game with the team we had at the time, but ultimately we decided not to release it to the public for a whole bunch of what I can assure you are very good reasons. It was really more of a tech demo than a game, just proving that some things we wanted to achieve are possible with current hardware. But in a nutshell, it didn't work quite the way I'd hoped it would. If I was independent, it probably would've made it out the door anyhow and died on the Internet like so many others, because I like to release ideas to see if anyone else can build off of them. But this was EA's property. A lot of my past games were like that, where they didn't quite work but I put them out anyhow because at least then it didn't feel like my time was completely wasted. *Citizenship: The Book: The Movie: The Game: The Experience* sold probably 120 copies, but that was also what it deserved, and I know Geoffrey Pignus used some of my code to help make *Eye Gouger*, which was actually pretty great.

WIRED: Can you say anything else about that first game that didn't pan out?

Reyes: I called it *Utopia* while we were making it. It was based on some of the procedural generation concepts that made their way into Arcadia, an attempt at using the natural formation of neural pathways as a sort of, I dunno, game engine. There were always some weird bugs with [*Utopia*], but as a proof of concept it was a success in that it helped me get the green light on Arcadia and convinced people that my budget made sense. Budget and HR and all that crap were a big part of my job, too, until I realized I could hire a person to deal with all that for me. In any case, *Utopia* served its purpose, but as a game it was kind of . . . *Utopia* was never actually fun to play.

WIRED: You mentioned your family earlier. Have they gotten to use Arcadia yet? What do your kids think about you making games?

Reyes: They like it. My oldest one's fairly into it, and he's definitely helped me out a lot with focus testing. He's a smart kid and knows his way around a game, so if he thinks something's a problem, then it probably is. My middle child isn't so into games, but my littlest one is really involved with them already. He's pretty young, so what he gets out of the experience is different than his older brother, but it's proven that Arcadia, as a platform, works regardless of age. There's stuff on there just for kids, so we've made sure that age and literacy aren't necessary for usability.

WIRED: All the press surrounding Arcadia has talked about it more as a platform than as a game per se. Do you see it more as a platform like Windows or Apple OS? Or a social network?

Reyes: It's always been difficult to define what exactly a game is, in the same way that it's difficult to say what art is. They're nebulous concepts, and I'll have to go with the "you'll know it when you see it" explanation. Really, the only difference between a game and any other activity is the addition of rules. I've heard complaints for years about the way pundits trivialize our political system by turning it into a game, but really that's all it ever was, with arcane rules and winners and losers just like basketball or *Super Mario Bros.*

The other key part of a game is the psychological aspect, right? It's about performing actions in order to achieve concrete goals. You have positive and negative response stimuli. Functionally speaking, the only difference between games and the rest of the world is that most games have rules that prevent anything truly awful from occurring: you can't just hit someone in a basketball game or you get a foul. The genius of the game systems that came out decades ago was creating trophies and achievements that go beyond the games themselves, creating a metagame. In a way, Arcadia's an expansion on that concept using procedural techniques based upon user input, all supported by advertising rather than purchases.

You're looking at me like that doesn't make all that much sense. I guess the short answer would be yes, and the more lengthy one is why can't it be that and still be a game? The only thing that ever kept Windows from being a game is lack of a goal. But if every time you double-click you score a point . . . well then now the same interface is suddenly transformed. In Arcadia, I added the goal, which is, of course, more games.

WIRED: Now that it's finally making its way online, do you have any ideas for future projects?

Reyes: Keeping Arcadia updated is going to be a big deal. That's a job on its own, though it's yet to be determined whether or not I'm the man for it. And Arcadia's coming out because it's playable, usable, enjoyable. Not necessarily because it's done. I don't just mean the way it iteratively creates new games, because of course that part will never be finished. I'm talking about some of the features it's supposed to have that aren't part of it yet. Key, key features. After five years, more or less, of production, EA wanted to put something out there that can earn a profit, and I certainly understand their point of view. It's just that what we're putting out isn't finished yet, at least not in my mind. And I'm not telling you anything that's news, either. My opinions on this are public. Arcadia is great as it is, a landmark, and I don't think anyone will be asking for their money back.

WIRED: Of course not, it's free.

Reyes: Poor turn of phrase. What I mean is I don't think people will be disappointed, even with some key parts still not even in alpha.

WIRED: So how is that going to work? Will you be patching it or releasing expansion packs?

Reyes: Patches, certainly. Part of the essential design for the system is that it's meant to be updatable, not something where you have to buy a new version every year. We want to get it into as many hands as possible. And, to be honest, you'd be a sucker not to use it, as either way you'll be using your computer to keep in touch with your friends or read business emails. Why not score a few points while you're at it?

WIRED: We shouldn't hold our breath for any new games from you, then? It sounds like Arcadia will be taking up all of your foreseeable time.

Reyes: I'm hoping to put some time towards a few more little games like I used to do, especially since now I can make a design doc and have someone else do the hard work of programming the damn thing. Anything I make will be added to the rest of the program's game library, so you could purchase them or earn enough Arcadia points to get them for free. Some parts of *Utopia* would be fun to get out there, for instance, once we get them working properly.

And although the program procedurally creates new games based upon the library, it still has to have something to build off of, right? Games for me have always been a collaborative process, a form of communication between the creator and the player. So I did help with some of Arcadia's initial games, the baseline that things will be iterating from, basic shooters, sims, platformers, etc. I wanted to make sure that Arcadia had the fundamental language already built into it. But beyond that, some of the guts of Arcadia aren't quite there yet, and at the moment that's what I really should be focused on. The ghost in the machine isn't quite as aware of players as it should be, mostly due to technical problems that, given enough time, I'm convinced we could solve. Right now it's all divided between multiple servers, and I want to find a way to integrate everything as much as possible, give it one brain, so to speak. And while the system is modular, it's still complex enough that sometimes you can't tell whether the addition of the slightest cosmetic change will ruin the entire system. Then again, the complexity, the small patterns that grow into something bigger, are why it's a project that interested me so much in the first place, and it's also why Arcadia, to me, feels more "real" than anything else I've ever played, even if it's not what a lot of people would traditionally consider a realistic game, or even a game at all. *Pong* doesn't feel real because it's a simplistic version of something we already understand. But when it comes to a concept or a philosophy or a feeling, those higher-level ideas, I think abstraction is valuable, and something avant-garde can feel conversely more familiar. The system itself, and how it fits together, is always far more important than graphical fidelity or frame rates. Format and form have to fit together.

WIRED: Care to give us a preview of what those patches might entail?
Reyes: You know, I've got quite a few ideas for the future, and some of them we're even testing right now. But I don't want to say too much this early, because we might just scrap them tomorrow and start working on something else. Whatever comes out, though, I assure you will be really cool. We've set the bar high and don't mean to disappoint.

17

Ever since she awoke in the hospital six years earlier, Teresa had had a recurring dream, though it always started differently. Sometimes she would be in an office doing some undefined job, sometimes she would be back at school, sometimes she would just be attending Mass with her grandparents, and usually it was even better than real life, her mother and father reunited, or she'd see that boy again, the one she couldn't bear to think about while awake, and he would be as happy and whole as when she first saw him in high school. Then her face would begin to itch, all around the sides of it but especially at the top, right at her hairline. She would try to ignore the irritation at the front of her scalp, but soon it became so irresistible that she had to touch the itch. She'd maybe try to hide scratching it, play it off as just a small irritation, but then she'd start tearing at it more and more. Eventually there'd be a little give. She'd scratch a tad too hard and a seam developed. The seam grew, a deepening line circumscribing her face that she could do nothing to prevent. She tried to hold it on with her hands but nothing helped, and when it hit a certain point, all of the skin came off like hot cheese on a slice of cheap pizza.

Although the dream became less frequent as Teresa grew older, it never disappeared entirely. Whenever she'd forgotten it and began wondering why she was so paranoid about going out in public, that night it would return, her face's fragile remains in her hands once more. After months of putting up with it, pretending she didn't lie awake sometimes in fear of what she'd see after closing her eyes, Teresa reluctantly told her grandparents about the dream. They had asked her during breakfast why she looked so spooked, her eyes wide and face bloodless. They said she looked like a zombie, and she told them that she'd had this night-mare and afterward spent the rest of the interminable night awake, too afraid to go back to sleep. They did their best to reassure her, Granny T adding that it was probably meaningless, maybe a sort of variant on the classic dream about teeth falling out. But later that afternoon, they knocked on her door and asked whether she would feel better if she spoke to a doctor about this, if perhaps concrete medical expertise could dispel the dream once and for all. Teresa agreed, even though she knew how much a consultation would cost them. Anything to know that it was, as her grandmother said, "just a meaningless nightmare."

The earliest available appointment was three weeks later at Presbyterian Hospital, a cool, modern building with abundant natural light and potted plants that contrasted with its patients' pallor. After a lengthy wait, Teresa and her grandparents followed a labyrinth of hallways into a tiny, fluorescent-lit room with a chair, a bed covered by butcher paper, and a small blue shelf. There was hardly enough room for the three of them, but Teresa wanted both of them with her, having hated hospitals ever since the months and months she spent in and out of them after the accident.

Finally a doctor entered the room, an overbearingly positive man who looked straight out of a 1950s film and stressed that honesty above all was his policy. He made small talk with her grandparents, then exam-ined her face with a light on a stick. He said it looked good, that he would never have known it wasn't real, then corrected himself, saying that of course it was real, he simply meant that it wasn't "typical." Then without missing a beat he told her that while he could be fairly certain that this dream scenario would never happen, he couldn't guarantee it.

"Transplants are strange," he said, his fingers caressing her face in a way that made Teresa flinch. He didn't seem to care that her grandparents were inches away from him, glaring. "Why the body rejects some and not others is difficult to fathom. Occasionally, a body will reject a transplant much later, for reasons we're still trying to uncover."

He prescribed a cream for her to rub into the almost imperceptible seams of her face, a strangely viscous substance that he warned her to use sparingly because it was mildly carcinogenic. She was supposed to rub it in once every day, but to keep it near and reapply whenever her face felt dry or flaky.

The doctor then advised her that she shouldn't worry herself about this, that she should live her life and enjoy the operation's success. If something did go wrong, it would likely not take a form like that of her dream but rather something far more grotesque. Still as cheerful as when he first greeted them, he said that the transplant might turn green and putrefy from the outside as the host and graft fought each other in a painful fight to the death. Fifteen minutes after they entered the examination room, Teresa began to feel that with every breath she took in public, someone might see her literally fall to pieces. Her grandfather drove home, a long, silent drive during which the three of them knew that there was nothing to be said. Granny T put her arm around Teresa, and neither of them cried, but everyone knew that the visit had been a mistake.

Although she was only a sophomore when the accident happened, Teresa never went back to school. She rarely saw anyone besides her grandparents, too afraid of her face suddenly malfunctioning. She couldn't bear the idea of becoming a freak, a victim. Before her mom's divorce, the move to Albuquerque, the crash, the operation, she'd dreamed of being famous. Not for a specific thing, not for acting or singing or being married to a prince of England, just famous. Invited to parties with other stars, her picture on magazine covers and fashion blogs, her name on the lips of strangers. Walking down the red carpet and offering bon mots on talk shows, admired by billions just for being herself. She still wanted that, but now the fear of having her face drop off or bubble up with green pustules kept her from even leaving the house.

For a while, Teresa's anthropophobia hadn't seemed like a big deal, more like an eccentricity. It was only when it compounded with other problems that her life began feeling untenable. It began as a sort of general malaise, just something in the background, and most of the time Teresa could easily ignore it. Everyone, she was pretty certain, spent some of their lives pretending that they were happier than they actually were, and she supposed that she was just one of the unlucky ones who had to do it more often. Showing up and looking sullen, immediately spurring questions. "What's wrong?" "What's her problem?" It drew attention, which only made things worse. Staying invisible had been one of her primary goals since moving to Albuquerque, but sullen girls get noticed, get judged. When she went to Mass on Sundays, one of the few reasons she ever left home anymore, Teresa made sure to smile, to wave at people she recognized after services, to walk to the sanctuary without losing her composure despite feeling like collapsing from the weight of their gazes.

She didn't know what brought this on. Maybe it was just a part of aging, or maybe it had been the isolation, day in and out with little human contact aside from her grandparents. Most of the time it was just a dull throb in the back of her mind, but sometimes it would bubble to the surface, reminding her that she was worthless, that her very existence was a waste of the world's rapidly decreasing resources. In her room, she had the freedom to do anything she desired, four walls keeping the rest of the world completely at bay, but all she wanted to do was lie in her bed and cry. She'd curl up beneath a worn quilt her grandmother had sewn together and stare straight up at the ceiling, or the underside of the quilt, or the inside of her eyelids, wishing that either the feeling would go away or she would.

Slowly the malaise grew worse. It transformed from a presence, a pressure she could sometimes force herself to ignore, into an ache that surrounded her, enveloping everything she did. It seemed to feed on inactivity, so she started trying to entertain herself in her room, fighting the overwhelming urge to lie in bed. She'd play violent video games, or work out using her grandparents' old stationary bike and yoga tapes purchased online, until she was too exhausted to move. She'd crank up music as loud as she could without irritating her grandparents, singing along with Gravedigger's angry, vindictive rhymes and trying to tap into their emotions rather than her own.

But then, after so many explosions, so much singing and jumping up and down while waves of bass propelled her around her tiny room, she always ended up back in bed again. Alone again. Without fail, the pain returned, and with it the reminder that there was no escape. There was so much time to fill, and nothing worked forever. Eventually she remembered herself, and unhappiness came roaring out. Teresa felt like she was running a race with no finish line.

What she couldn't figure out was what, fundamentally, she was doing wrong. All of the television shows and movies she'd grown up watching made it seem like she should be happy. The meaning of life, the path to contentment, was pretty much what she had. Teresa had no real cares. While she wasn't filthy rich, she certainly had enough money since she didn't pay for rent or food. When she saw a dress she liked, she could buy it. When she saw a trailer for a movie, she went and bought a copy online. She knew that the one thing she didn't have, which everyone on a screen seemed to have scads of, was friends. But that wasn't a problem she knew how to solve, and for a while it seemed perhaps more insurmountable than her steadily growing unhappiness. She had complete and total freedom within her room, but that seemed to mean nothing. She was always still stuck there with herself.

When finally the pain went beyond an ache, left her feeling battered at the end of every day, Teresa decided that she had to try something else, something new. Her very existence had become so unbearable that she was willing to attempt something drastic.

After a night of crying in bed, too agonized to fall asleep and too miserable to get up, she began looking for a job. She didn't need the money, but she thought of those other women on TV, the breadwinners, the ones who seemed content because they nailed the big contract or won the case. Satisfaction seemed to accompany a big paycheck, and that might be what she needed, to move past being subsidized by her grandparents and become an adult.

Teresa needed a job that could be done at home on her computer, but found herself surprised by how few of them weren't simply robotic tasks repeated ad infinitum, and even some of those asked for more qualifications than just a GED. She stumbled into freechatgirlz.com from an ad on Craigslist boasting flexible online hours and high pay for any willing female, the only requirement being an Arcadia account. Her dismay about the ad's trick (it never mentioned nudity or she wouldn't have followed up on it in the first place) gave way after a few days of agonizing depression and countless other false leads, scams to get personal information or work that paid far below minimum wage.

So out of a nagging curiosity, she visited the site, and found herself surprised both by how legitimate it was (not a single popup ad) and how little women had to do to get paid. It wasn't about painful orgies or humiliation. Half the videos she saw were just women, frequently but not always undressed, talking to a camera about their day. She felt that she could do that, and after a few days of exploring the site, she registered an account. At first she broadcast for only two minutes. A day later she sat there for five and even took off her shirt, leaving her bra on. Two weeks after finding out about freechatgirlz.com, she did her first hour and exchanged her newly earned Arcadia points for nearly two hundred dollars.

While Teresa still felt paranoid seeing people in person, still struggled just to make it through Mass even when shepherded through the church by her grandparents, all of that was gone online. She was being seen by more people, far more openly, but the computer felt safe. She always felt in control, could close down the live stream the moment she felt an itch at her scalp. Hers was the only face she ever saw on the screen, and that mattered.

Her grandparents never questioned how she was getting money, likely because she spent most of it on digital items, and they had no idea that she was suddenly living above her allowance's means. If they had worries about what she spent all her time doing inside her room, they kept it to themselves.

The problem came when she closed the stream: almost immediately the pain rushed back like a tsunami. She started streaming longer and longer sessions, and even tried leaving on her stream while asleep until users began to complain. Worse, though, was that the numbing effect of her new "job" began to wear off. As her sessions became more routine, no longer an event she needed to psych herself up for, their balm slowly left, unless she was actively broadcasting.

It was March when they sat down for dinner, a posole soup mixed with red chile that made the entire house smell delicious, and Teresa announced she was searching for work. "Not that I'll take anything, I just . . . I think maybe I'm ready to get out there."

Even her grandfather looked up from his bowl and smiled. "Is there something in particular you have in mind?" asked Granny T. They both suddenly looked younger, more hopeful.

"Not really. I'll probably just see what's available and go from there. To be honest, I don't even know where to start." Teresa didn't really know whether she was ready to take this step, but knowing what unhappiness awaited her after the meal, alone in her room, she was willing to find out.

18

It was Steve who came up with the idea, but he'd be the first to tell you it wasn't entirely original. Years ago a fringe Baptist preacher named Reginald Shepherd Haight claimed to have been told by a higher power that the end of the world would come on March 19, 2027, and there was nothing anyone could do to stop it. He said that the end would arrive in the form of a premillennial rapture, and that following the ascension of only a few hundred thousand devout followers, the world would become hell on earth. Natural disasters would lead to disease would lead to war would lead to the destruction of the planet and all humans still on it. Life for those who were forced to struggle through this ordeal would be worse than death, and suicides would soon outnumber births. The ocean tides would turn red with blood and before 2100, every last human being would be exterminated.

When Haight's predictions never came to pass, he was briefly apologetic but didn't miss a beat in using his newfound publicity to support a campaign for public office. This had been his third prediction about the end of the world and, by then, most of his followers seemed completely unmoved by its failure to arrive.

"If this put the fear of God into one individual, if one person was converted and gave up their wicked ways to embrace the path of godliness, then Reverend Haight's revelation was still a true one," said María Sánchez of KOAT *Action 7 News*. Overall reactions to the entire affair were mixed, but the immediate forgiveness of churches across the nation kept him from becoming a national joke for more than an evening, after which his opinions were treated as seriously as before. "The reason why God foretold the rapture rather than springing it upon us is so that we have time to prepare while still in this world," he explained in an interview on CNN. "It's not about the event, it's about the life we live before then. For each of us, personally, the end has always been at hand."

Even at nine years old, Steve was pissed off about the prediction and remained so for years to come. Following Haight's proclamation, Albuquerque was plastered with advertisements for the end of the world, each filled with vivid imagery of infants drowning and women crying over graves. Few mentioned following Christ and celebrating his good works. Instead they focused on tornadoes and earthquakes, bodies shredded with bullets and families screaming in terror, noxious green gases that coated the air and choked everyone who inhaled them. They spoke in definite terms about the rapture and what would occur when the trumpet sounded, of rape and murder and God's anger at what had become of the peaceful world he'd created.

The ghost of those billboards stuck around long after the anticlimactic arrival of March 20. Steve's dad, in one of the many predestined-to-fail lawsuits he filed before his deportation and subsequent disappearance, tried to sue for false advertising. But this came to nothing when the case was dismissed in summary judgment without even coming to trial. The judge found that religions were always full of unverifiable claims, but that didn't make them culpable when those claims failed to pan out. Faith necessitated unverifiable, possibly untruthful, claims, and for the same reason that the Catholic Church couldn't be sued when wine did not molecularly transform into blood, Haight couldn't be sued when the rapture failed to arrive on schedule.

Disney had a far worse experience with Haight's vision—although most of it occurred before he moved to the 505—when his family converted and began attending a megachurch in Los Angeles. The Díaz family gave away all of its earthly possessions in preparation for the event, selling their house and cars for donations to the church. Disney, young as he was, couldn't process his family's move from a large five-bedroom house to a tiny apartment. His parents told him this would only be necessary for a short period, that they'd soon move somewhere much nicer, fully convinced that the rapture would whisk all three of them off to heaven. He ran away from home several times and his constant desertions eventually resulted in a custody battle between his parents and grandparents that ripped the Díaz family apart. He moved with his grandparents to Albuquerque, only to learn upon arrival that the city was even more saturated with ads for the upcoming rapture (now long past) than Los Angeles was.

Disney's family wasn't the only one thrown into a sort of panic, and just the year before there were similar claims from a vaguely Hindu cult about an end of the world resulting in a mass suicide moments before a colossal meteor was prophesied to crash into the earth. Over eighty thousand died in the ceremony. Meanwhile, reports of rising global temperatures continued. More astral bodies were discovered in near proximity to Earth. Disney would never admit it, but there were reasons, although perhaps no more so than at any other time, to believe that the endpoint might be near. The year 2012 had come and gone, but some said that only meant the end could happen any day now. All guarantees were void.

Many billboards around Albuquerque detailing the precise date and events of the failed rapture stayed up for years, especially in the poorer parts of the city where they were only painted over when corporations were willing to pay for something else to go up. Steve's house was located almost directly beneath one of these billboards, and he saw it before and after school every day. Upon his arrival in Albuquerque, Disney and Steve became almost instant friends, but after his first visit to Steve's house, Disney refused to return. He thought that Steve's fascination with the rapture and other end-of-the-world scenarios was perverse, and this remained a sticking point between them. Steve said he didn't give a lit fart what Disney thought and that the guy should go cry to his grandmother if he couldn't take abstract statistical analysis at face value.

The entire affair left Steve wondering for years why the news media virtually stopped for a week when an unreliable preacher spoke about the end of the world for the third time. The nation, and in fact much of the world, waited with bated breath for his predictions to be proved true or false, while thousands of scientists around the world had verified that climate change was real, that it was destroying us every moment of the day, and the only thing that could slow it down would be an even greater catastrophe hitting the human race, be it a meteor or disease or geothermal nuclear war. Wasn't there a more logical way of thinking about the problem than listening to every half-baked prophet who talked his way onto a chat show?

Thus was born the Big Board of Apocalypses. Steve's first version of it was literally a large piece of poster board like the name implied, not because he liked working on paper (he didn't), but because it was more or less necessary for displaying a math project, in his case one focused on giving a practical application for graphing nonlinear phenomena. He'd hit the books and documented every historical apocalypse he could think of, from the death of the dinosaurs to the xenocide of the Neanderthals to the great flood. Then he graphed them based upon the period of time between each catastrophic event and used a nonlinear regression to estimate when the next cataclysm should theoretically hit. As projects go, it was relatively simple, and it spurred on his theory that the end of the world wasn't some ineffable, mystical thing you learned through prophecy but a predictable phenomenon like anything else. And while there was always a statistical margin of error, that didn't mean you couldn't draw conclusions.

The main problem, he found, was that historical sources could only document events that had happened on Earth or, at best, in the solar system. But events on Earth were frequently unprecedented and didn't necessarily give a good sample as far as statistical likelihood was concerned—the Permian-Triassic extinction event wasn't caused by a Pakistani dirty bomb set off in New York, triggering a retaliatory strike that angered China and soon escalated into a nuclear apocalypse. The reverse was equally problematic, since a stellar black hole would have so completely destroyed a planet that we would never know of its existence.

The difficulty in finding a truly accurate algorithm for predicting the probability that a certain day might be the last caused Steve to change his approach entirely. Rather than looking for the likely date of the next mass extinction, Steve began inquiring into which apocalypse would finish us off.

This transformed the BBA into a sort of betting table, listing the odds that any individual apocalypse might be the one to destroy humanity. Steve considered there to be a roughly 1:12 chance of the world's ending as a result of a meteor, whereas there was a 1:2 chance of a nuclear apocalypse. This was explained with a note: "Like, is there a country that *doesn't* have the bomb at this point?"

After a few months, Steve divided the board into various groupings, which he created after seeing a roulette table and noting the various betting combinations. E.g., if you were curious about the likelihood of a religious end of the world but weren't picky about whether it was Ragnarok or rapture or Kalki (an argument still raged over whether this category should include alien invasions, but other than a few of |3ə's absolute extremists, the general consensus was no), you'd find that the board's caretakers considered them to be pretty unlikely, with a group chance of just 1:25. Still, this was much higher than the chances of just a rapture or some otherwise Jesus-inflected end, which were put at 1:842.

As with most of Steve's projects, he almost immediately lost interest in the BBA after creating its first fully functional version, but he bequeathed its code, algorithms, and guidelines to the clan, since many of the Baby Eaters had become fascinated by the concept. Devon began a new thread on it in the clan's forum, and pretty soon it was more or less administering itself. Members found new research about one of the apocalypses, posted it online, and adjusted the odds accordingly. They'd even post about "signs" of the apocalypse, whether the eight Aztec omens had been repeated or Christianity's sixth seal had opened up. Just a few months after it became public, the BBA had become one of the clan's pastimes, something members updated while just shooting the shit between games, a metagame itself that they participated in despite knowing that there was no true way of winning.

Steve's initial eschatology chart included only ten different scenarios, but the current board maintained one hundred forty-four, though admittedly a lot of those toward the end were pretty much jokes. Being demolished to make way for a hyperspace bypass was given a $1:10^{63}$ chance, while Trouble with Tribbles was given a $1:10^{65}$ chance, both deemed significantly likelier than the Planet of the Apes scenario's $1:10^{68}$.

Mostly the BBA was filled with the real concerns of clan members, possible ends that they'd seen on the news or read about online. It listed artificial intelligence singularity and gray goo, nuclear warfare and nuclear winter and doomsday devices, nuclear meltdowns and massive oil spills, supervolcanoes, supernovae, stellar or rogue black holes, meteors, gamma-ray bursts, anoxic ocean events, a worldwide EMP, a super short-circuit causing an electrical arc that fries the world, climate change, solar expansion, solar storms, galactic cannibalism, the Big Rip, the Big Crunch, the Big Bounce, the Big Freeze, global dimming, methane burps, a vibration at the resonant frequency of the Earth's crust and/or mantle, a disease pandemic, Gulf Stream shutdown, colony collapse disorder, zombies, agricultural pesticide crisis, mega-tsunami, hypervelocity stars, vacuum metastability, cosmic radiation, heat death, magnetars, WWIII, dirty bombs, nuclear terrorism, Civil War II, fossil fuel depletion, alien invasion (enslavement or attack), super-resistant bacteria, overpopulation and/or mass famine, experimental physics accident, overconsumption, geomagnetic reversal, repositioning of the rotational axis, superdrugs, televisual mind control, voluntary human extinction, etc. etc. etc. etc. etc. etc. etc. etc. etc. etc. etc.

Steve's loss of interest came not just from a desire never to invest too much effort into one project—he liked to think of himself as an idea man, not necessarily a follow-through man—but also because the Big Board's current betting-style format had never fully diverted his interest in the earlier question: *When* would the last day finally hit?

Devon was the only person with whom Steve shared his discovery that, as far as he could tell, we were all living on borrowed time, saying something oblique about humans being the cause of a sixth mass extinction that would more than likely include humanity itself. When he heard this offhand comment as they walked from calculus to English together, Devon assumed that Steve was joking—it was, after all, Steve who suggested they not rule out the possibility of Tribble-based Armageddon. His friend hadn't found religion or changed his life in any observable way since the two had known each other, and if you were absolutely convinced that the end was just over the horizon, you'd have to adjust, to find some sort of peace with your own existence. You couldn't just hang around playing video games, pretending tomorrow would be just another ordinary day, could you?

19

Holly used to dread Autumn's questions about who she ate lunch with, what they spoke about. Her mom searched for cracks in her stories like an interrogator, hoping for any hint that Holly had ditched campus to wander Central or smoked pot beneath the bleachers or any other stereotypical rebellious teenager bullshit. This never happened, though, and not because Holly was particularly good at lying. The reason was simpler than that: Holly had never skipped a class, never been absent from a club meeting. Three years of perfect attendance that didn't count for crap. But she'd felt a certain responsibility about it at the time and an incredible weight of guilt when she even considered ditching—somehow her parents managed to instill in her the guilt of a traditional Catholic or Jewish upbringing despite their mutual atheism.

These days she felt the same responsibility about painting, and she'd resolved to make it her job, to treat it with complete seriousness. That no one else cared how she spent her time, even Robert, made the guilt of shirking it even worse.

"Painting" meant mixed media, watercolors and oils and acrylics, sure, but also ink or cutouts or whatever the project at hand required. She locked herself up in the studio so that she had no easy way of escaping work, but this only seemed to make things worse, to spur on the creativity of her procrastination rather than her brushes. It didn't even need to be good work, either, she just needed something to prove that her time hadn't disappeared like water into the studio floor's drain.

When she was younger, Holly used to work whenever inspiration, that fickle bitch, had struck her. She would crawl into bed at eleven o'clock and, while half-asleep, begin thinking about colors and shapes and maybe people she'd seen earlier, or events in the news. Out of this she'd know exactly what to create next, and a compulsion would enter her head that wouldn't leave until she'd put something on paper. She'd reluctantly force herself out of bed, stuff blankets into the bottom of her bedroom door to keep light from exiting the room, then walk in complete silence into her closet. It would take her a full minute to close its door or else the ancient rollers would screech, and then she would stuff its cracks with dirty clothes before turning on a flashlight. Still half-asleep, she would work until her alarm went off, listening with headphones to NPR or old radio dramas, an eight-hundred-page Dickens or Trollope novel compressed into an hour with commercials. At school the next day, she would feel near collapse.

After Holly left Albuquerque, she felt that to be a professional required discipline, time set aside specifically for creation without any interruption. Some music or a movie in the background, sure, but her primary focus had to be the work. Her ideal studio was a pure environment, a haven from the usual intrusions of life that inhibited an artist's best work.

She still kept a sketchbook in her purse, filled with lists of ideas and pencil drawings, sometimes miniature versions she meant to expand later and sometimes just random doodles made while waiting in line at Starbucks. But she used it less and less, instead trying to compartmentalize her life. When she was here in the garage-studio, she was at work, and she wanted to allow herself to exist in the rest of the world without always worrying about capturing it on an easel. She wanted to look at a sunset's splendor without wondering how you'd create those colors with paint, to walk over train tracks without thinking about how they crosshatched their way toward the horizon.

Lately, though, it seemed like every day she thought less about her work while inside the studio, though when she left it, her work, or rather her lack of productivity, subsumed everything. It didn't help that Robert seemed to have no problem of the sort, that an endless stream of ideas flowed directly from his head into his computer and then into a gallery. His only struggles were technical problems, more like puzzles than anything else, and he always seemed to solve them. She knew she shouldn't be jealous, but didn't know what to do about it besides spend more time locked in the studio, pretending he wasn't a hundred feet away but still completely aware of him.

Today, like yesterday, she watched a movie—for research, she supposed—while absentmindedly glancing at flowers on the Internet. In a sense they were models, and she browsed everything from Impressionist sunflowers to photographs. She knew she needed one in her painting, but deciding which one and how to display it had dragged on for hours. Mostly she just wanted to watch the goddamn movie, one of those witty old Hollywood productions that she thought was directed by Ernst Lubitsch or possibly Billy Wilder. She hadn't started watching until after the opening credits were finished and was determined to watch to the end without looking up the movie's name. If the movie lasted until after four o'clock, she could release herself from the studio, another day's work finished.

Holly's purse vibrated atop the wood table on the other side of the studio, and she rushed to answer before it hit voice mail. She picked up her phone and flicked her finger across the screen without even checking to see who called.

"Hey?" said Holly.

"Got a minute?" said Gideon.

"Um . . . kind of. I'm in the middle of some work right now, but it's no biggie, I guess. Why, what's up?" Under no circumstances would she admit to him that she was lying on a couch watching a movie. When she'd moved in with Robert, he'd built a carport over his driveway and had his garage converted into an over-the-top luxurious studio for her, then outfitted it with a couch, a drawing table, a new drain for hosing the place off, a full-size refrigerator, and even a skylight so it wouldn't feel so depressing. It was almost a miniature apartment of her own, attached to his mansion but separate, and they had an unspoken agreement that he would stay away from it unless invited, though recently he seemed to ignore this part of their arrangement more and more.

"No, it's cool. You can call me back later when you've got some time. It's not an emergency or anything."

"No no, it's fine. I haven't heard from you in . . . at least a few months? Longer? I dunno, at least since like the summer or so."

"You know me, I get busy with things. I figure we spent enough time together growing up that my voice is probably like fingernails against a chalkboard."

"No, I love you plenty. It's not my fault that if we're together for more than five days at a time, I will more than likely stab you through the eye with something pointy. But I'd do it with love."

"And I love you, too, Ms. Stabby."

"So what's up?"

"I don't need anything per se. Can't I just call to chat?"

"Okay, we're chatting. Any topic in particular, or should we just continue talking about the way we never talk enough until eventually we render the entire conversation moot?"

"You drew it out of me. I did have something in mind."

"I figured."

"Right, so . . . I've been having these weird dreams, right? Do you ever remember your dreams?"

"Sometimes. I mean, yeah, of course, everyone does."

"Well just . . . I had this super lucid one about dad. Like, I thought I was over all of that, I never even think about the guy anymore. And then bam, it's like he's at my door asking to come in. Just banging away."

"Umm . . . okay . . ."

"It just, God, it was so real. So I've been thinking about him and also, like, some other things, connections and all. How that even happens with a guy like me—I mean, a guy like him. Anyhow, I was just wondering if you remembered anything about the way mom and dad got together?"

"Umm . . . no. I don't tend to remember things that happened before I was born. Just because I live in T or C doesn't mean I've gone all mystic and shit. That's really more of a Taos thing, Robert would never let me hear the end of it. But I've heard some stories."

"I was just thinking, like . . . I don't know, up until he left they seemed so stable, right? Like, up until he disappeared, it never even seemed like divorce was on the table."

"I don't know about that . . ."

"I mean, they seemed as if they fit together. Like, some people, you just know that they'd be good as a couple. But then I was just thinking about how it never made sense that they were even a thing in the first place. I mean, dad's not exactly the sociable type. Or the wooing type. AP's got this AI program that tells you whether a logo is aesthetically appealing to the average consumer, and it's significantly more emotional than either of them."

"He was plenty emotional when you broke his hard drive."

"The way a tank squashing protesting students is emotional."

"Why can't you just ask mom? I'm sure she'd love to hear from you. Especially about this kind of stuff."

"That seems mean. Like, do you want to be the one to remind her about dad and everything?"

"Depends on my mood." Realizing she'd missed a chunk of the film, Holly opened up a new window and began searching for what

Lubitsch movie featured Gene Tierney. Or at least which movie that looked like a Lubitsch film featured Gene Tierney.

"Ha. You know mom, she'd tell me as if nothing was happening, honestly and precisely recounting what she remembered. She'd be clear and concise and speak in perfect grammatical sentences like that AI program. After hanging up she'd be in tears and for the next week, she'd be putting in twenty-hour days."

"So what? That's her choice."

"Really? Just talk to me for a second. Like, I can just picture dad then, scrawny little computer nerd talking really fast about games and frame rates and all that, but even worse because it's not tempered by years of family."

"Well, I think it was just one of those college things. He was an older guy and she was a younger woman and soon enough they were an item. Other than the age difference, I can't imagine it was too different from what happened between you and Sandra."

"Yeah I get that, but I mean like what were the specifics of the whole thing? I know they were in college but like, how did he do it? Do you know what words were said, if they were at a party or a club or something?"

"I think they were at the Hillel center. I think? I'm not sure why I would know this any better than you do." Not only was she right about it being Lubitsch, Gideon seemed to be in an unusually good mood. Maybe he was getting along with Claire, as unlikely as that sounded. Not that she should judge, but the speed at which Gideon moved from first wife to second had always struck Holly as at the very least unhealthy. She assumed they fought a lot, but didn't really know anything about their lives together.

"Because I never gave a crap about our family history. And I mean I know how mom tried to raise you Jewish for a little while before she went full-on atheist, but I didn't think she'd be able to get dad within, I dunno, a hundred feet of the place. He's not exactly keen on religion."

Holly heard knocking at the door. She stood up from the couch and unlocked it, not at all surprised to find Robert on the other side. His hair was slightly damp, so he must've just gotten out of the shower. He never dried himself enough after bathing, would drip water all over the floor of the bathroom and even trail it around their house rather than spending an extra fifteen seconds toweling off. He claimed it was so dry here that the water would evaporate almost the moment it stopped flowing from the faucet, but two weeks ago, she'd slipped on it and nearly cut her head open on a bathroom cabinet. After that he'd said he would be more careful, but his clothes were still damp and a tiny puddle was growing on the studio floor.

"Let me think . . . yeah no, it wasn't there," said Holly, waving him in. "I think they met in the library or something, and she was checking out books for class. Really stupid titles like *The Job of Doubt: The Role of Jewish Skepticism in Shaping the Chosen People*, really theory-heavy academic books for a religion course, and he was just paying attention to the books because he needed an excuse to talk to her."

Robert walked inside holding a glass of lemonade in his left hand. "Want some?" he silently mouthed.

She whispered back, "No, I'm fine. Why are you here?" She didn't want him to see her shirking work.

"Dad worked at the library?" said Gideon.

"Just thought you might want some," Robert whispered, still smiling and making no attempt to leave despite her obvious displeasure. "I want to show you something cool when you're done."

"Well, he got paid for it," said Holly into the phone. She realized Robert could see her computer screen running a movie, so she closed it, embarrassed but doing her best to hide it. "I can't imagine he did too much actual work, but I think he'd go to the checkout desk if there was a girl he thought was pretty. So he did that and saw mom digging up stuff on Jews and shit and used that to ask her out."

She covered the phone's microphone with her hand. "That's great, really. But it's not a good time."

"No problem," said Robert, no longer whispering. "Sorry, I just thought maybe you could use something to cheer you up. I'll just leave it here, didn't know you were in the middle of something." With this he turned around and shut the door behind him. Of course that was the point of the studio, that when she was in here she was always in the middle of something, but it never seemed to matter to him. It made her feel like her painting was a hobby, while his sculptures were real work because they brought in money. And what did he mean by "cheer you up"? Was she that much of a drag these days?

"She said yes just like that? There was no big production or anything? I mean, do girls respond to that sort of thing?"

Holly took a moment to remember what they were talking about. "Umm . . . I don't remember ever hearing anything else. He took her to the Hillel House at UNM and they talked about, I dunno, Judaism and stuff. I think dad may have accidentally convinced her that he was in fact Jewish, despite the whole Mexi-Catholic background."

"You sure it was an accident?"

"I mean, maybe it wasn't, but why would she care about what religion he was? Anyhow, they had dinner and kept going out. I've never really heard anything about how it went from there. You know how focused dad could be when he set his mind to something, though. Assuming he went after mom with the same intensity he did with any project, I can see why she stayed with him. But I'd prefer to stop there, if you don't mind—if you want info about when dad put the moves on her or whatever, I'm going to have to hang up the phone."

"Yeah, of course. But what about, like, when they moved in together?"

"Is it family history trivia night at the local pub or what? You never cared about dad while he was around, but a dream makes you want to hear his life story?"

"Keep humoring me or I start asking about you and Robert. You know the story grandma used to tell of how they met?"

"Oh yeah. Sure," said Holly. "You want me to tell it again?"

"I think I remember the basic gist, but I'd like a refresher."

"Well, if you recall, mom was at UNM at the time and was about to graduate. She was either headed back to Vegas to find a job there while staying with her family, or if dad married her, she was going to stick around."

"Okay," said Gideon.

"Of course she didn't tell dad about that or anything. That was just in her head."

"Goddamn, why do women always do that?"

"Do what?"

"Not tell you what the rules are. It would all be so much easier if you just told people everything. Like, 'if x, then y.' Instead it's all a bunch of guessing."

"Women aren't computers. They don't have algorithms where you can just enter in the correct data to get the correct response. They have this new thing called 'feelings' that I'm sure will be thrilling to your people in a couple thousand years when you've evolved enough to have them."

"Fine, fine. So she was deciding where to stay."

"Right. And so dad's trying to get her to stick it out in Albuquerque, not knowing her conditions or anything. He thinks it's time she finally meets his family—"

"Okay, I get that, but how did meeting his family turn into 'let's all play a cruel joke on you'?"

"I'm not exactly privy to dad's thoughts on things, but if you recall, he never could resist a stupid joke. He's your gender, you should be closer to him than I am."

"That's not how it works. Fathers love their daughters best and mothers love their sons. It's basic Fraud, or something," said Gideon.

"It's Freud."

"I know what I said. So did he ever mention anything to you about it?"

"No. The only time I remember talking to him about any of this, he said he didn't remember it and then went back to work. I think the only person who ever talked about it was Grandma Reyes," said Holly.

"Okay, so then . . . ?"

"So then mom goes over to grandma's house, and she's waiting there for him, since he's late. But the thing is, dad's convinced grandma to speak only in Spanish and to pretend like she doesn't know any English at all. Grandpa's in on this, too, for God knows what reason, and he's translating what she's saying, but kind of having fun with it too and making it pretty obvious that he's not translating everything she says. He's also pretending that his English is pretty bad."

"God, that's fucking nuts. I wonder when mom learned he was an English teacher."

"So then dad calls and says that something big has come up with whatever he's working on, some game probably, and he can't make it there," said Holly. "So she's stuck with them for dinner on her own."

"How did she end up finding out that it was a joke?"

"How long could they possibly keep it up? After a really awkward dinner, their neighbor comes over to see if they can watch her son for an hour or so, only she's speaking in English. At this point mom's just pissed off as all hell and she leaves the apartment. Grandma Reyes told me she thought it was the funniest thing she'd ever seen."

"What did mom do?"

"I know her and dad had some sort of big fight. She started packing up to leave, and she was still at it when he got home. But I don't know if it was any different from any of the fights while we were around, just a lot of yelling and threatening and all of that. I guess it somehow ended up with them engaged."

"God, I wish I'd thought of something like that. Such an amazing prank," said Gideon.

"If you'd thought up pranks like that, Claire would've had you neutered."

"She already did, remember? You were there for the ceremony."

"Ha-ha. So is there anything else you need to know?"

"No, that's great."

"All of that because dream-dad wants to bother you?"

"It was a really weird dream. I mean, I would've sworn . . . anyhow, thanks for the info. Send my best to that trophy boyfriend of yours."

"Adiós."

"Adiós."

Holly tapped the phone to hang it up and then glanced at the time. It was 3:50, too late to get anything started anyhow, so she wasn't going to try. But she also didn't want to see Robert, so she spent half a minute browsing other old comedy flicks before choosing one essentially at random and purchasing it with three thousand Arcadia points, happy to see she still had some left from her younger brother's Christmas present and so wouldn't need to dip into an ever-decreasing bank account. Maybe in an hour or two, she'd feel up to the task of heading back to the house.

20

The first day of Police Academy might have been the toughest day of Teresa's life, but afterward she was so tired that if she dreamt that night, she didn't know it. The Academy wasn't run like an academy at all—at least not like the private school by that name on the east side of town—but like a boot camp. While theoretically it had an academic side, too, Teresa had no problem coasting through that part of the training. The only real challenge in their simple, memorization-based tests was concentrating after a morning of running and jumping, endless push-ups and sit-ups until she felt like she'd sweated more than her body weight in water. After that, most cadets seemed to forget their own names, let alone what the police codes meant.

Teresa felt sore all over, but she found that her aches kept her from drifting back to unhappiness when she got home. She returned home so exhausted she didn't even care to open up her RSS for a quick look at the day's news, not that she had much time for that. Class began at seven in the morning and lasted until six at night. Then she drove home, ate dinner with her grandparents, put on a rote show for her fans online, and collapsed into sweet oblivion. Other trainees dropped out, many by the second week, and then a steady flow of quitters until the Academy ended twelve weeks later. She understood why—training was far from bliss, but that was what she'd hoped for. The Academy left her numb, too fatigued to dwell on herself.

By the end of the first week, everything, from polishing her boots to running the obstacle course to answering the training sergeant in class, had become automatic. The Academy input directions and she output the appropriate response. Other recruits were faster, stronger, smarter, and more honorable, but these traits were, within the Albuquerque Police Department, just as looked down upon as being weaker or stupider. A cadet's job at the Academy wasn't to impress, it was to achieve adequacy, no more and no less. To become the human equivalent of an assembly-line car. Despite what Teresa felt were her obvious inadequacies, she graduated at the top of her class and was called by the head of training "a model officer." Had he not tried to hit on her moments after their final class ended, at which point strictures about dating cadets abruptly ended in what she later learned was called "the opening of hunting season," she might've even believed him.

President Haight had begun the largest series of nationwide reforms since the New Deal, and though he had similar aims as FDR, his methodology had been strikingly different. With help from a split House and Senate, both sides of which refused to negotiate, Haight—an arch-right-winger harboring a supreme distrust of large government—worked hard at either abolishing or defunding as many government projects as possible. When protested, he and his supporters responded with cries of "free market" and a call for private industries to pick up the slack.

Haight's reforms were swift and far-reaching, but the government's deficit barely budged. Instead, money was funneled into military, law enforcement, and above all Homeland Security, which transformed even more rapidly than the rest of the government following its massive budget infusion. The APD ballooned from twelve hundred to three thousand in just three years. With funding came higher expectations, though, which would've been more difficult to achieve had they not been coupled with lax standards for police brutality and a new Supreme Court interpretation of the Fourth Amendment.

The idea of a necessary warrant for a basic search was written into the Constitution. However, warrants were only deemed necessary for unreasonable searches. A series of suspicious fatalities resulted in Haight's appointing three new Supreme Court justices in the first year of his presidency, and when a case concerning the Fourth Amendment finally made its way through various appeals past the circuit courts, the new justices, alongside a few conservative stalwarts, found that a "reasonable" search was anything that a police officer, interpreted as an innately upstanding and reasonable person, considered necessary. Warrants were still necessary for "unreasonable" searches, but these soon became so rare as to make them virtual relics.

"The American way means freedom," said Haight, in another of his online press conferences that surpassed fifty million views. "And freedom has never meant that you can do whatever you want, with no consideration for other human beings. No, freedom is security. Freedom is walking down the street knowing you won't get mugged. It's going to a ball game without worrying about whether your car will be stolen. We all have personal freedom. You can do whatever you want and live with the consequences. What we don't have enough of in our lives is freedom from one another, freedom that means you can go to work in the morning without worrying that someone will hijack a plane and ram it into your building. That's the freedom I want for this country."

By the time Teresa joined the Academy, the police force had fully adjusted to its new role as a far more aggressive and authoritative agency. The Academy's turn toward a more militaristic training program was indicative of greater national trends. It used to be that every academy was different, but in order to receive funding, the APD and nearly all other agencies adjusted and shifted their focus toward molding identical candidates. Physical fitness was stressed, as was the chain of command. Discipline was beyond important; it was sacred.

Teresa's graduating class had fifteen success stories and something like thirty recruits who for various reasons didn't make the cut. Most of the dropouts had been due to physical fitness, but not all. The only man in the Academy she liked, a quiet African-American who particularly excelled at the Academy's endless memorization, left for what were officially listed as religious reasons. He put up with the Academy for more than a month, but when he was shouted at for not maintaining correct posture in the chapel after a day of particularly brutal exercises, he walked out, saying that the whole thing was a farce, there was no God in the Academy, and so their services were sacrilege.

The Academy barely left time or energy for socializing, which suited Teresa just fine. She'd expected it would be a boys' club and wasn't the least bit surprised that whenever the sergeant left the room, the male cadets turned into beasts searching for prey. They harassed the lisping cadet for weeks until one day he just didn't show up. Several of the men made a point of asking Teresa what she was doing after class every single day. One time, a man with a shaved white head came up to her and said, as loudly as he could, "You know, why don't we go out for a big hunk of steak . . . it comes with a milkshake when you're finished." The rest of them hooted and hollered from the other side of the room like a gang of baboons watching a male display his red ass to a female.

But there were still women who stuck through it all; in fact only one from their original group had quit. At first they were just names and performances. Rebecca was athletic, the first woman Teresa had ever seen do more than one pull-up, and even before entering the Academy could run a seven-minute mile. Kate had a photographic memory and seemed mentally incapable of forgetting a rule. After several weeks, though, for reasons unbeknownst to Teresa, Kate and Rebecca decided she was worth talking to.

The more she respected them, the more she worried about doing something to offend them. If these women stopped talking to her, she didn't know whether she'd return. That small amount of human contact, the miracle of people smiling when they greeted her, letting her laugh at their jokes and be privy to their sidelong looks when the sergeant turned away, was every bit as invigorating as the compliments she received online.

Cadets weren't permitted to speak with anyone outside of the Academy about the training until they finished, which meant that any snarking about it had to be done with fellow cadets. After class they'd chat in the parking lot, nodding to the only other female cadet as she passed them by without saying anything. Mostly they talked about other students; the guy who'd shaved his hair off was an ex-skinhead, they said, and the guy obsessed about his pecs had a small penis, obviously. Teresa just agreed with them and prodded them on, keeping the topic of conversation as far away from herself as possible. Rebecca and Kate seemed perfectly happy to leave her this privacy, which was one of her favorite things about them.

Everyone in class wore identical outfits and their training emphasized their interchangeability, but that didn't mean they had identical bodies. Rebecca liked to do this thing where she'd try to get the attention of their instructor, to make him crack and show some humanity even if it was just for a second. The rules were simple: one point for a glance, five for a stare, and ten for a double take. She'd lean forward, exposing as much cleavage as possible, or maybe during lunch put a lollipop in her mouth before bending over to pick up a dropped pencil. Teresa kept score while her friends bet on the results.

She kept her life off-limits, but was almost as circumspect about theirs because she didn't know, outside of what she saw on TV shows, how invasive friends were allowed to be. She'd been away from peers for so long that she spent half their time together worrying if she was doing something wrong. Rebecca and Kate seemed to think there were no boundaries, though, so Teresa listened and tried to respond as supportively as possible and hoped that was the right thing to do. She didn't mind being the quiet one, just so long as they kept talking to her.

She didn't even know until the last week of class that Kate had a kid, a two-year-old girl she'd named Nicole but liked to call Nicki or even Nickle. Kate had arrived at class in a panic, saying that she was looking for a sitter after her mom had come down with some sort of illness. "You have no idea how tough it is to find someone you can trust." She showed them a picture of Nicki, and the girl's skin and hair were dark like her mother's but with crystal blue eyes that Kate said were the only thing Nicki's father had ever given her.

At the time, Teresa stayed silent, thinking it was no business of hers. She wanted desperately to know what had happened to the father, but didn't learn more about him until two days later, when they were changing in the locker room and he called to say he couldn't watch Nicki the following day. Kate's mother was still sick and she'd been forced to ask him for help looking after Nickle when she'd run out of other options.

"Goddamn that greasy-haired gringo, thinks he's better than you just 'cause he got some fucked-up job from his dad," said Rebecca. "Let's go over there and pop his ass unless he starts paying child support. At least, once we graduate we should put on uniforms and give him a scare." She smiled as she mimed a gun with her hands.

Kate laughed, and Teresa gathered that they'd had this same discussion a thousand times before without ever doing anything about it. Kate explained that Nicki was an accident, though not as much of one as sleeping with the girl's father. She'd never meant to do that, it had just happened.

"You know the train that runs down by Second? Well, some dumbass had the idea of putting buildings right across the street from it. Big high-rises, and the idea was that as the train goes past, people on the train see the building and it's a billboard on the bottom stories. So people on the train are looking at ads on the building while people in the building see the train passing and notice the ads on its sides.

"But like it's a fucking residential building. I was living there with this guy as my roommate after my parents kicked me out—long story, not worth getting into. So the people running the projects, they put up this shaky-ass high-rise with no foundation too close to the tracks and until the APD hires me it's the only place I can afford. Same with this guy. I mean, turns out his family's loaded and he's just touristing, but I didn't know it at the time.

"Motherfucking train comes by at 6:00 a.m. every day and we're living in this tiny apartment, splitting the rent because we're both working shit jobs that pay nothing and I'm living in the bedroom and he's in the living room on the couch and that's it. But like, train comes by, making the whole place shake and knocking everything off the counters and there's no way you can sleep through that. And like I didn't have to start getting ready for work for an hour or so . . ."

"What happened to him?" asked Teresa.

"Bastard left the morning he heard me sneak out of bed to throw up."

It explained why half the time Kate walked into class looking more haggard than the living dead. She'd literally passed out on the track at one point, but stayed in the class because her physical performance averaged out with her stellar academics.

"You still not asking him for child support?" said Rebecca. "I say lawyer up."

Kate just shrugged and said, "It is what it is. I mean I've asked, but he ain't giving and you know I don't need his bullshit, I'll do just fine. All I need to do is finish up here so we can get our badges and start making real money."

Their last day of class ended early, but the three of them had decided to opt out of the large group event down at Kelly's, where the meatheads and sergeants would be getting drunk, and instead headed to the Chama taproom downtown. Kate invited the other graduating woman, in case she wanted to join, but she declined and, as far as Teresa knew, just headed home. That was the role Teresa had thought she would play, the loner, the one who was there just for the work. Nothing made her happier than knowing that when she arrived at the bar, her friends— because that's who they were now, the first ones she'd had since moving to Albuquerque—would be waiting for her at a table.

She found them sitting in the back, both with large pints in front of them. She ordered a Sleeping Dog Stout, because she thought the name was cute, and pretended it wasn't the first beer she'd ever ordered. They talked about how great it would be to start work the next week, and how they hoped to end up with each other as partners. They would right the wrongs of the streets and be that thin blue line.

"And let's not shit ourselves," said Kate. "We're gonna get mad paid."

They clinked glasses in cheers, and Teresa found that she finally had the nerve to ask how Rebecca and Kate had met each other.

"You remember that place Kate was talking about? It was this absolute shithole. I mean, we're talking third-world country—and at least some of them have drinkable tap water. It wasn't just her place, either, it was the whole goddamn building. And I should know, I worked for the management.

"I was a secretary for some real assholes at Kraft, just some real jerkwads who were in love with any sort of power they had over you. But at the time I was young and didn't know better, so I took their shit, thinking that it would give me job security.

"Now, we had a lot of complaints about the places over on Second. Some were real safety issues, some were questions about how exactly they managed to fill the walls of a building constructed in the twenty-first century with asbestos. Most of the concerns that reached the company rather than the supers were pretty serious, but we had the same form letter go out to the tenants unless it was a repair that would bring down the property value of the building. Everything we did was evaluated based upon profit margins, and unless a fix was cost-effective, we didn't do it.

"One of the tenants is in the hospital now because of metal poisoning. Turns out that to cut costs, contractors installed old plumbing that began degrading as soon as it was installed. Executives at my office knew all about this, but decided that the place would probably have such a high turnaround rate, considering its location by the tracks, that by the time lead poisoning began to show up in tenants, no one would know what was happening or where it came from.

"But of course, not everyone can move around, and one kid grew up there, and of course had years of lead or whatever pumping into his system. He ends up in the hospital, and it wasn't long before the family figured out what was happening. My boss sent me an email saying to send the family packing, to give them the form letter and close the door on their asses, so I go ahead and do that."

"Seriously?" asked Teresa.

"Well, not quite. I'd been raised to take orders like a good girl, but . . . I mean, that wasn't just like telling someone to wait a day or two and the electricity would come back on, that was pure fucking evil. Fuck that shit. I mean I hated this guy anyhow, he was always trying to get into my pants, even though he treated me like shit, and I knew that he'd been with some of the other girls in the office and I was like no fucking way. I figured I'd get him back for this, so I sent out the form letter with his message on the top, saying to 'blow the fuckwits off like normal,' to the entire building."

"That's how I met her," said Kate. "I was living there and she was standing up to the motherfuckers. She was fired, of course, but so was the dick who ran the building, and they had to pay off some of the families there for poisoning them. Not everyone, not me, of course, because of some shady doctor they'd brought in who testified that maybe chromium was actually healthy, but at least that kid's family got paid off, and they're doing all right last I heard."

"What about the kid?"

"He's still in the hospital, with these headaches and shit. I visited him one time, and he was saying the craziest things like that he could only see into the future now and has no memories, but he couldn't make any of it change. It was sad. They say he picked up some permanent neurological disorder from the heavy metal in his blood, but nothing can be done about it. Head's permanently damaged. I dunno, I think his family's happy to just move on and pretend none of that ever happened, including him. After seeing the kid, can't say I totally blame 'em."

"So is that why you wanted to become a police officer?" asked Teresa.

"Pretty much. I mean the pay doesn't hurt," said Kate.

"Hear hear," said Rebecca, raising her glass.

"How about you?" asked Kate.

This was what Teresa had feared for weeks. As the conversation's pause grew longer, she had to say something. "Umm . . . I guess I just wanted a job where, I don't know, something where I could look at people but they couldn't look at me . . . something where, I don't know, I have these problems with people, and I just thought . . ."

"What? You hear that, she's drunk off of one beer."

"Nah, it's cool. Everyone's got their own reason, and not everyone's as much of a loudmouth as us," said Kate.

Teresa looked at each of her two friends and saw that, while they didn't believe her or perhaps even understand her, they didn't need to know. They just sipped their drinks and waited for a natural shift in the conversation, as if she hadn't made an ass of herself. It was the first time since she was a kid that Teresa felt truly comfortable with people outside of her family or a computer screen. She felt like she was about to cry, but it came out as a laugh, one that she couldn't stop, though she tried. Then Kate and Rebecca laughed, and Teresa didn't give a shit that the people at the next table were giving them looks, because who fucking cared about them anyhow?

"Hey, I'm buying the next round," she said, hoping the night would never end.

21

Esquire
Published online at 4:00 PM on May 15, 2037
Third Time's the Charm
A Day in the Life of President Haight
By Austin L. Murray

"What are we doing about the current credit crisis?" asks the president. The man in front of him, the well-dressed Jeffrey Stamos, Secretary of Treasury for the past six months, stammers an answer that I've been told not to repeat here. Stamos looks to either side for support from the other secretaries, but none of them dares glance in his direction. By the end of the day, Stamos has been removed, not unkindly, by the president, and even before the official announcement is offered to the press, the hunt for a replacement has begun.

We're in a long conference room, with ornamental bookshelves lining the walls and a window behind the president that, in the morning light, casts him in an almost otherworldly glow. After the meeting, which goes on for another hour and a half, I take my unique opportunity, as one of the few members of the press ever allowed into this inner sanctum, and ask the president why he fired Stamos, by all accounts one of the finest economic minds of his generation. I watch as the president's gaze scans my body from feet to head, appraising me without revealing what he's thinking. He looks me firmly in the eye and says, "He may be smart, in fact I know he is. But there are plenty of smart people out there who are also brave enough to stand by their convictions. When I saw the doubt in his eyes, the sheer terror of telling me some bad news even though he knew it to be true, well, that was enough to tell me he didn't have the character for the job."

Such bold, immediate decisions got the man elected two—let's be honest here, three—times and earned him a sixty-three percent approval rating. More than just a decider, he is a doer, most in his element when making fearless choices that, good or bad, leave me in admiration of the man who made them.

Finished with his cabinet meeting, President Haight heads off to his next appointment. His bone-white bushy hair sets him off from the rest of the room and sways a bit with each step in an almost jolly fashion, and I can't decide whether it looks like the icing on a cake or the fin of a shark. While the cabinet scurries away to do his bidding, Haight is surrounded by Homeland Security agents who secure his restroom, thoroughly searching it with dogs before allowing him in. A man at the doorway hands him a copy of the *Wall Street Journal*, and he exits with it twenty-five minutes later, tossing the newspaper to one of his agents, who wipes it down for prints before sending it off to an incinerator. Several others rush into the restroom and clean it out, removing every fingerprint and speck of DNA he might have left behind. It's a small ritual, and one that occurs everywhere the president goes, but if you're not used to seeing it, the whole affair's quite a spectacle.

I follow his posse of security and aides as he heads to a smallish room and sits down to a cup of coffee and cantaloupe. A young aide arrives with a stack of briefs, and Haight waves it away with an authoritative gesture. From twenty-five feet away, I can hear him telling the man who left them to return with a one-page summary, because he couldn't possibly be expected to read all of that. The aide hurries away, stumbling as he leaves, and another one takes his place, this time dropping off a pile of bulleted lists. Haight nods at the man, who hurries off like the first, then begins marking up the notes with his slender, elegant handwriting. Occasionally he takes a sip of coffee or bites off a hunk of melon, but he never looks up from the papers. Five minutes later, someone walks up to the president's table with a tablet, and he spends a few minutes dealing with this latest interruption. The man holds the tablet while Haight signs a few dozen documents with his finger, writing out his last name in a resolute script that's the most recognizable signature since John Hancock's.

Once he finishes, the president looks back to the papers in front of him until one of the HS agents, presumably the head, walks up and informs him that it's almost time for his seven-thirty appointment. I've now been at the White House for three hours. Used to a journalist's more leisurely schedule, I'm completely exhausted, ready to call it quits already. But for the president of the United States, the day has still only just begun.

It wasn't unexpected to see Reginald Shepherd Haight rise to become a leader of men, but no one who knew him growing up would have guessed he'd have anything to do with politics. His father had been a Southern Baptist preacher in the small town of Crystal City, Texas, and so had his grandfather. Born the sixth of seven children, two of Haight's three brothers went on to be preachers as well. When I spoke with his oldest brother, Ronald, he told me, "We all knew from an early age that Reggie was going to go that way, even though [Reginald] claims he didn't. I remember when he was just six years old and he'd begun scolding his sisters for wearing makeup, saying it was just one step removed from selling themselves on the corner, and it was like right then I knew he was meant for it. Most kids are bad at some point, but not Reggie. There wasn't a moment of his life when he wasn't holier than a saint."

The Haights grew up poor, since Mrs. Haight didn't work and their father's church fluctuated between thirty and fifty members. While some say that Reggie learned to love big business after he finished seminary and worked at the First Baptist Church of Newark—which found its way out of bankruptcy through a sponsorship deal with Taco Bell—speaking with his family made it clear that this infatuation came much earlier.

"There were so many kids, and I didn't have the time or money to make 'em anything fancy," said his mother, Regina. "So as a treat, once every week or so, we'd pile the whole family into our big old station wagon and head to the McDonald's down the road, because it was the only place we could ever afford to eat out. They had a deal at the time where on Sundays you could get burgers for forty-nine cents each, and we'd buy two or three a person for most of the family. But Reggie, he loved those so much that he'd scarf half a dozen, easy. Back then he was so skinny he could just wolf 'em down. McDonald's was his favorite food, and he loved it so much that he wanted 'em to cater his wedding. When I told him that they don't do that, he said to just head down there and ask 'em for a few hundred burgers and come back with 'em when they're ready."

Haight only attended high school through tenth grade, at which point he dropped out and lied about his age to join the Marines. He toured Iraq for two years during the second invasion, and it was his time there that supposedly informed his exclusionist foreign policy.

"He hated it," said his brother Reynold. "Every week I'd get another letter from him about how he didn't think we should be there and . . . well, a bunch of stuff about the locals that I really shouldn't say. He just hated being away from American soil, stuck with all those heathens, didn't see the point of any of it. Every letter I sent, I'd just tell him to keep cool for another week and he'd be back in the States before he knew it."

When he returned at the age of nineteen, Haight was a changed man. Before, he'd been passive, the child sitting at the back of the class who had to be asked by teachers to speak up. He'd always been popular, but he wasn't aggressive. He returned with a purpose, extroverted and strong-willed, and the day after he was honorably discharged, he applied to seminary. No one in his family was surprised, and they all supported his choice without question. Not that Haight would have responded to any—he's never answered questions about his tour in the Middle East, and all records concerning this period of his life have long been classified.

Previously a bit of a wallflower, almost afraid of women, he began dating and soon met the woman who would become the future First Lady. "I knew it was something special from the start," said his mother. "He didn't begin going steady with her for a little while, but I knew when he was headed to meet her because there'd be a twinkle in his eye. I don't think, after he met her, that he ever seriously thought of being with anyone else."

Magdalene Pryce was tall, blonde, and blue-eyed. Pictures of her in her twenties look like they were pulled straight from a Sears ad, contrasting with the tall, gawky Haight, who even post-Marines had yet to fill out into his later imposing figure. (Cultural critic Wanda Embid likened it to "the body of the nation, clearly once muscular but allowed to transfigure into fat during old age. Perfect for picking up votes in Peoria.") She's changed as much as he has during their relationship, and though the GOP claims she does not have an eating disorder, before this I'd never seen an image of her without visible ribs poking out from a blouse or skin pulled tightly against her cheekbones.

Pryce grew up in Crystal City but didn't meet her husband until he returned home. She was reluctant to date a man who'd served in the military, but his frequent insistence that the country should leave foreign affairs alone convinced her to give him a chance, and when he left for seminary just four months later, she went with him as his wife.

At seminary, Haight learned early on that he was particularly good at public speaking and learning "dead" languages, both of which came as a surprise. The soft-spoken student found that when behind a pulpit, he suddenly wanted to scream his beliefs to everyone in the room. Even his instructors were astonished, and while some, who wish to be left unnamed, told me they worried about the content of his sermons, none had any doubts about his ability to hold an audience captive. He picked up Latin almost without trying and by the time he left seminary was, as he said, fluent in biblical Hebrew as well. Since then he's learned both Greek and Aramaic in order to facilitate his hobby of translating various deuterocanonical Christian texts.

"The Jews and the Catholics committed many sins against God," he explained to me. "I don't know how much church history you know, but there's an awful lot of bad blood when you go back. Even my own church, Southern Baptist, has some links with slavery—although I want to stress that this has never been a part of my own preaching. Probably the greatest sin they committed, though, was suppressing parts of the Bible that the church didn't like. We're talking about the Word of God here, things that came straight from his mouth to the pens of his followers, and they discarded these things simply because they didn't fit what the church wanted. That just ain't right, I tell you what.

"One of my most deeply held beliefs, now and always, has been that you don't get to determine what God says. You listen to God because he is better than you. Kinder, smarter, better in every way. Just because you don't like what God's saying, like in Leviticus with the homosexuals or First Corinthians and women, doesn't mean you can dismiss it. You are not the authority in these matters. God is."

Haight brought his biblical scholarship to the pulpit and told his believers about new symbols from on high that he'd excavated, regardless of unbelievers even in his own church. Many left, but even more joined in his fervor, and as his church grew, so did its profits. Sponsorships littered not just the church walls but even his sermons, which attracted donors such as Chick-fil-A and Walmart, and he managed to make the Heritage Baptist Church one of the wealthiest and most influential in the nation. On television his followers numbered in the millions, and when he began speaking about the end of the world, even skeptics grew a little wary.

President Haight doesn't preach anymore—unless, like some of his more dedicated followers, you consider the State of the Union address or a political rally a sort of sermon. He still attends church every day, and having a small chapel built into the White House was the first change he commissioned to the building. The resulting controversy was a signal of things to come, and when he exited the chapel during my visit, he had a few minutes to speak with me, which I couldn't resist using to ask about this renovation.

"If I'd have known it was gonna be such a big deal for some folks," he said, again staring me straight in the eyes, "I would've done it anyhow. That's how I feel, and I want everyone to know that's how I've always felt. Nothing says whoever comes after me has to keep it here, but if I'm going to be anything of an efficient president, we can't have me heading all the way out to church every day, blocking off the road and inconveniencing everyone. I don't force anyone to pray or attend church, and I've heard some Baptists say that this is what makes my beliefs a whole different sect. If my staff want to go to hell, that's their business, not mine. But I'm not going to make the American public pay for a few people's intolerance."

His chummy relationship with corporate America and his jingoistic disdain for the rest of the world have drawn a lot of criticism, but it may be this religious aspect of his governance that sets off his detractors the most. I ask him what exactly he does in the chapel, which he always has closed off by armed guards while he's inside.

"Oh, it's no big thing," he says, smiling broadly. "I've heard people spout the craziest ideas about what goes on in there. I read somewhere that I communicate directly with Jesus, and He gives me my marching orders, and in another place that I take a nap." He laughs at this with a broad, good-natured smile on his face. Other common theories propose that he communicates directly with the devil, that he's beamed directives from our reptilian overlords, and that he uses that time to masturbate privately so his wife doesn't find out. (Haight has preached that sexual acts either not between a man and wife or without both physical and chemical protection are sinful.) "All I do is kneel down at the altar and pray, like anyone else. No one talks to me, I don't hear any voices, because Jesus doesn't communicate like that. Then, when I'm done, I head out. Only reason I have the doors blocked off is so that no one interrupts me. You wouldn't believe how hard it is to get a few uninterrupted minutes when you're president."

As if scripted, an aide walks up to Haight and informs him that he needs to get to his next meeting.

The story of how Haight came to politics has been told countless times, but it bears repeating because of how often it's been misrepresented. Haight had been periodically predicting the rapture almost since the day he was ordained, but it wasn't until his 2027 prophecy fizzled out that he turned his eye toward politics. Had Enrique Díaz not lit Haight's church on fire, it seems likely that America would've taken a completely different turn, especially since his foremost competitor in the 2028 GOP primaries was the uncharismatic ex-general, Thomas Colson.

Following the conflagration, Haight continued preaching as a guest at a nearby church, but it wasn't the same. He missed the sponsors and the fireworks, found it strange to speak of Jesus Christ's torture without having a member of the congregation there to help him demonstrate the martyr's death with squibs. In an interview with *Newsweek*, Haight said, "The way I learned to preach, we could have an Audi given away to someone in the audience and free McDonald's burgers under every seat. I could go back to doing it the old way, and I did, but I wasn't excited about it anymore. I'm not one of those small-town preachers like my dad, I'm here to talk to the masses. And what larger mass of good-hearted Christians is there than the United States?"

Aside from giving a single sermon each Sunday, Haight devoted all of his attention to the presidential election, and after just a pair of debates, his support grew from almost nonexistent to overwhelming. At the time, few analysts understood how he appealed to both halves of the GOP, the wealthy backers who fund its machine and the masses of radicalized poor who feel victimized despite its largely white male Christian makeup. But Haight, by speaking to both halves of the party, was a natural fit, the most exciting speaker the Grand Old Party had seen since the days of Abraham Lincoln.

The rest, as they say, is history. Haight won the GOP nomination without breaking a sweat, and after his startlingly well-funded super PAC outspent the Democrats in advertising almost two to one, no one was surprised at his landslide win with sixty-four percent of the popular vote.

The installation of a church in the White House alarmed many, but no American president since Franklin Roosevelt has polarized voters like Haight. Parallels between the two men are easy to draw, despite their radically different political agendas. Like Roosevelt, Haight has brought more power to the executive branch and used it as a sledgehammer to force policy through a split nation, with obviously varying results.

The Great Wall of Freedom, the barrier that locked down the United States' southern border, looms large in this discussion, but its effect on the lives of most Americans has been symbolic or nonexistent. Less publicized but in some ways more important have been his union-crushing policies and the legalization of corporations as full American citizens, giving them controversial adoption and voting rights, among others. Haight has drastically cut taxes for the wealthy while keeping them the same for income levels below $150,000 per annum, and he has overseen enormous cutbacks of "entitlement" programs such as Medicaid, food stamps, veterans' benefits, government-subsidized housing, and welfare.

To many critics, the most problematic aspect of his policies hasn't been their conceptual grounding, but rather their lack of promised effects. To take one of his more radical changes as an example, cutting legal immigration quotas to just a fraction of the number previously allowed (7,000, down from 700,000) has done little to spur the economic growth Haight promised, yet the president has refused to consider other options. Even detractors admire Haight's conviction, his willingness to stand behind his words, but they've also pointed out that conviction needs to align with reality.

The elephant in the room throughout Haight's terms has been the economy, which none of his cuts and changes (some have referred to these as Haight's "Old Deal") have helped. It's a sad fact that the country's economy has been in a slump throughout the entirety of his presidency, and while much of this economic downturn was inherited from his predecessor—it's impossible to imagine someone as governmentally inexperienced as Haight rising to power if the country had been in good shape during the 2028 election—he's been given an abundance of time to fix it, with largely disappointing results. According to supporters, Haight's policies have kept the nation from complete and utter collapse, but his equally vocal detractors claim that they've kept the nation from any sort of recovery, with some even saying he's intentionally damaged the economy in order to stay in power.

Even with the stagnant economy, it's hard to argue that his presidency has been unsuccessful, especially since Haight has somehow wormed his way into a third term and become a beloved figure. No man in the past seventy-five years has done more to reshape the nation, and though recovery seems to be ever on the horizon, voters no longer seem to care whether or not we get there.

Every religious voter I spoke with, including Muslims and Jews, told me that they had a great deal of respect for his faith. But more than that, his policy of isolation and noninterference spoke to them. His extreme government deregulation is frequently bad for average citizens, according to nearly every reputable economist, but it's none- theless ideologically sound and truly American. While it may be an extreme simplification to distill his complex ideology into such a short explanation, to Haight it isn't the people en masse who are important. Rather, it's protecting the rights of each individual that matters, allow- ing them to pretend that the parts of the world that they find unpleas- ant—the poor, the sick, other races, etc.—truly don't exist. It's about telling them that the only people they should be responsible for are themselves.

Toward the end of the day, the president finally has time for an- other quick interview. Knowing that I'll never have a chance to speak with him again, I decided to forgo the questions my editor wanted me to ask, all of which are more politically oriented, and instead take a cue from Haight and go with my gut. While Haight's not one of those politicians who avoids questions, he's answered people about policy countless times before, so I figure anyone who wants to read about the GWoF or the expanded powers of the Department of Homeland Security can find plenty about those topics online.

First I ask him about the end-of-the-world predictions, which first brought him mainstream notoriety. What does he think about having missed the mark, and does he still believe it's on the way?

"I've learned, finally, I guess you could say, that I should keep my mouth shut about those things. I still study the texts, old and new, and believe I know when it's coming, but if it doesn't happen again, I don't want people to get up in arms. People tend to forget that it's a blessing that we're here at all, and we should thank God for letting us live another day. The other thing they forget is that the end, whether our own personal death or the world's, is a glorious thing because it brings us closer to God. It's not something to cause panic, it's something to make us reevaluate our priorities."

I ask whether he's disappointed about not having any children. During their midtwenties, the Haights tried to conceive a child, but a doctor's visit confirmed that, in a particularly unfortunate twist of fate, both parents were infertile.

"Of course I'd love a child, of course I would. But God deals us all different hands, and for some of us that just isn't in the cards. I like to think that I'm a bit of a father to all of America, though. Some people adopt a child or two, but me and Magda went ahead and adopted the whole country."

Finally, I ask him a question that's been on my mind ever since his "third" election last November, when he ran as vice president for Senator Leonard Paradis who, immediately after being sworn in as president, resigned so as to allow his vice president to take over again. Did Haight, a devout Christian, think that this was ethical, and did he have plans for a fourth term using the same constitutional loophole?

"Well, loopholes are as American as apple pie. It isn't like I did anything illegal, and it isn't like I feel that there's a real ethical injunction against being president. It's not like killing a man; only serving two terms isn't one of the Ten Commandments, at least not in my Bible. As far as my plans for the future . . . well, I don't know if you've heard those pundits talking about how I just ignore Congress, because that's anything but the case. Most of my ideas get shot down in Congress, so now in my third term, I still haven't achieved half of what I set out to accomplish in my first. My feeling now is that so long as the people want me in here, I have a duty to try and make this country as close to heaven on earth as I possibly can."

With that, he stood up, offered me a firm handshake, and sent me on my way. He was off to dinner with Senator Fisk from Nebraska and several of his constituents, while I was asked kindly, but firmly, to leave the building. I acquiesced, looking backward for a last glance of the president striding down the hallway as his HS team wiped down the room. His majestic belly rumbled as he chortled a greeting to the senator, and while he was turned away from me, I could see the joy on the faces of the citizens he embraced in his immense hugs. I considered the candidate I voted for in the last election—the slim, almost lizard-like governor of California, how he would've greeted these guests, his awkward handshake and hunched posture—and I wondered whether I had made the wrong choice.

22

How many nights a week do you go out socializing?
__5+
__3-4
__1-2
√_1 or fewer

It took a while, but even Gideon began to feel lonely. The walls of his house had become so comfortable, almost a part of him, that the idea of leaving frightened him—even if he didn't think someone would rob him out there, mug him, kill him, how could he be sure? He wanted to see people, of course he did, felt himself slowly rotting away without them, felt himself questioning his humanity sometimes. Sometimes Gideon realized he was talking to himself and didn't know how long it had gone on. It terrified him, but he just didn't have it in him anymore to try to leave.

Not that there weren't emails and work meetings, projects and demos and endless tasks to accomplish. He kept busy, wrote and edited and reedited every work-related communication that came his way, obsessed over the most minute details. After he'd been awake for thirty-something hours, though, half-drunk on Scotch and Red Bull, he began to suspect that some of those messages he'd received weren't even real. Were people on the other end of those emails? How could he determine which ones were real and which were computer-generated? Was his computer really even connected to the world outside the apartment?

In the light of the next "morning," a relative term he used for whenever he woke up after a dozen or so hours of sleep, these delusions seemed ridiculous. Still, after enough time alone, a lot of ridiculous things felt possible, especially with an employer like Anonymous Propaganda, where fantasy not only became reality, it also turned a tidy profit. The only real interaction he had with the rest of the world was through his computer, with which he paid rent, purchased food, corresponded with his boss, and kept track of the employees working under him. Every day it seemed like the emails were a little bit odder than the day before. While they always made sense, they seemed a bit less than human. Who or what was this Micah Jackson, responding to his concerns about Gravedigger's servers for the next concert? Gideon remembered hiring him, but they'd never met in person. Did he have any concrete evidence that this man really existed, a reason to believe he wasn't a computer program interpreting Gideon's messages and sending back responses that felt almost, but not completely, right?

After four months inside, every communication felt like a conversation with a network of sophisticated bots. Even videochats felt like talking to CGI images of his coworkers. Gideon knew that these were crazy thoughts, that the problem likely lay on his end of things, not theirs, but it was impossible to tell. The Turing Test breaks down once you can no longer remember what normal human behavior even is.

Gideon didn't know whether he'd been dreaming or awake when the phone rang.

"Ahoy hoy?" His voice came out raspy, like he'd taken up smoking.

"Hey, this is Holly."

"What's up?"

"Not too much. I just had a computer question I thought you could answer, and while I was at it figured we could, you know, catch up a little bit. Do that whole sibling thing we talked about before."

"We suck at that whole sibling thing," said Gideon. "Remember? Though I appreciate the effort."

When he'd called Holly two weeks ago, it had been mostly to hear another voice, one that couldn't be faked. He'd also been wondering about relationships, whether what had gone wrong with his had been due to a bad beginning, whether he could've stayed together at least as long as his parents if he'd done something different, but really it was just about the human contact, such as it was. Holly told him things a bot never could have, things he knew were real. That was all it took, a few words of her voice, and he felt more alive. He sat up in his chair and put on a clean-ish T-shirt. It didn't even matter that what she'd said made little sense, as Devon was a hell of a lot more computer savvy than he'd ever been; whatever the excuse, it was obvious that on the other end of the line was a real person.

"What's on your mind?" he asked.

"I've been taking photos of some of my paintings to put online, right? Or use as a portfolio or whatever. I guess I've been thinking that I need something I can send out to people who can't come all the way out to bumfuck Truth or Consequences. Robert's always been saying I need to do some publicity, and ultimately I have to make a sale, right? Or somehow get noticed."

"Yeah, that makes sense."

Gideon moved his mouse, waking his computer screen to windows still open from last night or maybe ten minutes ago, he couldn't really say. Open on his main monitor was an online dating service questionnaire. Just because he'd answered a few questions did not mean, he assured himself, that he would necessarily use the service. He was just interested in seeing what it was like, whether he still had something to offer the opposite sex. He just wanted to talk to a woman for a few minutes, that was all. In order to keep himself from being tempted to leave his self-determined exile, Gideon had input his location as Albuquerque rather than Stamford.

How often do you masturbate?
√_Multiple times a day
__Daily
__Almost daily
__Several times a week
__Several times a month
__Several times a year

"So my camera's supposed to beam them right into the computer," said Holly. "And it says it's done so, and I'm pretty sure I believe it. But for the life of me I can't figure out where it puts them."

"You've got a Mac, right? So it's either in your photos folder, which I assume isn't the case or you wouldn't be calling me, or the camera installed an application folder with some dated sets of your photos and hid them in there."

The dating program was linked with Arcadia's main social networking system. All you had to do was opt in when you signed up, answer a few quick questions (two of which asked whether he would allow the installation of unrelated third-party programs that paid to be part of the package), and the program automatically began pairing you up based on whatever weird algorithm someone had decided was a good way to match up humans. He'd chosen an Arcadia-based platform because he would have access to hundreds of pictures for each person he was matched with. It didn't matter that he never planned on making contact, he just found it interesting to look at snapshots of their lives. He could make stories out of them, imagine a night in their lives from six still frames. Whether she'd gone home with the guy she danced with in the third picture, whether they'd stayed together, what it was that ultimately broke them up and made her sign up for the dating program.

"Hey, you should send me some of those pics when you find them," he said. "You've never let me see your stuff since you hit puberty."

"I . . . yeah, I guess I could. I mean, if you're really interested. I thought you weren't into that sort of thing, that you're more into the whole soulless, corporate marketing genre."

"Hey, just because I like being paid doesn't mean I don't have taste. Being a Reyes is why I don't have taste."

"Ha."

"Really, though, I mean just because I think most art's a load of crap doesn't mean I don't want to see my little sister's stuff. I'm not a monster."

"Okay, I'll send you something. Maybe you can tell me what's wrong with it. Though actually, please don't. What are you working on these days, anyhow?"

How important is music in your life?
__Not at all
√_A bit
__A lot
__What do you mean, music IS my life!

"Uhh . . . you ever listened to any of Gravedigger's stuff? I know Devon's into it." Gideon wanted to say to her that it was his, to lay claim to being an artist like her. He didn't know why, had in fact never felt this way before, but talking to her sometimes made him feel insecure about his job. He knew she didn't mean it, but the jab about his taste actually hurt. It felt like, in exchange for his effort, he should get some form of recognition besides money, something he could show off to his family or, perhaps, women.

"Not really. Pretty much all the rap I've ever heard was just violent, misogynistic bullshit . . . I guess that kinda turned me off from it."

"Some of it is, I'll grant you that. But not everything. And it really speaks to a lot of the country. I mean, when's the last time any rock album went platinum?"

174

"Umm, I don't know. I really don't listen to much new stuff."

"I know, sorry. Didn't mean to badger you. Just trying to say that the kids really dig it, and so do some of the critical tastemakers. Pretty big across the board."

"You make it sound kind of interesting. So what do you have to do with it, then?"

Are you interested in one day having a family?
__Yes
√_No
__Not looking, but if the right person comes along . . .

Everything. I design the beats, I write the rhymes, I approve the album art, I direct the music videos. "Oh, I kind of work . . . I work with his marketing people. You know, corporate stuff, that sort of thing. Kinda have my hands all over the whole project."

"That sounds pretty interesting. I figured you spent your time optimizing billboard placement or search terms."

"Yeah, it's fine. Not too exciting, I mean I still have a boss I have to answer to and all of that. I guess I opted out of the big, prize-winning stuff, but the pay is pretty damn sweet. And unlike the Wall, it doesn't lead to any death threats."

Gideon waited a few seconds, still unsure why his sister had called but hoping she wouldn't hang up. The only thing he could really think to say was to test her, to ask something only the real Holly would know, but he held himself back. He flipped through pictures of a couple girls he'd been matched up with, then looked back at the questions.

How religious are you?
__I attend religious services regularly
__I attend services sometimes

__I don't attend services but I believe in God
__I'm not sure if I believe in God
√_I don't believe in God

This girl had red hair and green eyes, which made her look like a model. Maybe better, because a model would never have freckles like hers. Every picture of her seemed to be at a club or a party, surrounded by friends. And while he felt like he would've killed to be with her, he couldn't imagine a life with all those people constantly around, drinking and dancing. Fun for a night or two, but so exhausting. He glanced past a few more pictures and then never thought of her again.

"So what's up with you, other than preparing this portfolio. How's Robert-o?"

"Robert's fine . . . better than fucking fine, I guess. Hell, he's doing super great. He's doing so goddamn well that sometimes I cannot fucking stand it."

My ideal vacation is
__A trip to an exotic location
__A cabin alone by a beach
√_Alone at home, marathoning a season of *The Room Downstairs* with a case of wine
__Nonstop clubbing with celebrities
__Visiting friends and family

This one had dark skin and long, beautiful hair in an elaborate braid that looked like it was straight from a movie, with little braids tied into bigger ones and the whole arrangement clearly taking an ungodly amount of time to style. All of her pictures were with work friends, sitting at an office. He couldn't put together what her job was from the pictures, but from the lack of anything interesting in her cubicle, he suspected accountant or something like that. Clearly the guys in the office were all over her, but she either ignored them or was oblivious to their attention. Gideon thought she looked fun, nice, kind even, but he didn't want a woman who was all about sixty-hour weeks like his mom. He didn't know what he wanted, but that wasn't it.

"Fuck, I don't know how much longer I can deal with this. Smiling and being the good girlfriend when all my stuff is just shit. Everyone here treats me like I'm his pet, some poor girl he adopted. And I know I shouldn't care, but I do."

"If it isn't working, you know what I say: just leave. Worked for me."

How close are you to your family?
__Very close
__Close
√_Not particularly close, but we stay in touch
__Distant
__I don't have one/no longer have one/don't wish to have one

"Well how do you know when it's right to say good-bye? Was there a tipping point or something? Did you just . . . know?"

"I haven't exactly been on, you know, that end of things. But I would guess that at a certain point, it's the only choice that makes sense."

Gideon tried to give his voice the sound of wisdom and experience, to embody the sage older brother that his sister could turn to for worldly wisdom. He didn't feel the role at all. In fact Holly seemed to have her head screwed on much better than anyone else in the family. Still, this was clearly the real reason why she'd called rather than, say, doing a one-minute Google on the subject of camera connections. So whether he felt it or not, he had to give her something that would feel like actual, usable advice, something she couldn't get by just posting a question in Arcadia somewhere and hearing what a bunch of jackasses thought.

"But until then, I think you should wait it out," he said. "It's one of those things that's hard to define, but you'll know it when you get there. Have you talked to him about this?"

"Yeah, but it's not like he has any real choice in the matter. He just tells me he respects what I feel and all that crap. Sometimes I wish he was more of an asshole so I wouldn't have this problem."

"You'll be okay," said Gideon. He didn't want her to end up alone and unhappy. "Seriously, just give it some thought and whatever happens, you'll come to the right conclusion. Don't panic, let the adrenaline subside and take things slowly. It'll become clear."

"Thanks, that's . . . that sounds like good advice. On a totally unrelated matter: Thinking of heading back to Nuevo México anytime?"

This one was . . . he recognized her immediately, sitting alone in her bedroom, with posters and books he could recognize even in a thumbnail, looking bored as she stared at the computer screen in front of her. She had shorter hair, so the picture had clearly been taken a few years ago, but it was definitely her. He had access to only two other pictures of her: one, mostly out of focus, sitting alone on a bench; the other, eating out with a couple of . . . cops? She was out there, and he could find her, this perfect woman who might be able to make everything right again.

"I hadn't been. But I have to admit, now that you mention it, the idea is extremely tantalizing."

23

Now that she had other responsibilities, her chats (as she usually thought of them, though often there was very little chatting involved) had become soothing again, almost therapeutic, a fugue state between sleep and her public self. The electronic whirr of her computer's fan kept her from completely losing herself to the shows she put on, but they were still the most relaxing part of her days, a time to unwind and enjoy the adoration. The best moment came at the end of every session, when she turned it off while they begged her to stay, whined that they needed just one more glimpse of her skin.

Last night, though, as so often these days, she'd missed that part. Now that she had a work schedule, she usually streamed just before falling asleep, and because of this sometimes Teresa was unaware of when exactly she was still online and when she was dreaming. Or, as had sometimes been the case, when she was doing both, her camera still sending signals to anyone connected but her eyes closed, offering the Internet yet one more tableau of a naked woman's body divorced from her thoughts. Teresa's mind, on the other hand, was both cognizant of the screen flashing one hundred twenty times a second and in some other world entirely. Sometimes it seemed as if there was little difference between the two, that both were fantastical and somehow completely removed from reality, despite the way she could see and feel and remember what happened within them. The Internet was a collective dream with the power to make fantasies come true or turn life into a nightmarish hellscape, with little rhyme or reason behind its whims.

When her phone's buzzing alarm woke her, she found her stream still running, and despite her inactivity, there were still several hundred people watching her. Had they been there all night? And if so, why? She closed the window without saying anything and wondered how much of what she remembered was real. She'd been talking about the idea of moving out, living on her own. Followers offered suggestions of where to visit, then began offering to put her up in palaces of luxury around the nation, the world. She laughed at this, because it was a cute game, just a fun fantasy for both sides to enjoy. They treated her as a sort of princess who needed rescuing from herself, and then she'd dreamed of just that, of being gone from her room and surrounded by luxury in Paris, in Tokyo, on the beaches of São Paulo. The alarm reminded Teresa that none of this was real.

She showered and dressed in uniform as quickly as she could, then headed to the main house for frozen waffles she could eat on the drive to work. It hadn't all been a game, though; she really did want out. Her grandparents offered her their normal morning comments—"Aren't you going to be late?" and "Be good today, nieta," and "Watch out, it looks like another scorcher"—while she raced to her car, trying to ignore the guilt she felt about her desire to leave them. Putting in nine hours like anyone else and getting a paycheck made her feel almost like an adult, but she still feared living alone. So while she spent the evening idly chatting with strangers about moving, giving them new fantasies about her, for the time being nothing changed.

She arrived at the station and met up with her partner, who drove them out to a speed trap on Pennsylvania near Candelaria, where they spent the rest of the day. She wiped a line of sweat off her forehead as the unrelenting sun baked everything beneath it. Teresa took off her cap and fanned herself with it. She wished her partner would turn on the car so the air conditioner would kick in but didn't want to say anything.

Mark sat beside her in the driver's seat, his eye to the radar gun. He was sweating, too, but his right eye was closed and he didn't seem to notice the trail of saltwater snaking down his face, dripping off his chin and onto his black pleated pants.

She was supposed to be observing him, "learning about the job firsthand from an experienced individual," to use the sergeant's phrasing, but nothing was happening. There wasn't anything to observe. As the junior partner, she was mostly there just to add another presence, another body out in the field. Until officers had been on the force for at least six months, they were supposed to shadow their partners, so she sat there, supposedly alert for anything and learning from her partner's vigilance, but her mind drifted from the task as she struggled to stay awake.

She hadn't expected the day-to-day life of a police officer to be this boring, and spent half her time on the job browsing on her phone, which Mark didn't seem to mind, or for that matter even notice. A couple of days earlier she'd felt so comfortable outside her room, sitting with Mark at another speed trap, that she'd even begun thinking about dating, and since then had spent a lot of time idly browsing Arcadia's dating services to see what might await her if she decided to take that plunge. She didn't use her real name when streaming, so it seemed safe enough, and some of the men on it were kind of attractive. It was more the idea of being with someone that appealed to her than meeting them, which still seemed pretty damn intimidating. Each picture of a man was a different world, a different reality that maybe one day she'd be brave enough to explore.

"He's only going six over," said Mark, sighing. "Not worth the effort."

"Yeah," she agreed, not really knowing which car he was referring to.

Her favorite thing about the job was the almost complete anonymity it offered. If you were a homicide detective, you might have some leeway in your dress or your manner, but patrol officers, while in uniform, were simply part of the police apparatus. No one saw a human being in the black and blue; they saw the APD squad car and the baton, the badge, and the gun. A walking reminder of law and order, a physical embodiment of uncompromising rules. It satisfied her desire to see other people while remaining unseen. Even to her fellow officers, she was Officer Llantos—Teresa was still asleep back home, tangled in green cotton sheets.

Except in the richest neighborhoods, cops were of course universally loathed. But that meant no one would look in her eyes, stare at her face. Because any cause for search was reasonable, she could count on being left alone. Even people they helped, the victims and those in need of assistance, frequently shivered in fear when they appeared. The only people happy to see a police officer were those with absolutely nothing to hide, no inner guilt whatsoever: practically no one. Those without guilt, they'd been advised in the Academy, were the most dangerous of all and most likely sociopaths.

Mark had made it clear on their first day together that he had no interest in learning more about her. "This is a professional relationship, and we will keep things professional." It was part of his spiel, something he said to every junior officer assigned to him for fifteen years, and in the office this had gotten him a reputation as a complete hard-ass, to put it lightly. Rebecca called him "Officer Buttstick," but his attitude suited Teresa just fine.

"Hey, I mention we're going to need you for a night bust this weekend?" asked Mark, not taking his eye off the radar gun. A small salt lake had formed on the dashboard.

"No. What's the deal? Meth lab bust? Smuggling illegals into the country? This is my first time doing anything like this."

"Nah, nothing so big. Don't need to worry about that sort of thing until you've got a few more months under your belt and a new assignment. No, a friend of mine working on prostitution asked if I could show you the ropes in one of those cases. Thinks you might be good there. Always useful to have more women working in vice."

"Okay. So what do I have to do?"

"Show up is all. I'll be there, too, you just follow my lead like normal. Here, I'll show you the tip-off." Mark pulled his phone out of his pocket and slid his finger across its face. He navigated through a few screens and handed it to her.

albuquerque > gigs > event gigs
Dancers (female) needed for party (Albuquerque)
Date: 2037-05-16, 9:39PM MDT
Reply to: coyote@//ΛVΛ\ʃ|3ə.com

We are looking for one or more female "dancers"—you know the type (but it's not one we're willing to spell out here on craigslist because that would of course result in this post being deleted and we wouldn't want that, now would we)—for an upcoming party. Pay is negotiable, and we can provide transpiration to/from the event. The gig will only last from 10pm til 2am, though we don't expect you to be working for the whole time. Applicants must be attractive, reliable, and smart enough to realize what it is we're actually requesting in this ad. Please send photo and contact info to coyote@//ΛVΛ\ʃ|3ə.com.

• Location: Albuquerque
• it's NOT ok to contact this poster with services or other commercial interests
• Compensation: negotiable

"Usually we don't respond to these sorts of things. Craigslist is filled with 'escorts.' But I guess this one stuck out to them, and I can see why. I'm guessing they think it's entertainment for something sketchy, maybe a low-level drug deal or underground gambling or something. Anyhow, it's out of the ordinary, so I guess they're following it up."

"Late night . . ."

"Don't complain, you'll get time and a half."

"Nice, my first overtime. And you said you'll be there, too, right?"

"Yeah, but don't look so down, that's just how they run things. Show's you're doing well. Only been on the clock for a couple of weeks and already invited for some real police work. Hey, there's one. Looks like we may meet that quota after all."

24

"I get what you're saying, Eric . . . but doesn't Christianity already have a spokesperson?"

"No, of course not. Gideon, my friend, this is a revolutionary way of thinking about religion. That's why they hired us. They told me on the phone, 'We know there are a lot of agencies out there, but we want the firm who figured out how to finance the GWoF and got corporate adoption past the Supreme Court.' Or something like that, I can't be bothered to remember what they actually said, got a busy schedule. Point is, this is some big-league shit."

"No, I mean like Jesus Christ."

"What are you so mad about?"

"Huh? You know, the guy whose name is the same as the religion."

"Oh yeah. Him. Well he's certainly great and all, a real symbol for the people, definitely. Thing is, and you know this as well as I do, Jesus isn't around to do press appearances during the Super Bowl. He isn't out there campaigning for Haight's reelection or endorsing crackers in a television commercial . . . which is a damn shame because we had some great commercials worked up before the guys in legal put a stop to it."

"Sorry to interrupt Eric, but just so I understand . . . you want a person to represent Christianity. But not Christ?"

"Precisely. No dead people need apply. I know you are the man for the job, know you're hep with it, as the kids say, at least according to our research group."

"I don't even . . . what about the pope?"

"Did I say Catholic? No, boyo, I said Christian, and while I don't want to count the Catholic market out, hell, they're huge where you're from and always big in Massachusetts, a lot of their stuff turns the rest of the Christians off. You know, the mysticism and the smelly old relics and the guys wearing pajamas molesting young boys. You wouldn't believe it, but according to some of the testing we've done, the public would rather they were feeling up little girls. Public gets that. Public even respects that in some sense, gets some pity on their side. But boys, oh no, molesting children is one thing but being a gay pedophile is worse than sacrificing virgins to Satan. Six percent worse, if I remember correctly. And don't even ask about the Mormons or Scientologists, who apparently don't have too much to do with any of it even though they're still into crosses? Maybe you can explain that one to me."

"Umm . . . yeah, I don't know, they're kind of their own thing, but I'm not really that knowledgeable about—"

"Okay, fine. Right, so we're talking about staying away from the Catholics, I mean unless they pay up like the rest, which, God willing, won't be a problem. But our clients at this point, whom I'm legally forbidden to name to you, are the Baptists and the Methodists and the Non-Denominationalists, hell, even the Episcopalians and—God help us—the Church of Christ-ers. And now that you mention the Mormons, I think I should probably find out if they want in on this, too. Everly? You hear that? Get me someone over with the Mormons, I want to find out if they're looking for a new PR campaign. Sorry, Gideon, gotta get that down before I forget. Anyhow, there are a bunch of others in there, too. I'm looking at a list, and it says the Congregationalists are paying a pretty penny, and I'll be honest, I don't know if anyone over here in the office knows who they are. Maybe you can help me out with them, too, while you're at it. Oh, and the best part is, because it's churches hiring us out, we're getting a hefty tax write-off for the whole affair, which Schwartzwalder will just fucking love."

"I don't really know who they are, either. What exactly is the 'whole affair'?"

"You're a little tired, I can hear that even over the phone, and I understand that, son, I really do, but you've gotta stay quick, gotta keep on your toes. It's all about making a spokesperson who can show up on talk shows and appear in guest spots, maybe voice a game character or pop up in the next Disney movie as a talking walrus."

"I'm, uhh, happy to help out with the project, but I don't really want to take my eyes off Gravedigger."

"I'm not saying you've done bad work there, in fact quite the opposite. I think it was really your effort that made the project a success, but it's time you transitioned into something else. When I hired you, it was because your work on the GWoF made me think you were an idea guy, and I don't want my idea guys stuck micromanaging. I can tell you're getting a little bored with that stuff anyhow. Had your success, got it running smoothly, and now you're coasting. An idea man like you can't just coast, you have to keep moving. You're like a shark, you stop swimming and you suffocate."

"I really feel like I'm—"

"I understand, I understand. You won't be taken off your old beat immediately. You can keep an eye on Gravedigger, make sure the next release is a hit, goes a couple platinum or diamond or whatever, but I want you to find a replacement. Let someone else manage the virtual star. It keeps bringing in dividends, for sure, but it's not going to have the growth it did early on—there's a finite number of fans, I always say. Finite number of people in the world, you have to remember, and how many of those even listen to music? When you hit the limit, you have to recognize it. Nothing wrong with your work, but that project's just not gonna grow much more. That's the problem I always have with bankers, they think they're working in a system with infinite returns when we've got some real-world limitations. I'm only concerned about the real world in front of me, the concrete things I can touch. That's why Jesus just won't cut it."

"That makes sense, I guess."

"Damn right it does. Reason why I want you to head up the Prophet Project is because you've got experience building up personalities. The Wall was clever, but Gravedigger was more than that, it was also a lot of hard work. You backed that idea with a lot of elbow grease, and I respect that. Some damn good micromanaging, and that's what I like to see, not just a bunch of ideas being slung around without any follow-through. This time we need to figure out a real person, though, can't leave this one on computer screens. Need to build someone who can be touched, who's got a firm handshake. Hai—our clients are adamant about that fact."

"Couldn't we just pick anyone, then? I mean, you kind of . . . what about the president, for instance?"

"Knew you were a smart man. I always told 'em that, whatever they said about your working methods, about you needing to come into the office once in a while. I asked our client that myself. I said, 'That's a great idea to create a new icon for Christianity. The president's a religious man, a patriotic man, shouldn't he be the face of the religion?' Thought I'd use some synergy there, get the ball rolling much quicker. But I was told they think he's too old for the job. They want someone younger, someone who can stick around for a while. Like what Tom Cruise did for Scientology, just without all the crazy. Gotta have someone young, someone without all that end-of-the-world baggage. That works for politics, I always tell our candidates that you want some sort of a threat there, want to tell them that if they don't elect you, the Iranians will start sending in the nukes. People think threat, they think power, and they vote for that power. But we need someone softer, need a Christian who they'd go and have a drink with, maybe a casual fuck with. He wouldn't need to call 'em back, but they'd have a good memory of the night and laugh about it later. Sure, he'll quote the Bible every now and then, kiss babies, and do some glad-handing, but I want someone who'd look good on a red carpet. Got some tech boys working on boots that could help the guy walk on water if they're still not convinced. Important thing is that he's getting 'em into churches."

"Isn't there a small matter of, like, scripture? I mean, the Bible's all about God and Jesus and that sort of thing. There's nothing in there about this . . . prophet?"

"Son, religion is just a different type of story, a narrative people happen to base their silly little lives on. People kill for it and die for it and do all sorts of crazy shit for it, but that doesn't make it any less a story. And what do you do when you need to change their lives? Why, you just change the story is all. Don't worry about that step, our clients already have the fundies in their pockets and have assured me it'll be no problem. You find us the candidate and we'll rewrite the narrative to fit them."

"So I'm in charge of this project?"

"Not yet, no. Officially there is no Prophet Project. Just need you to start the research, get people looking in the right direction. Need to figure out if this guy is the next Messiah or if he's still talking about Jesus. Is he black or white, or maybe Hispanic? They're a big vote, and seem like religious folks to me. But then again, if he's not white, then you'll probably get a lot of hicks calling to have him lynched. Could end ugly, could result in a shooting, gotta consider that angle. I can get my risk analysis boys onto that right now if you need it. What clothes is he going to endorse? Probably going to need some really clever ways of staying away from the whole abortion question, because I don't think our backers are going to know what to do with that."

"Is there money in the budget for a research trip?"

"Hell, with the deep pockets on these clients, there's money in the budget for a research trip to the moon. Could get a close-up look at the newest ads, ha-ha. Anyhow, fly wherever you want, do your research from the Bahamas for all I care. I gotta run, nephew's got a play or something in a few minutes and I keep getting texts about it from the wife. I'll have my secretary email you some of the preliminaries to get you up to speed on the whole shebang. The important thing is that wherever you go, you get started on this ASAP."

25

Holly let the stroke linger, enjoying the way her smooth sable marten brush caressed the coarse canvas to create a line that was close to, though not exactly the same as, how she'd envisioned it in her head. She took a step back, looked at the canvas from farther away, and wondered what to do next.

She couldn't continue. A drop of thick oil paint fell from her brush onto the floor while she stood there thinking and rethinking what she'd spent the week creating. What if the next stroke would ruin the entire piece, would create another disappointment? Each one held that possibility. Every movement she made was an earthquake that could bring the entire structure tumbling down into disaster. She couldn't even remember when she'd last been happy with something she created, and it had been a struggle even to start a piece lately, the pile of recent failures growing exponentially at the back of her studio.

Early last week, Holly had thought she'd finished working on the painting that she'd been struggling with for the previous month, and it still rested on her easel on the far side of the room. Its inspiration had been Robert, though in a circular enough manner that she didn't feel guilty about the way it "commented on" (i.e. attacked) his work. After she'd first moved in, enjoying the bliss of life away from her family and all the nonartistic endeavors that used to suck up her time, she'd coaxed Robert into letting her see his earlier work. His older sketches weren't that good, but they always had a strong point of view. He tended to draw exaggerated faces, reducing people and items to objects of ridicule through cruel physiognomy. His attitude toward the subject was almost always nasty. A few exaggerated lines and he transformed anyone into a monster.

After seeing Robert's work, Holly'd stopped enjoying drawing faces. Every line she drew, every speck on the canvas meant implicit judgment on the subject. And it was rarely complex judgment, either: the basic tools were hagiography or snark. This last work had been an attempt to move past her hang-ups.

So she'd taken a picture of some random man off Arcadia, someone she'd never met or heard of. Then she'd painted her version of his portrait as accurately as she could. She spent hours, days on his portrait, making sure the skin pigmentation was just right and that the shadows made his cheekbones look as pronounced as they were in the photo. After all that painstaking time on his face, Holly carefully crafted a background behind him that she thought fit his features. It was a sort of lounge setting, and she thought the room's dark lighting made the cracks on his lips look like he had experience and wisdom.

Afterward, she'd painted over his body and face with white, negating any possible judgment lingering in her portraiture. Finishing the still-unnamed painting had made her feel cheerful, like she still *was* a painter.

But then she'd realized her mistake: she could still see the shape of that face, could therefore judge the man it was supposed to represent. The silhouette was still there. Holly spent hours making it more ghostly, blending his afterimage into the background, but nothing could get rid of the implicit criticism, the damned simplification, even though she couldn't make him out any longer. She could paint over the entire work at which point it was questionable whether it would still be a painting of a man or just a blank canvas. Robert wouldn't've hesitated—he could've sold the hell out of a seemingly blank canvas with that much backstory. But she was not Robert.

So she'd decided to try a more direct approach to portraits, and even five minutes earlier it had seemed like this new one might break the streak, might be something truly worthwhile, but now she couldn't even take its presence in the room. She took the unfinished, perhaps unfinishable painting off the easel and faced it toward the opposite wall. The man it was supposed to capture was a friend of Robert's who'd commissioned this work, and she didn't know what to do about that.

"He saw some of your stuff online and really liked it," Robert had told her, though she knew this was, if not a lie, then certainly a half truth. The only way his friend might have discovered her work would have been if Robert had led him there, had put him up to it. It was a sweet gesture, kind of, but just made her feel worse about herself. And it wasn't like she could say no. She had to act like this was something she wanted to do or else she'd be the jerk here.

Holly lay down on her crusty, paint-spattered couch and rested her laptop on her chest, looking for any distraction. She didn't know what she'd say when Robert asked how things were going. She knew she'd lie, but that didn't help her feel any better. She hadn't been able to talk to him about work in a long time now, because every time she did, she explained to him that she didn't know what was wrong, and he just said that the next piece would turn out better. Did he really think those words were true, or that they meant something? Here he was winning awards and his only words of consolation were essentially, better luck next time.

Holly knew she was losing perspective, but she kept forcing herself into the studio, kept a routine. What other option did she have at this point? While working on this portrait over the past few days, she'd started looking back at her older paintings, trying to figure out why she'd liked them so much, but when she dredged them up she found each one more disappointing than the last. Everything looked amateurish now, and the ones that she'd thought weren't half bad, really, the ones that she could stand for someone else to see if it was absolutely necessary, now seemed dreadful. She browsed back to her website, with its well-designed selection of her best work, and took it offline. It wasn't like anyone was interested anyhow, even though her prices, as she'd stated, were negotiable. It wasn't about the money, it was about the fact of having a sale, of someone being interested enough in her work to purchase it. Robert and his friends didn't count.

Holly began drafting an apology email to Robert's friend, hoping to explain that she was just too busy to complete the project but would be happy to refund his three hundred dollars. She didn't hit send, though, because then Robert would ask about her new big project, what was taking up all of her time. He'd feign excitement—there was no way he could be excited, right?—and she didn't have it in her to come up with something. When she was outside the studio all she could think about was work, mostly how disappointing it was but also ideas for what to do next. Here, though, all she could think about was him, their relationship, the way all they seemed to be able to do together was watch television on the couch in silence. Whenever she spoke during one of his programs or movies, he either hit pause, making her feel like an interruption, or looked at her with visible unhappiness. But then, she was the one who shut things down immediately if he wanted to talk about work—whose fault was it, really, that the one topic he was willing to share about, to treat seriously, was also the one topic that she avoided like the plague.

So she stood up and walked back to the painting. Holly decided she would finish it now, this very afternoon. It didn't matter how good it was, it would be done and she could move on to something else, something possibly less disappointing. She placed the painting back on her easel when a knock echoed through the room.

"Robert, this better be important," said Holly. "I just remembered the secret to life, the universe, and everything and I want to get it down before I forget it." She hoped that this time he'd brought more than lemonade, that it was a bottle of wine.

Another knock.

"Goddammit, you made me lose it. Guess no one will ever get to know. So much for eternal happiness."

Holly walked across the studio to the door, happy for an interruption but wishing it would be literally anyone else. It was so much easier to be in a relationship when the other half wasn't around.

She unlocked both the deadbolt and the handle lock, wondering why she'd ever had them put in. For someone to steal from you, you had to have something valuable. She pulled the door open, and standing in front of her was a tall, thin man with graying hair who she hadn't seen in five years.

"Dad?"

26

Autumn had driven Devon to Steve's house down in the valley. Devon was supposed to be staying over with his friend that night, though he had no idea what exactly that would entail. They'd been playing *Dungeons & Dragons* since fourth grade, when Steve talked their teacher into believing that its combination of math and storytelling would be a great tool for learning of some sort, and that was supposed to be the main event for the evening. Devon had spent a few hours planning out a campaign on his tablet's simulated graph paper, and skimmed through the core rulebooks to refresh his memory on the game's basics, but the constant hints of a surprise Steve had been dropping all week kept him from getting too excited about things. Devon didn't like surprises, and as far as he was concerned, the unexpected was nearly always bad.

They pulled into the overgrown dirt path that functioned as Steve's driveway, and his mom parked the car while Steve seemed to spring out from his house. Steve's eyes passed over their BMW approvingly, and Devon tried to ignore this. It wasn't like he'd chosen to be wealthy, that's just how it was.

"Hey, Mrs. Reyes," said Steve, speaking to Autumn's rolled-down window. "Thanks for letting Devon stay over."

"I'll see you tomorrow. Have fun," said Autumn. Devon picked up his enormous army camo backpack and hurried out of the car. The

BMW's spotless white paint and chrome hubcaps felt so out of place here; he pretended he had nothing to do with it.

While she sped off behind them, Steve's body language changed immediately. "Okay, I've got the keg in the back on a dolly, but you've gotta help me with it."

They walked around the side of Steve's house, past his beater car and tall stalks of uncut yellow grass to where a squat gray keg sat with two bags of ice and a tap on top. Devon had never been certain whether Steve and his mother owned the place or rented it or were squatting, but he also barely knew his friend's family, and Steve had always been cagey about his background. He doubted that even the Baby Eaters at AHS knew that Steve's parents were illegal immigrants. And when Devon caught Steve, despite claims of US citizenship, paying a school secretary for certain changes to be made to his permanent record, both of them pretended it never happened.

"I knew you were getting beer, but . . . a keg?"

"A pony keg, but I'm not really expecting anyone outside of the usual suspects. Why, you think we need more?"

"No, I mean that seems like a lot. Maybe too much. Not that I'm an expert in these things . . ."

"Ahh, well I've also got some vodka and tequila, just in case." Steve walked through the house's back door and returned a moment later with a cloth grocery bag filled with bottles and cups.

"And some Coke and Mountain Dew for anyone too much of a wimp to drink this shit straight," he continued.

"Vodka and Mountain Dew?"

"Is not a drink for pussies. Or anyone else, really. I suggest you stick with the beer."

"What is it?" Devon said. "I thought we were just playing some *DnD* down in the tunnels, not like hosting a party or something."

"The finest, cheapest beer that money can buy. Devon, my friend, as much as I would love to host a party with you, we would need a whole shit-ton more booze than this. This is just to keep us loose all evening and into the morning. And while I don't expect anyone else to come along, we did invite a few other people, and we'd want them to be comfortable."

"Whatever. Just know that I'm not letting you drive me drunk."

"I hope you still remember how to ride a bike, because that's how we'll more than likely be getting back. Help me get all of this in the trunk and then we'll fit in the bikes."

Steve unlocked his car door, got in, then reached across the seat to unlock the passenger's side. By the time Devon had his seat belt on, they'd backed out of the driveway and "Flibbertigiblet" was playing on the speakers. Gravedigger sang, "Hey there Mr. President, I'm not your little sheep/find us schoolmasters that can teach/children learn your lesson's lie/I play pretend but fuckin' die." Bass beats shook the car and rattled its doors.

After parking at a residential street near but not quite at the north UNM golf course, they got out and lifted the dolly and pony keg down to the ground. Steve pulled a flashlight and several larger battery-powered lanterns out of the back of the car, and they wheeled the keg across the street and down to the golf course, bumping it over dirt and dry grass.

"So how far is this place?"

"Like, I don't know, fifteen minutes if we don't make a wrong turn."

The tunnels were covered in graffiti. Most of it was crude, just pictures of naked women and stick figures of hated public figures being disemboweled, but occasionally they passed magisterial paintings every bit the equal of the panoramas that businesses spent thousands on downtown or on the GWoF—though none of the figures beneath the earth held Jell-O pudding cups or implied that a conquistador making peace with Pueblo Indians had something to do with Panasonic. Steve told some of his favorite stories about tunnels, urban legends he swore were true about mole people and the kid who got lost down in the university's steam tunnels after a *DnD* session that sparked a witch hunt, with parents burning their kids' fantasy books on the assumption that satanic forces had something to do with rolling twenty-sided dice. None of it was new to Devon, but Steve's urban legends sounded more exciting and possible among the subterranean shadows and echoing footsteps. As they neared Hell, the drawings began to taper off. The last, an image of the Virgin of Guadalupe staring down a monumental wall and looking ready to break into tears, stood a good hundred feet from the threshold.

From here, it became darker and darker until it was no longer dark but a sheer, tenebrous black. They entered a circular room with a cathedral ceiling that rose to a point, supported there by a straight, slender stone pole. There were four entrances, each huge, none of the others visible from theirs. The room had no windows or cracks, and the walls were blackened: light seemed to dissipate before it had a chance to reflect. It was warm in the center of the room. Pete was waiting there and had already set up folding chairs around a large stone table at the far side.

"See, it's as awesome as I said. Hey, Pete, come help us carry this shit and you can have the first drink." They dragged the keg over, tapped it, then sat down at the table to get started.

Jeff arrived, then Disney and finally Billiam. While waiting for them, Devon poured himself a beer into one of the red plastic cups Steve brought along and pulled out his notes. It was the first real alcohol he'd ever drunk, and he didn't know what to expect. He'd always shied away from the stuff, not because of any sort of puritanical belief system but because he feared losing control. *DnD* had always appealed to him because characters were defined by set numeric values, were in a sense no more than a series of statistics assigned to a nominative value, achieving goals by exceeding the values of dragons and ghouls. This was a world he understood, a world he could control because he understood the math, the symbols. Alcohol seemed to diminish those values, to make people quit min-maxing and instead make stupid decisions. How could you win at life if you weren't optimizing your values?

But this was a special occasion, and while Devon hated the taste of whatever godawful shit Steve had bought—had to force the sickly, bitter liquid down his throat, since his first instinct had been to gag—after just a few minutes he understood why people liked it so much. It didn't make him feel less in control, it was as if the world itself were bending a bit to his will and pleasure.

"Hey, how about we play a drinking game?" asked Disney, who five minutes after arrival was already on his second beer.

"Later. Finish making your character so we can play." Devon feared that he wouldn't be able to keep up and would embarrass himself. If he wanted to play drinking games until he threw up, he would've gone to that party the night before, hosted by a student whose parents made an "agreement" with the cops not to investigate the overwhelming volume of the music and lines of sloppily parked cars. Instead, he'd joined in a raid and was happily surprised that everyone else from the clan had made the same decision.

"No, wait, that's a good idea," said Steve. "How about this: every time someone rolls a one on a d20, they have to do a shot or chug a beer."

Half an hour later, they finished their characters. Devon's head was swimming, but he was able to keep it together enough to start. In-game, the party awoke to the cackles of a mad wizard who'd captured them. He explained his grand experiment of stripping their souls from their bodies in order to fuel a dark immortality ritual. But the ritual had to be done during a full moon, and the wizard left in order to prepare. The player characters (PCs) needed to escape his dungeon or suffer the dire consequences.

Everyone seemed to be having a blast, and the story began taking on a life of its own. Steve played as a double-dealing gnome with a vengeful hatred of all elves, and Billiam's PC was an elf with a tendency to stumble into him "accidentally," saying that he "hadn't seen him there," that the only gnomish he'd ever learned was for communicating with his gardener. Jeff nearly died once, when a gargoyle in one of the wizard's towers turned out to be alive and not a statue at all, but he made his saves and the rest of the PCs helped him recover and transform the winged monster back into a pile of gravel. By then everyone was getting pretty drunk, but Devon slowed down with the beer and felt content rather than queasy.

Over the drunken babble of his friends, throwing around plastic cups and spinning dice and calling each other so fucking stupid for spilling their drinks, Devon heard the sound of a quick bass beat echoing around the room. Everyone else cheered for some reason while Devon felt his heartbeat increase in panic.

"What's going on?"

"I thought I'd mentioned a surprise," said Steve. The silhouette of a slim female figure became visible through the tunnel entrance they'd used earlier.

"That's the, she's the surprise?"

"I think her name is Tiffany or Aurora or some bullshit like that, but I don't think she'd mind if you called her 'Surprise,' so long as you don't skimp on the tips. I did tell you to bring cash, right?"

"I thought that was to pitch in for booze."

"Don't tell me you're one of those guys who doesn't tip. That's some low-class shit, especially from you, Mr. Moneybags-Reyes."

She was dressed as a secretary, but with a low-cut blouse and a skirt so short that you could see her panties if she so much as moved a leg. She pranced all the way across the room's scarred cement floor in glistening six-inch black heels, stopping only to place a set of speakers attached to her phone near the pole in the center. She wrapped her legs around it and twirled. Devon couldn't believe this was happening right in front of him. Not in a movie. Not on a computer screen. After a moment of hesitation, he followed his friends, who headed toward her, hooting and laughing away their anxiety.

"Hey, I know you didn't have this in mind," said Billiam, speaking to Devon without turning his head from the show in front of him. "But we just thought you needed to have some fun for once. We're down here alone, no one's gonna know or judge. Then, after we're all finished, she goes home happy with a big wad of money, and we go back to the game. It's all just good times, no harm done."

"Just think of this as the bonus level," said Disney, slipping a bill onto her boom box. "Giving me an erection: five hundred Arcadia points unlocked."

Her dance lasted five minutes. All Devon saw was movement, spinning that left him hypnotized. Whenever he glanced away from the curves of her legs and her barely concealed chest to her face, he saw a blank, unmoving smile that scared him for some reason, so he stared back at her limbs and absorbed their movement. Steve walked up to her with a green-capped syringe, placed it at her feet, then handed Devon a plastic shot glass full of tequila. He put a matching syringe into Devon's other hand, and Devon shook his head no, he was feeling fine already. Steve shrugged, and Devon found himself sitting back on his folding chair, his friends cheering while she started unbuttoning his pants.

Someone refilled his shot glass, but he didn't really register it among the music and the shouting and the feeling of her dancing, rubbing, touching him. Even when the bright lights blinded him and everyone else seemed to disappear like rats scurrying into a sewer, he didn't think to get up off the chair and run away with them, or even to put his pants back on. He couldn't remember how to stand up, so he sat there bewildered with his cock standing upright like a flagpole.

Devon awoke in the back of a police car with vomit on his face and in his hair. It felt like the sun's rays were burning a hole through his head, but before he had time to orient himself and figure out what time it was, he'd passed out again to the sound of voices yelling that the little shit had better lick the seats clean if he ever hoped to get his wrists unlocked.

27

After graduating from the Academy, Teresa saw Kate and Rebecca much less frequently, a simple result of them all being rookies and the management doing its best to integrate new recruits with the rest of the department. This wasn't just a matter of training. Older officers could be lazy and terrible, but they could also be professional, honorable, and thorough. Any sergeant worth his bars knew who the screwups were and tried corralling recruits toward everyone else in the hope that they would be a good influence. There was also a question of morale, given that new officers were most likely to be unhappy with the realities of day-to-day police work, and when left to themselves, bitched and moaned and sometimes quit, or in a few cases even started strikes.

Unlike the people Teresa met on the street, other police officers could and did look her in the eye, so Teresa never found herself comfortable among them. Her face started itching when they tried to joke around with her at the office or asked if she wanted to meet up after hours. She was still comfortable around her friends, but the moment anyone else spoke to her, she made an excuse and left.

"She's just shy," she heard Rebecca explain once when she thought Teresa was out of earshot. "Give her some time. She's about the nicest chica I've ever met, just easily spooked."

"Then should she be a cop?" one of the male officers asked.

"It's not like that. She's a great cop, I'm sure. Way better than you, at least."

Teresa wished her friend didn't have to stand up for her. It embarrassed her and made her feel like a child, but she couldn't do anything about her own behavior. She pretended not to hear any of this, that she didn't have a reputation. The job was perfect when she was out in the field, an anonymous pillar of law and order, but the office was all about bullshit politics and personal connections.

Conversely, Kate seemed always to be off for sick days and showed up late constantly, but she still managed to be the most popular recruit, especially when it got out that she was single. It didn't even seem to bother their colleagues when she brought around her daughter, and men courted her favor by bringing little Nicole candy or pastries, which Kate ate herself or distributed to her friends, wondering what they were thinking buying a two-year-old those kinds of foods. Sometimes it seemed like the less she was in the office, the more she was doted upon when around.

"The force is keeping me in the projects," said Kate, bitching in the women's locker room. "The money's great, but daycare means I don't get to keep a cent of it."

Mark explained how common moonlighting was to Teresa one day during a routine house call, when they found it had been called in by an officer barely older than Teresa, working as a nanny (or "au pair" as he called it) during his off time. "It's no biggie," Mark said. "A lot of people do two or three jobs their first few years on the force."

"Can't they just work overtime?"

"You're shitting me, right? There's so many officers. It's hard enough to get full time."

Teresa began listening for these second jobs when she was stuck in the office. Lorenzo said he used to drive a school bus during the day and then worked the night shift, resting between the time that he dropped kids off and picked them up. This lasted for three years until he was fired for falling asleep at the wheel and almost slamming the bus's thirty thousand pounds into a reinforced concrete wall near Rio Rancho. "Had I not been a cop, I probably would've been behind bars," he said, laughing.

When he was young, Connor worked at a GameStop until he blew up at a client for trying to return a scratched disc the day after he'd purchased it. "I could tell that he bought the game, went home, loaded it into Arcadia and played for thirty hours straight, then drove back and tried to return it. If he hadn't scratched it up, store policy said we had to accept it. But it looked like crap, so I said no, and he yelled at me, and I yelled at him, and I dunno, I was tired and couldn't help myself, pulling a gun on the little fucker and hitting him a couple times across the face. Goddamn, those places are hellholes, no wonder physical media went the way of house phones."

Everyone just assumed that Kate's haggard appearance meant she was working a second job, not to mention raising her daughter without any help. Maybe she should've asked Kate about it, or maybe Rebecca, but despite their friendship, Teresa thought it would be rude and intrusive to ask what exactly it was. If Kate wanted to bitch about her other work, that was her choice, but if not, she was going to respect that, too. Rebecca once said that she worried about her friend burning both ends of the candle, and she gave Teresa a knowing look as if it was common knowledge what she was talking about, but Teresa just let it pass. So when they shined their floodlights down those pitch-black concrete corridors and found Kate there, dancing without any clothes on for a bunch of fucking kids, no one was more surprised than Teresa.

Teresa, Mark, and two vice officers crept down the tunnels as silently as possible, leaving their flashlights off in hope of not alerting their prey to their presence until it was too late to get away. The moment the lights went on, though, almost everyone scurried off like cockroaches and ran through back exits that seemed to lead in every direction. The vice men made halfhearted attempts to follow them, but returned almost immediately, shrugging.

The only one they grabbed was nearly passed out when they booked him and read him his rights, a moon-faced boy with short black hair. He seemed barely to register their presence, which the vice men said wasn't a surprise considering the needle they'd found on the ground beneath him. They seemed thrilled about this discovery, said it would make their jobs a lot easier.

Teresa was barely listening, though. Soaked in sweat from the room's strange heat, Kate stoically ignored what was happening and put her clothes on as if no one were there with her. No one even hand-cuffed her. Mark just walked behind her as they exited the tunnels the way they came. The vice officers in front of them talked and laughed, but the rest of the entourage was silent. Beneath the light of a bright crescent moon—with its massive Xfinity logo glaring down on them— Kate stepped into the back of their squad car without being asked, never turning away from their gazes or acknowledging that Teresa was even there. Teresa wanted to say something to her friend, to reassure her that this was all somehow a mistake, but that felt like such an obvious lie that she opted instead to say nothing.

Teresa waited with Mark on the side of the golf course, not ready yet to get into that car and do their job. She turned to Mark and asked him, "Did you know about this?"

Mark looked down at the ground. "No, of course not . . . well, yes, they told me earlier today."

Teresa grabbed his uniform and pulled him toward her so that he had to look her in the face. This was, in fact, the first time she'd ever looked anyone besides her grandparents in the eyes since her accident, and the shock of seeing herself reflected in them was almost too much. "Then why the fuck didn't you tell me?"

"Because I wasn't supposed to. She's why they put you on this case, don't you see that? We can't just have police officers turning tricks on the side. I guess the brass wanted you along to send some sort of message."

"The message that they're motherfuckers?"

"The message that this is a serious job and not something you can play around with. Kate's an embarrassment to the force. As soon as they found out about her, they wanted to put a stop to it, but they needed proof. Well, they got it, and they want you to know that you need to play by the rules, too, and be a full-time cop."

"I'm not a whore."

"And I'm not saying you are. Listen, I don't know two shits about why they sent you. It could be that they want to fuck with you. It could be Lieutenant Davis hates you because you're not white—you wouldn't be the first. I don't know, and you don't know, so don't try to lay the blame on me. I'm just doing my job, wasting my evening busting up these kids' little get-together the same as you."

Teresa turned around and went straight into the car's passenger seat. She sat in silence as they drove back toward the police department. She wouldn't let him, or anyone, see her cry.

"Hey, I know it feels like shit to arrest your friend like this, but it could be worse. They haze everyone, make sure that you know where you stand in the department, make it so you don't forget that you're just another peon for them to toss around. For me, a couple weeks in, they had me send my own mother back across the Wall."

"You're an immigrant?"

"No, my mom was. I was born here. I have people call me Mark, 'cause it makes my life easier, but my name's Marcos."

"I thought a mother could stay if she had a child born here?"

"No, she can stay as long as she's the guardian. I was over eighteen. I guess they knew about it the whole time, let me get through the

Academy's background search without a hitch, all the while planning that bullshit to keep me in line."

"Why didn't you quit? Fuck those shits."

"Same as everyone else. I need the money."

"And your mom?"

"It was tough on us, I won't deny it, but she understands. She needs the money, too."

28

The New Yorker
Published online at 9:00 AM on September 27, 2037
Eric McTeague and the Art of Publicity
How Anonymous Propaganda Created an Empire While
Convincing the World It Didn't Exist
By Austin L. Murray

Eric McTeague is a workaholic. His friendly, almost-too-symmet-
rical face may have adorned the cover of *Businessweek* and the
front page of the *Wall Street Journal*, but it's not on account of his
looks that he got where he is today. According to McTeague, his
success is even simpler than that: it's a matter of work ethic. Born
to a lower-class family in Philadelphia, he realized early on that he
had to work harder than other children, and that drive to succeed,
to push fiscal earnings higher every year, is why some have described him as the American Dream made flesh. Of course, nothing
is quite that simple—or else we'd have a nation full of McTeagues
rather than one lone, glittering morning star—but I'm not going
to be the one to contradict him. If there's one thing most industry
professionals have learned about McTeague, it's that he seems
to be right about practically everything, time and time again. And
sterling personality that he may have, his almost prophetic ability

to predict trends is the real reason why clients keep returning to Anonymous Propaganda.

Despite the country's lapse into permanent recession fifteen years ago, his company has shown profits every year since its founding. One of his secrets to success, according to McTeague, is that because his business doesn't rest, neither does he. "I started adjusting to a daily three-hour sleep schedule when I was in middle school," McTeague says, "and sometimes I have trouble figuring out how everyone else makes do with less than a twenty-hour day. How do they find time in their lives for, you know, living?"

I can tell that McTeague is kidding when he says this because of the broad grin on his face, but there's certainly a modicum of truth to his sentiment. It's hard to imagine how a person as young as thirty-five could have constructed an empire like McTeague's if he hadn't been gifted with extra time.

First amongst his accomplishments, and certainly most public-ly known, remains the Great Wall of Freedom, to most outsiders the pinnacle of his empire, its crown jewel. The Wall could practically be Anonymous Propaganda's logo. (Incidentally, the company doesn't have one.) Working with the young designer Gideon Reyes, he put together the edifice that President Haight called "the greatest single thing our nation has ever built, or probably ever will build." It's the only American structure that's visible from space, and it would cer-tainly be the apex of anyone else's career. But McTeague and his company haven't slowed down, and today it seems less like his greatest project than just another milestone.

"The Wall is impressive, no question about it," says McTeague. "That being said, it's big and kind of obvious. I mean, not to short-change the idea or the execution or anything, but the G.W.O.F. is a teensy, tiny bit derivative, know what I mean? I like the ideas no one has come up with yet. Hell, my favorite projects are the ones that no one even knows exist."

McTeague offered only vague hints about what these might be, but it was clear that his company's most famous works, like the G.W.O.F. or ads on the moon were, if anything, slightly embarrassing to him. "Let's be blunt: the best publicity, the best product of any sort, is one that you think you're choosing yourself. Anyone can run a splashy PR firm. Marketing isn't exactly one of the subtler sciences, right? But the real mavericks out there, the guys doing the work I want to compete with, are the ones you only hear whispers about. The ones whose ideas sound so crazy you dismiss them as unbelievable. Only, of course they've already been executed."

Following McTeague through his workday is a confusing affair, and not just because he seems to have so many projects in motion at once that it's easy to lose track of what's going on moment to moment. Research into liminal and supraliminal advertising makes sense when I hear the words, but what exactly it means is difficult to fathom. Even less clear are AP's links with biochemical engineering projects and research into something called subatomic particle conjoinment, which I decided to risk sounding like an idiot and ask about because the name sounded so intriguingly obtuse. "In layman's terms," he explicated, "I guess it's a way of trying to harness the interconnectedness of everything in the universe in order to facilitate the . . . production, I guess you could say, of certain expensive base metals. Lithium, for example." Who they're working with on this, and why it needs marketing, is impossible to guess.

As fascinating as a lot of AP's projects sound, most of McTeague's days are spent in meetings. During the sixteen-hour workday when I shadowed him, McTeague had just one forty-five-minute block of time that wasn't spent speaking with either employees, investors, or customers. (He had meetings with Warner Music, Halliburton, Burt's Bees, and the lozenge division of

Pfizer—consulting with AP about how to spin a rash of customers choking on its peppermint cough drops, a predicament McTeague described as "the trickiest problem I've worked on in months.") He managed to keep a keen eye on the company's disparate projects, sometimes offering small suggestions or advice and sometimes overturning a few metaphorical coffee tables. What impressed me most was his universal enthusiasm. He was as excited speaking with investors about a tax loophole in Turkmenistan as he was considering a bold new advertising campaign set to capitalize on the hormones released by Sanmuert water bottles.

"Whatever I'm doing, it's making money. I'm not too concerned which side of the business it comes from, so long as we're seeing dollar signs. Diversification isn't just a theory here, it's a way of life."

I asked McTeague whether he missed being on the front lines, developing advertising campaigns himself, but he seemed nonplussed.

"You're asking if I'd go back to being the little guy with no money, being told what to do, rather than the suit in the big office? Hell no. I like it up here. You might think I have less creative freedom now that we're owned by investors, a public corporation in the eyes of God and the country, but it's just the opposite. The way I learned it growing up, freedom in America means having the money to do what you want. Anyone can have an idea. Executing it takes resources."

It would be simplistic to say that Eric McTeague's addiction to work is in some sense driven by tragedy, but that doesn't mean it's not the conclusion many have drawn. McTeague married young, only a few months after dropping out of Harvard to start Anonymous Propaganda, a name that's since become synonymous with the man who founded it. His wife still in school, McTeague felt an incredible amount of pressure to succeed, especially when he found out she was pregnant.

"I was actually working twenty-hour days, seven days a week," says McTeague. "Even I know it was stupid, and I wasn't doing my best work. But I didn't know what I'd do if the company sank. I didn't have any plan B, so I just worked harder."

McTeague continued with this schedule even after his daughter was born, at which point his wife, Blair, insisted that they take a trip, hoping finally to get her high-strung husband to relax. They'd never had a honeymoon, so it would be their first vacation together.

"It didn't feel selfish because we had literally never had a vacation together, just us and no work. Never," says Blair. I can see the tears welling up in her eyes, but she continues. "If we'd taken her with us, it wouldn't have even been a vacation. Not that my justification makes any difference."

The McTeagues hired a nanny to take care of their daughter for the two weeks they would be in Australia, but unfortunately, she was running late. The nanny called to tell them that she was on her way over to their house. Due to car trouble, she wouldn't be there for another twenty minutes. The couple waited for as long as they could but decided to leave before the nanny arrived rather than risk missing their flight. When I ask McTeague about this, he tells me that he doesn't want to talk about it, except to say that it was "the worst decision I've ever made. Sometimes I feel like it was the worst decision anyone has ever made. It was an accident."

Upon arrival in Sydney thirty hours later, the couple became frantic when no one answered either their home phone or the nanny's cell phone. Moments after the nanny had hung up, she merged onto the freeway and was sideswiped into a concrete barricade by a texting driver. According to the police report, their daughter was still in her jungle-themed playpen when they found her, with evidence of seizures, severe cerebral hemorrhaging, and complete asphyxiation as a result of isotonic dehydration.

The report mentions nothing about wounds sustained from their pet dog, let alone limbs gnawed off and eaten as they were in some of the grislier versions of the story. According to Officer Jeff Hadley, who handled the case, all of that was added later.

"Still," says Hadley, "people will believe what they want to believe."

Needless to say, the McTeagues were devastated. Blair told me that following their daughter's death, they've never tried to conceive again, and that having another child would "feel like we were trying to replace her." But after several weeks of mourning, Eric began channeling his frustration into his work.

"Maybe some people just aren't meant to have children, you know?" says Eric. "That's one legacy you can leave to the world, but I've come to accept that it's not the one for me. Just because I don't want another child doesn't mean I can't leave a lasting effect and, as stupid as this may sound, make a difference in the world."

McTeague's first big project following the tragedy was creating what was eventually named the Center for Innovation, Testing, and Evaluation, or CIT-E as it's most commonly known. McTeague refuses to acknowledge any direct influence his own life has had on any of his multitudinous projects, saying, "I'm just here to deliver on a contract with a client. My ego isn't supposed to be involved." Still, it's hard not to see the specter of his daughter's death in CIT-E's unique emptiness—in essence, McTeague's creation is the world's first intentional ghost town.

The American Southwest has always been littered with ghost towns, cities that were once thriving communities but have since lost all, or nearly all, of their population. In CIT-E's home state of New Mexico alone, there are nearly a thousand documented ghost towns in various states of decay. Some of them have almost completely disappeared from the face of the earth, mining communities forgotten a hundred years ago, while others have become kitschy tourist traps. But prior to CIT-E, what marked all of them was their inexplicable nature and their mystery: What happened to these boomtowns, what caused them to go bust? Conversely, while CIT-E was designed as vacant from the get-go, unlike every other ghost town, its clients at the RAND Corporation, Halliburton, and elsewhere would describe it as a glowing success.

CIT-E is vacant, but it's also in effect the world's largest laboratory. Twenty square miles in size, the town is outfitted not only with roads and buildings but also water lines and a power grid, enough that the area could comfortably house over 350,000 people. Or, according to McTeague, "something like 2,800,000 robots." The area was founded as a testing ground for corporations (and, to a lesser extent, universities and government agencies) looking to research everything from the effectiveness of billboard campaigns to surveillance systems and improved power grids. The entire area is run from an underground control room where hundreds of engineers and programmers have ample space to analyze the events taking place in the virtual city above them and decide whether or not the robots' increasingly sophisticated artificial intelligence is responding in a way that truly reflects humanity, or if there's still something missing from the programming.

"I think," says CIT-E's chief engineer, Gene Stackwell, "that [McTeague] didn't want to work with people when he designed it. I think he wanted to figure out a way of doing the pure research that he loves without the difficulty and emotions that come from dealing with other human beings. There are much worse ways to cope with loss."

When I mention this to McTeague himself, he disagrees with this analysis. "I had this idea in my head for a while and suddenly the current level of technology made it seem feasible. Sensory development and AI had finally gotten to the point where it could reasonably replicate human behavior, and I just wanted to be the first one to go all the way with it."

McTeague notices my skeptical look, and decides to explain a bit more. "Humans are, of course, unpredictable. No doubt about it. That's one of the greatest things about us, that however much you think you know the species, or even know a single person, they'll always surprise you. But given enough computing power, you can factor in levels of randomness, and within a reasonable degree of certainty, they become predictably unpredictable. At that point, from a phenotypic view of what's transpiring, there's little difference between our machines and humans.

"We know that inside of those robots, it's just silicon programming, without anything we'd consider conscious thought. But we're not looking at that, what we're concerned with is just behavior, rather than something internal, and because of that there's no reason to believe that this approach doesn't work. And since pretty much everything Anonymous Propaganda has fielded since CIT-E's creation has been market tested there, I think I can safely say that it works brilliantly. We may not know or understand the reasoning behind why people do things, but we do know that they do them, and in a way, that's all that really matters."

The truth of that matter is that most of what I saw at Anonymous Propaganda was the same as what occurs at any other office. Men in suits puttered about, worrying about deadlines and expectations. Women dressed in office grays and blacks walked from their computers to the printer and back to their computers again in an endless cycle. Unsurprisingly, they made me agree before arrival not to write about the exciting parts.

"We treat nondisclosure agreements the way born-agains treat the Bible," says AP's vice president, Joshua Schwartzwalder. "We may not be the best publicity firm out there, but we have fewer leaks than the Pentagon."

One of the advantages CIT-E has offered is a remote and secretive location to test AP's pilot projects without giving notice to the prying eyes of the public. "Not everything can be tested out there," says McTeague. "Even I can't pretend that throwing up a wall halfway through CIT-E can prepare us for the effects of the G.W.O.F. But on the other hand, you'd be surprised how much can be tested, even if our methodology for testing lunar advertising was just a big spotlight that shined in the sky. Before Comcast first appeared up there for everyone to see, we had two years to determine for sure that its negative backlash wouldn't be worse for advertisers than the rise in brand recognition."

"Most of our business is the same as any other firm that does PR and advertising," adds Schwartzwalder. "And I like to think we do a pretty good job at producing TV spots, web spots, press releases, et cetera. But the rest of what we do is based upon the supposition of people believing that they're making choices on their own. It's like a magician's force. We're the ones who stack the cards, but the moment you find out about it, the game is up. That's why we're so careful about keeping quiet."

I was hoping to find out whether it's true that President Haight employs the firm on a million-dollar weekly retainer, or that AP has been working with Monsanto on a whole new medium for "organic" advertising. The rumors that surround the company have almost eclipsed its known work, and it's common for the Internet to attribute any coincidence to "probably just an AP press stunt."

Still, while I can't say anything in particular without getting myself sued into oblivion, I will say that in my short time at the office, I was able to confirm that at least some of the rumors are true. I'll leave the guessing to the conspiracy nuts online.

By the end of the day, McTeague is exhausted. "I've been told I have a concentration level rarely seen outside of Ritalin addicts. Still, working a full load tires me out the same as the next man." McTeague turns off his laptop and puts it in his briefcase alongside a pile of papers. He makes another stack on his desk before dropping it onto his secretary's desk for tomorrow (she works long hours, though she's long since left the building).

I ask McTeague why he's taking so much home with him. "Well, sometimes I have some extra energy, and I want it focused into my work, not some other bullshit. I'm not exactly a guy who has hobbies."

Before leaving, McTeague's secretary told me that, just down the hall, her boss has what's affectionately called his guest suite, a room he stays in when he's too tired to drive home, an occurrence that apparently happens several times a week. I ask McTeague why he isn't sleeping there tonight. "Despite what you may think, I do love Blair, and it's nice to see her more frequently than, you know, once a week. And she's pretty busy, too, so it can be hard to make our schedules match up. But seeing her can be more energizing than a new contract with Electronic Arts.

"It would be easier, you know, if I didn't have to rest some of the time. Think how much more we could get done in a day. And even I know that I'm living on borrowed time—my doctor's told me on a number of occasions that my lifestyle's not good for my heart. Eventually something's gotta give, and I'm not exactly a person known for moderation. Hell, maybe that'll be my next project: figuring out how to let us all stay awake more and live longer. Now I've just gotta figure out how you test out the effects of sleep deprivation on a machine that doesn't rest in the first place." He laughs, and I know he's joking, but something tells me that if anyone were to solve this impossible problem, McTeague would be the one to do it.

29

How long could she stay in the kitchen, ostensibly brewing tea, before it became rude? And why the fuck did she care whether she was rude to the man who'd abandoned her? Holly poured the kettle's water into a pair of mugs—made by "authentic Native Americans" in the "old way" and purchased by Robert in Taos or Santa Fe or wherever—and headed back into the living room with them in hand. Did even Emily Post know proper manners for dealing with the return of a man who once gave a big middle finger to your entire family? Holly felt conflicting urges, either to hug him without letting go or throw the tea in his face and watch as the scalding liquid blinded him and left him crying on the floor. She did neither and set the tea down on a coffee table between them, slouching into a chair opposite her dad, already exhausted.

Juan Diego cleared his throat. He looked uncomfortable, but she'd decided not to make this easy for him by speaking first. After an achingly long pause, he took a sip of his tea, put it back on the coffee table because it was still too hot to drink, and resigned himself to speaking.

"So, I'm not sure what I'm supposed to say here. You're looking well."

"Umm, thanks. I guess." Holly remembered that she was still in her work clothes, an oversize T-shirt and old, now-too-small jeans she wore without buttoning the fly. She surreptitiously brushed her hair to feel for paint. "These are . . . I've been working."

"Of course, of course. I've seen some of your work online. You were always a talented artist, but I'm glad you stuck with it. Maybe I can see some of your finished stuff later?"

"Yeah, sure. Not that it's very good, but—"

"—I'm sure it's great, no reason to pretend otherwise. You need to learn that half of success is just having confidence. No more self-deprecating. You're talented and people should know it. That's nothing to be embarrassed about."

He'd been in her home for less than five minutes and already she felt like a little girl again. They'd reverted back to their old roles, with him lecturing her about the world and gently chastising her into doing what he thought was best. She didn't know how to squirm out of these positions, how to create new identities for them to speak from. And hearing him talk to her like that was also so comforting that she didn't know if she wanted things to change.

"You . . . you look good, too." He looked, in all honesty, like her dad. Nothing more or less. A tad more gray hair, deeper lines beneath his eyes, more sag to his skin, but she had to make an effort to notice. He was as tall as she remembered, though instead of dressing as sloppily as he used to, he wore an old brown suit and carried a briefcase, like some old-fashioned door-to-door salesman. Holly tried to think of how she'd draw him, but she couldn't see past her father, couldn't manage to reduce his face to lines and shading on a canvas. He was subsumed by their relationship, or rather its absence.

"Thanks. And thanks for the tea, it's very good."

"It's some sort of fancy green tea Robert buys that's supposedly made by the Navajos or something. I think that's probably bullshit and they just empty out tea bags into a clay jar before selling it for five times the price, but it's not bad . . . Robert's my boyfriend, as I assume you figured out since you tracked me down here."

"Yeah, I've managed to keep up with your life, at least lately. But you know, Holly, I didn't come here just to make you uncomfortable." In actuality, he looked even less comfortable than she felt. Juan Diego had never been the rock of their family. That was Autumn, who managed to raise three children while becoming a tenured professor without slacking on either front. But that perfection had always made Holly feel like everything her mother did was cold and methodical. In order to make her life function the way she wanted it to, Autumn had to plan out every moment of her day. Juan Diego had vacillated between absence—too busy struggling with a work deadline to even feign raising his family—and being the warm center of their house. Holly had argued with her mother, but she'd admired her father.

"I guess," said Holly, realizing that if she wasn't the one to act, this conversation could go on forever without either of them saying anything. "I guess I'm just surprised to see you again. Ever. I thought that if you didn't reappear by the end of the year, then either you'd died, or you might as well have. I mean I knew that you were out there, somewhere, but it was kind of . . . theoretical, I guess. Giddy once joked that we should throw you a wake, because at least then we'd get to move on . . . though I don't think he ever told mom that."

Juan Diego took a moment to sip his tea again, and stared into it while speaking. "Holly, I'm really sorry. I have to confess that, yes, I am old. Age is . . . unimportant in some aspects of life, but in others it's inescapable, the most important thing. Particularly when it comes to our proximity to death."

". . . and that's it?" she said, trying to make eye contact.

"I'm not saying that it's enough," he said, his gaze fixed stubbornly on the tea's surface. "I'm just saying that it's difficult for me to explain why I left to someone who hasn't been there, who can't understand. I want to apologize for leaving, but I can't say that I regret the choice I made. In a way, it was no choice at all."

"That's just . . . no choice? You had a family, three kids, and you went and disappeared to God knows where. I don't see a gun at your head right now, so forgive me if I think leaving for five years warrants a better explanation than that." What felt so unfair about her father's absolute desertion wasn't the fact that he left them, disappearing as if he had no past at all. That was still complete bastardry, of course, and everyone Holly knew had consoled her about it, told her that they understood if she needed some support or time off or a shoulder to cry on, whatever she wanted, they would make happen. All she had to do was tell Lisa, or Stephanie, or any of the other girls with older siblings who always seemed to have a ready supply of substances, that she needed something to get her through the day, and they wouldn't ask any questions. She'd text Lisa, "Let's talk about agriculture after school," and head over to her friend's house that evening, and if Holly got real wasted, they'd sob together, lie on Lisa's thick queen-size mattress, and talk about how it was all okay because nothing could hurt them there. Holly had to fake the tears, but that was always easier when she'd had a few hits. The only downside to scoring this way was that if she didn't cry when Lisa started crying, it seemed possible that maybe her supply would dry up, or worse, Lisa would think she was a bad person.

No, what felt unfair about Juan Diego's disappearance was that he left before she had the chance to run away herself. Fuck midlife crisis, Holly had been making plans to leave since she was twelve, when she'd put together the first of her "survival packs" and begun studying maps and drawing plans. She had loaded a backpack with rope and matches and canned foods, an impressive (though not particularly sharp) Bowie knife she'd bought from some skeezebag at school by making out with him at lunch, and miscellaneous items she thought would help her travel to New York or San Francisco or Paris or wherever else she'd decided that week. She sat down and explained to her favorite stuffed bear, Lola, why she'd have to go it alone, that she had what it took to make it in the cold, hard world around her, and that whatever choices she made later in life, Holly would always love her.

But then, when the moment to set out arrived, she couldn't do it. At dinner she spent the entire meal staring at her parents, wondering if they knew how close they were to never seeing their daughter again—or at least not for many years, after which she'd make a surprise visit and delight her siblings with tales of adventurous living on her own—but they seemed completely oblivious.

The urge to run away never truly left her, though, and after one attempt fizzled, she began planning another, with a different theoretical itinerary. This continued until Juan Diego disappeared. After seeing how hurt her mother and brothers had been about him leaving, pulling the same dirty trick was the last thing she wanted to do. He was the reason why she kept in touch with Autumn and the boys; every call home was in part to spite her father.

"I understand your anger," he said. "I didn't mean to say . . . I guess this is kind of coming out confused. I'd prepared a kind of, not a script exactly, but a—"

"—let's go off script. Just tell me what's going on."

"You're right, you're right. It's been a while since I've dealt with people who . . . rather, the point is that it was a big thing for me, too. It wasn't a casual decision, leaving everything behind. It was difficult. I know it was hard on everyone else, of course it was, but I didn't just idly decide not to come back one day. But when I thought through everything as logically as possible, when I took apart the cold, hard facts of what was happening to me, the relationship I had with your mother, the amount of time I had left in this world, I didn't see any other option."

"What the fuck do you mean? What was the reason? Was it a woman?"

"No, it wasn't like that. There was this rule where if you wanted to stay on the company's health insurance plan, you had to have an examination every year. I hated doctors, always have. The way they treat your body, it's as if you're not even there. They poke and prod you like a butcher wrapping up meat. But if I didn't visit the doctor, we couldn't stay on the company health plan, and a scare we had with your younger brother was one of the reasons why I stayed with EA, even when my aims and theirs weren't exactly aligned. Every year I jumped through their hoops and made my visit.

"This time I went in expecting everything to be normal, with the same doctor I'd had since starting at EA. I always hated doctors in general, but mine was pretty good, a no-bullshit guy I always felt I could trust. This time Dr. Chang asked me to have a prostate exam as part of the affair, and I assented." He finished his tea, putting his head back as if he were chugging a beer.

"And?"

"Everything was fine, he said. He told me he'd call in a few days about blood work and to exercise more, drink less."

"I don't get it. I thought it was going to be like where he found cancer or something. But that was just an ordinary exam."

"No, you don't get it. It was almost an ordinary exam, almost the same thing I had to do every year. But the prostate exam was something new, something I didn't have to get the year before but would need for the rest of my entire life. I arrived home and ate dinner with the family. I don't remember what day it was, maybe we played a game or watched a movie. Yes, I think that was it. But I kept thinking about that exam, what it meant. The way Chang looked at my charts a year earlier and thought, 'This is all a guy like him needs,' but that year he looked and thought, 'I'd better check out this old man's prostate because it may well be cancerous.' The next day I couldn't get out of bed."

"That's fucking ridiculous."

"I don't disagree. But it's true, I couldn't get out of bed, I just laid there thinking about it, not knowing what to do."

"I don't remember that."

"You probably thought I was at work or something. And I'm pretty sure you had your own life to deal with. When you're a teenager, it's hard to think too much about other people, especially your parents."

"You left me, all of us, because of a motherfucking prostate exam?"

"No, I left because I remembered I was dying a very unhappy man. Slowly, of course, but like everyone else, I was dying. Steadily, unavoidably. I know that it's unforgivable, that it was pure selfishness, but I decided I would do anything, anything at all, to change that. To stop from dying altogether."

30

Gideon finished parking his car in the airport's cavernous four-story lot. "I like it there, I really do," he said into his phone, pulling a rolling suitcase from the passenger's side seat. "It's just that things are busy. I plan on making the pilgrimage as soon as an opportunity presents itself, but one of the main differences between school and the real world is that I don't get random vacations just thrown at me."

"All I'm saying is it's been a while since you've visited," said Devon, whose voice sounded even higher over the phone, "and I could really use . . . Shit's fucked up. I don't really know what I'm doing and like, I could really use some advice and . . . Fuck I can't . . . You should check out my new place. It's pretty fucking sweet."

There had never been a time in Gideon's life when passing through airports was not a hellacious chore. The entire airline apparatus—its planes designed in the 1960s still in use via the magic of duct tape and last-minute welding—had always seemed incompetent, but it was the airports themselves that irritated Gideon most. His brother's call was a pleasant reintroduction to the strange world outside his apartment. Had it always been this windy outside? Had the sun always been this bright overhead? Had he just forgotten how close cars came to crashing, constantly, and how terrifying it was that his emaciated muscles and reflexes were all that stopped him from becoming permanently and painfully enmeshed in these machines?

"I will, really, but like I said, those days come out of my ridiculously limited pool of time off, days that could be spent lying around and doing the most glorious thing of all: nothing." Behind him, Gideon spotted a bomb-sniffing dog and its two handlers garbed in Homeland Security's intimidating black-and-white military uniforms giving his car a once-over. He tried to ignore the search, despite how immediately invasive it felt. The minute you purchased a ticket, you became a suspect, essentially under government jurisdiction. Gideon stemmed his curiosity about what else they had planned for his car and stared resolutely forward. You could never tell what the Homeland Security fascists would do if they noticed you watching them. If anyone had secretly rigged his car to blow up, it was too late to do anything about it now.

"If I'm over there, it means a lot of family time and, while I love all of you from the deepest, blackest depths of the bottom of my heart, that doesn't sound like much of a vacation to me."

"What if I were able to finagle a trip to visit you instead? Really, I just . . . I need to talk and . . . Fuck, I don't know how to do this. Maybe you could even introduce me to Gravedigger? Then I could return home and regale the rest of the family with stories of your life and they'd be perfectly content hearing about it secondhand from me instead, all without you having to sacrifice your valuable vacation days. It'd make mom happy."

Inside the terminal, the line for Southwest's ticketing counter looped back around itself twelve times—not bad. He'd arrived six and a half hours before his flight's boarding time, and by the standards of a major airport, this was nothing. JFK and O'Hare now had mobile beds available right on the premises so that waiting passengers could stay overnight without losing their place in the security line.

"Umm . . . well anything's possible, I suppose. But the guy's pretty shy, it's not just a publicity thing. I guess shy's not the right word, he's very secretive. Or, I don't know, he just likes his privacy a lot. Can't say I really blame him."

"Well you can ask, right? I mean, no harm in finding out."

"Sure, I'll ask for you, but don't hold your breath. Celebrities aren't like you and me. You can't just meet them like they're ordinary people."

"That's ridiculous, why not?"

Gideon had always loved the way people in old movies would arrive at airports and, moments later, be in the air. Where were the retinal scans? Where were the full cavity searches? Where was the mandatory Pledge of Allegiance and declaration of religious background? Above all, where were the large men holding automatic weapons, pulling people out of lines for "enhanced interrogation" sessions?

"Because accessibility is the opposite of celebrity. They're an image, made for display on screens, not something you can just feel and see and smell. To be a celebrity is to live in this world without ever touching it."

Gideon had one airport memory from when he was very young. It was so long ago, he couldn't remember anything very clearly. He wasn't sure whether Devon was alive yet or not. Gideon, Holly, and their parents arrived just an hour and a half before their flight time. His parents treated the whole affair like a joyous outing until they hit the security line. From what he recalled, they'd forgotten to bring an ID for Holly and security wasn't going to let them through. His dad first argued with them, then yelled at them until they pulled him out of line. Security brought him to a glass box and searched him and Holly while the rest of the family waited three hours until the police arrived to try to make sense of the situation. Juan Diego screamed at the guards for searching his baby girl, saying that they'd touched her inappropriately, while the security people responded that Juan Diego was clearly a terrorist. Gideon couldn't tell for sure if it was a memory or just something he'd made up, but they never ended up flying that day, and the whole thing had taken so long that he'd fallen asleep until it was time to head home, giving it all the half-remembered haze of a dream. That was the only time he recalled anyone in the family trying to fly until he left for college. Even then only Autumn came along, and she hated it so much she didn't visit again until graduation.

"I don't really care about all of that. I don't need to touch the guy or find out what brand of toilet paper he uses. I just want to see him in person, to look at him with my own eyes instead of through a camera."

"But that's part of what makes Gravedigger so special: that you can't. That no one can. He might as well only exist on screens and in glossy magazine spreads. You've watched talk shows, right? I'm sure you've noticed that the bigger the star, the less of themselves they have to reveal. A B- or C-lister will have to tell a story about changing the baby's diaper or a weird sexual hang-up. Something that makes them seem more human, something the audience can latch on to for identification. An A-lister is beyond that. You can't identify with them because they're almost supernatural."

"Seriously, he doesn't have to reveal a thing. I just want to see him, nothing else. I sit quietly in a corner for two minutes. I don't say anything. He doesn't say anything. Two minutes, then I leave and can tell people I saw him in person. He's been to prison, right? Like maybe he could help me out with—"

"I'm not saying I won't ask, I'm just saying it's super ridiculously unlikely that he'll let you near him unless you're on the same level. Think of the president of the United States, the ultimate A-lister. Unless people are on the same level as him, the best they'll ever get is a handshake in the White House, and I've heard the security procedures for that are even worse than for flying. They're never going to get a conversation with him because for all intents and purposes, he's not even a person. Gravedigger's like that for rap, and the moment he starts doing two-minute appearances for kids is the moment he's no longer on top. He gives up a piece of his aura the moment you get to say he acknowledged you."

It was no secret that defending the airports, whatever that meant, was one of Haight's most popular pet projects. While there had never been any disaster as dramatic as 9/11 during Gideon's life, that didn't mean there hadn't been a few hijackings and extremely close calls. Following a relatively minor incident in Italy and the somewhat more spectacular "triangle of fire" disaster in China, the president began calling the increase in airport security "a mandate from the people." Subsequently, enduring the airport rigmarole without becoming incensed about it was deemed patriotic and respectful of the American way of life. Even Democrats had trouble arguing against the idea that in today's day and age, requiring passports for domestic flights just made sense. After all, wasn't it known that terrorist cells existed in the United States already? And what about sex offenders, how else could we track them? Likewise, noting the religious and political convictions of every American who flew was simply the most intelligent way of conducting security investigations. The dark hoods with white insignias donned by Homeland Security were more than a symbol of the department's newfound power. With every agent cross-deputized as a federal marshal, the hoods were a way of saying that America wasn't fucking around anymore.

"Fine, I get it. Whatever, you always have excuses, I'm sorry I asked. But that's not really why I called, it's tha—"

"Really, I'll try. I'm not saying I'll succeed, but who knows. And again, think of the president. You remember that whole international incident with the French when he refused to speak respectfully to their president? He can do that because he's attained that uber-A-list status. 'The only person I call Sir is the Almighty Himself'—that business is some pompous assholery, no doubt about it, but it also got the fucker reelected."

From the corner of his eye, Gideon noticed a pair of hoods heading purposefully toward his position and felt his heart rate jump. His mind raced to think of anything suspicious he might have done recently. Obviously some of the porn sites he visited might have been tagged by the NSA and added to his HS profile . . . but why him? Surely half the people in line must have something like that in their browser history.

There were four of them now, marching forward at a measured pace, and while he couldn't be certain who they were focused on, their eyeless visages made his panic grow worse. It was probably the god-damn phone call, he realized, talking about the president. Their sensi-tive microphones could've heard from a mile away. "Devon, I've gotta go. Now." He hung up. Oh fuck oh fuck oh fuck.

Every word on the phone could have put another nail in his coffin. Homeland Security didn't use Miranda rights. Sometimes the people they apprehended just disappeared: no body, in a cell or in the ground. They were just gone.

One of the goons put an arm on the brown-skinned woman stand-ing two people in front of him. Gideon exhaled. He tried to get a better look at her face to see if he recognized her, but she looked like any other fortysomething woman of likely Middle Eastern descent, and really it was her own fault for wearing a sari or whatever the hell that was, rather than something Western. Homeland Security hated people who didn't Westernize, said that resisting integration was a form of mild sedition. The guard spoke a couple of quick words to the woman and escorted her to a metal door that Gideon hadn't even noticed until now. He was careful not to stare as the woman began crying, but he kept watching with his peripheral vision and couldn't help but flinch when he saw one of them Taser her in the shoulder as she passed the threshold. The woman immediately went limp and the door slammed shut.

Gideon forced himself to breathe normally. Sure, he was Hispanic, but he looked pretty white. And if they hadn't grabbed him yet, he was probably in the clear.

That left Gideon at least a couple hours of waiting in the first line, then another couple before the search. Unwilling to see Devon, Gideon wracked his brain to think of anyone in Albuquerque that he did want to catch up with. He decided it was high time he met up with his old friend Ralphie. He hoped Ralphie still had the same number. They hadn't talked outside of Arcadia in half a decade.

31

There was no denying it. Norman Loyola Raphelson IV, or Ralphie, as he'd been called since even before birth, was fat. He wasn't big boned, he wasn't just a bit thick in the thighs, and he certainly wasn't pleasantly plump. He was obese in the most literal meaning of the word, "a real porker, but in a good way," according to his mother, whose love and fondness for her son couldn't be overstated. His dad, equally doting but more keen to poke fun at his family, once corrected Gideon when he'd called Ralphie gravitationally challenged. "The challenge," he'd said, "would be escaping his gravitational pull."

Gideon now sat with his friend on a wooden bench outside of what Ralphie had, on the phone, called the Brainbox. It turned out to be an enormous backhouse built on his parents' property, a one-story building, square and squat, seemingly constructed with frugality and speed in mind, rather than quality. Despite this, it had a fresh coat of paint and looked like it had been maintained with care and affection. There were flowers planted in the corners of its miniature yard. What might have been built as little more than a glorified tool shack now looked almost like a quaint cottage from a children's movie.

"So what do you actually, you know . . . do?"

"Drugs, mostly," said Ralphie. "I mean it's not like I have a particularly wide range of options. Okay, so maybe my options are very wide, but limited as far as scope is concerned."

"Umm . . . so your parents pay for everything? I thought you mentioned online at some point that you were raking in the dough. I thought you'd moved out or I wouldn't have asked about crashing with you."

"Well I would have, really, except it's difficult for me to do my own shopping. If I walk down an aisle to get cereal, I'm well aware that I've effectively erased that aisle for the rest of the shoppers. You can look away, that's fine, I'm not ashamed. I guess it's been a while since I've been more than just a voice in a headset. Anyhow, I'm a realist. My parents buy the groceries and do some upkeep on the place, but we don't really live together. That's why they were so happy to find this house, which allows me to live close to them while maintaining my own space. It's a mutually beneficial relationship: they get to see that I'm safe and well cared for, and I don't need to worry about finding a car large enough to get me to Smith's."

"What about the drugs?" asked Gideon. "I mean you're online a lot, and you always sound clean. Or at least not super fucked up."

"I am clean. Pretty much all of the time, actually. That's a key part of being a dealer."

"Shit. So, am I going to be a suspect on a police report just for being here?"

"Gideon, my friend, from the sound of it, you've never gotten high, have you? I mean sure, you went to college, you smoked a little weed. I'm pretty sure you smoked some with me at some point, but you've never done enough to get truly toasted, have you?"

Ralphie hadn't been born fat. Until he was thirteen, he'd been pretty scrawny, with skin so translucent that people swore you could actually see through to his ribs. Despite his lack of heft, Ralphie was fairly athletic, and like a lot of incandescently white children, he just shrugged off the burns as he hopped from basketball to baseball to football, depending on the season. Ralphie was even fairly popular, one of the first boys in Jefferson Middle School's seventh grade class to have really and truly made out with a girl.

The resulting hickey was a mark of honor around his neck for a week, the spoils of a victory that only increased his social standing.

Then he suddenly jackrabbited through puberty in a matter of days, and accompanying the bodily changes, he'd also, practically overnight, developed an intense and unyielding fear of the opposite sex. One day, in the middle of first period, where he'd long sat next to the stunningly developed Ashley Tierzo, Ralphie sprinted out of the classroom and across the courtyard to the pair of vending machines sitting adjacent to the cafeteria.

Then Ralphie disappeared from school for a while, and it was only later that Gideon learned about his gamut of therapies. Not for Ralphie's fear of women—that ended up being relatively straightforward and largely solved itself as Ralphie ballooned into each new weight class. But even as the spark that ignited his food addiction disappeared, his hunger remained. If a glance from a girl walking down Central no longer sent him fleeing into the Frontier for a greasy burrito, that was because Ralphie was more than likely already there, with a huge plate of carne adovada and sweet rolls.

Food addiction isn't like alcoholism or drug abuse. You can't go cold turkey. Food Addicts Anonymous emphasized abstinence from particular foods, which worked well enough for those whose addictions were less extreme, who mostly just needed someone to point out their bullshit and keep them on the path. But it was pointless in extremist cases like Ralphie's, who followed the guidelines and, instead of pounding back Snickers, bought and ate twelve bags of carrots for lunch, turning him yellow for a week and off carrots forever.

"So what are you, then?" asked Gideon.

"I'm just an everyday enabler," Ralphie said. "I don't push. I don't worry about what happens if someone quits using, and I don't sell to people I don't know."

"And they just come to you?"

"Pretty much. I offer a select few a safe place to do drugs. You never mentioned why you came to town, but if you're looking for some easy, part-time work, I could use some help keeping watch here."

"Watch? Like, keeping a lookout for the cops?"

"Really, chill out, Gideon. The cops aren't at my doorstep. No, I'm talking about something more like a lifeguard. Most of my customers are pretty casual users. They're not addicts, they have day jobs and families and everything else. Most of them are cubicle monkeys like you, people who spend eight to twelve hours a day typing emails to their bosses and filling out TPS reports. They just want to unwind. My business is providing a safe haven so that no one will fuck with them if they're in, say, a k-hole or something."

"A k-hole?"

"You seriously grew up in the 505 without knowing what a k-hole is?"

"Dude, you know what I did growing up. I'm guessing you still have the d20s to prove it."

"Damn straight I do, but still."

"I've been busy, okay. I've had other things on my mind than fucking drugs." Gideon didn't want to go into detail and hoped Ralphie wouldn't ask. He'd come to his friend so he wouldn't have to talk to his family, so that Autumn wouldn't give him that pitying look of disappointment she offered up at the slightest sign of imperfection.

"Well you have never seen people so completely fucked out of their minds as when they enter a k-hole. It is the be-all, end-all of drug experiences. You use enough and you effectively shut the brain off from the rest of the body. It's like a hallucination but it's of a higher order. Rather than just tripping out, you become one with your mind. The problem is that people on Special K are pretty helpless. They're shut in a dream world, unable to move. And you can get stuck in a k-hole for a long time. Like more than five hours. I know of one guy who paid for his shit with some fake presidents, and when they found out, they tracked him down to his house. Unfortunately, he'd already shot the whole load into his veins. They cut off the guy's arms while he was still in the k-hole, so he wasn't even present enough to plead his case."

"Now you're just having me on."

"I'm not, though I realize it sounds crazy. I still know the guy. Hearing him explain why he couldn't play in my poker game anymore was one of the main inspirations for founding the Brainbox. He was awake the entire time they were sawing off his arms and cauterizing the stubs. Can you imagine that? Awake, just watching it happen. Only to him it wasn't happening to a person, let alone himself—the whole scene was abstract shapes and designs, like the swirls you get when you close your eyes and stare at your skin from the inside."

"You talked to him about it?"

"Yeah. By the end I guess he'd worked out that it wasn't a hallucination. That it was happening to him, right then. But he still couldn't stop them, so he just laid there waiting for control over his body to return. I just wanted to make a safe place for people like him, where they could come and get high out of their fucking minds without worrying about someone taking off their limbs while they're out of it."

"But at a profit."

"I am one hundred percent American, Gideon, every last ounce of me." Ralphie thumped his arm against his chest. "I like to think of myself as a sort of all-American factory. I eat bananas bought from South American dictators, candy bars made in China by peasants chained to their workstations, coffee grown in the fields of what were once Tanzania's jungles, and I convert all of it into raw American material. Refusing an opportunity for profit when one presents itself is positively unpatriotic."

"But how do you stay away from all the guns and shit if you're purchasing drugs for your clients? You say the cops don't bug you, but surely other dealers do."

"I have my own source that's not reliant on Colombian cartels or Afghanistan warlords. Like everything else in the building, what I sell is pure USA. It's produced by some folks right here in the 505, retired lab scientists or whatever from Los Alamos. It's some potent shit, not like the kit-kat you'll find anywhere else. Anyhow, enough about drugs, you're still . . . working in PR, right, for Gravedigger? Goddamn, I'd love to meet him. What are you doing in town with me when you should be up in a big New York high-rise? Visiting la familia?"

"No, and in fact I'd rather you didn't tell them I'm around. I don't want them up in my business right now and would like to keep them thinking everything is hunky-dory in NYC."

"Sure, but then why *are* you here?"

"Officially I'm on leave right now. I just finished up a big project. Well, maybe not 'finished,' but they took me off a big project. Unofficially I'm here for research on the next one. And even less official than that, I'm looking for a girl."

Ralphie and Gideon hadn't been particularly close while growing up, although they'd long known each other. After running out of that eighth-grade science classroom, though, Ralphie changed. He could no longer hang in the circles he used to, because at the cusp of adolescence, anyone halfway popular had just one thing in mind: sex. Everyone wanted some, yet no one knew how to get it. Suddenly girls were catty and boys raised bullying to new heights. Kids snuck out to get drunk on 40s at Netherwood Park and the golf course in the hope that somehow this would lead them to the opposite sex, although no one knew exactly how.

Ralphie sure as hell didn't, and while he tried to continue hanging with his old group, his presence was just too weird when girls arrived. By sitting at a distance, Ralphie found that he could keep his cool, until the moment one of the girls grabbed a pal of his seemingly at random to go make out with on the other side of Netherwood's looming semicircular hill, at which point, he left as quickly as he could in search of the nearest Milky Way.

While everyone else at Jefferson was drifting through parks and ditches like vagrants, grabbing each other at every opportunity, Gideon was stuck a

good fifteen miles away in the far Northeast Heights. And however lenient—
or at least apathetic—his family might be, there was no way he could finagle
a thirty-minute drive in the dead of night. He frequently spent evenings lying
awake considering possible excuses to get out—babysitting overnight, an
emergency group project!—but nothing ever sounded remotely convincing.

The exceptions were sleepovers at friends' houses, but the type of guys
who still had sleepover birthday parties were on the other side of an uncross-
able chasm from those actively pursuing each others' bodies. Kids who
spent serious time setting up six-person *Warhammer* battles with hand-
painted miniatures weren't also figuring out how to undo a bra. Gideon
and his friends were interested in sex, but in a sense they'd already given up.
At least, for the moment. Instead of booze and expired condoms, Gideon
arrived at his friends' houses with a bag full of his father's *DnD* books and
polyhedral dice.

Ralphie was left wondering what to do with his newfound free time.
Seeing their son suffer, his parents bought him a new PC and every game
console they could find, and he dived right into them. Early on, he was
interested in the same things as everyone else, but his isolation gradually led
him to the indie game scene, and after a decade of knowing Gideon as an
acquaintance, Ralphie realized who Gideon's dad was—a bona fide living
legend—and reached out to him about, "you know, hanging out together."

"Dude, you're more than welcome to crash here," said Ralphie. "I've got five
caves, that's what I call the rooms in the back, and I can just reserve one for
you while you're here. You'll have to come to the front if you want to use
the bathroom or the stove or anything, but you'll have a bed. And I'd be
happy to sell you whatever you'd like at cost."

"Thanks, that would be great. I don't think I'll need the drugs or whatever, but I appreciate it."

"I'll leave you some samples while you're here, just in case you change
your mind. So, what's the new project?"

"You know Jesus?"

"I know *of* Jesus, yes," said Ralphie. "I wouldn't say we're formally acquainted, although some of my clients have told me they've become so while out back in the caves. There was one guy who bought too much and ended up somewhere deep, and when he came out he went completely straight edge. He's a born-again now."

"He saw Jesus in there?"

"Maybe. Or God, or Allah, or Muhammad, or whatever other eternal power. Certainly he saw something. So what's with the whole religion angle? I know we only talk online, but you never sounded like you'd joined a cult."

"Shit, I couldn't be less interested in the religious aspect of things, but my boss still wants me on this project. I'm supposed to be looking for some sort of new spokesperson for mainstream Christianity. I guess someone thinks that Jesus is too old-fashioned or whatever. Anyhow, I'm here to figure out who's supposed to be the next leader of the flock so that they can have him, I dunno, throw out the first pitch at a Yankees game or whatever."

Ralphie raised an eyebrow. "Not sure I can help you much there, but that sounds like some interesting work. Just don't tell my parents what you're up to, they'd probably ask me to have you leave."

"They know about the drugs, right?"

"We don't discuss it, but without a doubt. I'm not exactly the world's most secretive human being."

"So they're cool with that, but not with me looking for the next Messiah?"

"Probably. Maybe not, but I don't think you should try and find out."

"That's fine. Do you still know the guy who found religion in the back of your little shack?"

"No, not as such. I guess religious enlightenment doesn't look too kindly on this sort of thing. But I can probably track him down for you."

"Thanks. I've gotta come up with something to show my boss. Who knows, maybe he's the one."

32

Becoming a Part of the Criminal Justice System
Game Walkthrough and Guide by DevolChildə

Wake up. Your head will feel . . . not exactly fine, but only woozy, no pain, no jackhammers like in cartoons. You won't know where you are. Think to yourself, wherever I am, it's certainly not home. **AVOID: thinking to yourself, I'm not in Kansas anymore. You're better than that.** Your head will rest on concrete that feels colder than ice. Despite its pocks and rough surface, it will be soothing to the touch, almost as good as a pillow. There will be nothing else to put your head on. Your bowels will be raging. You will wish beyond anything else that you could keep your body from churning like some demented whirlpool, but there will be nothing you can do.

Lie on the floor for what seems like hours, days, listening as people talk and yell in the background. A loud metal door will clang open and closed, but don't open your eyes until your insides have become too much to deal with and you have to use the toilet. The room you lie in will be dimly lit, but still too bright for your eyes, so squint in pain and notice that there are at least a dozen other men in this cell with you. Notice that you are the youngest one in the cell by at least five years, and also that there is no barricade of any sort between the metal toilet in the far corner and the rest of the cell.

It will only now occur to you that you are, in fact, in a cell.

Ignore everything else and spend most of the rest of the morning on or in front of the toilet. Feel embarrassed about this, but ignore the looks of the heavily bearded men nearby. Pretend you are alone. **Pro tip: when that fails, pretend that you can pretend you are alone.**

You will still be wearing your clothes, despite their unrecognizable stains yet far-too-recognizable smell, when the shuttle bus picks you up. The shuttle will be white and unlabeled, almost pleasant from the outside, as if it's ready to take you and your cellmates—because that's what they are, it will dawn on you, cellmates—to somewhere else. You won't even be sure where else, and while the shuttle is initially reassuring, that will end once you walk inside. Its floors will be metal and from the back, where you enter up a ramp like freight, like cargo, there will be no seats, just bars from the ceiling to the floor for you to hold on to. The security windows will be laced with metal wire and the front of the van will house two uniformed men holding assault rifles.

These will be the first assault rifles you've ever seen in person. They will be smaller than you've imagined, smaller than video games make them seem when they're hovering in front of your screen as an indication of your character, but far more frightening. The men carrying these assault rifles will seem to think nothing of them. No one with you will seem to care about them, either, but you won't be able to help internally flinching every time one of their barrels haphazardly crosses your path.

Your ride will take fifteen to twenty-five minutes, speeding you from downtown past where you thought the city ended.

Ask one of the other prisoners, *Where are we going?*

The prisoner will respond only by laughing.

Pretend you didn't ask and watch the city and everything you've ever known recede behind you as the shuttle bus pulls into a gate. Act as if all of this is normal, expected. Pretend you are as nonchalant as everyone else in the bus, even though internally you will be doing your best not to cry. Do not cry. Do Not Cry.

Pro tip: when you cry, face away from the other prisoners and guards.

Men with handguns will ask you for your fingerprints. You will give them without thinking or responding in any way that will draw their attention. Other men will ask you your birthday, Social Security number. They will ask you your hair color, your eye color, even though you are standing right in front of them. They'll ask you your height and ask you your weight, even though they have just measured both. They will have you sign forms you don't have time to read. You will sign them as quickly as you can, writing your name in an illegible scrawl and putting initials wherever indicated. They will take photographs of you and blood samples and urine samples. They will take a retinal scan. You will comply with whatever they say because there is no reason that you can think of not to comply. You will be asked about medical or psychological problems and respond that you have none, though you will wonder whether you are in fact telling the truth. You'll wonder how many people in here are fucking crazy and whether they answered the same way you did.

You will realize that your wallet and keys and phone are missing. They've probably been gone since before you woke up, but now is the first time you'll have the cognitive abilities to notice. You will put your hand in your pocket to check what your clan, the Baby Eaters, are doing on Arcadia. When your phone isn't there, you will momentarily worry about it being stolen. It will take you almost five full seconds to realize exactly how stupid this is. **BOSS STRATEGY: don't ask the guards when or if your possessions will be returned to you.**

After half an hour you will be taken to another room, a room with one metal door and no furniture. The floor will be tile but whatever pattern it may have once displayed will now be scuffed beyond recognition. The floor of this room will be dirty, but you will sit in the far corner, away from the other prisoners in the room, and try not to make eye contact with anyone else from your shuttle as they slowly join you. You will consider asking one of the other prisoners what will happen next but be unable to get up the courage.

The room will smell bland but dusty. With nothing else to do but sit, you'll become aware of your own smell, the stink of puke on your clothes that's only grown worse. You will wish you could brush your teeth because your mouth still tastes acidic, like fermented orange juice. You'll wonder, given how badly you smell to yourself, what it's like to be someone else in the room. You will wonder if this has in fact been a blessing, since despite being the smallest, weakest, youngest person in here, the other prisoners have given you a wide berth. Wonder about the lack of any camera in this particular room. Wonder about the brownish-red stains on the wall behind you.

When finally given your orange jumpsuit and a chance to shower, feel grateful. Worry, momentarily, about the chance of shower rape. Be grateful that no one in your group so much as looks at each other once naked.

Enjoy the feeling of synthetic fibers on your skin because at least they are clean. Your jumpsuit should feel almost like a tarp and seem virtually waterproof. While not terribly scratchy, the strangeness of its texture will be distracting. Wonder about how they managed to give you a jumpsuit several sizes too large and the man next to you, who would fit it perfectly, a jumpsuit far too small.

Wonder why no one looks good in orange. No one.

You will be escorted to your cell, which will be the most cell-looking enclosure you could possibly imagine. You will be in disbelief about how much it looks like a television set, to the point that you look for cameras, in the halfhearted hope that perhaps this has all been a big hoax, a reality television show. There will be cameras visible, but they are simply white, swivel-mounted security cameras. **Pro tip: this is not a reality television show.**

You and another prisoner, one you have not met before, one referred to as Navedo by the guards, will be in a cell together. Wait in silence with Navedo. Navedo will be large, maybe two hundred twenty pounds, perhaps with unkempt facial hair, but with a kind face. Navedo will seem just as uncertain as you are.

After an interminably long period, introduce yourself to Navedo. Navedo will say hi.

Ask Navedo if he wants the top bunk.

Navedo will say he doesn't care.

Give Navedo the top bunk anyhow, as a sign of respect of some sort, and lie down on your own bunk. Try to sleep but be unable to do so due to the noise and light of the room. Your back will feel terrible from sleeping on concrete last night, and now you will want nothing more than to relax, but it will be impossible to do so, even though Navedo seems to be the best cellmate you could have asked for.

At dinnertime, go to the meal. Fill up a tray with a hard roll, rice, gravy, beans, and an orange. With an almost completely empty stomach, this will feel like a blessing, up to the moment you taste the gravy. In the end, you will only be able to force yourself to eat the dry and stale roll and the orange, but regret this overnight when your stomach feels ready to mutiny and strangle you out of its own sense of irritation and entitlement.

The next day you will wake up almost as disoriented. Be ready to wonder about your phone call. Navedo will still be lying on his bunk and unwilling to leave the room when the hallway's fluorescent light signals you to get up.

Ask him, *do we get a phone call?*

He will groan in response.

Ask him again in twenty minutes, *so what's the deal with phone calls?*

He will say, *how should I know?* He will seem even unhappier than you are, so leave him be while you head to the cafeteria. This morning, you will eat everything on your plate, everything you can touch. You will feel even sicker for this later, will spend an uncomfortably large part of the day sitting on your metal, lidless toilet while your roommate exits the room to visit the chapel and wherever else.

When you have time later, and even though it's just a day it feels like you have endless amounts of time, infinite periods of time because you're still disconnected from Arcadia, you should speak with a guard about the phone call. He will laugh, then ask how much it means to you.

I thought it was a right, you'll say.

He will laugh again. **Pro tip: movies are liars.** You will decide that talking to him is pointless and wander on your own. Eventually you will come across a payphone asking for $1.50 a minute, which will seem incredible given that all of your money was taken away before getting in here. There will also be a bulletin board with bail bondsmen listed, though you will be unsure what exactly it is they do. There will be a line at the phone, twelve people waiting at this hard plastic relic, this payphone that might be the only one left in the city. Decide that maybe this is all too much, and more importantly, that you don't even know who to call anyhow. Reject calling your mom right now, and internally laugh about the idea of getting in touch with your father. Gideon or Holly? That motherfucker Steve? The truth, you will realize, is that you are alone in here and finding the phone was completely pointless.

Head back to your room and consider what else to do. You will be unclear on how much longer you will be stuck here, and so desperate that you even consider joining your roommate at the chapel.

It seems quaint to you, oddly old-fashioned that this jail should have a church, and even odder that prisoners go there to pray or whatever. **AVOID: mentioning this to Navedo when he returns to your cell. It will create an uncomfortable situation between the two of you for the rest of your stay.**

Wallow in your own unhappiness for the rest of the day. Nothing else should feel appropriate to the situation, certainly not going to worship a God you believe in minimally, if at all.

By the time guards pull you out of your cell a day later, it will seem like you have always been here. The guards will take you and twenty or so other prisoners to what appears, at first glance, to be a typical corporate conference room. You will sit around a large table with a lacquered faux-wood finish while a man who introduces himself as your probation officer greets everyone around the room. He will begin talking to people, not you, in a succession around the room until a projected image appears on the far wall. You will recognize this projection as an Arcadia chat program, and won't be able to hide your surprise when a fully robed judge appears on the other end of the screen.

Your turn with the judge will come somewhere in the middle. The probation officer will be told your crimes, which will be unlawful possession of a controlled substance with intent to distribute, underage drinking, and soliciting prostitution. Your probation officer will discuss these charges for between two and five minutes with the judge, at the end of which you will learn that there is a recommended bond on you for five thousand dollars.

Panic over the five thousand dollars. Be fully aware that you do not, and have never, owned five thousand dollars, despite the ridiculous wealth of your family.

Following your conference call with the judge, you will be taken to a room with multiple phones. Again, a bulletin board will list bail bondsmen and, after observing several other prisoners calling these numbers, do so as well.

Be completely unclear on which bondsman you should call. When the bondsman answers, she (it will be a she, and this will surprise you though it should not) will tell you that you need to give her five hundred dollars. This you can do. But you will wonder how to get her the money. The bondswoman will tell you it can be wired directly from your account, if you know the number, but you will not because that is a crazy thing to know. Instead, she will ask if someone else can bring it to her, and you tell her that your friend Steve can, in a check, but you don't know how to get ahold of him. Eventually she will agree to post your bail so long as you give her the five hundred within twenty-four hours of your release. This will be acceptable, doable, but you will wonder what would happen if you could not round up the money.

Less than an hour later, you will be transported back in the white van headed downtown. Your roommate Navedo will not be in the van with you, and you will wonder why that is, but never think of him again afterward.

You will be given back your clothes, which smell even worse than before, and most importantly your phone. Swipe it and enter your password. At the site of its home screen, feel like a full person again, like you have suddenly been cured of blindness. Text your friends for a ride home. You will see Disney's old primer-colored automobile, dubbed "The Boat" by Steve because it looks more seaworthy than roadworthy, turn the corner almost half an hour later. He will make a face at the way you smell but otherwise stick to small talk as he drives you home. Your mom will not be there to ask questions, thank God, so after putting your clothes in the washing machine and taking a shower you will feel ready to pretend none of that ever happened. Send five hundred dollars through PayPal to the bondswoman without ever meeting her and sleep soundly for the next fourteen hours.

A week later you will receive a letter in the mail from the State of New Mexico. Your mother will want to see what it says, but you will snatch it away and glare at her for asking. When she brings it up later, say it was just junk. It will be obvious that your mom doesn't believe you. Open the letter in your bedroom once she's asleep and read what it says. Realize that until opening this letter, you felt that that weekend was just a bad dream. You will want to burn the letter, but instead read it over and over again, even though it tells you no new information.

The next day, go downtown to the state public defender's office. **Pro tip: it will be impossible to find parking, so don't despair at paying five dollars an hour.** Once in the office, you will fill out a financial affidavit determining whether or not you qualify for a lawyer. You do, because everyone does, and will be assigned one at random. You will not meet with this lawyer in person. You will be told a name and then, several weeks later, receive a nonpersonalized email from the State Public Defender's Office repeating this information. You will wonder whether there is something you should discuss with this lawyer, but choose to do nothing. Spend the rest of the summer in Arcadia. Go to college. Continue acting in public as if none of this ever happened.

In late October, approximately five months after you were arrested, you will receive another letter from the state. Fortunately, by this time you will have moved out from your mom's house and it will arrive at your new one, a block from Bataan Park, shared with two of your friends. You will be the only one who takes in the mail anyhow, so it will be easy to make sure no one else sees this letter. You will read words like "indicted by a grand jury" and "required for a formal arraignment" and not be able to tell what any of this means. You will read a date to appear for the arraignment.

You will be prepared for the arraignment, you really will, but when the time comes, you will not be able to force yourself to go.

Instead, you will be playing a competitive match of *Duty Calls* on-line with your friends. When the bail bondswoman calls the next day and chews you out for not appearing in court, thereby threatening her livelihood, you will not know what to say.

I don't think you've been treating this seriously, the bondswoman will say.

You will say that you have.

Have you even been in contact with your lawyer? she will ask.

Not exactly, you will stammer.

BOSS STRATEGY: don't tell the bondswoman you are sorry. This will only cause her to yell at you even more.

The bondswoman will require another one hundred dollars from you to guarantee that you will show up at the next arraignment. Even so, when you do show up, she will be angry with you. You will tell her it was an honest mistake, but she will just grunt and ignore you.

The judge will be even less happy than the bondswoman. He will be an older man, white and balding but trying to hide it and sweating profusely all over his head. He will threaten to increase your bond, which will seriously worry you because of how expensive all of this is turning out to be. Eventually the judge will calm down, slightly, and read your charges and the possible penalties. The penalties will include five years in prison. You will begin sweating even more than the judge, shivering. The room will feel far too cold, even in your unpressed suit. The judge will set a deadline for "motions," and you will have no idea what this means.

After the arraignment, you will finally hear from your lawyer. He will leave a voice mail on your phone requesting your presence immediately. Visit his office the next day. Your lawyer, a surprisingly large man, a man you would not want to face in a dark alley given his size and the amount of hair on his white knuckles, will tell you to plead guilty. He will lay out the facts of the case: you were caught red-handed, the prostitute has accused you of giving her ketamine, your blood-alcohol level when the police picked you up. He will say that the state may go easy on you for a first offense. If you plead guilty.

You will leave the office not knowing what to do. You will be afraid of living the rest of your life as a felon, of having to tell your mother and face your family. You will be well aware by now that felons receive no financial aid for college. Your lawyer will have told you to get back in touch with him as soon as you've made a decision, that he needs an answer soon. Very soon. You will go home and get on Arcadia with your friends, destroy zombie invaders in a MOBA until you fall asleep on your keyboard, and pretend none of this ever happened for as long as you can.

33

Gideon's phone vibrated on the side table, and after seeing his sister's name lit up on it, he switched it to speaker mode so he could stay slouched in a beanbag chair. "Hey sis. To what do I owe this pleasure? More camera problems? Scanner problems? Perhaps some other technological problem that only a man with a liberal arts degree and a passing knowledge of computers can help you with?"

The room he stayed in was small and plain, with just a mattress, two beanbag chairs, a small table with a lamp on it, and a television set hanging against a wall—also a few diapers under the table, which he decided not to ask Ralphie about. A glorified closet, really. He'd been using Ralphie's bathroom on the other side of the house, which was large, luxurious, and far less in use than he'd initially feared. He'd initially assumed the accommodations would be a bit nicer, considering Ralphie's claims about the quality of his clientele, but apparently they didn't care. Business seemed to be bumping, with new houseguests arriving constantly, but no one ever bothered him. They flitted into their rooms and then left however many hours or days later, never making a ruckus. Usually he heard a television or music playing through the walls for the first fifteen or twenty minutes after someone arrived, but then things would go quiet, and the next thing he'd hear from them would be the door opening as they left.

"No, it's nothing like that. It's . . . something serious." Her voice cracked as she said this.

"I'm sorry. What's up? Is it about Robert? Do you need some kind of help?"

"No, I just wanted to tell you that I heard from, saw, actually, I mean he was visiting so I guess I—"

"Dad?"

"Yeah."

He didn't know how she expected him to react, so he stayed silent.

"I know," said Holly.

"Seriously? I mean, I kind of thought . . . How did he look?"

When Gideon returned after visiting a local parish, he'd discovered a selection of Ralphie's samples on his table. The THC, he'd learned, calmed him down, and had been vital in helping him back into the world so he could speak with the myriad of parishioners, pastors, and other Jesus freaks. He'd thought that by now he would be back to normal, that he'd had enough weeks since leaving Connecticut that talking to so many people wouldn't be a problem, but it was. Especially when talking to religious people, Gideon always felt like he was being judged.

"I don't know. He looked okay, I guess. Older, of course, but mostly the same. I guess it's been a while so I don't remember exactly how he looked before, but I'd never really thought of him as old before. He was an adult, older than us, sure, but now he's, he's definitely old."

"Like he was hobbled, using a cane or—"

"No, just normal old. Like if you saw him at a grocery store, you'd know that next to his driver's license he kept an AARP membership card. I didn't see him drive, but I'm sure he doesn't do it fast anymore, or if he does he's probably been in like a dozen crashes by now. He seemed . . . slower. Worn down. Do you remember how it used to seem like he was either asleep or half jumping with intensity, even while sitting at the computer? It wasn't like that anymore, it was like he was really tired. We sat around and drank tea."

Gideon remembered his sister at five years old, having a tea party with her father and her teddy bears. He shook this image out of his head, unsure if it had even happened or if it was one of those things you just make up about your childhood. Juan Diego had never really liked playing make-believe with his kids, had always preferred games. He'd never liked anything that didn't have rules you could master. Gideon remembered when he used to play basketball with his dad on a hoop they'd nailed up above the garage. His dad used to let him get nine points or spell out H-O-R-S, perhaps to appease Autumn, but he'd never let Gideon win a game.

"Okay. But . . . so like, why did he visit you?" Gideon had to admit to himself, he felt a little hurt. Holly hadn't been his dad's favorite, right? It felt like he was being rejected these days, passed up, even by his dad. "Hell, if he's going to visit someone, shouldn't it be me? I'm the oldest son. If this were the bad old days, when he died, I'd get all his money and title and you two would just be fucked."

"Ha. I don't know if it was necessarily favoritism, though maybe. After all, I'm pretty awesome, especially compared with you two dweebs. But no, he said something about trying to see you, too, but maybe you weren't home or available or something? I didn't know what to make of that, since you've always been as weird a hermit as the rest of us. Anyhow, I'm sure you'll see him soon, and I don't know, maybe you can tell me what you think of the whole thing. I was, I'm going to be honest with you, mostly just pissed off."

"I'm sure. I mean, of course you'd be angry, no one's happy. The dude's a shithead as a father."

"He was okay as a father."

"Really? Was he? Because I don't know if you're remembering things correctly."

"Yeah, leaving was a dick move, but—"

"He wasn't the most attentive parent before that, either."

"I know, I'm not trying to defend him, God knows I would never fucking do that. So the guy has some big fucking midlife crisis, boo fucking hoo. We all have problems, that doesn't excuse shit. God, Devon wasn't even a teenager then, was he?"

"I don't think so, and he still has the maturity level of a five-year-old. So like, did you talk about anything else?"

On his laptop Gideon scanned his spreadsheet of possible candidates. Each one seemed less interesting, less promising than the last. He just really couldn't make himself give a fuck about any of this. All he wanted to do was follow Teresa around, or watch her online. He closed his eyes and tried to make himself comfortable in the beanbag, but however he moved, it felt like his back was about three degrees away from snapping. His body just didn't like sitting anymore, and even driving, Gideon found himself squirming in his seat, unable to make his lower back feel comfortable again. He reluctantly moved to the cot, resting his phone against the side of his head.

"Kind of? You'll have to talk to dad yourself, but that's what I was getting from the conversation. He had this crisis that sounded like just a normal fear of death sort of thing. Did his equivalent of hitting forty or fifty or whatever arbitrary number freaks people out these days and just flipped. Mortality, impending death, wasting his life. The whole shebang, like he'd read a book on the subject and decided to go with the most obvious symptoms. I guess he made some bucket list shit and spent a fortune traveling around the world in disguise."

"God, if mom hears about that, she'll kill him. She was always saying they never went anywhere, did anything. Sometimes she'd say that he tricked her while they were dating into thinking he was the type of guy who went out and did stuff, then the moment they got married, he never left the house again for anything but work and groceries."

"Well, unless you decide to tell her, I don't see why she would ever hear about it. It sounds like he might want to be involved in our lives again, but I got the definite feeling that he's planning to stay the hell away from mom. I have no idea what's going on there, exactly."

"I don't like to tell her much about my life or anything, but still, I feel like she deserves to hear about what happened to him. I don't know . . . Did he say anything else?"

Not that Gideon wanted to be the one who told Autumn about Juan Diego's return. Holly could deal with that. Autumn and Holly were always fighting anyhow, but Gideon had always been the one who apologized, even when he felt he was in the right. When it came down to a real confrontation, he preferred to run.

"So he spent some time dicking around, doing all the stupid activities he wanted to do before he died. But of course unlike most people he's really fucking rich, so he could go off and do everything. Like, the moment he wanted to swim with dolphins, he just had his travel agent book the arrangements and hopped on a plane to the Atlantic. Thought that getting all of that done would make him 'happy' in some way."

"God, do you remember when we were young and we all had to pile in the back of the minivan?"

"Sadly, yes, despite all the hard work I've put into repressing those memories. Maybe I should try hypnotism."

"And that time when the air conditioner broke and dad took a wrong exit and we had to drive like fifteen miles before we could turn around?"

"Yeah, there was a little while there when I honestly thought we wouldn't make it. That we'd run out of gas and die of dehydration. Or maybe dad would get so angry he'd somehow make the car explode."

"Ha, yeah. That was awful."

"So he was on like this idiotic quest to 'find himself,' some bullshit like that. But then I guess he finished his bucket list."

"Is that why he came back?"

"No . . . I mean a bucket list is kind of like a scavenger hunt, really. Just because he finished the one he started with didn't mean he couldn't just write up another list of things to do. It sounds like he finished one, still felt unhappy, still hated the prospect of dying, and tried it again. And whatever else dad may be, he's a creative guy, so he had no trouble filling up a dozen more lists. It sounds pretty stupid to me, but I guess he spent quite a while doing that, just going through these experiences to mark them off and be able to say that he'd lived a full and complete life, that he'd done what he'd always wanted to do and could be content. If you measured lives by the number of hedonistic experiences, then I guess he would've won. I don't even think he really wanted to do a lot of it—like since when was he the kind of guy who fed dolphins?—but he made himself anyhow, because if he didn't, it wasn't like he'd get another chance."

Even flat on the cot, his back ached. Gideon turned over onto his stomach and felt a tiny bit better, but still wondered what had triggered these problems over the last few weeks. Maybe it was psychosomatic, maybe hearing about his dad's age was triggering things. These days he didn't know what to trust, including his own body and brain.

"Do you think dad's cracked? I mean, did he look kinda off?"

"Are you asking if he was obviously deranged, babbling about traveling through time with a bone stuck in his beard? No, of course not. He just looked exhausted, like he'd aged twenty years in five years' time. Other than that, he just seemed . . . I don't know, like dad. Though he dressed kinda weird."

"Weird like how? Because it sounds like he's gone off the deep end. He was always pretty intense. They say there's a thin line between genius and insanity."

"I know, but he wasn't crazy. You shouldn't listen to everything the tabloids say. He was neither locked in an asylum nor working at the head of some evil government conspiracy. He just said that he was finished with all that, the bucket-listing stuff, and so he went back to work for EA. He said he wanted to finally complete the work he started fifteen years ago."

"Arcadia 2.0? It's real?"

"I don't know, he didn't say. But he asked me to come down there and work on something with him. Said he'd seen my paintings—God, I never should've put them online—and wanted me to design part of the game. Textures or something, I assume? I don't know. He offered a lot of money . . ."

"What'd you say?"

"I said fuck no. I let him say his piece, then I told him that he's not welcome at my house again. If he wants to talk more, we can try I guess, but he can't just come barging in and presuming we can start back where we were before. And when I said I wouldn't go with, he asked me if I was happy and that kinda caught me off guard."

"Well, are you happy?"

"I don't know. I guess not. I mean, how are you supposed to know something like that? Then he asked me about things with Robert, if I didn't want to work with him on Arcadia because I wanted to stay with my boyfriend or whatever."

"What did you say?"

"Fuck, don't you start, too."

"I don't mean to, like, pry."

"I told him I don't know. Really I just want to do my shit and not have to deal with any of this. Then he gave me his email address and told me that if I ever changed my mind, or just wanted to talk again, to contact him. He said there wasn't much time left, and I told him he wasn't dying as fast as all that."

"Was that it?"

"Kind of. Toward the end he started ranting that I should really start eating organic, or local, or something like that. He seemed super worked up about it, but you know dad. Remember when Gram . . . you know, and he went on that crusade against ellipticals and exercise? God. I guess he's found a new fixation. At least that part seemed like the old dad. The rest of it, I mean, it was so weird. I hugged him before he left and it just felt wrong. It was like hugging a tree or a toaster, not someone you grew up with, not a parent. Then he left. He looked disappointed in me, or maybe in the visit, which is fine. That makes sense. I mean, he's got plenty of money and can do whatever he wants, so I don't know why I feel guilty."

"What if the thing he really wants now is his family again? Together, like before he disappeared."

"Then tough shit—no one gets to have everything they want. That's fucking life. I mean he's still my father, I haven't forgotten that. If he needed help, like he was dying in the wilderness or something, I would give it. And maybe if I felt like he was truly contrite, then I might forgive him. But what I will never do is let him into my house and pretend that all of this never happened."

"Well, thanks for the heads-up. I've got some work I gotta get to . . ."

"Yeah, I guess I do, too, though I don't think I can see straight enough to do it right now. Take it easy."

"Yeah, try to think about something else. At least now you have some sort of resolution with him."

"I don't see how this is resolution. I sure don't feel resolved about anything."

"Didn't you wonder whether he was alive? Didn't you have things you wanted to say to him, things you'd rehearse in your head while unable to sleep at night?"

"Yes . . . I did. But I didn't get to say them. It's not like I could. I mean, he asked me if I was happy, but he was the one who didn't look so good. I thought I'd just be able to scream at him for a while and maybe he'd cry or we'd hug or something like that. But in person, it wasn't like that."

"Well, maybe that's what you needed. That sort of . . . lack, I guess."

"I feel old now, too. Like a real adult. I'm sorry I kept you on the phone forever. I'm gonna take a bath and try to get past this somehow."

"Good idea. I'll talk to you later."

"Later."

Gideon hung up. His room was finally dimming with the sunset, and he thought about sleeping but felt too awake after the call. The news was huge, but he couldn't think of what it really meant for him, if anything. Gideon pulled his laptop over to the cot and looked at the spreadsheets again, but they were just as pointless as before. He deleted the entire file, knowing it had all been a waste of time. If there were other candidates in this city worth telling Eric about, he would've found them by now. The only person he could think of for the job was Teresa. It was made for her, just like he was. No one else was worthy.

34

On the corner of two intersecting residential streets sat a squat, brown building made of adobe and covered with stucco in a style favored only by those who'd moved to the Southwest to live out some fantasy of an authentic lifestyle. Locals preferred buildings that had good, solid bricks supporting their walls and any other color of paint—brown was too ubiquitous already, a color that coated the South Valley in a permanent sludge. After it rained, the building's walls were indistinguishable from the ground and almost seemed to grow up from it, another hill of indistinguishable marrón. But this was an old building. Its founders were poor and, like the people who used it, couldn't be picky about their materials. That it still stood, after generations of wind, hail, thunderstorms, fires, and occasional acts of vandalism, was some kind of miracle.

Teresa approached the entrance at the same torpid pace as her grandparents, whose half-walk, half-shuffle gait grew slower every year. Finally at the entrance, she placed her hand in a font of holy water and made the sign of the cross.

Watching her grandmother repeat this after her, Teresa wondered what this ritual was supposed to mean. She'd been doing it since she first began attending church services, but she'd never heard anyone explain why, besides that their own parents and grandparents did it when they were little. That it was ritual for its own sake gave this small act importance for her. Wetting their fingers wasn't done for penitence, nor was it a requirement for members of the church. It was just an invocation to the ceremony, and to Teresa the service began the moment her fingertips were moistened and she felt the oily water slowly evaporate on her temple. Her skin itched, just by putting pressure there, but she ignored it.

Inside, La Iglesia de San Daniel felt even smaller, and Teresa liked that it could only comfortably seat about sixty people. That during Christmas and Easter services, when everyone who studiously ignored it the rest of the year crammed into its single room, parishioners were forced to stand up, packed uncomfortably close to one another. Attendees couldn't zone out during the big Masses, falling asleep in the back pews like people over at the megachurches on the outskirts of town. Here you felt the presence of everyone in the room, the heat of their bodies and the stink of perfumes intermingling with sweat and dust falling from a roof that was little more than dust itself. For days afterward they'd have to air the whole building out, give it time to recover from so much concentrated humanity.

Teresa glanced at who else was here and chose a pew toward the front so her grandparents could see and hear what was going on. She knew, at least by sight, every person in the parish, but after anointing themselves, her family didn't speak to anyone. If they ran into friends of her grandmother in the parking lot, they would greet them, maybe catch up briefly about their families and work, and make arrangements to have lunch together during the week, but inside it was silence.

With the exception of the altar, the church was almost as plain from the inside as it was on the outside, despite the glimpses of color from yellow and blue flowers in the sanctuary's vases. A large crucifix adorned the far wall. Teresa pulled down their kneeler, unpadded and made of the same plain, light-colored wood as the rest of the building's furniture, and tried to make herself comfortable. It made Teresa's knees sore, so must have pressed against her grandmother's legs like burning knives, but the old woman never complained or offered a look of discomfort.

They knelt next to each other with closed eyes, but when she was younger, Teresa had kept hers open and watched her grandmother mouth mysterious words, words that in her youth Teresa believed were either a secret prayer that only true believers knew or else messages that went directly from her mouth to the ears of God. She'd never known what to say when she knelt but knew that the act itself had to be observed. It was all part of a greater whole. Her grandfather leaned in silence, sitting since his old knees and back prevented him from joining them on the kneeler. He looked serene, tension visibly leaving his brow. Teresa didn't know what she was supposed to think about, and this blankness led her mind to all the things she knew were unworthy: concerns about her job, the handsome man sitting four pews down who only attended semiregularly, the suddenly unbearable scratchiness of her turtleneck sweater against her chin. These thoughts flooded in, so she concentrated on having no thoughts, repeating the word "nothing" to herself over and over again until it echoed so loudly around her mind that it kept everything else from invading.

They waited on the pews. The sound of footsteps on tile and kneelers squeaking on ancient hinges filled the room. A single violin note pierced the air, and Teresa sat back in her seat. The church's band fluctuated, but usually it featured just a violinist or two, a pianist, and a handful of singers. Both the pianist and the first violin were gifted, and Teresa had heard people saying at Christmas Masses that they'd like to return more often just to hear the performances. They never did, but that didn't mean the sentiment was less true. She barely knew the musicians' names, but she still felt that she knew them intimately, or at least the part of them that came here to worship. She could hear it from the violinist as rosin blistered off his bow, the way he added variations each week to the same songs so that even if you'd fallen asleep during a sermon, you'd receive a holy commentary, still hear someone praising the Lord.

Luis and Theresa were part of the San Daniel community, but their granddaughter was not, at least not in any real sense. All of their friends were members, the friends who hadn't fallen by the wayside. When either of them was sick, they'd both stay home together, and rather than watching the service on television like a lot of Catholics, they waited for friends to come over afterward and give a detailed recap of the service, every week essentially the same as the last.

Teresa never told Rebecca or Mark that she attended church. Not that she would have lied about it if asked about it directly, but she was careful to keep it from coming up. She didn't know why, but her Sunday mornings at church felt intensely private and personal.

A woman stepped forward from the first row and spoke. "Good morning. My name is Angela, and I want to welcome all of you to the ten o'clock Mass at La Iglesia de San Daniel. If you can please take a moment to greet those around you."

Teresa and her grandmother turned to each other, gave half smiles, and said, "Nice to meet you. I'm T(h)eresa," which always made them both giggle. Laughter and crying were welcome here, maybe even encouraged. Only small talk seemed out of place. She shook hands with her grandfather, who offered a bit of a grin, and then she turned and greeted as many others in the congregation as she could reach. At other churches, the opening speaker would also ask the parish to silence their cellphones for the service, but here that wasn't necessary.

The Eucharist looked like a wheat wafer, it tasted like cardboard, and it smelled like stale crackers. But when the bread and wine of a Catholic Eucharist were consecrated, they remained the same physical substances they were a minute before yet were completely transformed into the body and blood of Christ. Both holy and base in the same manner that the faith's Messiah was both God and man. It was as simple as that, yet also what effectively separated Catholics from everyone else.

"Take this and eat this; this is my body," Jesus said, and transformed the bread, then and forever afterward, into a hunk of his flesh. "All of you drink of this; for this is my blood," he said, and the wine became the liquid of life that circulated through his veins and arteries. And it was only by eating the divine body itself, not just some loaf of bread, not a mere symbol, that a Catholic received the Eucharist.

Nobody was supposed to leave until the priest did, but even with a congregation this small, many exited early. Even Granny T squirmed in her seat as the priest finished the final prayer. Afterward, they stuck around in front of the church, blocking off the sidewalk and traffic, making conversation.

The congregants were ecstatic. A crotchety old man, usually incensed to leave his house, smiled and made jokes about his age. A single mother working two and a half jobs relaxed for a few moments and let her children buy donuts in the foyer. No one brought up the readings from Mass. No one commented on whether the priest's sermon had been insightful or just hot air. After Mass, it suddenly felt like there was so much to live for. Everyone was planning for the future, talking about picnics, dances, the new diet they'd suddenly decided to go on and were certain would work this time.

When Teresa exited San Daniel, it felt like she was leaving a movie theater at noon. Everything was more radiant than she remembered. The world suddenly looked far more real than it had before, two dimensions transforming into three. It made her want to pick up her grandmother and run off to a field with blooming wildflowers, some sort of hyperreality like characters had on television, because everything else felt unworthy.

When they arrived home, Teresa felt herself relax for a few hours. Work didn't seem so bad after all. Maybe they really were the long arm of justice, at least in a way. Maybe it didn't matter that she'd arrested one of her only friends, put her in prison and probably fucked up her life and her child's life, had done nothing to stop it from happening. Maybe that was somehow for the best. Everything happened for a reason, right?

She went to her room, opened Arcadia, pulled up *Pentadrome* (an easy-to-learn, difficult-to-master puzzler), took off her top, opened her channel, and began streaming so she could pay for the week's gas. It didn't matter that tomorrow she'd be in the squad car again, working with her partner to arrest supposed criminals for offenses she was increasingly uncertain they'd committed. The love she felt wash over her after a service left her really and truly free until the next morning, when guilt would crash over her so hard that once again she'd struggle to pull herself out of bed.

35

Gideon woke up early to follow her and maybe, possibly, get up the nerve to approach her. The possibility filled him with adrenaline, and he skipped his usual coffee, feeling like an explorer sent by Spain or Italy or whoever to lay claim to new land.

He sat in his rental car with the engine running and the air conditioner on full blast. In a way it was already better than any relationship he'd had before, since Gideon only needed to interact with her when he wanted to. He could close her stream at any moment without being asked why he wasn't giving her enough attention, why he wasn't listening to her, why he hadn't taken the trash out and picked up the groceries. But he couldn't help his desire to punch through that two-dimensional image and get at something more. She'd become his El Dorado, but he *knew* she was real.

Stalking was, he thought, an elegant word, evoking sleek cats on the hunt. But it had undergone such an ugly semantic shift that he tried to keep it from invading his mind while he watched her and what were clearly her grandparents enter an old, powder-blue sedan and turn south toward the river.

He straightened his sunglasses and shifted the car into drive. He dawdled through traffic and nearly ran into a car making a late left turn in front of him, distracted by what he could see through their back window. Even watching the back of her head filled him with excitement. He imagined the way she would speak to him, not as Giddy, as his family called him, or

GetItOn, the screenname that she knew him by (one of several he used in her channel), but simply Gideon, said in a sultry voice while fingering her long white stockings.

They parked in a small dirt lot behind an old, grubby church that looked ready to collapse. Since arriving in Albuquerque, he'd visited more than a dozen churches, all of them huge, monumental buildings. Yesterday, Hoffmantown had looked from the outside like a modern-day re-creation of the Colosseum.

Gideon parked as far away as he could without losing sight of them, scraping paint off his rented Hyundai on a cinder-block wall. He cursed at himself and hoped he didn't draw notice. The girl exited the car wearing a simple red dress that brought out her warm brown skin, making her positively glow even without makeup on. She looked even younger in person. Too young? What would that even mean?

She seemed pensive as she walked slowly up to the church with her grandparents. None of them said anything. Gideon realized he'd never seen her interact with another person before. Online she'd never even mentioned other people, let alone her family. He couldn't guess why she still lived with her grandparents, but it couldn't just be money—he'd probably tipped her enough on his own to pay for an apartment.

Gideon hesitated at the church's threshold. There was no chance of her recognizing him, of realizing that he'd spent hours staring at her on Arcadia. Should he pretend he was just another anonymous bystander, or let on that he knew her intimately, had spent hours studying every aspect of her body—at least, a version of her body transmitted across electromagnetic pulses?

He noticed other people waiting behind him, apologized, and headed in. He took a pew at the back of the church so that she couldn't see him, but then a tall man with long black hair flowing past his shoulders sat in front of him, obstructing his view. He moved, only to have another person get in his way. The goddamn church was too small. Finally he found a spot near the aisle where he could see her clearly. She was kneeling down next to her grandmother, who was mouthing words at a furious pace, but the girl just stared forward until a woman approached the podium and started speaking. She sat up, and Gideon lost himself in the raven-black swirl of her hair.

The first time he ever actively pursued anyone was in college. He'd met her in an intro English class he took as a freshman, when he was still undeclared and the course seemed like an easy way to kill a graduation requirement. It wasn't until after they had finished their first assigned book that he even noticed Sandra. She rarely spoke up and wore baggy sweaters to class. She seemed completely bored by the string of transcendentalists, misplaced idealists, and pure egoists that made up the early American canon. After their first class together, he asked Sandra out and, to his surprise, she accepted.

He felt the same uncertainty now, sitting at the back of this strangely unadorned cathedral. Why had he even come here? In all likelihood, she had a boyfriend, someone who grew up without the endless comforts of his own life and who would defend her honor with more than words. Gideon loved her, of that he felt certain, but enough to fight for her, to risk being maimed or murdered? Probably not.

Before this assignment, Gideon hadn't been in a church since his grandparents had dragged him there as a kid, but he still knew most of the words, and it was easy enough to follow the crowd as it sat, stood, and knelt. The warmth inside the building made him comfortable, cozy. He tuned out entirely during an epistle, enjoying the archaic words that had no bearing on his life.

He kept waiting for her to turn her head, even once, but she never did. By the end of the Mass she seemed like a part of the ceremony itself. She was what had been missing from all those other services he'd attended. She was worth worshipping.

He probably stood out in a small church like this, where everyone knew everyone else. If he stuck around afterward, he'd have to explain himself, who he was, why he was here. And while he liked the atmosphere, the songs, the whole communal vibe, he didn't plan on returning and didn't want to lie to a priest. He'd done enough of that the past few days.

36

BizWatch.com
Published online at 2:32 PM on August 17, 2037
New Marketing Opportunities Available in Meat and Produce
By Austin L. Murray

Once again those revolutionary minds at Anonymous Propaganda have come up with a whole new market for advertisement: on the very food we eat! This November, AP plans on rolling out its new line of fruits, vegetables, and even meats with advertisements embedded in the products without the use of any additives or dyes. Fortunately for us, the founder and creative director of AP, Eric McTeague, was able to take some time out of his busy schedule to talk with us about the new opportunities that produce marketing can offer.

"Businesses have always been looking for a more direct way of reaching consumers," McTeague says, "and what could be more direct or straightforward than advertising in the very things we need to survive? It doesn't take a genius to see that these new advertisement opportunities will be more direct and memorable to consumers than a mere thirty-second television spot or a video pre-roll."

Pricing for these "food spots" has yet to be finalized, but Anonymous Propaganda promises that as its program grows, there will even be opportunities for locally targeted spots and perhaps even pricing low enough to be affordable by local chains.

"I think people underestimate exactly how far GMO technology has developed during the past ten years since the FDA and its many speed bumps were removed," McTeague says. "While this sort of structural-level manipulation used to be the stuff of science fiction, now our simple patented process can put your product's logo onto the next season's crop with just a few weeks' preparation."

For McTeague and the rest of AP, it's a literal growth market out there, and according to him it's only the next logical step in what has already been a very fruitful relationship between the firm and Monsanto, whose mutual stock purchases had investors surprised not long ago. Although early detractors have claimed that no one would be willing to pay for an apple or pear with a logo on it when old-fashioned fruit is still around, McTeague says that advertised produce will move in the marketplace due to its rock-bottom, advertisement-subsidized prices.

During our interview with McTeague, we also managed to glean some exclusive information about the first round of sponsored products, which have been under heavy consideration. "Of course, we're not going to allow these ads to be sold carelessly. You won't see any firearms or cigarettes popping up on tomatoes anytime soon." So who are these first advertisers? "Unsurprisingly, we were able to get a great bid from Apple. Beyond that, I think you may be surprised where Coke and GM chose to put their advertising. But that's more than I should have said."

Consumer focus testing has been unanimously positive for these products, and while the pilot program will begin in the Southwest, expect a national rollout of Monsanto/AP's produce line by the end of the year.

Don't just sit there, join the conversation! No need to register to comment, just let us know what you think. Have fun, but please keep it clean and stay on topic—inappropriate remarks will be removed.

37

Six months ago, Devon had his eyes on UNM's honors program. But after the arrest, and the two nights he'd spent in jail crying and alone, he felt lucky to still be enrolled, and worried that might change soon if he ended up with a felony on his record when things finally shook out. He'd been told by his public defender that he should plead, take the rap not just for underage drinking and prostitution but also for giving the woman ketamine. He'd been told by the bursar that he wouldn't be kicked out of school with a felony (despite her apparent desire to do so), but his financial aid would disappear. If he wanted to stay, at that point he'd have to tell his mom. No one had told him it would be all okay in the end, probably because even he could see that was patently untrue. Still, that was all he wanted to hear, even if it was a lie.

He hadn't spoken with Autumn about any of it, hadn't even hinted that his time with Steve had gone awry, because he wasn't sure what to say. "Hey, mom, I was arrested for getting drunk and hiring a stripper and giving her drugs. Oh, and how was your day?" He'd tried to tell Gideon, but he hadn't been able to come right out with it. Maybe if he could email his family and then disappear from their lives entirely it would be okay, but to face them and explain just how big of a disappointment he was? No, it just wasn't fucking possible.

And truth be told, truth be completely fucking exposed and put right out there on the table, naked, where its harsh light was impossible to look away from, he hadn't even wanted to go to college in the first place. But high school was over, and what other options did he have that wouldn't mean even more wasted hours doing meaningless work; if he wasn't in school, Autumn would expect him to find some sort of job. The saving grace for UNM was that Steve and all of his friends seemed happy enough to take the path of least resistance through college, to float through classes while their real priorities were on their phones and tablets and souped-up gamer rigs back home. Devon couldn't just tell Autumn he'd prefer spending his life stabbing virtual vampires with stakes or planning raids for the motherfucking Baby Eaters. But he couldn't just stop and treat classes seriously, either.

Devon looked back to his friends to see what they'd been up to during the professor's strange presentation on the chemical composition of a human body, complete with a tank of water, a bag of coal, a box of chalk, and other props. Steve was screwing around on his laptop with some image in Photoshop and eyeing the goth girl toward the front of the room. When he noticed Devon looking at him, Steve rotated his laptop so Devon could see his drawing, a fairly realistic rendering of the girl down on her knees in a pentagram, worshipping/blowing a demon with Steve's face. Super juvenile, but it still made Devon stifle a laugh.

A line of drool trickled down Disney's chin. He'd propped up his head on his arm so that you'd have to struggle to notice that his eyes were closed. Pete took notes, largely an automatic function for him, but looking onto his paper, Devon saw that they were mostly about the class itself and the professor rather than the material.

- *Does Majewski really think people don't know he's bald, or does he require the toupee in order to get the courage to stand in front of us?*
- *Majewski's gotta be making like half of those numbers up.*
- *I'm pretty sure that if I don't get him out of here fast Steve's going to show his picture to that girl.*

His friends all seemed calm, happy even, and Devon just wished he could feel the same, that he could just be an ordinary student ready to half ass his way through a great four or (realistically) more years of college. But when he was offline, it was difficult to think of anything but the charges, the inevitability of it all coming at him with impossible speed. In an attempt to distract himself, he looked back down at the bottom of the lecture hall where Majewski was struggling to pick up the bag of coal.

"But these are just the building blocks," said the professor, "the utter basics of what we call life—a phenomenon that I want to stress has no fully encompassing definition, no one aspect that religion or philosophy or even science can agree upon. It's the most important thing in the world to us, yet no one has figured out what it really is. For your homework assignment, I would like each of you to simply consider the absolutely extraordinary fact that if you dunked this bag of coal into the water in precisely the right way on a molecular level, you could come out with something alive. Something that thinks, feels, and loves just the way you do, with hopes and dreams and consciousness, something with a capacity to grow or reproduce. Or die."

Majewski unceremoniously dunked the bag of coal into the fish tank, making a splash large enough to wake Disney and dampen several students in the front row.

"More likely, though, you'll just end up with a tank full of soggy coal."

38

From: Gideon Reyes <gideon.reyes@anonprop.com>
To: Eric McTeague <eric@anonprop.com>
Date: October 14, 2037 3:07 AM
Subject: Quick update

Hey Eric,

Your secretary said you were busy doing god knows what for the next few days and were unable to talk, so I just thought I'd send you a quick email update on how the project's coming along. Tell me if you want to talk about things on the phone or chat online next week.

I've come across an initial snag as far as potential candidates are concerned that I think may warrant a change in tactics. Most of my time so far has been spent meeting with local parishioners and some of the religious leaders, trying to suss out potentials and generally scouting out what the local attitude is towards this sort of thing. My feeling is that if we want this to be a success, we don't need to work at getting the big guys behind it (we know that we can count on their support), we need to make sure that we're delivering a product that the plebes are happy with. One of the things I learned when working on the Gravedigger project, was that if you're in with Citadel, Cox, Infiniti, et al. you can manufacture a single. But if you want to sell an album and a tour and a lifestyle and all the rest, you need content that speaks to the masses. That goes doubly on this one since we/our clients want to stay completely invisible, so we need the appearance of a grass-roots movement. Or at least something grassroots-adjacent.

Unfortunately, most of the priests I've spoken with and the more devout (or, so far as I could ascertain, seemingly devout) churchgoers were a little incensed by the idea of anyone representing the church at large. The word "sacrilege" is a bit toothless these days, but that's definitely the vibe I was getting. Megachurchers didn't seem to mind nearly as much, and one preacher seemed to think that any nominee other than himself would be an insult, but you could smell the sleaze reeking off him from a mile away. And just in case you're worrying, let me stress that I didn't come out and tell them what we're considering, I just asked questions about leadership in the church, nothing about becoming our miracle man.

Of course, none of these setbacks means that we can't make this happen, only that it might not be as simple an affair as we'd hoped. A couple things we might want to consider:

As you pointed out, Gravedigger's virtual approach won't work here for obvious reasons. However, if this plan is long-term, rather than something the churches want us to crank out by the end of the year, we could take the slow route and begin raising a child. There is some precedent in this, and all we'd need to do is create a puppet corporation that would have ownership (guardianship). I know the country's still split on corporate adoption, but it would only make it more compelling if the kid came from that background. Spin it as them being raised by an evil, soulless corporate environment only to reject it and turn toward Jesus, leading the Christians to new levels of righteousness, etc. Or however else we want to play it.

Should this plan be deemed too slow, another way to choose our person would be to up the spectacle. I'm sure you're familiar with the "reality" competition formats used for finding pop stars, basketball players, and CEOs. There's no reason that can't work here, too, we just need to figure out the events, points system, etc. and rig the person we want to win. After that, we just make sure that any skeletons that may lurk in the closet stay put. The advantage this route has is that even our initial search for contestants would receive a great deal of media coverage, and I'm willing to bet the show could bring in some killer ratings. Plus, by doing it as a program on national television (simulcast in Arcadia, of course), we'd be starting our spokesperson off with an initial fan base of millions.

I'm not saying that these are the only routes we could take, but at the moment they both seem like the most promising ways of doing this. Tell me if you've got any other avenues you want to pursue. For the moment I'm going to continue with research until you want to move on to the next step. I still really need a timeline from you, though, before I start putting together anything like a full-on proposal.

Oh, and I'm going to stick around here in NM for a while, unless you've got any objections. It's been nice catching up with family and friends, and I feel like you get a real "heartland" point of view here that would be impossible to find at the coasts.

-Gideon

From: Eric McTeague <eric@anonprop.com>
To: Gideon Reyes <gideon.reyes@anonprop.com>
Date: October 14, 2037 8:44 AM
Subject: RE: Quick update

Sounds like you're doing some good work down there, so don't worry about hurrying back. I can practically hear the paradigms shattering!

I want to say upfront that corporately sponsored parentage is one of those things we've tried to stay away from ever since the PepsiKid fiasco. I see what you were thinking, but it's not worth the bad publicity. Also, it's surprisingly expensive, as anything with children usually is. Glad as fuck I had my wife's tubes tied, and I'd rather not spend time babysitting one unless a client absolutely insists.

That being said, I like your idea of keeping an adoptee away from visibility until a much later time. I don't think Cola would've killed himself, at least not in such a messy, visible way, if they hadn't made his entire life into a string of commercials. It might be tricky, but one of our other clients might find this idea useful, and from what I hear, they're much less averse to long-term planning. Unfortunately for Prophet, most of these religious people seem a bit shortsighted and really want some immediate, concrete results.

That leaves us with your second idea, which I prefer anyhow because, as you mention, it has built-in publicity. I think we can safely assume that Fox would be willing to air the show (and the rest of News Corp would cover it as if the whole thing were news), and I think it could pick up some easy traction from there. What I particularly like about this is that the kind of people who watch these shows are the same demographic we're looking at to give us support for the Prophet! At least, I believe so. I'll have to ask the research boys how much overlap there really is between reality TV audiences and red-state Bible thumpers. I don't expect the NYT or any other elitist rag to get behind what we're doing, but if we can show that the masses really go for this sort of thing, then I think we can move into the next stage of research.

I haven't sent you a timetable yet because I don't have anything definite from the client. Still, I would like to have something to show them in three weeks' time. Broad strokes. We don't expect you to have any figures, just want to give them the overall game plan. After they approve the proposal, we'll start getting serious about dates. Don't be afraid to think really big. That's what we're best at, and the client's got some pretty deep pockets. Leave subtlety to the other firms, ha-ha!

Oh, and if you see any of those corporately sponsored foods out there, don't eat them. All of the products in the pilot program were supposed to have been recalled due to some unforeseen problems, but it looks like a few of them were purchased before anyone noticed. I'm sure you weren't enticed by saving a few bucks, but better safe than sorry!

-E

39

Autumn chose the first one entirely by aesthetics. The toned muscles in his shirtless profile picture, the expensive haircut, the rakish smile that suggested he was looking for a good time and nothing more. If she hadn't done her research, she would've assumed he was a spambot, a lure to trick fifty-year-old women into giving up their credit card and Social Security numbers. But he was real and, as she suspected, just looking for a quick fuck. He was perfect.

They spent the weekend in a motel on Central, one of many that still advertised "Color TV" in neon but had added to this a worn sign saying "Free WiFi" underneath. Afterward, she never saw him again. They didn't even exchange phone numbers or email addresses. It hadn't been particularly good—of course not—but it was still what she'd wanted.

The second was less pretty. He looked like a normal, well-dressed thirtysomething middle manager. He paid for dinner and drinks and opened his car door for her before driving them to a house in the North Valley. They fucked, and he tried to get her to stay over, but instead she took an Uber home and wondered why these men seemed as bad at the whole affair as the teenagers she'd been with in high school, or her husband after them.

There was the redhead with the red Corvette and the red cardigan, who seemed unaware of his personal color scheme but was at least legitimately good in bed. There was the man who wore a tuxedo to dinner and seemed to think he was James Bond, though in fact he made a living managing the Chili's on Menaul and Louisiana. The man who insisted on going down on her even though he wasn't any good at it, and the man who tried to get her to go down on him by pushing her head so hard she thought he'd break her neck. The sixtysomething man who looked nothing like his fortysomething photo and might have had early (or perhaps normal) onset dementia. Three men in a row who seemed uncertain how to put a condom on, even though they were all at least thirty-five years old (and one nearly as old as she was), and a guy who tried to slip it off during sex, prompting her to walk out on him. Two of the men she was with told the same anecdote, literally word for word, like they were reading off cue cards, and one seemed to think that buying her dinner entitled him to anal sex, which—no.

Most were unmemorable, either in bed or in person. Dull, obvious, prototypical men. It took her only half a year running the gauntlet of their slight, meaningless differences to wonder why she'd been interested in reentering the dating pool in the first place.

In taking an early retirement, Autumn hadn't really considered what she would fill her time with. She'd promised herself not to micromanage her children's lives, never to become more involved than they wished. This was the same policy she'd held to since they'd hit puberty, and while she was ready to offer any and all support they might desire, they rarely seemed to want any. Now her oldest son was living in New York with a second wife he probably couldn't hang on to for much longer, and her daughter was going broke with some con-man artist, pretending she had no cell reception. Even Devon either disappeared for entire weekends or stayed locked in his bedroom. Something had changed him, but he wasn't willing to say what. She missed when they were all little and dependent and willing to talk.

But what else was there, now that she had all the time and money she could hope for? Autumn's interest in what was streaming on Arcadia lasted for less than a weekend, and knitting was so boring it made televised baseball look exciting by comparison. She'd taken up gourmet cooking for one, and while the results were certainly enjoyable, she found the overall process almost as dull as the knitting. She'd lived for her work and her children, and now what was left?

Fortunately, she liked sex. Even, it turned out, bad sex, which was key, because very rarely was any other kind to be found. Even after half a bottle of red wine, she couldn't turn off the part of herself that was fully cognizant of the mechanical nature of these physical sensations. She could practically feel the hormones flooding her mind with desire. But if her head was still in charge, at least it was working in concert with her body for a change. Even the most pedestrian of men brought something to the table, another smell in his hair, another taste from his kiss, another playing field down below. It was fun, and that was enough.

Sometimes, when she was headed home afterward, she'd imagine what the AdMRI machine might show her if it could get a reading during those evenings out—the electrical impulses sent from her nerves, the map of her feelings—so she could replicate them without all the messiness of an awkward ride in a stranger's old Hyundai in the middle of the night. But that wasn't her project anymore. She'd sold it, ironically enough, to the same man who had helped her discover her sexual capacity in the first place, so many years ago. And in exchange she'd ended up with this new lifestyle that was, in its own way, just as disappointing and frustrating as academia or publishing—or marriage.

The interchangeable men became dull after a few months, and masturbation just wasn't the same. That essential spark that sometimes ignited between two people was so utterly lacking that she wondered whether it was just a Hollywood construction. But it had happened to her before, so it must be real, even if it was nothing more than a pattern of electrons snapping in her brain. She wanted that pattern again. After so many misfires, she'd begun suspecting that maybe the problem wasn't her, but the algorithm itself. She was using Arcadia's matchmaking program, but how good could that program be, designed on a system created by a man whose understanding of romance was flawed to the point of nonexistence?

She couldn't access Arcadia's matchmaking algorithms directly, but she did have access to profile information, her own experiences, and large-scale information dumps that other dissatisfied users had posted. She spent days combing through spreadsheets of data about these people, data fields about creativity, happiness, intelligence, and other variables. Metrics were the only way for computers to understand the world, even when it came to something as ineffable as human personalities. Over time, she arrived at a theory about why the program didn't work, perhaps fundamentally could not work. To be matched up by Arcadia profiles was to pay for the service, through points or dollars or thousands of ad clicks. And the only way for the program to make money was for people to keep using it. Matches were intentionally bad, planned for obsolescence. The point of Arcadia wasn't to set you up and make you happy. It was profit.

So Autumn created her own program. Sifting through profiles, she made the decisions she assumed Arcadia wouldn't. This took time, but time was something she had now, and the work was more interesting than the dating had been. She hadn't initially thought to consider a variable for gender, and fixing this error took just a matter of minutes, with new fields for gender and sexual orientation. After correcting this oversight and running the program on herself, her output was a list almost exclusively filled by women.

Autumn's first date with a woman was almost as disastrous as some of the ones she'd had with men. Lacey was curt and demanding, though physically attractive in an "airbrushed for daytime talk shows" sort of way. She seemed to have absolutely no interest in anyone but herself. They met at the downtown Garcia's for lunch. Lacey drank three margaritas and had difficulty staying in her chair. She wanted to drive Autumn home—whose home, she hadn't specified—but when she stumbled into the restroom, Autumn slipped out the front door.

Instead of giving up, she simply adjusted her program and tried it again. She was less interested in the next date, though, than in finding out whether her program was working correctly. Still, her expectations for Subject #2, Brianna, were low.

They met at a basement bar in Nob Hill. The room was dark, with wood paneling along the walls and miniature tables. Slightly too-loud music played in the background, and the bartender was dressed like the place was a speakeasy, shaking his drinks to make everyone aware that he was expending maximum effort. It was a younger crowd than anywhere else she'd been on these dates, and she felt acutely out of place.

Autumn barely knew what she was looking for, had only glanced at this woman's photo moments before heading out. On the far side of the bar, a waving hand led her to a table where a small woman with short brown hair was quizzically half smiling at her. Autumn approached the table, introduced herself, and sat down.

"I was worried I wouldn't be able to see you," said Brianna. She laughed nervously. "It's so dark in here."

"I'm glad you did," said Autumn, unsure what else to say.

Brianna's hair was longer on one side than the other, with bangs covering her left eye, and Autumn wanted to push them away from her face to get a better look but also liked the mysterious air they gave off. Brianna seemed uncomfortable, unsettled by the strange social dance she was participating in. It was refreshing. Subject #2 was better than she'd hoped. Autumn could feel her posture and facial expression changing, even as she tried to remain impassive.

They sat in silence for long seconds. Autumn found Brianna's shyness cute. The men she'd been with always filled the silence. That was what dating was, she'd relearned, an attempt at waiting patiently until the other party gave in and took you back to their apartment or a hotel room. No one approached the table, and Autumn searched for something to look at besides the woman sitting across from her. Was she supposed to make eye contact? Why did she suddenly care so much?

"God," said Brianna. "I feel so old here."

Autumn laughed. Brianna looked to be in her midthirties. "You feel old? I feel ancient. I remember when this nonsense was cool twenty-five years ago, and I hated it then. All I could think about when I first walked down here was how out of place I am."

"Right? You know, I don't know that anyone's coming to serve us. Why don't we just leave?"

Autumn agreed, and as the overloud music receded behind them, Autumn wondered whether the date was over.

"To be honest, I'm not even hungry," said Brianna. "I get so nervous about this sort of thing that I just . . . god, I shouldn't be saying this."

"No, it's fine. Let's do something else then. Let's just walk. And talk."

"That sounds much better," said Brianna, half smiling again. Autumn desperately wanted to see her smile fully.

The early-evening sunlight was only now beginning to tuck into the West Mesa along the horizon. They walked toward it. Cars and motorcycles sped past them, bus fumes spraying and then dissipating invisibly—unnoticeable but ever present. They laughed at window displays and traded comments about the people they passed.

By the time they made it back to the bar where they'd first met, it was dark and the neighborhood was alive with drunken students and people who wished they were drunken students. Autumn drove them to a restaurant on the other side of town. Over sushi she learned that Brianna was a computer programmer—because of course she was—but also an activist, at least online. "Kind of a white-hat hacker," Brianna said. "I guess."

Autumn shared that she had three children, but avoided bringing up Juan Diego or Arcadia, though she figured Brianna probably knew who her famous ex was. They talked about recent movies and news, the conversation flowing easily.

When they finished eating, it was almost eleven. They'd been together for four hours without so much as holding hands. Autumn drove Brianna back to her parking space. They hadn't exchanged numbers, and it had become increasingly evident that they weren't going to sleep together. But as Brianna stepped out of the car, Autumn got out, too.

"I don't . . . my friends made me do this," Brianna admitted. "Honestly, I haven't dated in a long time. But it's been fun."

"I haven't, umm . . . me neither," said Autumn. She hadn't dated, she'd hooked up. Until tonight, she hadn't thought there was a difference.

"That's nice," said Brianna, brushing her bangs out of her face. "Means less pressure on me, because you don't know what you're doing, either."

"Ha, that's right. For all you know, tonight's been great. An experienced dater would've left me back at the restaurant."

"Or maybe tonight just really has been great."

"Or that." They waited in silence outside of Brianna's car. Autumn wondered what she was supposed to do to keep the night from ending. Or whether she wanted to let it end. "Can I, can we do this again?"

The next Friday they went to a movie together. The following Wednesday they met for dinner. A month later, Autumn wondered how she'd ever lived without Brianna.

40

Gideon woke up sweating from the burning rays of light on his forehead, even while cool air streamed down from a vent in the roof. The combination of hot and cold made him feel slightly nauseated. He had forgotten how bright the sun was in the late afternoon. He'd been living in Ralphie's backhouse for weeks—why hadn't he purchased a blackout curtain yet and hung it over the window? He felt betrayed by his body for reminding him how uncomfortable the world could be while awake. If possible, he would've drifted back asleep. Maybe it was a sign he should find a hotel?

Gideon lifted his laptop from the ground and opened it. Teresa wasn't online, and he had no new messages. He closed the laptop, walked to the other side of the house, and took a shower, his nausea dissipating with the caress of warm water cascading from his body and into the drain. He shaved for the first time in weeks, thinking that he'd better get a haircut soon, too. He'd always neglected his grooming, but if he was going to ask Teresa out, he needed to start things off right. She'd seemed to respond well to his casual hints about knowing Gravedigger, so it was only a matter of time.

Ralphie still wasn't awake when Gideon exited the bathroom, so Gideon left and headed to his car. Hungry, he drove down to Central and headed to the university campus, where he parked beneath the fading yellow roof of the Frontier, one of the few parts of the city that never seemed to change. He had eaten here at least once a day since arriving back in Albuquerque.

Gideon walked through the restaurant's back door and made his way to the ordering line, which was backed up all the way to the building's second room. If UNM was the city's brain, then the Frontier was its gut. And while not everyone gave a shit about science and art and higher education, everyone loved cheap, tasty food, so the restaurant was about the most diverse destination in the city. He stood behind a graying university professor and in front of a fortysomething Chicana with green, blue, and red hair, at least five pounds of metal piercings hanging from her face.

After five minutes of waiting, he ordered a breakfast burrito, smothering it with green chile before finding a place to sit. The table he found was across from a pack of middle school kids shoving and flirting and pouring salt, pepper, and sugar all over their table. The Frontier was always loud, sometimes excruciatingly so, and the background ambience of a hundred conversations was just what he needed to keep his mind from obsessing about her. He couldn't allow himself to get nervous.

On the wall in front of him, John Wayne's gigantic, unfeeling eyes looked down at him. Without thinking about it, he'd ended up in the John Wayne room. Other rooms in the Frontier were sprinkled with Wayne, too, but here they coated everything like a cowboy wallpaper. No one knew why the owners had this obsession, whether it was a benign predilection or a political statement or what. They were known to be hard right-wingers who considered the Frontier a profitable investment and nothing more, a couple who'd simply ascertained that it was easier to make money from the hippies and burnouts and tenured professors that they hated than to discourage their presence. Some said that John Wayne's visage was meant to send a message to all of the gutterpunks and hobos who visited, a paternal white male presence to remind everyone who'd really claimed the southwestern frontier. When asked by the *Alibi*, the owners just said, "We thought they looked all right."

Gideon felt slightly traitorous. Years ago Holly painted a portrait of Wayne in the hope of having it placed on the establishment's wall, one of her many failed schemes to get her work noticed. Everything that adorned the Frontier was a gift, but the proprietors' choices as to what to keep seemed random. The Wayne portraits were, almost without exception, terrible, and most other pieces in the restaurant were abstract or Santa Fe–style southwestern cliché. Every now and then a new one would go up or an old one would get taken down (to be destroyed? taken to a home collection?), but there was never any explanation, let alone fanfare. Most clients never noticed the change.

The manager arranged for Holly to meet with the owners during one of their regular visits, but after staring at her painting for just a few seconds, they rejected it. Holly channeled her disappointment into a new piece, *Tyranny #1*, which featured her John Wayne standing in the same triumphant pose as in her original painting, but over a pair of corpses, Native American and Hispanic, ashes dropping from his cigar onto the forehead of a young girl. Autumn had called it childish and too blunt, to which Holly responded, "That's the whole fucking point."

Gideon tried to ignore the painted, artificial eyes while lingering on the burrito, eating it as slowly as he could manage, scooping up every last piece of green chile with his fork. As he picked up his tray to leave, he felt a hand on his shoulder and looked up to see a man with a slightly wrinkled face and wearing an ill-fitting brown suit. He immediately recognized his father. His tray hit the floor, though he didn't even register that he'd dropped it. "Oh. Hi, dad."

"Got a second?"

"Uhh, yeah, sure. Just let me . . . just let me clean this up."

"That's not your job," said Juan Diego with a frown. He was holding his own tray with one hand. "Let's move to another room. Someone else will deal with that."

"Sure, I guess," said Gideon. He followed his dad to another room and ignored the eyes of everyone who'd seen him drop the tray. They sat in the far corner. A couple sat several tables away, so close together that Gideon assumed they had their hands in each other's pants.

"Holly told me you two talked," said Gideon.

"Did she say anything else?"

"Not really. She said something about you wanting her to work for you, and that she declined."

"That sounds about right."

"She also said you disappeared because of some sort of midlife crisis. She was pretty unhappy about the whole thing. I don't know what exactly you intended, but I don't think it helped. At least, I haven't been able to get ahold of her since we talked about it."

Juan Diego slowly cut into a half order of enchiladas, then drank from a large orange juice as if this were all normal. When Gideon was young, they rarely ate out, but when they did, the Frontier was the perfect place for the Reyes family, given both their budget and the fact that a few more screaming children made no difference to the atmosphere. Gideon didn't pick up a taste for spicy food until he was older, so the first time they ate at the Frontier, the only thing he ordered was orange juice. It was the greatest taste he'd ever experienced (though purportedly fresh, everyone said they sweetened it with heaps of sugar). After that, whenever his dad visited the diner, he always brought an orange juice home for his son Giddy. He couldn't tell whether Juan Diego was trying to remind him.

"That's not because of me."

"Are you sure? Because she may act tough, but she's not as hard as she'd like you to think." Even when she was in elementary school, Holly had always gotten in trouble for talking back to teachers. Later, some schoolmates told Gideon they thought his sister was a stuck-up bitch, but he'd known that they were just unhappy that she didn't pay any attention to them. She was content with herself, and that tended to piss people off. "Devon was too young for you to . . . I don't expect us to find out how it's affected him until twenty years from now, when he's in therapy five days or a week or blown up a bus full of children. But with Holly, that cut deep."

"I told her I'm sorry," said Juan Diego. He took another bite and a swig of orange juice. "What else can I say? I'm here saying it to you, too."

"Dad, I can't just . . . I know you feel that way now, but . . . so what? What does that even mean?"

"It means I wish I hadn't hurt you. Do I wish I hadn't left? No. It was important, and I think it's paid off, but I do wish there hadn't been all that collateral damage."

"That's one half-assed apology."

"You said that Holly told you about my . . . choice."

"She did."

"I'm old, son. I may not look it, but I am." He looked extremely old—the same man, for sure, but wrinkled, with deep circles around his eyes and a receding hairline. Juan Diego had always looked youthful to Gideon before, always seemed ready to bound to the computer with a new idea, which he'd toil on for the next ten hours with only a pot of coffee to fuel him. Sitting across from Gideon, looking tired in his brown suit like a sad sidewalk preacher, was the same withered man who'd waited at his doorstep months earlier. "I'm not going to last much longer. Neither, I should add, is anyone else."

Gideon watched as his father finished the enchiladas with the same single-minded intensity as he did everything else. "I don't know what I'm supposed to say here. I mean, are you in a doomsday cult now? Is that it? Wearing your 'the end is nigh' suit? Have you found Jesus or something?"

"Of course not, son, don't be stupid," said Juan Diego. He seemed angry. Growing up he'd always been mellow, largely disconnected from their lives. If the Reyes children needed disciplining, he suddenly had a work project crop up, even in the middle of the night. "This world is dangerous, as I told your sister. You need to be aware of certain things.

I would've thought you'd know that, working for who you do. Speaking of which, I also have an offer for you. A job. Doing something you used to love, not this manipulative, Big Brother bullshit."

"How much do you know about my job?" Probably everything. It was well known within AP that the company had links with EA. They were both part of some complicated corporate mess he didn't fully understand. And even if he wasn't being informed, it wasn't like Juan Diego had ever been one to give a shit about the ethics and legalities of hacking.

"Enough. You used to be truly creative, son. Your sister doesn't care to use her gifts for money. She may be perfectly happy making paintings that no one will see until she's buried in the ground, but you seem uninterested in using those gifts at all. I don't think that's really you, though."

"I don't need handouts. Or nepotism."

"You haven't even heard what it is. I'm asking you to come help me beta test Arcadia 2.0. You used to love doing that when you were a kid, and you were pretty damn good at it. I want you with me on this project."

"I'm not ten anymore. So no, I'm not interested."

"Is this about the girl?"

"What girl?"

"Does it even matter? What you're feeling isn't love. You've been married more times than I have."

"After all you did, you're going to berate *me*?"

"Again, I'm sorry. But I'm just trying to be honest with you. I'd like to get your trust back. Let me ask you this: Why weren't you happy with either of your wives? They were perfectly fine women, I'm sure, or you wouldn't have married them—no one put a shotgun to your back."

"How would you know? I distinctly remember your absence at my wedding, it got drunk on the punch and made a fool of itself." He hadn't even invited his father because he wouldn't have known where to send the invitation. He'd kind of hoped that Juan Diego would show up unexpectedly, and when that hadn't happened it was like being abandoned a second and then third time.

"No, I wasn't there." Juan Diego seemed truly contrite. Gideon felt the anger seeping out of himself and didn't like it.

"So I fucked shit up. Whatever."

"I know the feeling. But if you knew they were pretty great, why weren't you happy?"

"I don't know. It just wasn't . . . I was happy for a while, then eventually I wasn't. I can't explain my feelings, they just happened."

"That's called being human. You adjust to a situation and before long you find a new equilibrium. That's just how these heads of ours work. It's like if you were a corporation. If you make a five percent profit this year, you can't just have a five percent profit next year. Two years in a row of five percent profits is the same as zero percent growth. The reason why a company cheats, breaks laws, finds loopholes, is that constant growth is an untenable bitch. The same with a person. You can't become more in love every year, it doesn't work like that. But when we're not growing, we're dying."

"Is that why you left? We weren't paying enough dividends?"

"I was perfectly happy with all of you, but I wanted more. I don't work for EA, I make them work for me. You remember our house on Calle del Monte, how poor we were? You remember shopping for beans and rice, big bags of generic cereal that never quite tasted the way they were supposed to? You must remember that leak in the roof of Devon's room that took six months to fix because we didn't have the money for repairs? I learned that you beat the system the same way the system beats everyone else: you take advantage of it, ruthlessly and methodically."

"Whatever. I don't want the job, and I really don't want this family history lesson. Dad, it was great seeing you, but I'm headed out." Gideon stood up to leave.

"Just listen for five more damn minutes. This decaying lump of flesh is why we're always searching for more, it's why I left you all," said Juan Diego, gesturing at his body. "But I've sorted it out, I think. With this project. But I want your help."

"So you've found the Good News, only it's just another goddamn game? Really, dad, this is nuts. I get it, you're dying, mortality, wah wah wah. It's sad. But I don't have time for this."

"I'm not nuts. You don't have to decide right now."

"Dad, there's no decision. You can't just pretend I'm ten, helping you with your chintzy little games. You cut us off from your life, and we can't go back."

"This isn't about me, it's so much bigger."

"It is *clearly* about you. It's always about you, about the way you left the family, about the way some scars never heal."

"They can if you take the next step, if you're willing to trust in the future. We can create organs in labs, skin grafts from your very DNA to replace whatever's been damaged."

"God, dad, maybe get help. But leave me alone."

"Fine, I'm not going to force you. But do me a favor and leave the city. As soon as you can, I want you to get out of here. Go back east, or head to California. I told you, there are danger—"

"Good-bye, dad." Gideon walked toward the Frontier's back door, where an antenna bounced a microwave beam of light onto his body that reflected at a different wavelength into a sensor and commanded the door to open, which it did with a pleasant whoosh. From there he walked to his car without looking back.

41

Devon awoke and shielded his eyes from the light passing through the blinds. The sun was setting, a dim redness in the west that looked like a smear over the horizon, muddying the tops of houses. He stayed in bed until it was clear his body wasn't going to let him fall back asleep, then struggled through dressing himself. Twenty minutes after waking up, Devon wandered outside and checked the mail: junk for Steve, junk for Billiam, junk for someone named Rodrigo Barela, and State Attorney's Office for Devon.

His bowels suddenly felt like they were about to explode, so he rushed back inside, tossing the junk onto an already cluttered coffee table on his way to the bathroom. While waiting for his body to feel better, Devon glanced in the bathroom mirror and noticed his shirt was on inside out. And backward. With a groan he took it off and fixed it, feeling tired of everything in the goddamn world.

Finally returning to his room, Devon placed the letter on his desk, where it sat unopened next to three empty Red Bull cans and a mostly eaten bag of Flamin' Hot Cheetos. He opened up a list of his Arcadia games. The clan had spent the last week playing a military shooter called *Rapture*, a standard post-apocalyptic team game about defending America with all the usual jingoistic bullshit that always entailed, but he didn't want to play anything that required interacting with other humans. There were more than twelve hundred titles in his library, but nothing sounded remotely fun. He filtered the list so it only showed his dad's old indie titles—*You Only Get One Life (Unless You Find the 1up)*, *Asymptotic!*—and began playing through them sequentially. That his dad actually made these, with their strange titles and even stranger takes on traditional game tropes and vocabulary, seemed even crazier now than when he'd been growing up. At Devon's age, Juan Diego had known what he wanted to do in life, and some of the early games were from when Juan Diego was in college or earlier. Some had literally been knocked together in his parents' garage, writing his own engine in assembly language and then self-publishing online. That drive seemed unfathomable to Devon. None of the games were particularly polished, and almost all were dated, but he'd played through them so many times that it didn't matter. They allowed him to turn off his brain and concentrate on the almost abstract patterns of light on the screen, on the pulsating language of circular stimuli that was so entrancing because of its sheer meaninglessness. No games understood the simple pleasure of repeating X activity to achieve Y result as well as his dad's. Devon played until long after sunlight began creeping back into his bedroom again.

He took a break when his right wrist started aching from what he feared might be a steadily developing carpal tunnel syndrome. Devon ripped open the envelope, and while he didn't understand its enclosed letter's full implications, the phrases "grand jury indictment" and "formal arraignment" said enough. At the bottom of the page was a court date: October 26, the Monday following UNM's fall break. He put the letter back on his desk, not knowing what to do next. Onscreen his avatar wore a fashionable suit and sat on the couch of his immaculate estate doing nothing, waiting for input. The figure had the same nondescript facial expression as ever, a cold smile coupled with eyes that blinked with irregular frequency, but right now it looked lonely to him. Maybe he should change the expression, make the avatar look genuinely happy, excited even. Would that be weird? Or write a mod that made him breathe? The only sounds in the house were his own breathing and the whirring of his computer's fan, and the quiet was oppressive. For once Devon wanted to see people, needed to hear their voices. He needed some last hurrah before it was too late. Devon messaged the entire clan, proposing a pisser for the four-day fall break.

A pisser was a gaming marathon: no one got up or stopped playing, even to pee. Like a lot of these sorts of gamer trends, pissers were supposed to have originated in Japan but had never been documented there. The media just kinda assumed that crazy shit like that must come from there or Korea and rarely noticed that most really extreme ideas originated in the good old US of A.

"Except we have a bathroom in the house, so don't be that stupid," Devon wrote on the clan's event announcement.

Devon went back to sleep, and by the time he woke up he'd received enthusiastic responses from the rest of the Baby Eaters. Disney and Pete said they'd stop by the house, Jeff planned on partaking from Boston, and other clan members they'd never met physically would be playing from their own houses and apartments around the world.

With the news that everyone was interested, Devon wasted almost no time thinking about the inevitable. During one of his weekly trips home to do laundry, he snuck out an old suit that, though wrinkled, seemed like it would be acceptable for court. That was the only preparation he could bring himself to make.

He feared burning out on gaming before the pisser even began, so he needed to find ways of occupying himself until then. He started attending every class, even the biology section at nine thirty in the morning. School barely sucked up any of his time, though, so Devon began cleaning the house, which had been steadily transforming into a miniature Superfund site ever since they moved in.

Besides the half-assed routine he went through once or twice a year for his mom, Devon had never cleaned much of anything before, so he made up the process as he went along. He filled the dishwasher with a third of their pile of dirty dishes (they'd long since begun using paper plates and plastic utensils), only to learn, upon turning it on, that its seal was broken, and the device shot hot, soapy water all around the kitchen. He scrubbed the floor with rags, and by the end of the evening he'd finally finished, but now the stains on the cabinets and everything else were far too noticeable. He stuck the rags in the washing machine and collapsed into bed.

Two hours later he was awakened by the sounds of Billiam and Steve playing a shooter in the living room, and he dearly wanted to join them, but he stayed in bed and fell back asleep, feeling as he did that this should count for something, should earn him some karmic goodwill from the universe. A Get Out of Jail Free card, perhaps.

When Devon wandered back to the kitchen the next morning, cheese- and sauce-encrusted plates from the night before sat atop the clean ones he'd left drying. They'd long ago adopted a policy of letting spills and foods dropped go uncleaned, but still, the guys had to have seen what he was doing. As he spent the next day finishing the kitchen, cleaning the sink itself, the cabinets, the washer and dryer in the far corner, he couldn't help but feel like this disrespect had been intentional.

The mess wasn't a big deal, but it was the same with the drugs. Before the tunnels the only syringes Devon had seen were in a doctor's office, yet here he was, one step away from a felony, while his friend who'd brought them was throwing his popcorn kernels all over their—correction: Devon's—couch. The legal system was supposed to catch criminals, not bystanders. It was only a matter of time before the cops figured out what had happened and took Steve in, or Steve realized what was going on, made the sacrifice, and confessed. So Devon cleaned and waited, willing himself not to worry through sheer exhaustion; meanwhile, Steve's behavior underwent no change whatsoever.

A week after they'd moved in, the house's once-beautiful hardwood floors had become so scuffed that you could cut pictures into them with a knife and no one would notice. By Friday afternoon, they were waxed and gleamed in the sunlight, the whole house smelling like citrus and chemicals. Devon gathered the house's mismatched desks, tables, and chairs into a row in the living room and logged on to Arcadia. By the time Pete arrived early in the afternoon, Devon had already been playing *GMS 6.2* for several hours.

"You do this?" asked Pete, gesturing first to the floor, then to the whole room.

"Uhh, yeah," said Devon. "*GMS*?"

"Sure, whatever."

Around five o'clock, Billiam had wandered in from his bedroom, yawning and wearing only his boxers while he brushed his teeth. Soon Disney showed up with four eighteen-inch pizzas. He paused at the doorway and asked, "Can we still eat in here, or is there some sort of new 'don't shit the place up' policy?"

"Probably best to ask our new cleaning lady," said Billiam, nodding toward Devon and grabbing one of the pizzas.

"Hey, is Steve coming?" said Devon, trying to act nonchalant.

"I assume so," said Pete. "Doesn't he live here? Let's get in a few hours of *Undead Redemption*. God, I am so sick of *Rapture*."

"He's gone AWOL," said Devon. "Does anyone know what's up?"

"Nah," said Disney. The doorbell rang. "That's probably him."

No one made any motion to stand, so Devon opened the door to a large, thirtysomething man with thinning hair and a thick brown beard that went halfway down his chest. "Is this the Baby Eaters? The pisser?"

"Yeah. Umm . . . and you are?"

"I'm TeslaTank69."

"Oh wow, I . . . do you live in Albuquerque?" Devon had always imagined TeslaTank as a high school or college student like them.

"No, but I'm in Santa Fe, so I just thought I'd drive down." He looked expectantly at everyone in the room. "I mean, if it's okay."

"Hey, I'm Devon. Yeah sure, come in." They had always acted as if any member of the clan was welcome at their events, and posted their locations online, but no one had ever taken them up on it. Everyone greeted the man—his real name was Scott—then no one knew what else to say, so the group returned to gaming while Scott set up his computer.

Steve arrived shortly after midnight. Devon could smell the liquor on his breath, and he had a thirty rack of Coors Light in each hand. Without saying anything, Steve headed straight to the fridge and placed one of the cases inside. He ripped open the cardboard on the other case and tossed cans to everyone else in the room.

"I'm good," said Devon. "Remember last time?"

"So you got an MiP, big fucking deal," said Steve. He pointed at Scott. "And who's this guy?"

Scott spun around on his stool to offer Steve his hand. "I'm TeslaTank."

"Oh cool, cool." Steve headed toward Scott but stumbled, spilling his beer.

"Dude, clean that up," said Devon.

"Seriously? Like let me shake this guy's fucking hand first." He did so. "Hey man, I'm Steve. Glad you could come."

"Really? Just fucking do it, all right?" Here he was, ignoring Devon again.

"Chill out. Just give me a second."

"I can get it. It was kind of my fault," said Scott.

"You didn't spill the fucking beer," said Devon. "How is it your fault?"

"I don't mind, really."

"Nah man, I got it," said Steve. He grabbed paper towels from the kitchen and gave the floor a cursory wiping.

Devon put his headset back on and rejoined. They'd moved on to *Panopticon*, an asymmetrical team-based game in which a hoard of "terrorists" fought a handful of "government agents" who were outnumbered but had access to the other team's locations, voice chat, and even video streams. They played one map, but Devon couldn't stop thinking about the floor. While they waited for the matchmaking algorithm to run on a second map, Devon grabbed the cleaner and went over the spilled beer again.

Steve didn't even seem to notice, so Devon did his best not to care, either. This could be the last time he played with Steve, at least for a long while. He was determined not to let this petty business ruin the last really good time he might have left.

It wasn't hard. Hunched over his computer screen for thirty hours, twitch dexterity at the mouse and keyboard combining with the concentration required to memorize maps, strategies, and counterstrategies, six hundred milligrams of caffeine and three hundred grams of sugar in his stomach—Devon hardly felt like he was in his body. He was almost a part of the computer program, performing the perfect inputs for its outputs until distinguishing between the two sides of the equation became essentially impossible.

They half slept in shifts on their beds and sofas. Everyone else got so drunk they collapsed, but Devon chose his sleep intervals when he felt his abilities decreasing, crashing late Friday for just over five hours and again very late on Saturday night/Sunday morning. That second time, he'd found himself more than half-asleep yet still playing, lost in Arcadia, his screen's flashing lights blurring in front of him, the sounds on his headset speaking through his dreams.

When Devon woke up on Sunday, he could hear his friends' voices coming from the living room. He wore the same clothes he'd had on when the pisser began, and they smelled like he'd taken a hot bath in stagnant water. The sun was setting yet again out his back window, as if daytime had become just a series of fading light followed by endless evenings.

He stepped over his still-wrinkled suit, now lying on the floor with all his other clothes. The arraignment was closer now, and Steve still hadn't offered him an out. What fucking time was it, and how much longer did he have?

Devon wandered into the living room. Scott snored loudly on the couch, half-covered in an old skiing jacket. Pete, Billiam, and Disney sat at their computers. Billiam reclined in his chair with a keyboard on his lap and a saucepan full of chili on the table in front of him. Devon sat at his computer, moving his mouse to awaken it. He saw that it was almost 8:00 p.m. Fuck.

"Hey," said Pete. "We're just slaughtering some Swarm newbs, so it shouldn't be long if you want in next game. And Billiam's apparently doing his homework."

"Where's Steve?" asked Devon.

Billiam kept his headset on as he walked to the sink and soaked his chili pan. "I've been trying to get my reading done for English while we nuke some aliens. Listening to *Lear*, sort of. At least I think it's *Lear*."

"So no Steve? Seriously?"

"I'm testing this theory I saw online. Somebody on one of the boards was writing about this, like, I don't know, osmosis learning method. Okay, I'm in next game."

"According to this dipshit," said Disney, "he's hacking the brain. He's not even listening or paying any attention, he's just playing online with us. But somehow he's supposed to pick it all up even if he really spent all afternoon playing *Dystopic*."

"He's an idiot, that's all," said Pete. "And Steve is praying to the porcelain god."

"The fuck?" said Devon.

"It's scientifically based," said Billiam. "You know that old bullshit that you only use ten percent of your brain? That's categorically, like, empirically false. Just something idiots like to tell you as a motivational tactic. However, there is a limit to how much of what your brain's processing you can ever be consciously aware of."

"You sure about that?" said Devon.

"It's like you're building a computer from scratch. At the first level you're binary, right? On and off, life and death. And then above that there's machine language."

"No one fucking cares, I mean about Steve."

"Devon, chill out about Steve for a minute," said Disney. "What's your fucking deal with him lately?"

Devon heard the toilet flush. Steve entered the living room, beer in hand, deep bags beneath his eyes. "'Sup, sleeping beauty," he said. "You've returned to the land of the living. *Star Colonizer*?"

Devon desperately wanted to play, wanted the weekend to last forever, but he didn't have a choice. "Hey man, we need to talk," he said, forcing every syllable out.

"Just a sec," said Steve. He sat down at his computer and opted in to the next game, which began matchmaking.

Devon caught a whiff of Steve's breath, its acidic stink like fermented orange juice. "Seriously, dude," he said.

Steve gave Devon a nasty look. Devon didn't flinch. Steve made an exaggerated sigh, took off his headset, and stood up, almost half a foot taller than Devon and at least fifty pounds heavier. Steve took a drink of his beer and walked toward Devon's bedroom. Devon shrugged to everyone else, all either too engrossed in the game to care or pretending to be. He shut the door behind him, uncertain what to do next. Steve absentmindedly twirled the pop-top on his can.

"So I was wondering if . . ." Devon began.

Steve looked up but didn't seem particularly interested.

"God, why does this have to be so difficult?"

"Seriously, dude, I don't have the faintest idea what the fuck is going on," said Steve. "Wanna just spit it out so we can get back to the pisser?"

"It's just . . . the needles."

"Needles?"

"From down in the tunnels."

"Okay. Yeah?"

"You know I got arrested, right?"

"A minor in possession isn't a big deal, chill out." Steve stood up.

"Fuck yes, it's a big deal. This wasn't some nothing MiP charge, they say I was giving it to her. That's a felony."

Steve sat down and stayed silent for a few seconds. He dropped the volume of his voice to just above a whisper, though he still slurred his words. "I'm sorry, man. That fucking sucks."

"Dude, those weren't my fucking drugs. And you're going to tell them that."

"No, I'm not." Steve kept staring at his drink.

"Yes you fucking are."

"It's . . . that's just not an option. La migra, dude. You think you're fucked, I'd be deported."

"I don't give two shits what your excuse is. Your drugs, your whore. You're fucking confessing."

"You know what? Fuck you too, I don't need this bullshit."

Steve stood up and headed for the door. Devon blocked the way, but Steve pushed his one-hundred-twenty-pound frame backward, jerked the door open, and walked straight to the front of the house.

"Get your drunk ass back here," said Devon.

The others—their eyes still glued to their screens and their ears covered by noise-reducing headphone cups—didn't react. Steve left and slammed the door, waking up Scott, who asked, "Hey, is everything all right?"

"Everything's just fucking fine," said Devon.

Scott frowned but lay back down. Outside the window, Steve swerved away without even turning his headlights on, despite the encroaching darkness.

All at once, Billiam, Disney, and Pete pushed back from the tables. Pete took his headphones off and stretched his arms. "Hey, man," he said. "Are you and Steve in the next round?"

"Fuck Steve," said Devon.

"You let him drive drunk? I mean he's fucking wasted."

"Skullfuck him in his fucking face," Devon replied. He sat down at his computer and put on his headset. "Yeah, I'm in."

42

It was soon after GrendelFire78's disappearance that one of Teresa's other regulars started getting weird. With married couples, it was supposed to be a seven-year itch, but for most of the men who visited her channel, it was more like seven days. Her regulars, though, those few who stuck around for longer, were a different breed entirely. If she was having a particularly awful day, barely able to leave bed, she could count on StopDropnFuck making her laugh or H0rnerist patiently listening to her bitch about her problems. The regulars cared less about what she did than that it was her doing it, and many gave tips for practically anything. They'd talk to her about what she had for dinner and compliment her new top. They'd ask what she thought of the latest Batman movie. The only difference between these conversations and real ones was that she was always the center of attention. They made her feel like a sage who'd come down from the mountaintop to offer wisdom on why she liked Gravedigger's latest single.

What was most special about her regulars wasn't their loyalty, that they would curse any jackass who came into her channel screaming to see pussy. She could ban that motherfucker ASAP on her own. It was that at least a few had come to regard her as a person, not just a pleasure robot on the other side of an Internet connection. She'd include them in private shows even if they hadn't been tipping and looked forward to seeing their names pop up in the channel.

For a long time, though, she'd rarely thought of *them* as people. And because they never seemed real, it never fazed her that some regulars could get quite confessional. They talked about their masturbatory habits, their medical problems, the people they hated at work and home. The shield of anonymity let them open up in a way that would have been impossible face-to-face, even with a soulmate. Cumkwat told her about the time he woke up in the middle of the night and, after walking to the kitchen for a glass of water, came back to his bedroom with a knife. His wife slept on their king-size bed under a down comforter and his daughter lay in her crib beside it, her tiny head peeking out from beneath a handwoven turquoise afghan. He stood there until day broke, wondering if he should kill all three of them, trying to decide calmly and rationally what was best for his family. He'd kept staring until his wife, woken by a ray of sunlight hitting her face, opened her eyes and brought him out of this trance. It was the darkest moment of his life, he'd said, the realization that he didn't know if he wanted any of them, the only three people in the world he was sure he truly loved, to live in a world as horribly fucked up as this one. Since then, he'd been wracked by the nagging feeling that he'd made the wrong choice, that his hesitation had sentenced them all to years of suffering, that his daughter would die after ninety years of misery instead of happily at the age of two. Teresa knew she should've been disturbed by this, but she had difficulty picturing Cumkwat as someone who really did have a wife and a child and a knife he could've used against them. He might be lying, but that wasn't why she never thought of reporting him to the police. He was confessing, and she was absolving him by her very presence.

Then GrendelFire78 disappeared. No regular had ever done that before. Some had stopped showing up, but they'd said good-bye, responded to messages, and still had active Arcadia profiles.

GrendelFire78 had been one of the wittiest individuals she'd ever met online, particularly interested in telling fantastic, unverifiable stories about his hometown. He'd never rambled on about her beautiful body or her exquisite, sculpted face, like most of the others had. Post-operation, she'd never looked at mirrors, wanted to forget she even had a face. And he'd let her do that. So after his first week of absence, she found herself searching through obituaries, even though she didn't really know where he lived or what she was looking for. She considered each one a possibility. Could he be "faithful father of three" or "loving husband"? What about "His work in biotechnology was his true love"? He could be any of them. Or none.

The disappearance of GrendelFire78 and the PMs she began receiving from GetItOn occurred simultaneously, and eventually she decided they had to be linked. GetItOn's messages were different from the usual PMs she received from fans. They weren't lengthy, confessional rants or paeans to Aphrodite. His PMs were direct and jarring. The first one read, "You're in Albuquerque, right? I think I'm headed there." That was all.

She ignored it, pretended the message never existed, that it didn't matter. The version of herself that appeared on the screen wasn't in Albuquerque, it wasn't anywhere except this small room for maybe a few hours a day. It wasn't the same Teresa who spoke at breakfast with her grandparents, attended church every Sunday, and spent days roaming the streets in a squad car. Until his message, she thought, she had never mentioned Albuquerque, though evidently she was wrong.

GetItOn's next message, two weeks later, was, "I'm around now. Want to meet up for coffee or something?" Her immediate thought was *hell fucking no*. Yes, she was a trained police officer, but could there possibly be a more unbalanced meeting? She knew nothing about him, but he had seen all of her orifices, heard the way she sneezed at sunlight, knew what clothes she preferred. But then she thought about GrendelFire78, and she missed that wit. How coincidental was it that he'd disappeared right when this other guy started trying to meet up?

After that, though, he became more brazen, and more demanding.

GetItOn: I don't know how to say this, but I just think we were meant to be together. I know it sounds corny but it's true.

GetItOn: But listen, you don't even have to do this anymore. I'm doing pretty well for myself and maybe you could learn to love me. I just want a shot.

GetItOn: I have more than enough money for us both to live on. I know you love Gravedigger's music and I might as well be him. He was my goddamn idea. Just think about that for a second. You could essentially be with Gravedigger.

He just wouldn't shut up.

RonJeremiah: Damn, I know you must hear this a lot, but you are really fucking pretty. And I'm not just saying that because I can see your cooch.

RonJeremiah has left a tip

"Umm, thanks Ron," she said aloud.

GetItOn: Ron couldn't be more right.

GetItOn: If you don't want to be with Gravedigger, how would you like to be a star? I'm working on a project right now that could use a model.

GetItOn: Well, a spokesperson. I'm in PR and we could use a new face.

StopDropnFuck: Oh shit dude, that's a great idea. God I hate all those people on TV.

Guest839: Dude if you're just handing out contracts, I could sure as hell use a job.

SurlyD: Shut up, no one wants you.

"Umm . . . yeah, I don't know if I'm so interested . . ." Unless it would make him leave her be.

GetItOn: It's legit, don't worry. If you'll send me your email, I'll send you an application form. At minimum you'd get to be on national TV.

"I . . . um . . . I'll PM it to you later."

Guest60: I don't have any fake contract, but I do have $100 if you're giving out your email.

"Please don't ask for that again, you or anybody else, you, too, GetItOn, or I'm going to have to get out the banhammer. That puts me in a bad mood."

Guest60: Sorry, I was just joking.

"It's okay, Guest60, I forgive you. But I feel kinda tired now, I'm going to get off. I'll see you guys tomorrow."

She didn't send him her email, but after that he only became more insistent. When she didn't respond to his PM for two days, he wrote back, saying, "I didn't mean to seem aggressive or anything. I just want to meet up. No pressure. No games. btw, the app form I mentioned is online here http://43782dts.com/files/CPProject.pdf"

She wrote back with a single word—"no." Then she put his account and IP on permanent ban for good measure.

When he found a way around that, she knew that shit had finally gotten stalker-level serious. She considered quitting her stream entirely, which she should've done after that not-so-subtle threat from her partner about playing by the rules. But she'd be damned if she was going to let a bunch of police brass slut-shame her into some false morality, and she'd be damned if she was going to let this prick change her life, either.

The stream was the only thing that kept her going while she sleepwalked through the drudgery of life in uniform.

So fuck this guy. She PM'd him, saying she was ready to meet up, then cleaned her nine millimeter in anticipation.

43

RappersDelite.com

Hey hey, it's Milli Vanilli: Is Gravedigger a fake?

New Topic   Post Reply
Page 1 of 140 [2770 posts]   Go to page 1, 2 . . . 140 [next]

Author: ProBeats
Joined: Sat. Jan. 3, 2037
Location: The Rhythm Section

So last night I was hanging out on one of those sex chat things for whatever fucking reason (fwap), and one of the guys on it started ranting about how he made Gravedigger. As in, like, created him, not just helped the guy hit it big or wrote some rhymes for him or shit, but like the whole person. At first I was like this dude's drunk our crazy or whatever and just saying shit. But then I was like wait, this makes some fucking sense.

Has anyone, and I mean a person and not a publicist or some hack journalist, ever spoken with the guy? He only does shows online or in venues where the security is carefully controlled, and in public he's always hiding behind those masks. There's gotta be something to the way he made his name not from real performances or anything but due to a buncha fanboys in Arcadia.

I started digging around on this but most of what I found were just some conspiracy theories that are pretty easily debunked by his official biography. But then I started thinking, "Wait, that's his official biography, which was written by . . . his publicists." I tried to track down some of the sources for it and haven't come up with anything at all. Most of the people quoted pop up every now and then to say shit about him, but pretty much never on anyone else. This may sound stupid but I want to see a birth certificate. I want to see some verification that he's not just a studio-made wannabe. He's just too perfect, too radio friendly. What do you guys think, is there a real human behind that mask or is he just reciting rhymes given to him by Warner Music?

Author: Shadz
Joined: Sat. July 18, 2037
Location: Shadz

Goddamn you fucking shit you can't just make up fucking crazy theories and throw them up here. I've been to the guy's concerts and trust me, they're legit. Liek I can tell you for sure that just because you're seeing em in Arcadia, the music is being made totally live. I don't know what his studio time is like but neither does anyone else. I mean, how do you fucking know the Beatles weren't just given those songs either? It's a stupid question and you're wasting everyone's time by asking it.

Author: LegendaryJ
Joined: Wed. March 1, 2034
Location: Atlanta, GA

What does it matter whether or not he's "real"? He's signed to a corporate label. Whether or not Wyatt Collins Jr. is legit or not is pretty immaterial to me, since either way I doubt he's written a rhyme in his life. You shouldn't be listening to that shit—keep it underground. Fenix or the Live2Die crew could shit on a slab of vinyl and it would be better than anything Gravedigger's put out.

Author: NotoriousP.I.G.
Joined: Thurs. Oct. 1, 2037
Location: M.I.A.

Fuck you ProBeats, GDWAG 4EVA!!!!!!!!!!!

Author: TiffanyX
Joined: Sun. Oct. 25, 2037
Location: Playboy Manson

Would you like to get your penis enlarged? Because not only can you, we 100% guarantee that your lady would appreciate it, and we here at BigDix.com know that pleasing your woman is what you're all about. Everyone wants to be a big man, http://pen.is so come to BigDix where our new herbal supplement is guaranteed to grow you three inches in three months or your money back.

Author: StackAttack
Joined: Tues. May 26, 2037
Location: Connecticut

You know what, I was wondering the same thing after I read this interview he did with Slate. It just sounded . . . too good? Not perfect exactly, but his edges seem intentionally rough. All of his off-the-cuff comments were a little too much what you'd expect them to be. Here's a link to the piece I'm talking about: www.slate.com/articles/3423488. Also, the journalist's description of him without a mask is almost exactly the same as what you find here: www.rollingstone.com/features/gravediggerp1.html.

There's of course a few possibilities for why this is the case. It could be that the Slate guy copied the Rolling Stone guy, an old fashioned case of bad journalism . . . but when I went back and started reading through other articles on GD, they all started feeling eerily similar. I had trouble separating one from another because they hit on the same points. They describe him, sure, but I never get the feeling like the writer is in the same room as their subject. That may be why the same details pop up over and over again, prose about his facial structure and all that. They don't have anything else to go on besides what they're being fed, and whenever he's in public he's wearing a mask and shit. I mean, I know masks have a big history in rap, but you combine that with his whole online only performance thing and it makes you wonder . . .

Author: EpicEpoch
Joined: Sat. June 7, 2036
Location: The Dance Floor

The truth is out there . . . and it's that you dumbasses are nuts. You shouldn't be posting here on rappers delite, you should be on the conspiracy boards explaining your whacked out theories about how he's an emissary from the greys, preparing for an invasion foretold by the great and powerful Xenu.

I never understand why there's so much hate for the guy here. I get it, he's successful, while your favorite artists aren't, but he came from the underground like anyone else before getting signed. You want some articles about it? Here's a live write-up from the Voice: www.villagevoice.com/live/review/july8.htm and BuzzFeed's interview with him from before he had an album out: www.buzzfeed.com/mplayers/august235.html. If you're too lazy to click on it yourself, here's an excerpt:

Opening up tonight for Nostradahmer was Gravedigger, who—despite being almost completely unknown—blew the crowd away. He started out ferociously by rapping about the first time he got shot, which surprised the hell out of the venue's audience, even given their hardcore expectations, and continued with an ode to the way drugs fueled his music, which he called "Mead for the Muse." He ripped through a seven-song set, and while a couple of the tracks seemed incomplete, his performances were always stellar. This was a guy with fire in his belly, and I wouldn't be surprised to see a major label scoop him up before the end of the year. He didn't upstage the main act, especially since Nostradahmer gave his best performance in years, but he came damn close. It's a mighty stupid argument, and while you're free to have your own opinions, stick to the music.

Author: ShirleyBNasty
Joined: Sun. Oct. 25, 2037
Location: http://tablix.com

Is your woman disappointed with your performance? Have you found yourself coming up short? Tablix has what you need at just $29.99 a month http://tablix.com. Never leave her wanting more again.

Author: NightclubDwight
Joined: Tues. Feb. 24, 2037
Location: Nice, Nice

Now that you mention it, there is something eerily similar about that piece in the Voice and this one from Pitchfork: http://pitchfork.com/news/467963-nostradahmer-takes-atlanta-by-storm. Also, those aren't staff writers for either publication, they're just freelancers. I don't see Sasha Vierny covering any of his stuff early on, it's always these writers no one's ever heard of before.

Author: JayP423
Joined: Fri. Oct. 12, 2035
Location: Brooklyn, NY

That's because those places, and a lot of other publications, use interns for live reviews because nobody actually reads them. And trust me, there's no way something like that could get covered up. I've been freelancing for music publications for more than a decade, and while admittedly there's a lot of shady shit that goes down (payola is real, let me tell you that much), the reviews are legit. There's just no way someone could keep an artist as big as Gravedigger under wraps for that long.

And let's talk about your source again: a camwhore site. I don't think you're insane for wondering about Gravedigger's past. Some parts of it always seem more than a tad airbrushed to me, too, but that's true of every major artist. You dig a little bit and you'll always see some cracks in the surface, details that don't quite make sense. But that's because their publicist's job is to tell you a story. They need to give you a compelling story behind the album or it's all just noise, that's what gives the music its meaning. Sometimes

316

the music itself can do that, sure, but hearing from an artist that it's about their struggle with their father or growing up as a drug dealer gives listeners a key, a direction to take their interpretation. When things don't quite fit the story, they adjust here and there, give the bitch little nips and tucks until they do. But the bigger outline about an artist is going to be legit, and of course "existing" isn't exactly a small point that they're going to screw up.

Author: BigRalph
Joined: Sun. May 1, 2033
Location: The Fridge

I get what you're saying EpicEpoch, but you know how the internet works. If enough people and their networked computers agree that something's true, then the consensus is what everyone believes regardless of the concrete, verifiable "facts" of a situation

Here's my question for both sides: how could any of you ever know for sure that Gravedigger is "real?" Even if it's just an actor spouting lines, does that make the lyrics in any way less legitimate? The words and delivery are the same either way and so, frankly, is the performance. I have no reason to believe that this ProBeats is any more real than Gravedigger, let alone the person he supposedly talked to on the sex channel. Still, I have to admit that despite my skepticism and questions as to its relevance (either way, I'll be purchasing his next album), your idea has piqued my curiosity. Anyone here feel like hacking us up some government records to find out whether this Wyatt Collins Jr. fellow existed before 2025?

Author: EpicEpoch
Joined: Sat. June 7, 2036
Location: The Dance Floor

You guys completely misinterpreted me. What I was trying to say is that there is clear documentation, from multiple independent and might I add reliable sources, that Gravedigger is Gravedigger. I would much sooner debate whether orn ot you are a person, BigRalph, or just another screenname for ProBeats. Goddamn, guys like you are why I wonder why I spend so much fucking time explaining things like this to dumbshits online. This whole board is such a fucking joke.

Author: Bad_A$$
Joined: Sat. July 11, 2037
Location: NJ fo life

I like your farfetched story, ProBeats, and wish to subscribe to your poorly photocopied newsletter. Do you think that perhaps the Bilderberg Group is involved? If this links up to the Kennedy assassination the way I think it might, we may be onto one of the reptilians' biggest cover-ups since Waco.

Author: ProBeats
Joined: Sat. Jan. 3, 2037
Location: The Rhythm Section

Haha, laugh it up guys. Not that I meant this to be taken seriously when I wrote it, but all of you getting so pissed off about the very IDEA of him not being legit made me think that maybe I was onto something. Just consider it for a few moments and you'll realize that there are crazier things that have happened in music history. Until that tape played, no one knew that it wasn't Milli and/or Vanilli singing. Had it not been for mechanical failure they could've been bigger than Michael Jackson + Prince x Cher. Don't call bullshit unless you can prove, for sure, that he's a real person. If you've seen his face or knew him growing up, tell us about it. Otherwise, don't be so quick to jump down my throat.

Author: SlickTommy
Joined: Mon. March 23, 2037
Location: Williamsburg

i'm not saying i believe you or not, but when i asked some friends (who are also pretty big fans) about this last night, at first they laughed at the very idea . . . but then they started thinking about it and checking out some sources and before long they were noticing the same patterns that stacksttack pointed out. i feel like we should post links to this online and see if we can crowdsource things. maybe someone out there has the free time to really dig into this. i don't want to rule out that we're seeing things that aren't there, jumping to conclusions because we want to believe our own crazy theories. but what if we really are onto something? what if gravedigger is no more real than santa claus, ronald mcdonald, or jesus? or i guess, what if he's exactly as real?

44

From: Eric McTeague <eric@anonprop.com>
To: Gideon Reyes <gideon.reyes@anonprop.com>
Date: November 12, 2037 3:33 PM
Subject: Important

Gideon,

I have to say that I'm pretty disappointed in you. I realize you were frustrated about being moved off the Gravedigger project, but that's no reason to act out about this publicly. You're no rookie. You know the stakes we're playing with, yet you insisted on commenting publicly about your relationship with the project. Completely unacceptable.

As you may have surmised, we need to terminate your employment immediately. It's not that I don't have faith in your abilities. Your creativity has long made you a natural publicist, and an asset to AP. But I can't have disloyalty on my team. It pains me to think that you might take this as a threat, but I need to remind you that the nondisclosure agreement you signed when you began working here means that if we wanted to, we could sue you into bankruptcy for your next ten lifetimes.

But I'm not a vindictive man. I know we don't always see eye to eye. (Now that I think of it, when was the last time we actually met? Maybe why you didn't treat things seriously enough.) But I wish you the best of luck in the future. I had our lawyers consider what the next step should be, and we agreed that it would be best if we could work something out with you rather than dragging everyone's names through court.

Here's what I have to offer: you'll continue on as an AP employee up through the anniversary of the Wall's completion. It's good publicity to show that the company retains the person who thought the whole venture up, etc. etc. I want to see you put on your best public-relations face and head out there for the Thanksgiving festivities. Talk about how important the fixture is, how it shows corporations standing up for the rights of Americans, how it's helped international relations, all that good stuff. After that, you'll quietly leave the company with a small settlement and an understanding that should you ever speak about Gravedigger, the Prophet Project you've been working on, or even the GWoF, without explicit instructions from us, you'll be in violation of contract and subject to heavy (HEAVY!) penalties. I've attached a pdf with the legalese that we need you to sign and send back ASAP, effectively saying that the part of your life spent with AP is officially our property. Keep in mind that your hiring contract already stated the same. This new form merely updates the terms for new media platforms and some of the statutory changes of the past five years.

I hope there are no hard feelings about this. It's nothing personal, and I'm sure you'll land on your feet wherever you end up next. In some ways, I even envy you. Without a job to tie you down, you can go anywhere, do anything. Leaving AP could be the best thing ever to happen to you! There's no reason why we can't remain friends. Just be sure to get those forms back to me ASAP, or the lawyers have advised me to say that there will be no settlement and we will be forced to begin filing charges against you immediately, which I'd hate to see happen.

Eric McTeague
Anonymous Propaganda - Creative Director

45

Holly poured two glasses of red wine from a bottle labeled in French and written in a calligraphic faux-handwritten font she couldn't read. She'd pulled it at random from their wine rack, figuring that if Robert didn't like it, he wouldn't have purchased it. She took a sip, found it almost sour, and decided to let it wait before drinking any more. In the other room, Robert still wasn't ready. She poked at one of the asparagus stalks she'd cooked and considered eating it. How long could any of this take?

While she sat in the dining room, down the hallway and at the back of the house, Robert typed at his computer while humming loudly and tunelessly. Tonight was perhaps the biggest of his artistic life. She'd prepared a fancy meal, the fanciest she could manage, in his honor. The main course was saffron risotto with roasted duck, which she'd never made before, following along with a six-year-old YouTube video. Someone had gone to great lengths to film the entire process, but that didn't mean it wasn't a lot of effort.

Robert hadn't finished his work on time, was still tinkering with his presentation while the food slowly cooled to room temperature. Resigned, Holly headed back to the kitchen where she'd left her laptop, sitting down on an overly tall, chic bar stool to watch the event when it finally started. She opened a browser tab to MOMA's website, navigated to the live stream ("The presentation will begin shortly"), and left it open, meanwhile The rules were screwing around on her friends' Arcadia profiles and reading listicles.

A beer and a half later, MOMA's site began playing sound, so she jumped back to the tab where a man in a tuxedo introduced Robert, the guest of honor, who then appeared on a screen behind him. When the applause died down, she could hear Robert, both from her laptop's tiny speakers and muffled from the other side of the house, begin a short speech about anticonceptual sculptural realism. Despite living with him, Holly had little idea what any of this theory-babble meant, suspecting that it was just posturing in the hope that academics would write more about his work. She muted her laptop and heard the low-pitched sound of formless vocals from the other room, his arms gesticulating wildly on the screen in front of her. As he came to the end of his speech, Robert took questions from the audience. She didn't need to know what was being asked, the smirk on his face let her know that things were going well, that he had everyone where he wanted them for the big finale. After only a few months of living with him, she'd come to realize that it wasn't the art that he cared about, but what it made people think about him; the sculptures themselves were just a means to an end. And what an end it was.

The video on her screen panned over to the side of the stage where a colossal 3D printer began excreting a miniature of the conference she'd just watched. Robert had chosen a particular moment of the press conference and output, at one-eighth the original size, every last person and detail picked up by the group of cameras he'd rigged all around and above the conference hall. She thought it was awfully derivative of his earlier "¿Hay un tostador?" series, which had involved a working 3D-printed toaster, a 3D-printed printer, and a working 3D-printed minitoaster printed by the 3D-printed printer. This new tour de force featured a working projection of the conference that, while smaller, would allow future museumgoers to watch the event again, including the full creation of the exhibit they were in fact watching. God, he could be an exhausting twat.

A man with a tuxedo walked up to this new exhibit and placed a placard next to it: "Press Conference in Carbonite." Robert had been fretting about this part of the exhibit for weeks, fiddling with a constancy that belied his nonchalant interviews about "instinctive" art. She'd found his obsessiveness doubly annoying because, in addition to reminding her of her father, it made her feel guilty about how little work she was doing. So she'd decided to cook an elaborate meal as penance, and to give herself something quasi-productive to do that wasn't painting. Would someone who didn't love her boyfriend, and his megalomaniacal sculptures, spend hours sweltering in a kitchen for him? Possibly. Well then, the meal would serve as penance for more than one form of guilt.

Robert's presentation finished and he entered the kitchen with an ebullient look on his face, laptop in hand, like a child opening up a new game console on his birthday. "It worked," he said. "It actually fucking worked."

"Yay," said Holly, trying her best to affect some real enthusiasm.

Robert's phone rang just as she began to stand up and move to the dining room. He looked at it and said, "I think I should take this. More interviews." He gestured to the food in the other room, indicating she should go ahead without him.

"You sure?" said Holly, knowing there'd be no response. "I hope the interview goes well." She was speaking to his back.

She tried the wine, and by now it was excellent, spicy and a little earthy. She thought it probably cost more than she had in her bank account, and wasn't sure whether that made it taste better or worse. The risotto had gotten cold, so she reheated it in the microwave before picking at it slowly, hoping that maybe he'd return before she finished, though she was starving and all the alcohol she was drinking on an empty stomach was making her feel on the far side of tipsy.

She realized that Robert had left his laptop behind, a rare occur-rence since he was usually glued to it during most of his waking hours. She popped it open before she could stop herself and saw that an Arcadia browser window was open. She minimized this and opened up his email, not looking for anything in particular, just curious what he'd been up to.

There were half a dozen press inquiries about the talk, and she avoided opening them so he wouldn't see that she'd been looking. She scrolled lower and it was mostly the same, but eventually she spotted a name she recognized. It was Aurelio Luna, the gallery owner who'd invited her to exhibit at his space in Albuquerque. She didn't mean to snoop, really, but Robert had told her he'd never even heard of the guy. She had to open it.

From: Aurelio Luna <ALuna@arcadia.com>
To: Roberto Francisco Hernández-Romero <RFHR@gmail.com>
Date: April 18, 2037 12:32 PM
Subject: RE: Favor

The opening went well, and I could tell your chica was happy about everything. Some of her stuff wasn't half bad, either. Just next time you need my help putting on amateur hour, I could use more notice, as every time I have to do something like this it keeps the real artists from exposure.

Give me a call next time you're in town.

-Aurelio

She didn't scroll down to see Robert's original email. She didn't have to. She couldn't fucking believe what he'd done, or what she'd done, but the only way to bring it up would be to admit she'd been reading his emails. She'd half expected to find letters to a mistress or something along those lines, but this was much worse. Holly never would've agreed to show her work if she'd known it was just some dumb favor from Robert to try to cheer her up.

She closed the laptop and tried to forget what she'd seen. What did it matter anyway? She should just be happy that her boyfriend loved her so much that he'd go through such a charade for her.

Holly killed the rest of the wine she'd poured and walked upstairs to try to sleep. She couldn't help but feel guilty, unworthy of his love even though she didn't, at the moment, want it. She could hear occasional outbursts of laughter, so she shut the door behind her, tossed her clothes in the closet, and lay down to sleep.

After her father disappeared, Holly had decided that the most important part of a relationship wasn't love or communication or anything so high-minded as that, but just staying around. The difference between people with four divorces and eighty-year-old spouses who died within weeks of each other was a question of quitters. Now she wasn't so sure. Maybe some relationships just couldn't be saved. When Robert asked about her day after Juan Diego left the house, how the latest "masterpieces" were going (when they'd first met, his word choice had made her blush, but now it made her contemplate ripping out his chest hair), she didn't mention her father, that she still felt his presence in their living room even though Robert didn't seem to notice.

She'd thought at the time that her father's reappearance had changed nothing, but she knew that wasn't true. Seeing him had deflated the mythical version of Juan Diego in her mind. For the first time in Holly's life, he was no more than a person, an ordinary man, and while his disappearance still hurt, it didn't have the same hold over her that it once had. She'd given up on running away once because of him, and maybe that had been the wrong decision.

When she was younger, she'd had a recurring dream about being either the last one in her family alive (with the whole world doting on this tragic survivor) or, when she was a bit older, being the last living human on Earth. When she was alone in her room, she wrote stories about what happened afterward, alternative versions of herself that got to spend time with other families or make her way on her own, a child beloved by kindly hobos, the hobo princess. She'd use colored pencils to illustrate what she'd written, unhappy with the way her words came out, never able to encapsulate everything that was exciting or magical or just plain strange about her dreams. By the time she was older, the stories had tapered off, but she continued drawing these fantasy scenarios, leaving herself out because she was afraid that if people saw them, they'd say she was too solipsistic. She still drew the other families or the ruin-wracked worlds, but with an extra place setting at the table or a buckled seat belt waiting for her to arrive.

After her eighth-grade art teacher dragged her parents to a stilted conference about her work, Holly stopped drawing at school, but she never stopped at home. Her mother had agreed with the principal and teacher that perhaps drawings like these could be a warning sign, were Holly someone else's child. Autumn insisted, though, that Holly was particularly well-adjusted. Juan Diego claimed that the teachers had misunderstood entirely, that the cataclysmic scenarios Holly envisioned were in fact an image of utopian worlds that the teachers just couldn't understand. It wasn't their place to cast judgment on her art, and had anyone noticed the careful brushwork on the fire emanating from the exploding car? That showed real talent, and the art teacher should be focusing on that, rather than worrying about why all the crash victims' intestines were being chewed by radioactive vultures. Dad had always been kind of full of shit, but at least he'd always had her back, aesthetically speaking.

The next thing she knew, Robert turned in his sleep and reached out to grab her side. Holly maneuvered a pillow into his grasp, annoyed. She didn't know when he'd come to bed, but dawn light was creeping through the curtains. The sheets beneath her felt scratchy, and she knew it'd been too long since she'd changed them, that they were filled with dirt and dust and sweat that she wanted to extricate herself from. She wanted to extricate herself from everything, even though she loved Robert. Clearly. After all, what other explanation did she have for the last three years of her life? You could fuck a guy and not love him easily enough. You could even drop out of school and run away with him just for rebellion's sake. But you probably couldn't stay with him and all of his bullshit, see him day in and day out for years, without loving him.

But of course you could.

The thought of having to talk to Robert again made her want to disappear, and she realized she'd already come to a decision. Holly left the bed, stepped into the closet, closed the door, and dressed herself in the T-shirt and jeans she'd tossed in there the night before. Walking back through the bedroom she saw him, arm now firmly around the pillow, hair standing up like a mohawk. She didn't even say good-bye.

46

At the front of the class, one of the football players began his "grammar presentation" on capitalization. Stretching the topic to two minutes, let alone ten, seemed ridiculous, but the kid tried his best. Devon instinctively glanced to his left, where Steve usually sat, offering a snide look to no one before he caught himself. When Steve took off at the end of the pisser, he'd driven straight down Lomas toward his mom's house, but he'd driven far too straight. When the road eventually curved beneath an overpass, he'd smashed into a wall going what the police estimated to have been forty-five miles per hour. He'd suffered substantial head trauma—though how extensive nobody could say. Devon had spent days failing to convince himself that it hadn't really been his own fault.

"You always capitalize titles of things. Like books or movies. Or people. But you don't capitalize the whole thing. Like you don't capitalize prepositions, which are words like 'the' or 'is' or 'at.' The short words. You just do big ones." God, this was amazing. It was a tragedy, Steve missing this.

They found out the day after the pisser, though no one told Devon until the evening. He'd spent the day sleeping through both class and his arraignment. No visitors had been allowed until Wednesday, when Billiam drove them down to the hospital. Steve's mother was already there, but she declined to say anything to them and walked straight out of the hospital room when they entered. The doctors said Steve would be allowed to stay there for as long as he took to recover. Then he'd be deported with an impossibly large hospital bill to his name. They'd stayed for only an hour, but it was the longest hour Devon had lived since leaving jail.

At home, Billiam largely pretended things were the same as always. If anything, he was more active with the Baby Eaters than he'd ever been before, leading raids while the rest of the clan's leadership was AFK. He'd taken up drinking during the day, resting his legs on his desk and sipping from a bottle of Maker's Mark until he blacked out.

For several days straight, according to his profile, Pete's computer had been logged in to *Punchy the Pugilist Platypus*, a kid's game released back in 2024, and people in the channel commented that they thought something was wrong. His auto-reply message said, "Punchy and I are busy boxing bears." It was the only thing anyone had heard from him.

Devon had yet to figure out how he was supposed to react. He still went on his raids and daily quests, but he wasn't sure what he was supposed to be doing when he wasn't online.

He'd showed up to the second arraignment and met with his lawyer. His options were thinning. He'd been told that if he didn't take the plea, a conviction was certain, that he should accept the felony now and get it over with. A trial date had been set for December 11. He'd left saying he would think about it but didn't know what there was to think about. Both options were unacceptable, and his Get Out of Jail Free card was now unconscious and about to be deported. Ironically, Steve's accident made him care less about the jail debacle, but not much less. Feeling guilty, he went back to reading for his courses, but the schoolwork was so undemanding that it barely put a dent in his free time.

So he found himself spending hour after hour numbly rearranging the furniture of his estate. He was spending Arcadia points on vases and end tables rather than new games, trying to create the perfect setting in different styles. A pure minimalist apartment to clear his mind. A gothic castle to fit his mood. A suburban home pulled straight from old

Douglas Sirk movies that Holly used to watch. As soon as Devon had completed one, he'd realize that it wasn't what he wanted, so he'd start rebuilding from scratch, interrupted only by sleep, hospital visits, and classes, where the seat to his left sat vacant.

Yesterday the doctor said that he suspected it might not be long before Steve could pronounce syllables, but that it was still impossible to assess what long-term damage had been done. Even after a battery of fMRI, CT, PET, EEG, MEG, and NIRS scans, no one would answer Devon's simple question of when, or if, Steve would walk again, let alone what his memory would be like. What was he thinking, trapped in there? Would he eventually be able to drive again, or sense that his paralyzed left arm was connected to him? Was the person lying in that bed still, in a nonmaterialist sense, Steve?

The class ended. Making his way out of the English building, Devon pulled out his phone to call Holly. After seven rings, her voice mail answered. "I'm not in. Maybe I'm in the studio avoiding calls, or maybe I've lost my phone. Whatever, you know the drill."

"Hey sis, this is Devon. Umm . . . I was wondering if I could come out to see you sometime soon, like we talked about with mom. Been needing to get away from here and I thought a drive down south might be nice. Anyhow, tell me if that's cool—I'd be happy to make the trip, like, really soon."

Devon wandered over to the bus stop, trying to make himself care about stats and hotkey strategies, hoping that a few hours of Arcadia would keep his thoughts occupied, that staring at a screen would have the same draw for him that it used to.

47

Conference Room B: Anonymous Propaganda Headquarters
Manhattan

"Really, this is the best we could come up with? There's gotta be like . . . I dunno, a billion candidates out there, right? And this is the best we could do."

"We can certainly keep the search going, if that's what you'd like. What about Canada? I realize we don't want to look south, but what about north? They're all pretty clean-cut up there, right?"

"Canada?! Are you out of your fucking mind, Jenkins? Canada, that's the stupidest thing I've heard all day. Next thing I know, you'll be telling me we need to find a Croatian to fill the spot, or an African. No, if I hear anyone else say Canada, they're getting a ten-K fine and a rubber band in the eye."

"Ha-ha."

"You think I'm joking, Jenkins, try me."

"Mr. McTeague, I know you made me bring this box of rubber bands along, but may I remind you that you're running on fifty-plus hours without sleep . . . Are you sure you're not a little, er . . . punchy?"

"Punchy, Everly? No, I'm in my full fucking faculties. Never better, and I wouldn't undermine your boss, if I were you. Just take the minutes, like you're supposed to."

"Okay, sir."

"Right, so Canada is straight—ouch, goddamn that stings."

"Everly, please document Jenkins's fine and notify accounting after this meeting."

"All right, though this seems—"

"My aim works just as well on you, Everly. As I was saying, we need our prophet to be American, and we've been searching long enough that this shouldn't even be a problem. Let's run through everyone's top candidate. This McDowell fellow, what's his deal?"

"All-American football for Boston College, Rhodes Scholar, and from what I understand, a generally straight-edge man. Just look at his picture."

"Why, his teeth are practically gleaming. Who's his dentist?"

"Are you sure they aren't actually . . . glowing? Those look almost radioactive."

"Err . . . I don't know. I guess we could ask him."

"If you don't know already, it's not worth pursuing, although I must say they're also perfectly in line. I can't stop staring at them."

"So are his fingernails. It's almost hypnotic."

". . . ahem, but no, he's out. He's too picture-perfect, too much a mama's boy. People won't want to worship this guy, they'll be too afraid of being judged. Hell, even Jesus had a few years wandering around in the desert. Show me the next candidate."

"This is Dwayne Kiwali, a living embodiment of the rags-to-riches story. He was homeless until the age of six, when he was picked up and taken to an orphanage. There he was adopted by—hey, ow, what was that for?"

"Yeah, sir, that's not fair. He didn't say Canada, or even Toront—fuck, that hurts. Can I go to the bathroom to wash out my eye? I think that last rubber band had some gunk on it and it really burns."

"Are you crying, Jenkins? Because I won't have crying on my team."

"I'm not crying, it's just my eyes are watering because you keep—ow—hitting them with rubber bands."

"If I didn't want a Canadian, do you think I want some minority? You've seen the risk analysis report. You think that would play well in the South? Well, do you?"

"We had a . . ."

"Speak up, Mr. Hawk. Don't be shy."

". . . our country's had a black president, and many of the more fervent parishioners in the South are black. I'm just saying that this would be a way to tap into a—ouch. Really, sir, this is most unseemly."

"And we haven't had another one since. I don't care if this black kid of yours is the Messiah, the report says there's no way we can get whites interested in a Christian leader who's black. End of story. Let's finish off with the guys. Show me what you've got, Chavez."

"Well, I, uhh . . . can you take that rubber band off your fingers? Sir?"

"Just keep talking, Chavez."

"Okay. So my man isn't like those others. He's from a poor background and is the first member of his family to go to college—"

"I thought you said he wasn't like the others, Chavez. This is sounding a lot like Jenkins's Captain America."

"Ow, hey, what did I do?"

"Nothing, Jenkins. I just like the way you flinch. Everly, maybe we should start keeping score. One point for a head shot, five points for an eye, and . . . let's say ten points if I manage to get one into someone's mouth."

"Sir, this is getting ridic—ow!"

"Okay, Rebekah, keep talking."

"So unlike, uh, Captain America, he didn't go on to a Rhodes Scholarship or anything like that. He graduated and started a small business in his community, Ratigan's Shoes."

"Ratigan? The kid's name is Ratigan?"

"Derek Ratigan. He started this shoe store, and it's a local phenomenon. 'Wear Again Your Ratigans' is their slogan, because they recycle old shoes and fix them up, and it's become like a big thing to be seen wearing recycled shoes. And he also donates pairs to the local charity through his church and is well-known for his solos in the gospel choir. His generosity is really, I think, the selling point for Derek, and—"

"Whoa whoa whoa, slow down a second, Rebekah. He donates to charity *and* he started a recycling program?"

"Yes. He seems to really embody a lot of very Christian values without being patronizing about—"

"Stop right there, Mrs. Chavez. You seem to be mistaken. You yourself are a Christian, correct?"

"Born and raised. There were a few years where I kind of lapsed, but ever since my mother passed—"

"Wasn't asking for your life story, I was asking for your religion, because I think it's clouding your judgment here. While officially many churches still sanction charity, a majority of parishioners hate the very idea, consider it to be socialism at best, some sort of black magic voodoo curse at worst. I thought you received the same research as everyone else?"

"I did, but . . . are all those numbers about the demographics accurate? I was always taught in Sunday school that Christianity was about love and generosity and—"

"That's your mistake right there, Rebekah, though I'm glad to hear you at least read the research, unlike some people."

"Ow, sir, can I leave now? That one from earlier cut me and I can't stop the blood from coming out. Look, some of it already got on my sleeve."

"You can't stop the blood from bleeding, Jenkins, not 'coming out.' We have the whole glorious world of the English language available to us: use it. As I was saying, your pastor may have told a good story about love and charity and all that bullshit, but the stats don't lie, and they tell us that even the idea of recycling turns our largest demographic off. Recycling makes them think of climate change, which they don't believe in because if it were real, they'd have to do something about it. Makes them think of science, which leads to evolution and all those PhDs bossing them around and telling them what to believe. Okay, let's see what women we've found. Miss Kerr, tell me about your lead."

"She's thirty years old, not just white but also blonde and blue-eyed."

"Very nice."

"She's from a wealthier background . . ."

"How wealthy?"

"Umm . . . very wealthy."

"Speak up, Alice."

"Very wealthy, sir. I don't know if that's a problem . . ."

"Not necessarily. Don't ask me why, but eighty-six percent of the 'faithful' love the wealthy. Consider wealth to be God smiling down on a person or some such nonsense. Tell me more."

"Umm, that's mostly it, I guess. She's very charismatic, and I think you can see from these photos that her, umm, assets are enormous."

"What church?"

"Well, she's not a practicing Christian, but I don't think she's necessarily opposed—"

"What else does she do?"

"Pageants, mostly. Is that a—ow, goddammit, those things sting."

"I have to say, Alice, I'm almost as disappointed with you as I am with Jenkins."

"But sir, you said that the candidates' attractiveness was of paramount importance."

"It is, but I asked for a person with a compelling story and you brought me a blow-up doll."

"With all due respect, sir, if you took the time to speak with her, you'd understand that she's more than just a blow-up doll."

"Look, if we just wanted a pretty face, I'd start with the casting agents in Los Angeles. I expected some top-quality results, but none of you delivered. That only leaves . . . oh yes, Gideon's no longer with us. Well, Jenkins, show me what your ex-colleague found."

"I don't know about Gideon's methodology. After all, he's now—"

"Quit stalling, Jenkins."

"Well, I haven't met her, but according to him—"

"She's quite a looker. Gideon has some real taste. That face, it's almost unreal."

"Sir, I thought we weren't going for blow-up dolls. I don't mean to—fuck."

"Ha, a fiver. She's not a blow-up doll, she looks like some sort of, I don't know . . . Indian princess? There's gotta be a way of saying that that doesn't come out so racist."

"Native American princess?"

"Indigenous American chief's daughter?"

"You know what, forget it. What's her story, Jenkins?"

"She's from a poor family in New Mexico, was raised by her grandparents and is a practicing Catholic. I thought we weren't interested in them."

"I didn't tell you guys? I mean, they're not our primary target, but they're still fair game. I brought it up to them, and enough bishops like what we're doing that by the time the pope gets word, he'll have to at least offer lip service. They've paid their part like the rest of the clients. I've had Hoselton pitching everyone, and at this rate I wouldn't be surprised if the Reform Jews were with us by the end of the week. What else?"

"I guess she's a cop."

"You don't say. Now that really is something. A beautiful young girl who's religious—she's actually religious, right, Jenkins?"

"Yes, says here she attends Mass every week, though there's one potential problem. She apparently . . . she's also a camgirl for one of those online sites. Not too popular, we had to dig to find out. Gideon didn't mention it, but she seems to have a devoted follow—*ow*."

"So she's a pretty little hypocrite, is she? You know, that isn't necessarily a bad thing, might give us some leverage if she's hard to work with. And no one else needs to find out. Hell, even if they did, the virgin/whore thing's been hot for centuries. And a police officer, too, right? She may not be what I had in mind, but she sounds . . . Wait, did you say she was in New Mexico?"

"Yes, Albuquerque. Why?"

"That could be a problem. You know what, arrange to get her out of there ASAP, and I mean *ASAP*, Everly, you hear me?"

"Yes, sir."

"Fly her out here and we'll speak with her. If we can get her in time, that only makes her story better. I can see it now: 'Orphaned Messiah to Lead Christians to New Promised Land.' Practically writes the copy for us."

"Sir, she's not orphaned, I believe. Grandparents or—"

"Don't interrupt me. Yes, this we can work with. Have her taken out of there immediately. I'd like to think Homeland Security can handle this RV thing, and they've assured me it's under control, but I've run through the projections and you wouldn't believe how fast these things can spread if they get out of hand. Speaking of which, while the GMO ads got off to a . . . rocky start, I've been assured that particular problem has been solved. Our projections from CIT-E are fantastic, and I want us to go national on those before the end of the next quarter, so let's keep that in mind. What else . . . it looks like the backlash about the moon ads has completely died off, as predicted, and Chick-fil-A's latest PR disaster is fading away nicely. Is there anything else on the agenda or can we finally get out of here?"

"Sir, there's still the Gravedigger project that requires some—"

"Yes, Everly, I remember. I need ideas, people. Hawk, Chavez? Kerr?"

"You mentioned New Mexico. It's like they say, tragedy always breeds opportunity."

"I'm not quite sure I follow you, Alice."

"It seems to me like Gravedigger could be headed to the Southwest for his latest tour. Maybe he drives through the infected areas."

"There's a certain elegance to your solution."

"Thank you, sir."

"I want an outline of how we want this to work on my desk by the end of the day tomorrow. I'm thinking you send some tour dates over to *Pitchfork* so the whole world fucking knows about it, but make sure our favorite pseudonymous shill Mr. Murray is in control of the coverage. I want to see you figure out a way to really drum this up and make a big fucking event out of his 'death.' We're throwing a big cash cow under the bus here, and I want to see sales skyrocket after he's gone. And circulate some rumors about him being back in the recording studio so that we can start milking 'em for a couple dozen 'posthumous' albums. Okay, everyone, it's time to move your asses out of here and get back to work."

48

Given both the financial and logistical difficulties of visiting in person, Paul, Sonja, and their children and grandchildren decided to skip the traditional Thanksgiving get-together. They would eat turkey and mashed potatoes and that canned cranberry stuff that tasted wonderful so long as they didn't think too much about it, but the entire meal would be hosted online. And more than a week early. They'd discussed this the year prior, after their daughter Sandra's husband walked through their door complaining of the long trek and the "waste" of his time off. Paul didn't really like Jim, but he was a huge step up from Sandra's first husband, that Great Wall–building race traitor. Jim's complaints dominated the long weekend, though, and by the end, even Sandra and her sister Paula had joined in. When Paul began calling around in early September to tell everyone that they were going through with it, that it just seemed easier to meet in Arcadia this year, and meet the week before so as not to interfere with other Thanksgiving plans, he could practically hear the relief on the other end of the phone.

But even if their guests would only be avatars and audio streams, they still had to eat. The day before their makeshift Thanksgiving, Paul found himself staring into the refrigerator, wondering what they could fix for a meal while their avatars chowed through the customary feast. He hoped, as always, to find something irresistible, but there wasn't much besides baking soda and bread, a dozen half-empty condiment bottles and some not-quite-expired deli meats and cheese. It was the middle of the month, so he should've known better—they tried to go to the store only twice a month, since it was twenty miles away, and it'd been at least a couple of weeks since Sonja had stocked the fridge. Clearly another trip was due.

Paul shut the refrigerator door and sighed as loudly as he could, making sure Sonja heard it. She sat on a stool at the other side of their kitchen's bar, staring at her laptop. Sonja glanced up.

"What?" she asked.

"Do I need to say it?"

"I don't know, do you?"

"Our Thanksgiving's tomorrow, and unless there's some secret alijo you have hidden away . . ."

"If there were, I certainly wouldn't be sharing it with you," said Sonja. "Yes, I plan on going to the store in a bit. Why, are you thinking of coming with, for once?"

"Do I have to?" Both of them knew that Paul hated going to the grocery store and would make any excuse to avoid it.

"Fine, you don't have to. Just try to make yourself useful while I'm gone. Work on the decorations or something."

Paul was happy enough about staying home that it almost made up for the rather lackluster sandwich he had for lunch. Their move from Albuquerque to San Lorenzo had been his wife's idea, as Paul liked to remind her, so there was no use in blaming him for how far out in the middle of nowhere they'd ended up, or how long a drive it was just to buy a few staples. After all, she chose the house. And while he'd suggested looking in the area, it had only been a suggestion. Sonja had decided, and he was even fonder of mentioning this because it offered him an easy segue into saying, yet again, that the means of obtaining the house had been due to him. The house vindicated one of the few vices that Paul Chávez had allowed himself in life.

"La lotería? Estúpido, Paul," his wife would say. "Why don't you use that money for something useful? We never have milk in the fridge when I need it for cooking, and I'll tell you why that is, it's because you scrimp on the milk and bread so you can buy those tickets."

He'd respond, as he always did, by saying that he'd quit playing years ago, that she was only imagining things, until she found another ticket tucked away in the bottom of his wallet. It had gone on like this for decades, but despite the recurring arguments, he kept playing. It was the only real secret he kept from his wife, and that was one of the chief reasons he enjoyed it so much. He didn't drink, had quit smoking while they were still dating, and the thought of an affair hadn't crossed his mind since the moment he first laid eyes on Sonja. But playing the lottery made him feel like he was still independent, and the thrill of hiding it had long ago supplanted the thrill of the potential win as his motivation for purchasing tickets.

Although he rarely won—and since that had long since stopped being the point, it didn't matter that he seemed to dramatically under-perform even the lottery's notoriously low odds—Paul only liked to play when the jackpot was huge. Bigger than huge. He liked it when the jackpot was life changing, large enough that its winner could purchase an island or eat salads made of hundred-dollar bills every night. Paul looked down on the people who bought tickets every time they filled their gas tanks—they were just addicts. All he wanted was his infinitesimal shot at the big one. In the end he hadn't exactly won, either. He'd found his winning ticket, on the ground outside a bar, or at least that's what he'd told Sonja. He still felt bad about the lie, but if she hated gambling, she sure as hell wasn't going to condone stealing from some drunk preacher. And while he hadn't won the full Powerball prize, the $815,000 he'd claimed was still a fortune, more than they'd earned in a decade. A month later, they moved out of the South Valley and the small adobe house they'd lived in for more than twenty years, into a newly built two-story house on a half acre of land outside of Silver City. Five years later, here they were.

When he finally heard Sonja pull out of the driveway, Paul began making preparations online. They hadn't had visitors to their hub since Sonja's birthday a few months back, and the place wasn't properly decorated for the festivities. He began palette-swapping the room, and then he opened up Arcadia's store and began browsing cheap decorations, maybe some smiling toy pilgrims with their bootstrapped hats for the centerpiece, or a turkey painting for the walls. It wouldn't be the same as having his family there with him, but it would be something.

Sonja rarely drove, so her occasional trip to the grocery store afforded her a smidge of freedom. She complained that Paul never went with her, but that was to keep him from knowing how much she enjoyed it. When she really needed to get out of the house, couldn't take another hour cooped up at home, she'd pour milk down the sink, or break a couple of eggs and say they'd gone bad, then head out the door, reveling in the decadence of the waste as well as the lie. She suspected that Paul knew what she was doing, but he wouldn't say anything. He was a good man. Lately, she'd realized she'd have to cut out even that small vice, since they'd been running through those winnings much faster than either of them had anticipated.

When driving on her own, Sonja liked to crank the radio up as high as she could stand it and listen to the sort of thing that Paul hated, usually singer-songwriters with voices so soothing she forgot to pay attention to the lyrics. He only liked the music he'd grown up with, and while she didn't have much use for the new stuff on the radio, she was sick to death of the songs she'd been listening to for forty years. Sometimes even the radio was too much company, so she'd turn it off and listen to the rumble of her car's engine and the white noise of the tires. Alone in her car, Sonja felt truly relaxed, beholden to no one but herself.

Sonja pulled off the highway and turned into the Jewel-Osco parking lot. On entering, her eyes were assaulted by a flashy overhead banner announcing produce at greatly discounted prices in large, green letters. "Let Corporations Pay for YOUR Food!" Sonja pulled her shopping cart up to the display. Aside from logos printed on the cheeses, nothing seemed particularly different about the produce. The banner offered no explanation, so even though the price was right, she only placed one bag of apples in her cart. It's not like they'd get through much fresh fruit before it spoiled anyway. She moved through the rest of her list, staples and the usual Thanksgiving hodgepodge.

After loading her trunk with grocery bags, Sonja grabbed one of the apples for the drive home. It wasn't terribly good—a bit mealy on the inside, waxy on the skin and rather flavorless. Served her right for going down-market. Glancing at it, she almost swerved. There was a strange black pattern in the apple. It didn't really seem to affect its taste, but as she continued eating it, what formed inside was impossible to ignore. Imprinted on the pale interior was, of all things, an Apple logo. It wasn't perfect, her bites were uneven, but while its stem was a bit off-center, the shape was undeniable. She finished the rest of the apple on the way home, tossing the core, now just a blackened pillar like a pole of ash, out the window.

Sonja pulled off the highway and onto her community's main street, her patch of suburban desert affluence. With the exception of a pair of old farmhouses, the rest were made from the same sixteen designs. The developer's brochure had said that other communities—in Los Angeles and Phoenix and Denver and outside of Dallas—used the same designs. Sometimes she wondered what other people living in the same style house as hers were like. Paul said it was a ridiculous idea; weren't they acquaintances with the Inez family down the block, who shared the C model with them? She still had him build a replica on Arcadia so that she'd feel more at home there. She liked that her little avatar looked like a taller, younger, lighter-skinned version of herself, living in a house that was like their own but better decorated and cleaner.

Sonja had trouble sleeping that night. She woke up several times straining to breathe, and at 5:00 a.m., she woke again with her stomach roiling. Paul slept through most of it, and she was thankful for that. He'd make a big deal out of it, ruining the holiday. When he did wake up, she claimed to have had trouble sleeping, and Paul seemed to accept it at face value.

Paul posted the family invite at 1:25, in case anyone wanted to get online early, though no one else showed up until almost a half hour later. He sat at his PC with his headset on, proudly showing Sandra and the children around the house while their avatars hung up the children's virtual coats. Sonja sat at a card table on the other side of the room with her laptop and a plate of food in front of her.

"Mmm, this is really good turkey," said Paul, miming with his avatar. "So moist and juicy. I think it's your best yet." She turned her head and silently mouthed "idiota" at him, but he was biting into an apple and didn't notice. He made a face. She'd forgotten to tell him the apples were mealy, but she was glad he wasn't paying much attention to her, since she felt terrible. She left for the bathroom without saying anything.

She came to on the hallway floor. Paul was kneeling over her, fanning her, saying, "Oh thank God, thank God."

"What happened?"

"You didn't come back and the kids were asking about you. I came to check and there you were."

"How long was I out?"

"You left fifteen minutes ago. And I know you make fun of me when I stay in the bathroom for that long, so I just thought . . ."

"Are the kids still there?"

"Yes, I just told them something came up in the kitchen."

"Good, good. Let's go back to them."

Sonja explained to her children that there'd been a problem with the rolls, but everything was better now. Paul kept looking at her from the other side of the room, but she just smiled, and the rest of the afternoon went well.

Sonja felt relieved when everyone logged off a little before six. She made her way to the restroom again, then decided to lie down for the night.

"Do you think it's the flu?" asked Paul, pulling back the covers for her. She didn't answer, and hoped it was nothing more to worry about than old age.

49

Teresa arrived ten minutes early and waited by the restaurant's glass windows, taking shelter from the sun beneath a dark green awning. She already regretted wearing heels. She would've preferred to arrive late, but she didn't want to be caught off guard when so much about the evening was already unpredictable. So she stood uncomfortably, her legs beginning to cramp, feeling overdressed as countless schlubs in T-shirts and jeans walked past her on Central. She felt sweat gathering in her armpits and couldn't tell if it was from nerves or the heat. At least she had her backup plan in the car.

She'd fantasized about her first real date since the accident for so long that she hadn't been able to help dressing up for the occasion, spending an afternoon browsing perfumes at Nordstrom in Coronado. She knew it was a bad idea to encourage the kind of psychopath she was almost certain to meet, but distracting him into a false sense of security would only give her the upper hand. Tonight was all about control, even the creep knew that. He was just confused about who was *in* control. Teresa wasn't here for herself, she was here to stop him from repeating this, from stalking other women in the future. If she wasn't able to protect anyone as a police officer, wasting her days on meaningless violations designed to inflate arrest numbers, at least she could here.

She looked at her reflection in the window, surprised by the person staring back. The woman's hair flowed down past her shoulders without a strand misplaced. Her dress hugged her curves and showed off her toned legs (the shoes were certainly working there). Her face had the airbrushed look of a magazine cover, with a smile that hinted at a mischievous intelligence that Teresa didn't recognize as her own.

She turned and noticed a man wearing cargo shorts and a local radio station T-shirt, staring at her as he walked forward. She reflexively felt for the crease of her surgery. Everything was still normal. She looked back at him and he looked away, pretending he was only leering at the sidewalk, and for a second this felt ordinary. But the urge to run and hide, to duck into a bathroom and apply facial cream, was gone. He was twice her age and had disgusting body hair, but she wasn't worried about him. After he walked past, her face stayed put, the way it always had. No police uniform necessary, she was in public and in control.

Finally, a man wearing a polo shirt and khakis approached from the parking lot, an enormous smile plastered on his face, a bouquet of orange and yellow roses in his hands, average at best, with a cheap haircut and ill-fitting clothes that failed to hide a developing belly.

"Hi," he said. "I'm Gideon. Thanks for coming out to meet me. I know this is weird, but I hope you'll forgive me. I got you these."

He looked at her expectantly, as if the flowers should earn him goodwill, erase their history, but it only emphasized how forced this was. She thanked him for the flowers. He put out his hand but she ignored it. He had forced her here, and Teresa wasn't going to forget that he'd ruined one of the few parts of her life she had enjoyed. She'd kept streaming for a couple of days, but it was more out of habit than anything else. Until he butted into her life, it hadn't felt dirty, but now she felt naked online. Her computer's camera had become a spider, its thousand eyes all leering at her, telling her to touch herself again because that was all she was good for. But quitting had only meant more time alone in her room, slowly going crazy with no one to communicate with.

They walked into the Flying Star, which her grandparents still called the Double Rainbow after its name back in the 1980s. Distracted by her "date," who kept looking down at her like she was a birthday present, Teresa ordered the first sandwich listed on the menu behind the counter. She wanted to get this over quickly. He picked the same sandwich, smiling broadly at her. She started to return the smile, out of instinct, but stopped herself. This was going to be harder than she'd thought.

He insisted on paying, then asked her to choose where to sit. Teresa walked to the back, where there were plenty of people. She had her gun in her purse, but it wasn't *on* her, and that made her nervous. She'd learned, at the Academy, not to fool herself about getting into a fight with a guy who weighed double her one hundred five pounds. Ninety percent of fights went to the bigger body.

Finally deciding she might as well say something and get it over with, she opened with a simple, "So what do you actually do?"

He explained that he used to work in publicity and had been serious about signing her up as a spokesperson, that he was happy she'd sent in her application.

"Oh God, I'd forgotten about that."

"I can tell you that you're being seriously considered. And don't worry, they don't know how I met you. I just . . . when they said they wanted an angelic face, I thought of yours."

He smiled at her again, but this time she wasn't even tempted to return it. She touched her face along the sides, thought she felt seams, like it was ready to slip off at any moment. This was bad.

"Thanks, I guess. Used to?"

"I'm kind of temporarily in between positions."

Of course he was. She sat and pretended to listen while he babbled on about himself. He didn't seem to notice. When their food arrived, she pounced on the sandwich.

As their meal continued, the rictus on his face grew tighter, and she wondered if he was forcing himself to enjoy this charade. She half listened to an anecdote about his mother and the incredible lengths she went to in order to make sure all three of her children could do as many after-school activities as they wanted, ferrying them from soccer to art classes to basketball.

"Your mother sounds very nice," she said, one eyebrow raised.

"Yeah, she is, she is. That's the difficult part. Sometimes it feels like the entire world is screwed up except for her. Which is why I don't see her too often. I always feel like whatever I say, I'll just disappoint her. My sister always fights with her because she's a genuine optimist. You can't rebel against her. Made a profession out of figuring out what people want and giving it to them."

"What's wrong with that?" Her eyebrow couldn't go any higher.

"I don't know about you, but in my line of work . . . what you learn in marketing is the exact opposite. People don't think for themselves, they think what you tell them to think. And they don't do what's right—whatever the hell that means—they do what's easiest. There's no reason every one of us can't try to save the world, donate our time and money, go to church on Sunday, think about what we can do for other humans. But if I ask the average guy on the street what he really wants to do, he'd tell me he wants to drink a lot and fuck some girls. And he isn't even going to do that, because it's too much goddamn work. He's going to come home from his job, tired and exhausted, and turn on the computer to watch a rerun, then he'll masturbate and fall asleep. How do you make a living? Do you just go online, or do you have a day job?"

"I'm a cop."

"Oh, right. Yeah, I forget about that when you're not in the uniform."

"You've seen me in uniform?" Sirens went off in her head.

"Just like in passing, I mean."

"Uh-huh. Right." He'd gone beyond online stalking.

For another five minutes, she shoveled food into her mouth, gulping it down without chewing, like a bird. The other reason she'd arranged their meeting for the Flying Star was that you paid when you ordered, so as soon as they finished eating, she could walk to her car and be done with it.

Teresa pushed her chair back and hastily led the way to the door, past a bevy of college students with bags under their eyes. She turned and headed toward the parking lot while he trailed after her like a puppy, smiling. She looked at his face and realized that they had never been truly communicating. He saw and heard only what he'd been imagining in his head for so long. At least she'd tried.

"Do you need a ride home?" he asked.

"No, I drove here," she replied without turning around. They stopped at her car and Teresa looked back at him. His gaze was cast expectantly at her lips, and he leaned his head forward for a kiss. She contemplated leaning forward to meet him, thought about what it would be like if this were a real date instead of a terrible charade. But she apparently didn't get real dates, real kisses. She got face surgeries and schlubby stalkers.

"Look," she said. "I did what you asked, though it was against my better judgment. I showed up. You got your little fantasy date and ruined my life online along the way, so I hope you're happy with the result. Now, fair warning, you need to back off and leave me the fuck alone. Forever." She opened her car door and dropped the flowers he'd given her onto the pavement, kicking them aside. He darted forward to shut the door and pin her between him and it, but he was slow and she was very fast, nerves honed by an hour of adrenalized tension. She spun and grabbed the pair of steel handcuffs that lay on the dashboard, where she'd carefully positioned them. She pushed him back with her elbow, yanked the back of his neck hard enough that he spun around, slammed him against the car, pulled his arms behind him, and fastened the cuffs.

"That's not what I . . . I didn't mean you any harm. I just . . . listen, Teresa, I'm in love with you."

"Don't even call me that. I don't know how you found out my real name, but you have no right to pretend you know anything about me. I gave you a chance to fuck off, you entitled prick."

His face looked pained, like a smacked puppy.

"That's right, motherfucker. You think I came down here to fulfill your sick fantasies about meeting your 'dream girl'? I came down here to see if you were as pathetic as you seemed online, or if you'd be a stand-up guy and respect a girl's wishes once she was a real human being standing in front of you. Looks like pathetic won out. So consider this a warning, one I could be making with my gun if I were a less merciful person. If you ever try to contact me again, I will have you arrested. From now on, you're being watched. If you ever try to pull this with another girl, I will fucking know, and I will end you."

She stepped into the car and drove off as quickly as she could, watching as he waddled back toward the street, his arms stuck behind him, his mouth wide with shock and indignation.

50

In the early morning hours after Robert's talk, Holly had quickly formulated a plan and headed out, taking Robert's Visa with her. At Smith's she'd piled food into her shopping cart, without much thought at first. Milk, cheese, some new branded fruit, shelf-stable juices. Frozen foods were good, but canned was even better. She could put bread in the freezer. She'd need big jugs of water, too, just in case. Peas, beans, corn, carrots, and as many soups as would fit in her old Mazda. She had driven home and spent forty-five minutes unloading, putting as much as she could in the studio's fridge. She had stacked the cans in a corner, a technicolor display of labels climbing up the wall. The fruit, she realized, had been a mistake—she didn't even really like fruit, so it would rot and stink up the place before she ate it. She had taken it into the house and dumped it into a display bowl on the kitchen counter—let Robert deal with it.

Holly had two more stops. First, Gecko's, the art supply store whose owner had nearly gone bankrupt shortly before the local boom took over and allowed him to move to a large, former gift shop on Third. She had plenty of canvas already, but she bought more so that she wouldn't need to ration. The checkout clerk gave her a funny look when he saw Robert's name on the credit card, but she had said, "He's my husband," and the clerk just shrugged and said it was none of his business. From there she had driven to Lowe's for a nail gun and long, sturdy lumber.

Holly now laid the paints and canvases on the studio floor to sort out later. She looked at her watch. Robert would sleep for two more hours, so she went back to the house and cooked herself a quasi last meal of eggs, bacon, and frozen waffles. Holly hummed as the bacon crackled in the pan, almost dancing as she worked. She took her time eating, savoring the bacon's smoky flavor, soaking the waffles in syrup until they were half-liquid like she used to when she was little. When she finished, she placed two plates, two bowls, and a smattering of silverware inside the microwave, unplugged it, and carried it to the studio.

The skylight let rays into the room, lighting the dust so it glowed like little pixies floating among the canvases. Holly remembered that tonight there would be an eclipse, wondered whether it would be visible from the studio. She retrieved the nail gun and wood from her car, carrying the long pieces back into the studio. When Robert had converted the garage, he filled in the gaping car door and attached a conventional wooden one to the building's front. Holly began at the floor and placed each plank of wood above the last, rhythmically nailing to the beat of a rap album Gideon sent her a few weeks ago. She sprinkled each one with three-and-a-third-inch nails until she had no more left. The work went surprisingly fast. With the nail gun, she didn't even work up a sweat until she had to lift pieces of lumber above her head. She used a paint-encrusted stepladder to attach the last few, and where there had once been an exit, now there was an ugly patchwork of wood fastened to the wall with several pounds of steel.

No escape, but really the ultimate escape. This was what she'd always seen in Robert, Holly realized. Freedom from the world. But it wasn't what he'd given her, wasn't what she'd been able to find in their life together.

So this was how she would break up with him. She'd paint, finally without distractions, without worrying about their relationship and where it stood and her father and all the other personal bullshit getting in her way, and when she ran out of materials, then she'd decide what to do next. Maybe Robert deserved an explanation, but she didn't care right now. First she needed to decide whether art was really what she wanted, really something she could do. Everything else in the world could fucking give her a break.

Finished with her preparations, Holly felt invigorated. She'd stretched a new canvas a few days before, when she'd wanted to work but didn't have any idea what to do next, and looking at it from across the room, she now saw its potential, envisioned figures, a family, a whole city dancing with joy in the foreground of a volcano that lit the night sky with its eruption. She began painting and didn't stop until late that night. Exhausted and hungry, she heated up a frozen meal in the microwave.

At some point the next day, Holly heard voices outside the garage, someone banging on the door, screaming, and coughing. She assumed it was Robert, so she ignored the sounds.

She had everything she needed. Using the drain in the floor as a bathroom had freaked her out at first, though now she'd gotten used to it, running water from the sink's hose to wash the stink down as soon as she finished. Her wireless Internet connection quit soon after she entered, but Holly was pleasantly surprised when the power stayed on well into her second week (or so she assumed—she'd long since lost sense of time), at which point she presumed Robert had cut the cord. It didn't matter, by then she'd practically worked her way through the fridge and freezer. She would be eating beans and peas for the foreseeable future, but she'd long since stopped tasting food. Having become a conduit for the work, which piled up at the back of the room, she ate only for nourishment.

Some paintings were lush, some minimalist. Some were original, others a mishmash of influences. Holly was unaware, with no time to consider one before becoming obsessed with the next. Her clothes became so covered with paint that she crunched when she moved, so she stripped them off and wondered why she'd kept wearing them for so long. She began to paint with her fingers and then her hands, then her legs and her breasts and her feet and her hair and her head.

At night, she looked at the sky, the moon with its Xfinity logo, the stars, more numerous than they had been since she was little, staying at Hummingbird Camp up in the Jemez, far from cars and streetlights. Back then she used to draw effortlessly, realistic birds and trees for the delight of friends she'd never see again, had given them away without a second thought to anyone who asked. Holly closed her eyes and fell asleep almost instantly, dreaming of the next canvas, breathing in the sickly sweet chemical smell of a thousand pigments with nowhere to go.

51

When Teresa arrived home, Granny T was clearing dishes into the sink while Luis watched the news on their small kitchen TV. A calm broadcaster listed the damage caused by an earthquake in Indonesia in a practiced monotone, struggling to enunciate the names of cities he'd never heard of before.

"Sorry we didn't make you anything," said Teresa's grandmother. "We thought you'd eat out."

"No, I did. I just got back and . . . you know."

Her grandfather slowly stood up and turned off the TV. "Is anything bothering you?" he asked.

"No. I don't know, I'm just . . . Hey, you don't have to stop watching because of me."

"It's fine, the news never stops coming. I'll watch it later."

"You're not going to be up later."

"You got me." He smiled. "Okay, I'll turn it back on."

They watched in silence for several minutes. Granny T pulled off the yellow rubber gloves she used for dishes and joined them at the table as the weatherman reported a record high for mid-November, replacing last year's record high, and the sportscaster detailed how UNM's teams had fared against their rivals. She couldn't concentrate on the stories, but pretended to for the feeling of normalcy it gave her, the sense that everything was still okay.

"M-maybe there was something I wanted to talk about," she said. Her grandparents both turned away from the television.

"Honey, what is it?" asked Granny T. "It's okay. You can say anything to us, you should know that."

"I just . . . you know how I have to go back to work tomorrow? Well, I just don't want to do it anymore. I know this is going to sound childish, but I thought it would be one thing, right? Helping people, protecting, all of that. But it's not that at all, and I hate my boss, and I'm afraid to talk to most of my coworkers—and it's all just so horrible I can't stand it anymore. I mean I tried, I tried to go out there and do something, and it didn't help."

The television's continued drone made this somehow easier. She looked back at it, afraid of seeing what her grandparents thought. After a brief pause, though, they both started chuckling.

Her grandmother stood up and put her arm around Teresa. "Honey, it's okay, really. If you don't want to be a cop, no one's going to force you to. You don't have to do anything you don't want to. There's always something else. There's something for everyone out there. You have a family who loves and supports you, and eventually you'll find your thing."

Teresa was surprised to find herself crying. She wiped her eyes, careful as always not to push too hard on her face.

"Thanks. I think . . . I think I just needed to hear that."

"Give it more of a chance, though. See how you feel in the morning, and in a week, and if you're still unhappy, then leave. Every job has its ups and downs, you've just gotta get past this. Why don't you pray on it and see how you feel."

"I will."

The next morning, Teresa put on her uniform and began her commute to work, but midway through the drive, she pulled her car off to a side street and parked alongside Bataan Park. It was like every other park in the city, a rectangle of flat grass bordered by a walking path and covered by the shadows of immense trees. She walked around it, uncertain what she was doing but unable to head home or continue toward the station. A group of twenty- and thirtysomething men tossed a Frisbee as hard as they could at each other, laughing. Her phone rang, but she ignored it.

Eventually she walked across the street to a Walgreens to purchase bottled water. She wandered back to the park, lay down in its lush grass, and wondered what the hell she was doing. It was only ten fifteen and she didn't have any idea how she was going to fill the rest of the day. She walked around the park a few more times. It smelled both fresh and dead at the same time, alive with greenery yet choked with car exhaust from the busy street on its southern border.

She wandered onto nearby side streets populated only by empty houses, their inhabitants at school or work for the day. Birds darted among power lines. Bugs crawled from cracks in the sidewalk.

Her phone buzzed again, and Teresa pulled it out of her pocket, expecting a call from work. It was a number she didn't recognize, but seeking any form of distraction, she answered it.

"Hello?"

"Hi, is this Teresa Llantos?"

"Uhh, yes. May I ask who this is?"

"Hi, Teresa. I'm with Anonymous Propaganda, and we received information that you might be interested in working as a spokesperson."

"Oh, yes, umm . . . that. Yes, I might be. Could you tell me more about it? I'm a little . . . I don't know if I was ever told exactly what it was I was applying for, actually. Now that you mention it."

"Of course, of course," said the almost-too-friendly voice on the other end of the line. "That's because it's all very secret and confidential and *exciting*. It's a very exciting opportunity. I can't say anything more right now, but if you'll be willing to visit our offices, we can explain more about what this work may entail for you."

"Your offices . . . you're not in New Mexico, are you? Does this mean I got the job? It's a job, right?"

"Actually, we're based out of New York, but I can offer you transportation here for the audition. The only thing is, we're going to need a response from you right away."

"What do you mean right away, exactly?"

"I think Eri—my boss, the head of the project, he'd like to see you in less than forty-eight hours."

52

Here was the idea: Autumn would have all three of her children over for Thanksgiving, plus Brianna. That was it. None of Juan Diego's random relations, no aunts and uncles and the assorted fights that came with them, no preparation of dozens of dishes. It would be a small, intimate dinner where her children met her new partner. It might be difficult, replete with awkwardness on all sides, but it was time that everything was out in the open.

Brianna teased her, saying that meeting all three Reyes children at once sounded a little theatrical, but if that was how Autumn wanted to do things, well, she had no other plans. Brianna maintained contact with her younger brother, but she hadn't spoken to her parents in years. They were both proud churchgoers, flag-waving supporters of Haight who'd decided that the best way of dealing with their daughter's "lifestyle choice" was to pretend she'd never existed. During her sophomore year of college, Brianna told Autumn, her parents stopped paying her tuition and threw out or donated every item in her childhood bedroom. When her brother snuck her in for a visit a few months later, she found they'd already converted it into an exercise room and removed her photos from all of the house's walls. Since then, she celebrated Thanksgiving with friends or just marathoned movies.

Autumn found inviting her children to be far more problematic. At one of his occasional visits home to do laundry, Devon had agreed to show up (which had been more or less a given, but she still liked to make certain). "Sure, mom, of course," he said. But he didn't look her in the eyes, and he'd been avoiding her direct gaze for months. Either he was in the midst of a second, even brattier puberty, or his adjustment to college life was going worse than she'd thought. While he moved clothing from the washer to the dryer, she asked him what was going on with school.

"Oh, just class and all. I'm doing fine."

It was like speaking to a robot. She felt his evasions like a physical barrier. And lately, trying to get past them was just too tiring, too much effort for no results. Not knowing what else to do, she'd given him a look that made it clear she didn't believe him for a second, and left.

Gideon, on the other hand, wasn't even making a passive-aggressive effort—he was actively avoiding her. Not responding to voice mails was normal for him and had been for years, but she could tell from her read receipts that he'd opened her emails and Arcadia messages. He'd done this in the past, right before his first wife left him, so although it hurt, at least she understood it. After Juan Diego left her, Autumn had more or less lost contact with most of the people in her life, too. Maybe, at long last, his marriage to Claire was almost over, and maybe some good would come out of this after all. Eventually she decided that there was likely no point in trying to get in touch with him: he'd return to her and the rest of the world when he was good and ready, just like last time. Brianna could meet him later.

The real problem was Holly. She was missing, too, but unlike her brother, Holly usually responded to Autumn—perhaps snippily, especially during the past year, but usually with some degree of promptness. So it was only more disconcerting that Holly had not answered her phone or opened any messages from Autumn, hadn't posted or logged any activity on Arcadia whatsoever. It was possible that she'd simply gone offline, but her boyfriend's Arcadia presence was just as active as ever. Something was wrong, but she couldn't figure out what. Then, less than a week before Thanksgiving, Autumn saw a post on Arcadia about rumors of a virus in the southwestern part of the state, and she couldn't help but worry.

What began as one isolated rumor became a small news story became a series of rumors and editorials. One evening, after a quiet dinner together, Brianna asked her what was wrong.

"It's the tensest I've seen you since we first met," said Brianna. "This isn't about Thanksgiving, is it?"

53

Paul was waiting at the door when the paramedics arrived for Sonja.

"She's in our bedroom closet upstairs. She had some sort of episode and then passed out. I don't know, I think it's the fever. She tried to attack me and then tried to lock herself in the closet, but it doesn't lock. She's been having breathing trouble for a few days now, and stomach problems, and she passed out yesterday for a little bit. But then she was fine. Or better. We thought it was just the flu. Could it just be the flu? She did go to the grocery store a few days ago, maybe she caught something there? She's unconscious, please hurry." His babbling, interrupted by the occasional coughing jag, continued as the paramedics rushed up the stairs with a gurney and checked Sonja's vitals.

They sent him back downstairs to wait, and he staggered into his old recliner, feeling his bleeding face in disbelief. His first intuition that something had gone seriously wrong was when she'd woken him in the middle of the night, shrieking about bugs as she clawed her neck. He'd managed to calm her down and get her back to sleep, noting how hot she was. He'd been planning on taking her to the clinic in the morning, but obviously he should've acted much sooner.

When they carried her down on the gurney, there was a breathing mask over Sonja's face and ointment on her cuts. One of the men, whose expressionless pock-scarred face looked nearly as old as Paul's, said that she didn't seem to have had a stroke.

"What could it have been?"

"It's difficult to say. What were her other symptoms, again?"

"Nausea, difficulty breathing. And it sounded like she had some pretty bad pesadillas in the middle of the night. That's when she . . ." He gestured to her face.

"Quesadillas?" asked the younger man.

"Nightmares," said the older one. "We're taking her straight to Gila."

On the drive to the hospital, Paul's cough grew worse. Maybe it was stress, but he thought that was unlikely. The paramedics exchanged glances before placing another breathing mask over his face.

When Paul came to, he was in a hospital bed, listening as the nurse on the other side of the room talked about his upcoming weekend trip to Truth or Consequences. Paul could barely concentrate. He was burning up.

"Yeah, my prima lives there and she's been telling me about this friend of hers and, you know, I just need something to help me get over the breakup."

"You know," the other interjected, "Truth or Consequences was named after a game show. A lot of people think it's just a phrase, but it really was named after the show. And the government now uses it as ground zero to test all their new terrible experiments. How much pollution people can take, stealth advertising, alien genetic hybrids, mind control rays, stuff like that. You should really avoid T or C, unless you want the Truth *and* the Consequences. Ha-ha."

Paul launched into a coughing fit that built until he passed out.

The doctors at Gila Regional Medical Center in Silver City were absolutely baffled as to what they were dealing with and had even less idea how to fight it. By the time they thought to call in the CDC, they had twenty more patients with identical symptoms. Once the CDC arrived, they attempted to quarantine the hospital, but it wasn't nearly soon enough.

54

The_Creator: Hello, are you there?

Devon's first thought when The_Creator contacted him was that this was another one of Steve's jokes. It wouldn't have been the first time his friend had hacked the system, made an alias, and started screwing around with people.

Steve was gone, though, asleep or dead or somewhere between the two. Every couple days, Devon still visited his friend, who now walked with little assistance and even seemed to remember him. Or at least, he had some sort of positive association with Devon's appearance, although what that meant was anyone's guess, since Steve didn't seem capable of speaking anymore.

Neither could he write, despite having regained enough motor control to lift a pen and move it with reasonable accuracy. At the end of Devon's visit yesterday, Steve's neurologist said that he'd sustained serious and possibly irrevocable damage to the parts of the brain that controlled language. The term "global aphasia" had been used, but what Devon had taken away was that his Hail-Mary hope to clear his name in court on December 11 was a pipe dream.

Then last night Devon dreamt that he was the one recovering in the hospital ward. Men and women in white clothes kept opening their mouths and grunting at him. They grew increasingly angry at him for not grunting back. When he finally did, they covered their ears, grunting loudly until he stopped. Some of them thrust sheets of white covered in markings into his hands, then grunted at him until he grunted some more, which only made them angrier. As day turned into night and back into day, they just continued shoving things at him and screaming until he felt more and more confused, crying into his pillow because they neither gave him peace nor told him what they wanted.

When Devon woke up, the first thing he did was repeat his name over and over again to make sure he still could. Once he could think rationally, he decided it had clearly been an anxiety dream brought on by a shitstorm of trauma, past, present, and future—that stint in jail, a seemingly inevitable prison sentence, his best friend's accident and imminent deportation, his own responsibility for it. He couldn't help but feel like it was also an omen about Steve's chances at recovery.

While that body would always go by the name Estéban Vásquez, who knew if Steve, as Devon knew him, even existed anymore. Devon didn't really think so. Steve's physical state had kept him in the United States, but with his recovery stalled, they'd put a date on his deportation. One week from today, he would be gone, back to an extended family in Chihuahua he'd never met. So Devon had effectively managed to kill his friend and send his body back to Mexico as a criminal. Maybe his dreams should've been worse.

DevolChildə: Do you know me?
DevolChildə: You get your ass kicked by the Baby Eaters? It's just a game, man.

It wasn't abnormal for random people to contact him on Arcadia, although it happened infrequently. Half of the messages he received from unidentified accounts were spam; a few were people asking about the clan—usually about joining, though only a handful ended up doing so—and a few just wanted someone to talk to. The surprise about The_Creator was the admin account, signified by its avatar's glowing green aura. Since EA was known to have a beta-testing mirror of Arcadia, it was strange to see an admin hanging around the client side. Strange enough that it took Devon a few seconds to remember what the aura signified, since it had been years since he'd seen one on an avatar.

The_Creator: No, I didn't. Sorry about startling you. Do you have a moment, Devon? I know this is sudden, but I need to talk with you.

Far more surprising was seeing his name appear. Devon drank some Mountain Dew and thought for a second. If this guy was an admin, he should have access to everything about Devon that was stored in Arcadia's databases, so it wasn't too worrisome that he knew Devon's real name. Calmed, he responded.

DevolChilde: I guess so. How can I help you?
The_Creator: I just realized you wouldn't remember this screenname. I haven't contacted you online in years.

Devon struggled to remember anyone who'd left the clan that might (a) still be on good terms with them, (b) have started working for EA, and (c) want to contact Devon in particular. Devon was a good player, and was proud to say that he was equally skilled when it came to RTS or FPS or most any other genre, but he'd never been particularly popular, even within the group. It took him a few more seconds to realize that he'd been thinking about the question from the wrong angle entirely.

DevolChildə: Dad?
The_Creator: Yes.
DevolChildə: So this is . . . you? Juan Diego?
The_Creator: I'm sorry I haven't made myself clearer. Yes, this is Juan Diego. Now that I think about it, I'm not sure what handle I used last time we chatted online. Do you have a moment?
DevolChildə: Yeah, sure.

If his dad hadn't reappeared online, Devon didn't know how he would've responded. For the most part, he'd just pretended he never had a father from thirteen on, and barely missed a step. He knew that he was supposed to feel something, but he didn't, and in person that would matter.

The_Creator: I'm sorry I'm only contacting you online. It looks like time may be running short, though, and I haven't been having much luck with face-to-face meetings.
DevolChildə: You talked to my sibs?
The_Creator: They didn't tell you? I was hoping the three of you would stick together more.
The_Creator: In any case, it's not important. What I really wanted to do was apologize.
DevolChildə: For leaving us?
The_Creator: For everything.
DevolChildə: I see.

Not that he did, even remotely. Devon had no idea what the hell was going on, but as annoyed and suddenly exhausted as he felt, this was a distraction from Steve and the drug charges. And distractions were what he sorely needed.

The_Creator: I'm not saying you need to forgive me. But I'd like to

371

see you in person to show you something. A gift. The greatest gift.

The_Creator: I'm not asking for forgiveness because I don't deserve any. But I've figured out a way to cheat the system. To win against all odds.

DevolChildǝ: I'm not sure what you're saying. Are you doing ok?

The_Creator: I'm old, son. I'm dying, we all are, and that changed things for me. I couldn't deal with the family anymore, I couldn't stay there and pretend I was content. But I didn't waste my time, I've come up with a solution that will keep us from ever being apart again.

DevolChildǝ: What do you mean? Are you in a cult?

The_Creator: Just listen for one second. Myself and a few others, we've been trying everything, every idea, no matter how horrible they might seem, to stay alive. Some of the things . . . they may have had unintended consequences. In the end, though, I found a way out, but I don't want to go alone. I tried asking your brother and sister, but they wouldn't listen.

DevolChildǝ: So you're dying, and you've found religion? To be honest, I wasn't sure if you'd already died. That's what some people have been saying online.

The_Creator: I'm not dying, no more than usual. You like Arcadia, Devon, don't you? You've always been into games.

DevolChildǝ: Yeah . . .

The_Creator: There's a project I want you to work with me on. I need a pilot tester for the next version, and I want it to be you.

DevolChildǝ: And this is a religious game?

The_Creator: No, not really. It's basically an extension of Arcadia.

DevolChildǝ: Is this like a job, or something I can upload onto my computer and do from home?

The_Creator: Neither. What if you could really go inside, feel what it's like to be your avatar? What if you could stay there forever, where you're wealthy and have everything you could ever need, without coming out? What if you never had to feel your body decaying around you again?

DevolChildə: You lost me again, this still sounds like cult-speak.

The_Creator: It's not.

The_Creator: You understand how game emulation works, right? What a rom is? A rom is an exact image of a program, no more, no less. The beauty of them

DevolChildə: Of course I know what a rom is.

The_Creator: is that they can be extracted and used even when the intricacies of the actual program are far beyond what we understand. You can play a rom of a game even when the original source code has long since been deleted. If you copied a rom of Arcadia onto a similarly sized network of machines, you'd have the same program again, even if you have no idea how it works.

DevolChildə: So you're reproducing Arcadia, making a new version you need me to test?

DevolChildə: Why?

The_Creator: No, that was just an example, this is bigger than Arcadia.

The_Creator: The point is that with some programs the intricacies may be beyond human understanding. There's no reason to assume that human brains are built in a way that they themselves could ever understand their own complexity. We didn't evolve for that, we evolved in order to make little huts and hunt in packs and be ever-so-slightly more capable of using tools than any other ape.

The_Creator: Of course those insignificant changes made all the difference, but that's always the way it is. You remove a comma and suddenly your entire program works. Delete a few lines of dialogue from your play and suddenly a train wreck becomes a masterpiece.

The_Creator: Computers as we understand them are binary.

Or, in a few cases, ternary, but those are just some long-failing experiments. The brain itself is analog, it has subtleties beyond on and off. It works far more in parallel than any processor. Most difficult of all, its neurons that process information are the same ones that are having their synapses modified, effectively making them both cpu and ram at the same time.

His dad's messages arrived at a furious pace, each one right after the last, faster than Devon had a chance to respond. When they were little, Holly and Gideon used to call this "dadsplaining," and Devon had forgotten what it felt like. It felt . . . like home. Maybe he was more like his dad than he'd thought. Finally, there was a brief pause. Devon could tell his dad wanted him to say something, but he didn't know what.

DevolChildə: I heard that a computer would need to process something like 2 x 10^17 or something bits per second to be as fast as a brain.
The_Creator: That was an old, outdated estimate by someone who didn't know what he was talking about. The number is far higher, but it's unimportant because people don't realize that we already have computers that run that fast. The difficulty isn't the speed, it's the architecture. If it was just a matter of creating a supercomputer with the right parameters, at which point a brain magically assembled itself, we would've achieved that long ago.
The_Creator: Creating one from scratch is beyond our grasp, and probably always will be. But emulating one isn't.
DevolChildə: And you need me involved in pilot testing this emulation?
The_Creator: Yes. But it's not just that I need you, Devon. I want you there. If I could, I would have your siblings with us, too, but they weren't interested.

DevolChildə: What about mom?

There was a long pause.

The_Creator: She wouldn't be interested. Though I guess I hadn't really thought to ask her.

Then another.

DevolChildə: What happens with this emulation, exactly?
The_Creator: You'd be uploaded, at which point you're no longer linked to your body. You could inhabit a 3D scan of what you have now, or you could use any body made in Arcadia that's compatible with the 2.4.31191 patch.
DevolChildə: And then I'm just in there?
The_Creator: I think so. I believe so.

A final pause. Devon thought about Thanksgiving dinner next week. Telling his mom about the drug charges seemed unavoidable. The trial would be two weeks after that. He thought about the tunnels, and Steve in the hospital, and that he'd tried to get his friend to take the fall and now would never have a chance to ask for forgiveness. He thought about his rent and utilities, paying taxes, applying for jobs. Showers and shaving. Getting his hair cut and flu shots. He thought about telling Autumn that he didn't want to stay at UNM anyhow, that he didn't want a job, either, or anything else. That he was over all of it, all of everything he could think of, especially himself.

DevolChildə: Where do you want to meet?
The_Creator: I'm still up on Mesa del Sol. Just tell the guard who you are and I'll meet you at the gate.

55

Gideon heard a knock on the door and half jumped where he sat on the thin mattress. It took him a second to put himself together enough to shut his laptop, hiding the archived video streams he'd spent the afternoon staring at. He stood up to open the door, but the sound of a woman moaning continued, and he realized that he'd forgotten to turn the computer off or put it to sleep, so the video kept running. He opened it again and hit mute before answering the door, taking a second to compose himself and present the competent, respectable appearance of a man who hadn't been smoking weed for the past couple days.

On the other side of the doorway, Ralphie's oversize head looked back at him, tendrils of smoke filtering out from Gideon's room and into the yard.

"Dude, how much have you burned through? It smells like . . . I don't even know, it smells like a bong up and died in there," said Ralphie.

"How much did you sell me? That's how much I smoked."

"Well, shit. Why don't you come in, I've got something for you in the house. Let's leave the door open to air out for a few minutes. That's gotta be bad for your laptop or something."

Gideon shrugged and followed his friend back to Ralphie's side of the Brainbox. They sat down on an enormous couch for some co-op *Alien Invasion Force 3: Hidden Enemy*, while Gideon tried to explain that no, nothing was wrong, why was he asking. Given the handcuffs he still wore (not too much of an annoyance, once he managed to loop his hands around to the front of his body), he wasn't terribly convincing.

"Seriously, I've known you for ages and you've never been like this before. I just thought you could use someone to talk to."

"How about you break out a little more of that agricultural goodness first?" said Gideon.

Ralphie waddled to the back of his room and came back with a pipe made from swirling green-and-yellow glass. It was short and slightly knobby, with a curve at the end. Its bowl was fully packed.

"Here," he said. "It's a gift. I figure if you're smoking this much, you should have the right tool for the job."

"Thanks, though it looks like my grandpa's old dildo."

"And so it hath been christened. So, like, what the fuck's going on?"

"Well, my boss fired me, and the girl I came here to see told me to go fuck myself," said Gideon, lighting the bowl and inhaling until he felt a burn at the back of his throat and in his lungs. "That's about the size of it."

"Ouch. So?" Ralphie unpaused the game and looked straight at the television screen in front of them. Gideon followed suit.

"What do you mean, 'so'? So I'm taking a little breather, that's all."

"How long do you think this, uhh, little breather's gonna last you?"

"I don't know, man, I just need a little while to get my head straight. You know it's good you came knocking, because I really did burn through everything."

"That's cool. And I get you, everyone needs a breather sometimes. That's some heavy shit, for sure."

"Thanks, man."

"I just wanted to say that if you wanted to, you could come hang out for a bit. Maybe eat a decent meal for once. Dwelling's not good for anything. Just, I don't know, maybe it's time to think about what's next. No girl and no job seems like a great time to figure your shit out."

"I know, I know," said Gideon. "Just . . . it's hard. I think I just need more time. Time for myself, and, like, away from obligations and all that. I had a good setup back east. I'm thinking of heading back there. Maybe." It was the first time that the idea had popped into Gideon's head, but it seemed legitimate at the moment.

They played for a little while longer, not talking about anything but the game as they finished the bowl. Gideon didn't remember anything else until he woke up the next morning on Ralphie's couch, the smell of their butt sweat digging into his nostrils. He felt like crap, especially when he headed back to his room and saw his computer. The video had finished playing, but it was still open, and he couldn't help himself. After watching it again, Gideon tried to recall what it was like before he'd first seen her, what it had been like to have other interests. He couldn't. He spent much of the afternoon browsing camgirl sites, hoping she was still out there somewhere, maybe under a different screenname. He asked around on forums, but no one seemed to know anything. It was like she'd simply disappeared from Arcadia.

Around midnight he gave up and began a new search for someone to replace her. He didn't know exactly what he was looking for. He tried women who were similar, with skin like hot chocolate and long, dark hair, girlish laughs and dangerously intelligent eyes, but they only reminded him of the real thing. So he browsed every other combination of traits, blondes and redheads, different eye colors, skin tones, breast sizes. If his attraction had only been physical, then maybe he could find a new configuration of traits that turned him on, made him feel happy just to be on the other end of that fiber-optic connection. Nothing worked. Some of them were beautiful, enough to masturbate to, to temporarily forget the world to, but no one was her equal. Gideon fell asleep crying, wishing he could turn back the clock and just be content to have her onscreen, the version of her that he loved, the one he felt he knew. In two dimensions, Teresa had never disappointed him. Not once.

Two days later, having called in a final favor with Ralphie to get the damn cuffs off, he was waiting in the car across the street and about a block away from where Teresa and her grandparents lived, his headlights and dashboard lights off, the radio on. It was a little after 9:00 p.m., and he'd been sitting there since the sun went down more than half an hour ago. Dimly lit figures in the window offered him a silhouetted version of the people living inside. And this was what he'd become, a guy who wore binoculars while looking through windows. Since when was he that guy?

Gideon took a puff from Grandpa's Dildo while he waited, wondering how much longer before everyone went to sleep so he could see her again, just one more time. What then? He didn't know. Maybe he'd beg her to get back on Arcadia, promise to leave her alone if she'd just return to how they were before. Maybe he'd do something else, something worse, something unforgivable. Maybe she'd kill him simply for showing his face. Gideon just knew that he needed to be in her room, to see her at least one more time, on his terms.

Gideon focused on the radio, a Top 40 station. He switched to talk radio as soon as he heard Gravedigger's voice. It was a song Gideon had conceptualized about the struggle of life in the 'hood, some bullshit about wondering where the next shot's gonna come from, and he had to admit he felt some pride alongside his anger. But it was too much to deal with right now. He listened to a reporter from Florida droning on about the plight of the flood survivors and the trillions of dollars in damage caused by last year's cataclysmic hurricane.

"According to meteorologists, this sort of disaster has become all too common as climate change continues. One prominent meteorologist, Gregory Schumann of Penn State, has said that he considers living anywhere along the coastline to be tantamount to a death wish, that he sees no end in sight for these class-five storms, and that in fact he predicts it won't be long before the once-fabled class-six hurricanes become a sad reality.

"Probably the strangest discovery coming out of the storm was a new species of bird that washed up with the rest of the flotsam and jetsam left in its wake. At first assumed to be a raven, the bird's head had split in two. A fisherman spotted it from a gleam of light, which turned out to be from the bird's odd brain. Unlike other species, its cerebrum isn't gray but rather a reflective silver, that is to say, a natural mirror. It's been said that the president himself has requested to see this strange phenomenon, though he's unsurprisingly not made any plans to visit the area's wreckage given—"

The lights went off in Teresa's house, and Gideon snapped to attention. He grabbed a black ski mask (purchased with the binoculars from a suspicious Walmart clerk) and exited the car. The street was barely visible, the only streetlight more than a block away. There were no sidewalks, so Gideon walked along the road past chain-link fences and blue plastic trash bins, putting the ski mask over his head. He started sweating almost immediately, causing the mask's eyeholes to slump down his cheeks.

He crept to the backyard. Teresa's room was a converted garage, detached from the rest of the house. It had windows in the back, so he stood on his toes and peeked in. He couldn't see past a set of heavy curtains, but it was obvious that there were no lights on inside.

He hesitated at the door, then lightly knocked. After several seconds of silence, he knocked again, louder. Still no answer. He moved a molded plastic lawn chair from the backyard up against the house. He stepped onto it, feeling it bend beneath his weight, took off his shirt and wrapped it around his fist. Then he punched the window and was surprised when glass still broke off into his hand, the shatter echoing around the backyard. Fuck.

A neighbor's dog barked, and Gideon hid behind the converted garage, smelling the stink of his own profuse sweat inside the ski mask, unsure of how long to wait. The blood from his hand began to soak through the shirt and drip onto the ground, so he decided he'd probably waited long enough.

He stood back on the lawn chair, wiped broken glass from the windowpane, and pulled himself up and in, cutting both of his hands some more. He landed hard on the floor below, his knees aching. Out of breath and worried about the blood, he flipped on the light switch and was thrilled to find himself in a familiar space.

Here it was, her room, her film studio. He knew the posters on the walls and the figurines on the shelves, the stuffed animals and the photographs tacked above her desk. Here was her dresser, which she'd said was the same one her mom had used while she was growing up, and her bed, with its set of slick, dark green sheets that matched the curtains. He sat on an old sewn quilt and sniffed her pillow, which smelled of something light and fruity. He held the quilt's thickness beneath his fingers until he noticed blood dripping onto its squares. He attempted to wipe this off with his arm and pant leg, but it didn't work, so he stood up and made his way to her bathroom.

It was all so much smaller than it seemed on his computer screen. When he'd watched her online, it seemed like there was a whole world in her little studio, but the bathroom door would barely close unless he stepped into her bathtub, which seemed too small for anyone to lie down in. The room was humid, musty—odd for Albuquerque. Gideon's flesh stung as he washed it beneath cool water and pulled shards from his skin, finding them even embedded in his chest. He watched laces of blood stream down into the sink before it became a swamp of brownish liquid. The sink drained slowly, Teresa's hair caught in it. He dried his hands and chest halfheartedly on a faded pink towel, opened her medicine cabinet, and began sticking Band-Aid after Band-Aid onto his wounds. Eventually the bleeding stopped, but he was covered in stiff strips of plastic, the sink was almost overflowing, and almost every surface in the room was streaked with blood.

This wasn't how it was supposed to happen. She was supposed to be here. They would make up somehow, reconcile. She would apologize, explain that she'd only been frightened, or maybe playing a game, that was it, and what she'd really wanted was to see him again. She was supposed to be as acquiescing and sweet and charming and beautiful as she was online, only now he'd be able to touch her; she'd want him to touch her. She could even perform for the camera, only he'd be in the room, too.

Instead, there was this empty room, blood staining the carpet, towels, and walls. Gideon sat on the cheap, faux-leather chair at her desk. It was a child's desk, too small for the chair, and he felt, for the first time since entering, invasive, like he didn't belong here. He swiveled around and looked back at her room. What was there left to do?

Staring, wondering what he'd find in her drawers, her closets, every hidden part of the room he'd never glimpsed from her streams, he noticed something new. On the black, square table near her bed was a fruit basket and an open envelope. He pulled a letter from the envelope and read: "Thank you for sharing your granddaughter! America's going to love her! Please enjoy this fruit basket, on behalf of all of us at Anonymous Propaganda." Underneath, in a scrawl, he could just make out, "Mija, we wanted you to have these. You're the one that earned them!"

It felt gratifying to learn that his boss and colleagues had decided to go with his suggestion for the Prophet Project. It also explained where she was now, truly gone from him, off in New York where he couldn't find her. All this effort for nothing. Hell, maybe the door had even been left unlocked—why hadn't he thought of trying the door?

Gideon spent the next few minutes messing around in the closet, as if on autopilot. The marijuana made everything easier. He didn't need to rationalize, he just did what he wanted, no guilt screaming in the back of his mind. Her bras and panties were fascinating, almost magical, everything was, the socks and tights and even sweatpants. He took the largest shirt he could find and put it on, not caring that it still didn't fit him at all. It smelled like cheap detergent, the type that Costco sells in barrels, but it still reminded him somehow of her. It wasn't enough, though, so he grabbed a pile of clothes and threw it onto her bed. When he fell back into it, it felt good, like he'd achieved something.

He grabbed an apple from the fruit basket and bit into it. It was mealy on the inside, waxy on the skin, and rather flavorless, but he didn't care. There was a strange black pattern in the apple, and he was too hungry at first to think about it, but after several more bites it formed, of all things, an Apple logo. It was slightly off, a little ragged, but clearly the logo. Gideon worried for a moment that he was hallucinating. He finished the apple and ate through the rest of the gift basket too: Sunkist oranges, hard Kia pears, Delta Air Lines nectarines. The room was a mess now, juice spattered on the floor alongside blood and discarded fruit cores. But he didn't care anymore. He lay back onto her bed, surrounded by Teresa's clothing, and decided he'd stay as long as he could.

THANKSGIVING 2037

TERESA

Only a week ago she'd been in Albuquerque. Last Wednesday, she'd told her grandparents about the offer—how little she knew about it, how much it still seemed to promise. She'd packed her bags with Granny T, both of them trying not to cry as they fit an outfit for every conceivable circumstance into two large, Samsonite bags Teresa hadn't used since she first moved to New Mexico. Her grandfather had packed her a lunch so large that she hadn't been able to eat even a quarter of it, despite being stuck in line at the airport for the better part of a day. Only a week ago she'd been a different person. When she returned home for Thanksgiving, she'd be a star.

Teresa sat in a green room. She stared at the mirror in front of her without flinching for the first time in years, while a woman she'd never met before coated her face in makeup. She'd spent so much time with stylists and mirrors over the last few days that she'd begun to get over her fear. The room itself was familiar. The hair stylist earlier, the dress waiting for her on entry, these chairs and mirrors, all of this made sense, offered an element of normalcy. The rest of her life felt out of control, a stream of strangers telling her what to do next without explaining why, but here she understood her role.

"What if . . . what if something happens to my face while we're shooting?" asked Teresa. "What if there's some sort of, I don't know, allergic reaction?"

"Are you allergic to anything?" asked the woman. She was middle-aged and seemed to know what she was doing. She concealed the seams of Teresa's face so well that even in the magnifying mirror, they were impossible to find.

"I don't think so. What if my face just, you know, falls off?"

The woman gave her a funny look. Teresa sat in silence while she finished. She'd applied the doctor's cream without fail, and when she confessed about the accident to folks at AP, had been told by Eric not to worry.

"If this face comes off, why, we'll just get you a new one," he said, smiling broadly.

If what they said was true, this show was going to be bigger than big, a sensation. She was going to be internationally famous, so there was a good chance that someone would recognize her. But there was also a chance that no one had ripped any of her streams, that everything she'd done on Arcadia was as ephemeral as she hoped. There was no way of telling. As the show came closer and closer to airing, she kept waiting for someone to put a stop to this, to say they recognized her from the Internet, call her a whore, void her contract, but nothing of the sort happened. So far, there'd been no hitch.

The makeup artist put the finishing touches on her face, completing a look that a team of publicists finalized two days ago for her first appearance on the air. She wore a flowing, light blue dress that showed no cleavage but hugged her body so that it was impossible not to see that what it hid was well formed, and a pair of matching shoes with dyed blue leather that she could keep. She didn't really care for this much makeup, her face even less familiar to her than usual, especially with the new bangs. The haircut was attractive but indistinct, unmemorable, could've been almost anyone, which, she supposed, was the effect that they wanted.

With time to kill, Teresa opened the plastic grocery bag she'd brought with her and pulled out an apple, the last item remaining from her "lunch." She'd gradually been snacking her way through it whenever she felt anxious. She'd been put under "reality show quarantine" and hadn't been able to call or message her grandparents since AP notified them of her safe arrival in New York. No one had told her that this was part of the deal, but it made it easier to distance herself from her past life. Eric had personally promised that if things went well tonight, she could have full use of his private plane to go see her grandparents for a few hours of the Thanksgiving holiday. They'd be over the moon to see her again.

In the meantime, whenever she dug into her grandfather's "lunch" to find one of the packets of cheese crackers or a granola bar, she felt soothed. The morning she'd left, they'd received a fruit basket from AP addressed to her grandparents, and her grandfather tried to make her take most of it with her, saying they couldn't possibly eat it all themselves, although this was an obvious lie. She'd compromised by taking this one apple, leaving the rest for them to enjoy, and she'd forgotten about it. Now it was almost certainly bad, or at least mealy. She was about to throw it away when she caught the makeup woman's eye.

"Did you want this? It's a week old, so I'm not sure if it's the best, but . . ."

"God yes, thanks. I've been here all day and craft services was only set up for like an hour."

Eric barged through the door without knocking. "Ready for the show? I know you are, let's get out there."

She didn't have time to respond before he turned around and an aide gestured for her to follow. They walked down a short hallway before arriving backstage, where people wandered in every direction. The audience murmured on the other side of the set.

"Umm, Eric, I'm not really sure—"

"You're fine, baby, you're fine," said Eric, looking her directly in the eyes. "Just do like in rehearsal and read from the teleprompter."

He was right, she did feel fine. She had what they'd called "natural presence," and as with everything she'd done over the past week, this revelation had thrilled Eric.

"What if there's a problem with the teleprompter?"

"There won't be, so don't worry. Everything's just like rehearsal. Only better."

Eric smiled and wandered off, leaving her alone as the lights dimmed. The show's host, a celebrity she only knew from banner ads for game and variety shows, gave her a nod as he passed. The show's theme music engulfed the studio with a fanfare. She waited as the first two contestants were announced, then entered last, a spotlight following her to the middle of three lecterns, her name written on it in an elegant font.

The host began the show with a brief monologue about its importance, then introduced each of the "contestants" to the audience, who gasped and laughed at exactly the right times. The men on each side of Teresa could theoretically win the most votes from the home audience, but the scripts, makeup, hair, outfits, even the men themselves had been chosen so as to make her look as good as possible. Everything had been planned in advance. They'd lose.

The only unknown was Teresa's nagging conviction that her grandparents wouldn't like the show. Were they watching now? She hadn't told them specifics, had been as vague as possible about the job ("a new reality TV angle about clean living"), but they'd find out sooner or later. And she feared what they'd say. To them, religion was small and sacred. Personal. It wasn't game shows and computer-generated graphics, audiences and online voting and Arcadia simulcasts. Religion didn't have winners who received lucrative contracts or losers who'd go on to feature in TLC reality shows. But this was her chance.

When she smiled at the camera, no one could see the seams or the former camgirl or the scared cop. All they could see was her face, and as she caught a glimpse of it in the monitor, she finally recognized it as herself. What's more, she embraced it. Maybe she was born to be the Prophet.

The introduction concluded and Teresa found that she didn't need the teleprompter. The host asked about her favorite psalm, and she recited it from memory. He asked about her first communion, and she told the anecdote without stumbling over a single preapproved detail. The script she'd memorized made her funny in a self-deprecating way. The audience ate it up. The lights, the cameras, the people—they loved her, and she found that she loved them as well.

GIDEON

Gideon coughed, and everyone else in the room—three gray-suited men and one woman waiting to speak at the event, the interns bringing coffee, even the otherwise inattentive security guard stationed at the door—reacted as if he'd just insulted their mothers. One of the interns asked him if he felt okay, and Gideon wondered what that could even mean anymore. When was the last time he would've described himself as "okay"?

"The girl of my dreams rejected me, my boss fired me, and I just drove a few hundred fucking miles to get here. I'm having a bit of a time, all right?"

The intern sighed with annoyance. "No, I mean have you felt sick lately?"

"I just got through telling you I feel like absolute crap, so what do you think?"

The intern backed up. He looked ready to bolt from the room. It occurred to Gideon how young this kid was, in his light blue polo shirt and overlarge khaki pants. He probably didn't want to be here, either, fetching coffee for some bullshit speakers no one had ever heard of. When the Great Wall of Freedom first "opened," the president himself had been here cutting the red ribbon; now it was just Gideon and a few politicians who couldn't say no to a TV appearance, no matter how small.

"Sorry, I've just been smoking a little too much weed," said Gideon.

The intern visibly relaxed. The whole room relaxed. Apparently they'd all been listening in. "Okay, just making sure. You can never be too careful."

He began walking away. Gideon spoke loudly after him, "Hey, wait. Too careful of what?"

"RV. I mean, if it's real."

It had been an easy drive down to the Wall. The New Mexico passage was difficult to miss, a straight shot down I-25 past Las Cruces, then you veered off long before El Paso and what used to be the heavily trafficked border crossing before the GWoF's policy changes. Ciudad Juárez and El Paso were now sealed up entirely, and anyone moving between the two cities needed to take a lengthy, frequently multiple-day-long roundabout. Supposedly for security, really this policy seemed to be more a matter of spite. Haight famously disliked that families used to move between the two cities as if the border didn't exist. Whether or not it had been intended, the Wall worked both ways.

But that was the thing about the Wall: it hadn't begun as a political statement, but everything about it became political. Gideon had nothing against immigrants—hell, he was Hispanic, or half-Hispanic or whatever—so if anything, he was on their side, figuratively speaking. But beyond the clever joke of it, Gideon had come to think of the Wall as a truly great idea. He liked walls. He liked privacy. He didn't appreciate other people asking for his help. He'd felt defensive about it for so long because of the protests, the controversy, but as he grew older, Gideon had become fond of the Wall for more than what it did to help his career. What was wrong with trying to live peacefully alone?

He picked up his phone and Googled "RV." At first he didn't find anything but recreational vehicle dealerships and listings for where he could hook them up. He thought he must've misheard the kid, until he hit the "News" button at the top of his search and a flood of disturbing headlines filled his screen:

"Research at Georgia Tech Claims Illness a Hoax"
"RV Outbreak Said to Begin in Southern New Mexico"
"Scientists Say New Virus Fatal in Most Cases"
"CDC Says Cure for New Illness May Take Time"
"RV: Fact or Fiction? Watch Live Debate on CNN"
"Airborne Illness Cause for International Concern"
"France Closes Airports to US Citizens, Fear of Possible RV Infection"
"President Says No Need to Panic, Plague Will Only Harm Blasphemers"

Gideon didn't know which one to open, so he was tapping them at random when an announcement blared over the room's PA.

"THERE IS NO NEED TO PANIC. PLEASE MAKE A CALM AND ORDERLY EXIT." Spoken in a heavy Mexican accent and filtered by feedback, the message repeated again and again, so loudly that Gideon couldn't think straight. The other speakers began filing out of the room, and Gideon followed them simply to get away from the noise.

They walked a short tunnel through the Wall's thick concrete and out onto a foldout platform with a black lectern at its center, where they were supposed to have made a dramatic entrance over an hour ago. Behind them, temporary walls covered in sea-green carpet stood against the Wall itself, with a large portrait of President Haight on one side and an enormous American flag on the other, both dwarfed by the billboards and neon lights above and around them. Where he'd expected to see rows of folding chairs occupied by spectators and camera crews, there were only dropped programs and swirling dust. Past the chairs, cars were driving away from floodlights. Hundreds of people in desert-camouflaged hazmat suits and carrying large rifles streamed out of the Wall's only opening for hundreds of miles. Behind them, the gates' portcullis slammed shut.

Gideon walked toward the parking lot as purposefully as he could, ignoring the other speakers' panic, hoping no one would notice him. Then he heard someone yell. "They're locking us out here, with the disease!" A cacophony of shrieking erupted, followed by a boom of gunfire. Complete chaos. Gideon reflexively dropped to the ground and crawled beneath the nearest car, a white news van that seemed to have been abandoned. He looked back at the Wall and saw that the gunfire wasn't limited to the ground; explosions and shouting rang out from the walkways above. Then a body, dressed in American military fatigues, dropped from the top of the Wall, lifeless before it hit the ground.

The voice over the PA began again. "DO NOT BE ALARMED. THE WALL HAS BEEN QUARANTINED. NO INDIVIDUALS WILL BE ALLOWED TO PASS THROUGH. DO NOT BE ALARMED. YOUR COUNTRY IS BEING QUARANTINED."

Gideon tried to remain still. The commotion had kicked up a lot of dust, and he felt a burning at the back of his throat. He started coughing again, and this time he couldn't stop.

Gideon awoke beneath the van. Hazmats were visible on top of the Wall and patrolling around the stage, but the only sound was the desert wind's insistent whisper. He couldn't tell how many hours had passed, but only dim moonlight illuminated the scene around him.

He walked to his rental, staying low, making his way across the jumbled remains of an improvised parking lot. Every third car seemed either to have been in a collision or punctured with bullet holes. When he finally reached the far end of the lot, he was surprised to find the car untouched. He got in, turned the ignition, and began driving toward the road.

A spotlight appeared on the car and Gideon almost slammed into the vehicle next to him. A PA sounded, its metallic tone so loud that it made his chest vibrate. "DO NOT BE ALARMED. PLEASE EXIT YOUR VEHICLE AND REPORT FOR TESTING OR WE WILL BE FORCED TO RESTRAIN YOU."

It only took him half a second to decide not to obey. He swung the car wide in reverse, rearview mirror flying off as he slipped past another car, then shifted into drive and slammed his foot down on the gas. He tore past the parking lot and onto the highway, abandoned cars lining both sides of the road.

For a few seconds, Gideon thought he was fine. Then he heard a ping and a thud as a rear tire deflated, bumping him so much he hit his head on the car's low ceiling. He slowed the car to a stop and put it in park, coughing intensely. He could barely think about anything but getting his next breath, even as a military jeep pulled up and several hazmat suits exited it and began shining flashlights into his car.

"¿Parece mexicano?" said a muffled voice. "Tiene la tos. ¿Qué haremos?"

Fuck. Gideon wanted to explain to them that he was fine, an American citizen not worth the effort, but couldn't find the breath to speak. As his coughing grew worse, the last thing he saw was a pair of rifles pointed through the windshield at his head, though by then he would've happily welcomed the entire Mexican army if they'd make the pain in his throat finally end.

AUTUMN

From inside the walls, it looked like a normal city. There were buildings and cars, parks and fences and asphalt. Movement in the streets, identifiable traffic patterns reacting to lights and stop signs like anywhere else. But the shiny, perfect, self-driving cars and gleaming white robots weren't exactly normal. Nor was the giant gate they'd entered using Brianna's stolen entrance codes. Above their heads, a billboard read, "CIT-E: A Prototype for the Future."

It was difficult to believe that this was real. At least Gideon was away from it all in New York. And apparently Devon was under the protection of his father, scheduled to move into the EA studios today. That tidbit, courtesy of a stolen email Brianna had been lucky to stumble across, particularly stung, but at least he'd probably be safe there. So this was her Thanksgiving.

The helicopter pad they were headed toward was surrounded by cars, almost a hundred of them filling a small parking lot and lining the streets. They didn't look like the streamlined and spotless cars they'd passed on their way into the city. These were beaten up, with scratched paint jobs, dented doors, bumper stickers, air fresheners, Styrofoam cups failing to decompose in their holders.

Autumn parked several blocks away, and when she turned off her car, it was eerie and silent. No people were around, but it felt like they were being listened to, watched. They got out of the car without saying anything and walked down perfect, litter-free sidewalks to the helicopter pad. Next to it was a small building with an elevator and a single down button.

"So now what do we do?" asked Brianna.

"We wait," said Autumn.

"What if Holly doesn't arrive?" Brianna sat down in the small shadow cast by the building. "What if Homeland Security doesn't follow the orders?"

"From what you told me, these guys are good at following orders, and even better at not asking where those orders came from. There's no reason for them to suspect you hacked Homeland Security and sent those emails. They'll arrive. And then we'll go inside and, I guess, wait everything out."

Autumn sat down beside Brianna and held her hand. It was soft and perfect, and as she squeezed, Brianna squeezed back. Despite everything else, she smiled. It was temperate out, not a cloud in the sky. The sun's rays seemed to have weight. Birds chirped. Not a soul was around to notice them, to care that until they'd arrived, this city had been vacant. Maybe, if they were lucky, in just a few minutes more, it would be again.

"How long do you think we'll have to wait?" asked Brianna.

Autumn kissed her hand and tried not to think about it.

HOLLY

By the time a battering ram smashed through her studio door, she had long since lost all track of time. She'd lost all track of herself. As the orange hazmat suits burst inside, she was naked and almost feral, her body and hair so smeared and matted that they seemed to be made of paint. She barely noticed their entrance, her focus on a corner of the far wall that still wasn't finished, still needed another line of figures in the mural's background.

"I think we've found the daughter," said one of the hazmats, the voice rendered slightly electronic by the suit's speakers.

Another figure responded. "I don't think she's infected, at least I haven't heard about RV doing *this* to anyone yet. I think this is something . . . else. And if she really is his daughter, you know . . ."

"AP does not pay enough for us to put up with this shit. Ma'am? Ma'am! Holly?"

This finally drew her attention. Holly whipped around with a bewildered look, shielding her eyes.

"Miss Holly Reyes? Ma'am, can you confirm that you're Holly Reyes?"

"I—" she choked. Her voice came out as a growl. "I am. Holly. I'm Holly. Am I in trouble?"

"No, ma'am. Though we'll need to have your blood tested. To check for the RV."

"The RV? What RV? Blood test . . . I'm fine." Her throat hurt, her lips chapped and bleeding. She wanted to get back to painting, to what made sense. "And wait a second, you can't just barge in here. This is my space. Did Robert do this?"

Other figures yelled at her as she pushed past them to leave the studio. She stopped to stare at the outside world, the sun brighter and air purer than she'd remembered. There were no cars, no people walking their dogs, no people walking anywhere. The world was still, only the sound of birds and wind and emptiness competing with these intruders. What the fuck had happened?

She was forced into an orange suit and toward a waiting helicopter. A figure next to her said, "Please don't remove the suit. It's for your own safety."

"What the hell is going on? Who are you? Where are we going?"

"RV, ma'am. You know. Or if you don't, just be grateful. We're not really at liberty to say who we are, though."

"What about Robert? What about my family?"

"I don't know, miss. I'm sorry."

"How do you know who I am?"

"Again, we're not at liberty to say. But we had very specific, very detailed orders."

"I don't . . . where are you taking me?"

"That I can tell you. We're going to CIT-E. They say the bunkers are safe there."

DEVON

The large black box—more than seven feet long and maybe three feet wide, its sides unadorned, no logos or symbols to indicate origin or manufacturer—looked almost crude, like something built in shop class. Its black paint seemed to have been sprayed on, its dullness accented by the fluorescent lights above. A pair of long green wires wrapped around it like brambles, or thick veins.

A technician approached and opened its heavy lid. Inside lay a red velvet pillow at one end. It contained nothing else. Without looking at him, the technician covered his mouth as he coughed, exited the room, and shut the door.

He stepped into the box. There was no handle, so he reached up to the lip of the lid and carefully lowered it. He waited, tried to clear his mind, to ignore the smell of particleboard and paint, the scrape of the rough surface against the skin of his back. He heard muffled sounds. A few minutes later they went away. As time dragged on, he felt his lungs pulling harder, and the box began to feel softer, more comfortable. He closed his eyes, and wondered what it would feel like when he opened them.

ACKNOWLEDGMENTS

This book couldn't have been written without Heather Freeman's endless outpouring of love, support, and patience. I can't thank you enough for everything you've done for me.

Thanks to Jason Kirk for your enthusiasm and ability to propose perfect solutions to problems I didn't even know existed. Thanks to Jesseca Salky for somehow never losing faith in me, or this book.

Thanks to Ben Willow, Noah Gelb, Dailey Jackson, and the rest of my *DnD* crew back in Albuquerque. You taught me to love crafting stories before I even knew that was what I was doing. I know, I promised I'd start DMing again when I finished this book, but now I'm in the middle of another one, so maybe next year . . .

Thanks to Angie Cruz, Deirdre McNamer, and Alice Mattison for helping me with various sections of the manuscript and offering advice on what to do when I was lost in the middle of a sea of drafts with no end in sight.

Thanks to Katherinna Mar, Jim Joyce, David Prichard, Sarah Kovach, Jason Welch, and Chloe Stricklin for endless discussions about books, help with stressful workshops, and putting up with my terrible dancing and karaoke.

Thanks to June and Joe, who never questioned my desire to write even when it was obvious that this was a terrible career choice. Thanks to Pat, Sue, and Miguel for myriad reasons—I'm so lucky to have had all of you in my corner.

Thanks to Daniel, Matthew, the LAB, and Charlie Lupica; I wish I could see all of you far more often than I actually get to. Thanks to Vanessa Atler for not minding that I stole one of her stories; I hope you like what I did with it. Thanks to Blake Foley, my "office husband" from fifteen hundred miles away.

Finally, thanks to the many muses (mewses?) who helped me during my years of writing this book: Penelope, Tib, Lavender, Midnight, Jazz, and Blue. All of you have made sitting alone and writing all day far less lonely, and occasionally hitting ctrl+z after you walk across the keyboard is a small price to pay for your company.

About the Author

Photo © 2015 Miguel Gandert

Sean Gandert was born and raised in Albuquerque, New Mexico. He received his undergraduate degree from Yale University and an MFA in creative writing from Bennington College. A freelance writer and college English instructor, Sean's reviews and interviews have appeared in *Paste* magazine and other publications. An avid gamer, Sean currently resides in Florida with his partner and their three cats.